AVENGING ANGEL

A JOSEY ANGEL NOVEL

AVENGING ANGEL

A FRONTIER EPIC OF
LOVE AND VENGEANCE

DEREK CATRON

WHEELER PUBLISHING
A part of Gale, a Cengage Company

GALE
A Cengage Company

LIBRARY OF CONGRESS CIP DATA ON FILE.
CATALOGUING IN PUBLICATION FOR THIS BOOK
IS AVAILABLE FROM THE LIBRARY OF CONGRESS.

ISBN-13: 978-1-4328-8857-2 (softcover alk. paper)

Published in 2022 by arrangement with Derek Catron.

Printed in the USA
1 2 3 4 5   26 25 24 23 22

This is for my Isabel,
who taught me all I know about
being a father and who, despite my
missteps, fills me with a pride that's
"bigger than the sky and more than
the sand on the beach."

CHAPTER ONE

She thought watching her husband die would be the worst part. Now she knew better; he'd gotten away easy.

"Take off your bonnet."

Maria Larsson shook her head. She didn't trust her voice.

"I said take off your bonnet."

The man who'd murdered Daniel spoke the words slowly, enunciating each syllable as if only a lack of comprehension delayed her obedience. She breathed through her mouth to keep the stench of him from violating her nostrils and cast her eyes down, afraid to look at his face. His black boots were caked in the red clay he'd tracked into the bed of the wagon. He sat on a trunk packed with her finest linens and the silk gown she'd worn on her wedding day. She felt the weight of him on her heart, each beat strangled a little more until her blood stilled.

The steel blade of his long knife glinted in the light that seeped through the wagon's canvas cover. He'd been using the point to pick dirt from under his nails, but now he watched her. She knew without looking. She'd been married long enough to know a man's mind. He shifted his legs while he leered at her, the wooden trunk creaking beneath his weight. His voice came rough and hard, like rock scratching against iron. "I could cut it off, but then you'd have nothing to protect that pretty face from the sun."

She closed her fingers into fists so he wouldn't see them shake, her nails digging into her palms until the pain stilled the tremors. She untied the bonnet, pulled it from her hair, and let it fall beside her onto the grass-stuffed mattress. When they were too tired to walk, the children sat on the mattress, which covered boxes and sacks of provisions. The man had asked to see them when he'd led her into the wagon. Now he seemed to have lost interest in the flour, rice, and beans.

"That's nice. I like yellow hair." He swallowed. "Now take the ribbon out."

She did as she was told, feeling his eyes on her as she raised her arms over her head, as if her body were exposed to him through her calico dress.

Bitterly, she recalled that the thought of Indians had terrified her when she and Daniel left Minnesota because of the Dakota War. That had been in 1862, six years ago now. They had made a new home in Illinois, where Danny was born that first year and Astrid the next. They celebrated the end of the Great Rebellion with everyone else and looked forward to better days. Maria thought they were happy. When Daniel had told her his plans to go west, she'd been unable to sleep without recalling tales of scalped settlers during the uprising. Hundreds had been killed by the Sioux, some in ways that not even the brazen newspaper accounts would detail. Daniel had reassured her they would be safe in a large group, and Maria believed him, so long as they traveled with white men. When they departed Council Bluffs, the people in the other wagons seemed kind enough. Most were families like hers looking to homestead in Oregon and California. The others included hard men who'd banded together to reach the goldfields in Montana and soft men looking for work and adventure in the mining camps and cities growing out of the scoured dirt. They were good, God-fearing people, most of them, and Maria had never worried for herself or the children, who took to the two-thousand-mile journey at first like a summer of picnics.

Those days seemed long ago now. Maria sometimes wondered if God had abandoned them. Or maybe they'd abandoned God. For all the misfortune that had befallen them, she wondered if He was deaf to prayers uttered beneath a wagon's thin canvas cover. The trouble had started when the oxen sickened on the trail west of Ogallala. Daniel had blamed alkaline water from a tainted spring. Even after Daniel had fed bacon grease to the animals to counteract the effects, two of the beasts never recovered. With only a single yoke to pull the wagon, they had to throw out every furnishing they'd packed. Other families offered to carry some items for them, but they were limited in what they could take. Everyone had packed all they could fit into their wagons.

The loss of the oxen had slowed them, and no one could afford to wait. Accounts of travelers who'd arrived too late to cross the mountains before snows set in weighed on everyone. None of the stories ended well. Daniel, always vulnerable to the sin of pride, had urged the others to move on. To assuage their guilt, he vowed to press forward with longer days and no break on the Sabbath. They might meet again at Fort Laramie, where he could buy or trade for more oxen, he'd told them. Yet after the others had departed, Daniel couldn't push the oxen long or hard enough to make up for the slower pace. Heat cloaked the air, heavy in their lungs and on their weary backs. Daniel had worried the last oxen would break down.

With the sun high overhead, they had stopped for a midday meal and allowed the animals to graze and rest. Daniel had been unyoking the oxen when Danny saw riders approach. He called out in his excitement. At first Maria had welcomed the idea of company; riders might know how much farther it was to the fort. Then she got a look at them. She called back Danny and picked up Astrid and put the children in the wagon while Daniel had gone to meet the newcomers.

The three riders reminded Maria of the miners who had traveled in the train: rough-looking men wearing leather belts with holsters and guns at their waists. Each led a mule packed with goods. The oldest one, the one who did all the talking, had streaks of gray in his beard that reminded Maria of a wolf.

He had ridden directly to Daniel and introduced himself as Lucas Stoddard. The others were his brothers, Cyrus and Sean. Lucas Stoddard's lips stretched back into a wide smile, speaking with a hearty voice while his pale eyes surveyed their camp until they found Maria and pinned her to the spot.

The men had expressed gratitude when Daniel offered to share a meal. "It's not much," he had told them. "We don't cook a big meal when we stop in the middle of the day, but the animals need the water and time to graze."

The strangers helped Daniel gather water and see to the oxen. Together the men led the animals to a nearby field. Danny gathered dried buffalo chips, and Maria started a fire to make coffee and warm a pot of oatmeal and a stew of dried apples. She set out hardtack, and since there was company, she fried up some bacon. The sweet smell of the sizzling meat helped put her mind at ease.

The men had returned and washed up at the water barrel tied to the outside of the wagon while Daniel told the brothers of their hardships on the trail. His voice had rung with a cheerful tone when he told her Mr. Stoddard said the brothers would join them as far as Laramie.

The gray-bearded Stoddard, standing at Daniel's shoulder, doffed his dusty hat to Maria. She smiled uncertainly. "Won't that slow you down, three men on horseback?"

He offered his broadest smile, but his brows narrowed and his gaze sharpened like a blade. "We're not in such a hurry that we would strand a family in the wilderness." He turned to his brothers. "I don't think we could live with ourselves if we did."

The pair nodded in eager assent. They were smaller than their brother, thin and hungry looking, the runts in the pack. The youngest — she thought it was Sean — didn't look old enough for a beard. He had a large Adam's apple that bobbed in his throat with every swallow. Cyrus sported a wispy blond mustache that reminded her of a caterpillar. Both were too shy to meet her gaze, and she had tried to assure herself it would be good to have more men around to share the labors of the trail. *A larger group would be safer, would it not?*

With the food ready, Maria had excused herself to fetch the children. Astrid had followed after her brother in gathering more buffalo chips. Maria found them on the opposite side of the wagon, Danny flinging the patties toward his squealing sister. She was

13

about to chide the boy when she sensed a presence at her side and shivered.

It was Sean, his throat practically spasming with unstated agitation.

"You startled me," she said.

She eased away from his sudden closeness, but he stepped forward, his voice a whisper hot against the bare skin of her neck. "Better leave them to their play, ma'am."

Confused, she followed his gaze back toward the campfire where Mr. Stoddard had filled a plate with food. He offered it to Daniel, who initially objected before acceding to the newcomer's insistence. Her husband looked her way and smiled while raising the plate a fraction to acknowledge their guest's manners, as if to reassure her that all would be well. Maria had wanted to return the expression, but something in Sean's manner left her throat tight and lips pursed.

With the plate in Daniel's hands, Mr. Stoddard reached down as if to wipe his hands on his trousers. Sean gripped Maria's arm when she stepped toward them. The strength in his thin-boned fingers surprised her. She turned to the younger man, noting only in the corner of her eye how Mr. Stoddard's right hand came up with a pistol.

She blinked, confused to see him hold the gun to Daniel's head. It happened so fast her brain hardly had time to note the strangeness of the gesture before she shuddered at the pop that echoed across the clearing like a single handclap. A puff of smoke rose from the barrel of Mr. Stoddard's gun, which he returned to the holster on his belt in a movement so smooth he somehow managed to take the plate from Daniel's hand before her husband, open-mouthed with surprise, slumped to his knees and collapsed to the ground.

With the plate in hand, Mr. Stoddard turned to Cyrus. "No sense wasting a meal he won't enjoy."

The words hadn't completely registered in Maria's mind. No sensible thought could, for she hadn't believed the images her eyes had captured, a blurry daguerreotype displaying a scene that could come only from a fevered nightmare: her husband's body — *corpse?* — lying in the red dirt beside the campfire.

"Daniel!"

Maria had lost track of time after going to Daniel. She hadn't believed what she'd seen until she held him, his lifeless eyes staring at her with an emptiness that hollowed her, his blood on the hand she raised before her face confirming what she had witnessed. She covered his body with hers, rocking on her haunches as if she might shake him awake. Death had conveyed a great weight to him, as if he were no more animate than a stone. She disbelieved life could so quickly be extinguished — even a fire left a vestige of heat or smoke — but her doubts fell away with tears shed to no effect. She looked to the heavens. A high level of flat, ruffled clouds had moved in, blanketing the sky like a flouncy quilt and obscuring the sun. *Were God's eyes so easily veiled to the treachery of man? How could He have allowed this to happen?*

The men had left her to mourning as they tore through the camp, taking whatever they wanted. Thoughts of her children brought Maria back. Her mind had become so untethered from the moment she didn't know if the children had heard her screams or the gunshot that had killed their father. She stood to look for them, unsteady on her feet, forgetting Daniel's blood on her hands as she smoothed the folds of her dress, leaving smears across her waist and hips. She heard their squeals coming from the other side of the wagon and realized they must still be at play gathering buffalo chips. Her world had irretrievably altered, yet it was as if no time had passed at all.

With her attention diverted, Cyrus had dragged Daniel's body into the nearby brush. Clumps of moist red mud where Daniel's blood had soaked the hard ground were all that remained of him. She had turned from the sight and stumbled. Mr. Stoddard had caught her elbow and guided her to the wagon. Her legs functioned, but she had no awareness of their movement. "Will you allow me to bury him?"

"You can do whatever you want after we leave."

He had forced her to hand over the key to the strongbox where Daniel kept what little money they had. He hadn't believed her when she said they had no other valuables and made her show him the inside of the wagon. She had cringed to watch him rifle through the trunk that held her wedding dress, his murdering hands pushing aside the silk folds in search of something he might sell. She might have explained that they'd turned over what few bits of silver they'd owned to others to carry after the oxen died. How at that point flour and rice were more valuable than heirloom cutlery. But she had grown numb, her body cold to the world despite the afternoon heat and the suffocating air beneath the canvas cover.

She had heard Mr. Stoddard promise not to harm the children and to leave them with enough food to survive, but his voice sounded far away. She had nodded absently, her head woozy from heat and grief. Her focus returned only once it became clear Stoddard wasn't done taking.

Maria untied the ribbon and pulled the pins, allowing her hair to fall about her shoulders. She shivered despite the heat after a loose strand grazed her neck. Stoddard watched, his red, wet mouth like an open wound between the hoary beard.

"No need to be afraid. This is nothing you haven't done before. Just do what comes natural, and no harm will come to you or those little ones."

He shifted again on the trunk and leaned forward, closing the distance between them. She could smell on his breath cheap tobacco and the brandy she'd kept in her medicine bag. He gestured with the knife. "You won't be needing that apron."

She nearly choked on the bile in her throat, her mouth too dry to swallow. Her hands shook as she reached behind her, and the knot she'd tied that morning with steady hands defied her.

"Let me help."

He hovered over her, his arms reaching so that even though he didn't touch her she felt smothered by the stench of body odor and dried horse sweat. He took his time in untying the apron strands, his breath hot against her neck. Gripping the apron like a prize, he leaned back, a triumphant expression splitting his beard. White flakes of spittle had gathered at the corners of his mouth. She tried to avoid his eyes, but they seemed to hold her in place as he stared, and she flushed through her chest and throat beneath the blue calico dress that buttoned up to her neck.

"Those are a lot of buttons. Do you want to unhook them or shall I?" He turned the knife in his hand, looking eager to test its edge.

She managed to swallow. "Please, just take what you want and go."

His eyes, pale as river ice, looked her up and down before locking onto hers again. "I mean to do just that."

Her body tensed as he started toward her. She closed her eyes and held her breath. The knowledge that this man wouldn't stop taking until she had nothing left crushed whatever hope remained within her, and she cursed God. She felt Stoddard looming over her when a voice from outside the wagon stopped him.

"Lucas. Rider's coming."

CHAPTER TWO

Atticus Grieve saw the wagon from the trail and rode toward it, hoping he might get a meal he didn't have to cook himself. The long hours in a saddle over so many days had numbed his legs and ground his backbone to a nub. His arm ached from holding the tether rope on which a pack mule trailed behind the tall palomino stallion he rode. He'd named it Deuce because it was the second golden-skinned horse he'd owned. This one had been through hell and back and was the closest thing to family he had left. Deuce deserved a feedbag and rest even if he didn't.

On approaching the wagon, he was surprised not to see more behind the first and called out a hesitant greeting. Not many wagons traveled alone. Then again, there weren't many lone riders on the emigrant trail, either. Riding into a camp could be a tricky thing, and the smaller the camp, the more nervous its occupants might be. Grieve reassured himself there was safety in numbers — provided no one got shot in the introductions.

They were waiting for him when he drew up. Three men who, by the looks of them, had been on the trail as long as he had. A rustle of movement from inside the wagon alerted him to at least one more, but he held his eyes straight. He was the stranger here; better he check his curiosity until everyone felt at ease. His right hand rested on the saddle horn, near enough to the Colt '60 on his hip if it came to that.

The man in the middle stepped forward. He looked about forty, close to Grieve's age. He had a head of dark, unruly hair beneath a dusty dome-shaped hat. Gray speckled his wiry beard. A revolver hung butt forward from his belt on the left, as if he were accustomed to drawing while on horseback. Grieve wondered if he could shuck that six-shooter as quickly from the ground. Just in case it mattered.

"A good day to you," the man said, touching the brim of his hat.

Grieve returned the salute with his left hand. "Evening."

"What can we do for you?"

"It's getting late. I thought maybe I could

share your fire."

Grieve allowed himself a glance around the camp. Despite the hour, it looked like they'd let a fire burn out. Beyond the wagon, a pair of oxen grazed in a picked-over field at the base of a sandy ridge. Three horses and three mules were picketed nearby to find what they could among the coarse grass and brush. A lot of horses for a single wagon. Their ribs showed through their flanks, and Grieve wondered if the riders had run out of oats for their mounts.

The men didn't look so well put together themselves. Their clothes were so dirty Grieve figured they hadn't been washed or changed since they'd come on the trail. The speaker was the biggest of the trio. His hair hung to his shoulders so that the back of his neck never saw the sun. Or a bar of soap. He had a bulbous nose and pale eyes that never wavered from Grieve. The others were thin-boned young men with nervous eyes that alighted everywhere but on Grieve. These three plus whoever's in the wagon. With the canvas top pulled tight in the back, Grieve couldn't see inside. Maybe one man, he calculated; the wagon looked light from the way its wheels barely dug into the soft dirt off the trail. His back itched with uncertainty, as if a scattergun were pointed his way.

"I can feed myself," Grieve said, "even have some to offer if you don't mind plain fare."

"That's awfully kind of you." Despite the gun on his hip, the big man's manner was as hearty as a preacher working up to the offering. "Got a name, stranger?"

"Atticus Grieve."

"Where you from?"

There it was. An innocent question once, now rife with portents. Grieve didn't doubt his voice would give him away in time, so he saw no sense in lying. With the truth, he at least stood a halfway chance of a friendly reception. His odds might be even better than a coin flip. Maybe the men hadn't fought in the war. Maybe they asked just to make conversation. Three years had passed. A lot of people had gotten on with their lives. Some hadn't. Grieve knew that better than anyone.

"Georgia," Grieve said. "Near Macon."

The man nodded as if he'd guessed the truth. "I'm Lucas Stoddard. These are my brothers, Cyrus and Sean. We're from Arkansas."

"Pleased to make your acquaintance." Grieve waited. The younger men looked

24

toward their brother, who seemed lost in thought. Grieve gestured toward the field where the animals grazed. "Guess I'll just picket my mule and horse over with the others."

It could have been a question the way he phrased it, and he waited a beat before Lucas Stoddard nodded again and spoke: "I suppose we'll need to gather fuel for a fire."

Grieve took a wide berth around the camp. As he rode past the back of the wagon, still imagining the hidden scattergun, movement drew his eyes. Someone had loosened the ties that held the canvas in place. He couldn't see into the deep shadows within, just a face looking out, small and pale as a death mask.

Grieve unsaddled his horse and stripped the mule of its packs, piling his supplies under a canvas cover for safekeeping in a thicket of greasewood. He looped a feedbag over Deuce's ears and took his time brushing down the horse as he mulled his options.

Unsettled by the manner of these men, he contemplated moving on. Strangers raised the potential for a threat, especially so far from the civilizing influences of a town. Yet Grieve had found most emigrants, once they had a measure of a man, were pleased by company, either for the exchange of news or simply to break the monotony of conversation among the same people every day.

By the time Grieve returned to the camp, a woman was working over the fire. He interpreted her presence as a good sign that the brothers felt comfortable with their guest. She was a little thing, almost too clean for the trail. Grieve masked his surprise when Lucas Stoddard introduced her as his wife, Maria. He guessed her to be younger than her husband by nearly a score of years.

Grieve removed his hat. "Ma'am."

The woman offered a tight-lipped smile in return but held her eyes on the fire, a hot-burning blaze of dried brush and buffalo chips. She wore a high-collared blue dress without an apron. A smear of red clay stained the fabric that stretched across her narrow hips. Her uncovered hair, the color of corn silk, hung loose down her back.

"I've brought some things to contribute to our provender," Grieve said. "I'm afraid it's not much."

"All God's gifts are equal in His eyes," she said.

"Bacon, especially, I expect." He smiled, earning another tight-lipped response that

26

did not reach her eyes. A tiny crucifix hung on a thin chain around her neck. *A papist.* The few Grieve knew usually stayed to themselves. He expected she normally kept the cross tucked beneath her dress, but the chain had gotten caught in the folds of the collar. It glinted in the light from the fire as she leaned over to pour coffee.

He accepted a cup and thanked her. Stoddard already had a tin cup in his hands. His younger brothers were off washing after seeing to their animals. Stoddard asked, "Where you headed, Mr. Grieve?"

"At least as far as Laramie." Grieve blew on the coffee and sipped. *Real beans.* He'd never grown accustomed to the blends of roasted rye and other substitutes they'd been forced to drink during the war. He savored the taste. "How about you?"

"We'll be passing through Laramie on our way to the South Pass. We figure to get us a homestead."

"Never took up arms against the Union?" The Yankees said the war was over, but their laws continued to punish Confederate veterans, denying them the hundred and sixty acres of government land free to any other citizen.

A grin split Stoddard's beard. "Not my brothers. They were too young to fight."

They had returned from washing. Cyrus looked a shade paler with a layer of dust scrubbed from his downy cheeks. Beneath his vest he wore a red flannel shirt with a large tear at the elbow. He stood uncomfortably, shifting his weight from one leg to the other like he had somewhere else to be.

The boyish one, Sean, looked just as uneasy. He had a lean face and an Adam's apple almost the size of a child's fist that rose up and down in his throat steady as a heartbeat. Grieve wondered how he managed to breathe through the thing. Both of them looked to their brother as if awaiting instructions. All three men were still heeled. Grieve was glad he'd decided to leave his gun belt on, too.

"Supper's ready." Maria stepped back from the fire, leaving room for the men to approach. Grieve's stomach rumbled at the smell of bacon and potatoes.

Stoddard moved in first. "Let me fix a plate for our guest."

CHAPTER THREE

The rifle shone like gold beneath Montana's early summer sun.

"So that's a Winchester. I've heard of them but never seen one up close."

Josey Angel noted a trace of envy in the tone of his neighbor. Stephen Chestnut cradled the gun like a newborn, his rheumy eyes blinking in the light. It was the receiver, made of a bronze and brass alloy, that shone so brightly.

"I see why they call it 'Yellow Boy.' It sure is pretty." Chestnut whistled for emphasis. "Sort of puts my Henry to shame."

"I'll hear no disparagement of a Henry." Josey had carried the Winchester's antecedent throughout the war and all the way to Virginia City, long enough for him to feel the weapon was as much a part of him as his right arm, though some of the things he had done with that gun still haunted him.

Chestnut handed the rifle back. "It suits you."

"It's just a rifle."

"And I suppose you're just Josef Anglie-wicz."

"That's my name."

Chestnut cocked his head, exposing his narrow face beneath a wide-brimmed hat. "No more Josey Angel, eh? I suppose you have changed as much as people say."

"What do people say?" Josey smiled to soften the edge in his voice. He knew Chestnut meant well, but he felt an old sadness creeping up on him. He'd never appreciated the nickname, or the notoriety that came with it. Some names attracted stories like burrs on a saddle blanket. The stories could be more nettlesome than any thorns, until his life felt appropriated into a legend no longer his to determine.

"Just that you're different. You're a wealthy rancher now. A husband. A father."

"I'm still the same man, aren't I?" He posed the question to Chestnut, but it was something Josey wondered about as well. People had always taken him for younger than his years. They saw boyish qualities in his slender frame and smooth cheeks that Josey resented as a younger man. Yet now, when he caught sight of his face in the shaving mirror he still only needed every other day, his eyes went to the lines that stretched across his forehead like a plowed field and the deepening creases that bracketed his mouth. In quiet moments alone, his wife traced the branching wrinkles that extended from the corners of his eyes. She called them "becoming," a word that begged a question he never asked aloud. *Becoming what?* Josey wasn't certain he would welcome the answer.

Rather than answer the question, Chestnut looked off, as if wishing his wife, Myrtle, or daughter, Sarah, might arrive and prompt a new course of conversation. The Chestnuts had been one of the families Josey helped guide to Montana on a wagon train from Omaha. Beset by road agents and Indians, the journey had been hard on all of them but none more so than the Chestnuts. Burton, their fourteen-year-old son, had been killed after he grabbed a loaded rifle in haste and accidentally set it off. They'd had to cover the body so his mother wouldn't see what the minié ball had done to her son's face. Two years later, Josey still felt protective of the emigrants, especially Chestnut. A small-boned man with a wispy reddish-brown mustache and pallor better suited to indoor work, he'd been a banker before the war and decided to head west when it became clear the carpetbaggers would take all the profitable work around his Atlanta home. Josey had tried to persuade him to return to that occupation in Virginia City or Bozeman, but Chestnut was determined to start fresh. He'd taken up ranching sheep on the grassy foothills between the towns, not far from Josey's place.

With the women still inside, cleaning up after lunch, no reinforcements were in sight, leaving Chestnut to explain himself. "I guess I mean you don't go looking for trouble anymore."

"I never went looking for trouble."

"Plenty always found you, though."

Can't argue with that. Even after Josey had led the emigrants across the Bozeman Trail, surviving the start of what settlers now called Red Cloud's War, trouble had found Josey. He'd returned to Fort Phil Kearny, the main source of the conflict in what was about to be recognized as the new Wyoming Territory, on a promise to Colonel Marlowe Long. The Colonel had been his commanding officer during the war and a second father to him afterwards. He'd been wounded and remained behind at the fort while Josey and the settlers pressed on to Virginia City. Josey returned to fetch him but then, laid up with his own wounds, wasn't there when Red Cloud's warriors ambushed eighty-one men outside the fort, killing every last one — including the Colonel, who'd been carrying Josey's Henry rifle when he died. Newspapers back east published lurid accounts of the massacre, undermining support for defending the Bozeman Trail, and compelling the army to negotiate terms with Red Cloud. Josey's involvement had ended even earlier. Before she would marry him, Annabelle Rutledge exacted a pledge from Josey to end his fighting days. She had no wish to raise their child as a widow. Josey said the vows, and he had not killed a man since.

He now saw Chestnut's point; he wasn't the same man. The Colonel had labeled Josey's ability to stay cool when other men grew fevered in a fight as a gift. In those moments, Josey felt more alive than at almost any other time. Light shone brighter. Sounds grew sharper. Time telescoped itself in a way that left him aware of everything happening around him all at once. In the madness of battle, Josey felt he hovered over the chaos, like a hawk floating on the wind.

Then the moment passed, and Josey's "gift" exacted its cost. He recalled walking among the dead after a battle. They were spread in monotonous lines and clusters so that they were no longer individuals but a collective, the way pine trunks blend into a single tree line or cornflowers appear as a smear of blue in a field. But the dead are the opposite of those things, which please the eye and soothe the soul. The dead are ugly as nothing else. Faces made pasty and bloated. Misshapen limbs no longer recognizable as human parts. Josey hated them, these lifeless carcasses stripped of the myth of immortality that a boy will clasp to until the lie of it is thrust in his face. He can hold his nose and numb his mind to the dead in the moment, but their ugliness leaves a mark, a stain that spreads with every attempt to wipe it away. Long after he has forgotten the peace of the forest and the scent of the bloom, he will awake with the stink of the dead on him and know that it is his inexorable end he smells.

Josey had come to terms with the war by viewing it as a culling, something every generation endured until it lost its taste for butchery. Just as bees die off after summer's flowers wilt, Josey had expected his time would come when his usefulness to the world ended. On surviving the slaughter, he had struggled to live among people again. He turned to drink. Put himself in circumstances where death seemed certain. He would have gone to meet Saint Peter half a dozen different times if it hadn't been for the Colonel and Lord Byron, the freed slave who took up with them following the march through Georgia. The two of them looked out for Josey until he had been willing — or able — to look out for himself again.

Annabelle was the cause of that — she and the rest of the settlers he'd led across never-ending plains and waterless badlands. They'd extended their hands in friendship to Josey, and they'd rallied to his and Annabelle's aid when they were most in need. In caring for others, Josey had found the humanity he'd surrendered during the war. Now when he woke in the middle of the night, it was just as likely in response to his baby's cries as to the old nightmares. The responsibility of marriage and fatherhood left him with new worries, but they were fears that reinforced his humanity rather than diminished it.

The baby had been born before the end of May the previous year. Isabelle Mary they named her. Mother and baby couldn't have been healthier, leaving Josey feeling as useful as a saddle on a pig and anxious over the need to provide for this growing family.

Even before Isabelle came into the world, he had sent Lord Byron and their top hand, Willis Daggett, off to Texas to hire a couple of dozen drovers. Josey met them there as soon as he could after Isabelle's birth, and together they herded some three thousand head back to Montana.

Josey wasn't the first to make that sort of cattle drive. His new neighbor Nelson Story had done it a year earlier. Josey had met the man when he drove his cattle past Fort Phil Kearny on the way to Montana. It had been in Josey's head ever since to match the accomplishment. On his return to Montana, Josey found the butchers in Virginia City and the surrounding mining camps were so desperate for good beef that they paid ten times what it had cost him to buy the cattle in Texas. Josey and Byron kept what they couldn't sell on the joint property they called Angel Falls to raise their own herds on the lush valley grassland.

At twenty-eight years, Josey was a wealthy man. The home he was building for Annabelle would be the biggest ranch house in Montana, constructed of stone two stories high with a veranda that wrapped around the house so she could sit in the shade with their child no matter the time of day. Josey had once promised the Colonel a seat on that porch, but he understood now the old man wouldn't have been happy sitting idle and waiting for his time to run out. *God, I miss him.*

Guilt at challenging Chestnut's assessment of his character moved Josey to generosity. He swallowed his discomfort and held out the rifle. "Do you want to shoot it?"

Chestnut's face lit up like an oil lamp with an untrimmed wick. "May I?"

Still careful of the gun, he shot just once. If Chestnut had meant to hit anything, he didn't announce it, so Josey couldn't judge his aim. "The recoil's just like the Henry," Chestnut said.

"Told you." Neither repeater packed the punch of the single-shot rifles hunters used to kill buffalo. But Josey could fire off fifteen rounds in ten seconds or less with the lever-action Winchester. He found he rarely needed more power when he hit what he aimed at. "Keep your Henry clean, and you've got no reason to buy a new rifle."

Chestnut handed over the Winchester, and Josey slipped a new cartridge into the loading gate. Chestnut shook his head. "Afraid you're going to run out of shots?"

"You know I never like to leave a gun less than fully loaded."

"The war's over, Josey. When's the last

time you needed to shoot every round before reloading?"

A lopsided grin signaled that Chestnut was teasing him, but Josey's sense of humor had never extended to martial matters. "I don't concern myself with the last time," he said. "I look to the next time."

Josey gathered his gray Indian pony and waited for Chestnut to mount the old mare that was a few hands too big for the man. The Chestnuts lived in a large, well-chinked cabin near a bend in a stream. Josey had been there to lend a hand the day they built it, along with nearly every man who'd journeyed west in their wagon train. Chestnut had plans to build a frame house like the one he'd had back in the States after the next spring shearing — if his fortunes improved. He'd been losing sheep lately and feared wolves. With Annabelle and the baby in town visiting family, Josey had come to help. He looked forward to testing his rifle on a dangerous predator.

They rode into the hills and out of sight of the cabin. Josey listened for the rush of water from the stream near a line of trees that marked one border to Chestnut's property. He loped over toward the far side of the property, drawing up when he saw a row of thin wooden posts leaning crookedly against the horizon. He waited for Chestnut to catch up. "That supposed to be a fence?"

"It's new since the last time you were here," Chestnut said, still a little breathless from the ride. "My neighbor, Remy Bouchard, put it up after he moved in."

"He did a poor job of it." Josey's sharp eyes followed the line. "Where are the rails?"

"They're made of wire, Josey."

Josey trotted his gray pony to the fence so he could inspect the taut wires with thorn-like hooks that stretched between the posts. Following his gaze, Chestnut said, "They keep the animals from rubbing up against the fence and knocking it over."

Josey rode along the fence line, wondering if it would hold cattle. Chestnut caught up. "The wire fence is an idea Bouchard brought from France."

Josey grunted. In a lot of ways, he was still a shave tail when it came to ranching. Better with a rifle than a lariat, he still had much to learn. "A lot cheaper than wood rails, I expect."

They followed the fence until Josey saw something that made him doubt the day would deliver a wolf pelt. He pulled his rifle from the saddle scabbard, levered in a cartridge, and kicked his heels into Gray's flanks.

A trio of men were gathered on the opposite side of the fence. Two were mounted. The third worked at loose wires in the fence with tools, while a half dozen sheep grazed behind them. The men looked when Josey pulled up and asked, "Problems with the fence?"

"Nothing we can't handle." One of the mounted men, the oldest of the three, had answered. He wore a dark hat and a gray mustache as thick as a horse brush. He introduced himself as McCord, Bouchard's foreman.

Josey forgot the other men's names as soon as he heard them. He replied with his and Chestnut's proper names. "Mr. Chestnut's been losing some sheep. He feared wolves."

"Wolves are a menace," McCord said. The man at the fence had stopped working and watched.

"I'm not so sure," Josey said. "Before you finish mending that fence, do you mind if Mr. Chestnut comes over and checks the notches on those animals' ears? Wouldn't want for you to get any of his sheep by mistake."

"We've made no mistake," McCord said. He stared at Josey, the lines at the corners of his eyes creasing with concentration.

40

Josey heard the thrum of the wire in the wind that blew steady off the hills. A scattering of clouds passed overhead, casting long shadows across the ground. A black-breasted magpie, perched on a nearby post, sang out, the notes of its song echoing across the undulating field.

"Maybe we should go." Josey had nearly forgotten Chestnut. "I don't think those are my sheep, Josey."

"Josey?" The man at the fence looked up. "You be Josey Angel?"

McCord chuckled. "Relax, Jack. Haven't you heard? Now that he's gotten married and settled, Josey Angel's no longer a shootist."

Josey's gaze passed over the men. The other rider held the reins in his hand, but Josey felt certain he wore a holster on the hip hidden from his view. The man who'd been working the fence had taken off his thick work gloves but still held the wire cutters in his right hand. McCord sat motionless but for a twitch to the brush at his lip.

The wood rifle stock felt warm in Josey's hands, like a living thing. Recalling his vow to Annabelle, he heard her voice in his head, reassuring him there had to be a reasonable way to work this out. He said, "Killing men was bad for my soul."

The man at the fence smiled, as if he'd heard a jape. McCord's brush twitched again. "So why carry that fancy rifle? There are better weapons for hunting wolves."

"I prefer a repeater," Josey said, raising the Winchester as if to admire its gleam, though his eyes never left the men facing him. "You never know when you might go out after a lone wolf and find a pack."

McCord said, "Faced with a pack, I'd rather have the speed of a revolver. Care for a demonstration?" His hand fell to the butt of his holstered gun as the other rider pivoted on his mount, and the third man dropped the wire cutters.

Before the tool even hit the ground, Josey fired. Levered. Fired. Levered. Fired.

In an instant, the man at the fence screamed and hopped on one foot. The second rider tumbled to the ground after his horse reared with a squeal and ran off. McCord's eyes cast up toward the hole in the brim of his hat.

Josey cocked his head, allowing a pair of ejected cartridge shells to slide off his hat brim where they'd landed. He levered in a new shot. "I've got another twelve if *you'd* like more of a demonstration."

To Chestnut he said, "Pick up those

cutters and get through the fence. I believe we'll find Mr. McCord is mistaken about the sheep."

Chestnut had already dismounted. After snipping a gap in the fence, he said, "Guess you've never seen a real shootist work a repeating rifle."

The sheep, unfazed by the gunfire, continued grazing while Chestnut confirmed the notches in their ears were his mark. He waved them through the opening with his hat.

Bouchard's men had roused from their stupor. McCord held his reins high, so Josey could see his hands. The man who'd fallen rose on quivering legs. "I think he shot my horse," he said. The third man clutched at the bullet hole in his boot. "I thought you didn't shoot people no more."

"I said *killing* was bad for my soul." Josey waited while Chestnut remounted. "I'll shoot anyone who's got it coming."

43

Chapter Four

Annabelle hiked up her linsey-woolsey skirts as she picked her way across Wallace Street. Snowmelt had transformed Virginia City's main commercial road into a bog, requiring a keen eye and even sharper olfactory sense to distinguish plain muck from the leavings of the horse-drawn traffic.

She navigated her way onto the wooden boardwalk on the north side of the street. June sun gleamed against the windows of the shops, heralding, at last, a promise of summer. Men in suits walked without overcoats and doffed their felt hats as she passed, while the few women downtown on a weekday had shed their shawls.

Virginia City held itself to be the finest town in the territory, but whatever aspirations it once held for rivaling San Francisco or Denver had been doused. Just five years earlier, in May of 1863, a couple of trail-weary miners had set their picks and shovels into nearby Alder Gulch and discovered one of the richest gold deposits in America. Within a month, a town formed. Within a year, Montana became a territory. Virginia City sprouted into its capital a year after that. The population surged past ten thousand. The wagons, tents, and wickiups that housed the first businesses were replaced with wood-frame and even stone buildings, as sturdy as anything in her native Charleston.

Decline set in almost as swiftly as Virginia City's ascension. New gold strikes near Helena drew away many miners. Commercial mining operations, some using hydraulic hoses that scarred the hillsides with streams of pressurized water, displaced others. Chinamen worked abandoned placer claims, scratching out whatever gold dust remained — which wasn't enough to maintain the luster built on get-rich-quick dreams. After her father's mercantile business in Charleston had failed during the War Between the States, Annabelle and her family had come west harboring the same dreams of wealth. With the gold tapping out, civic leaders like her father hoped to sustain Virginia City's fortunes with business and government endeavors. Evidence of how difficult that would be stood at the corner: the vacant building that once housed the *Montana Post.* The territory's first newspaper when it opened four years ago, it had picked up and followed the miners to Helena. Whispers around town predicted the capital would move next. She shuddered to envision the ghost town Virginia City would become if that happened.

Annabelle stopped at the intersection while a buckboard loaded with provisions clattered past on its way to the dining houses on Jackson Street. She pivoted to face the sun, savoring its warmth like a caress against her cheek. She had left Isabelle at her parents' house, realizing now that it had been too long since she walked through town unencumbered by a child and all the accoutrements of motherhood. Isabelle had recently marked her first birthday and had weaned herself to solid foods. Josey declared this an indication that his daughter shared her mother's strong will. While Annabelle accused him of flattery, she secretly agreed.

Motherhood had proved a revelation — though not always in the glowing terms Annabelle heard from other new mothers. She'd been a woman with duties: helping her father with the bookkeeping at his business before she married; overseeing her late husband's plantation while he'd been at war. Yet she'd never known anything like the all-consuming responsibility a child represented. Annabelle's disposition played no small part in her exhausted state. After a miscarriage during her first marriage, she'd believed herself barren. Isabelle's birth was either the answer to prayers or proof of a cruel deception by her dead husband. Either way, Annabelle determined to leave nothing to chance with the care of her child.

"You take on too much," her mother often cautioned her.

But what choice did she have? Isabelle found comfort in no one else the way she did in her mother. Even now that she was off the breast, the child wanted only Annabelle to feed her. Almost the moment Isabelle was born, Josey had fled on a cattle drive he said would set their future. At least before he left, Josey had hired Mr. Pok, the Chinaman who had worked for Annabelle's parents. Mr. Pok had recently arranged for his wife and daughter to join him in America, and Josey built them a cabin on the ranch. The Poks saw to household affairs — it was a running joke that Annabelle, raised in a home with domestic slaves, knew how to cook only over an open campfire — but, despite Josey's encouragement, Annabelle had found no suitable candidate to be a nanny to their child. Her mother, of course, eagerly offered to help. While her mother had raised three children, Annabelle had to remind herself it had been more than a score of years since her mother had cared for a baby. So it fell to Annabelle, who wondered sometimes, even as happy as she was with Josey, if she'd understood what love really meant before she'd given birth.

And yet . . .

When she thought back to her days journeying west, she recalled how frightened, excited, and awed she'd been at each new discovery. Anything seemed possible — and just about everything had happened to her. She'd been held for ransom by bandits. She'd lived as a captive among Indians. She'd killed men who'd meant her harm, including the husband she'd thought dead. While such travails might have driven another woman to ensconce herself into the sturdiest place she could find, Annabelle felt stronger for everything she had endured. Now that she was a mother and had to think of Isabelle's future, she understood how much she'd asked of Josey. This man, who'd been forced to kill more times than she wished to contemplate, turned gentle as a kitten around her and Isabelle. He'd crisscrossed the country trying to flee memories of the things he'd done to survive the war before settling down with her to build a home. Yet there were nights when she awoke alone and found him looking out the window as if called by the mountains. Sometimes she imagined she heard the call, too, though she would not speak of it. She couldn't bear the thought of watching him ride off, wondering when — or if — he'd make his way back to her. Yet the thought of caging this man like a songbird didn't sit right either.

Josey Angel was no songbird.

The jangling of a wagon's harness broke Annabelle's reverie, and she crossed Jackson Street. A young woman in a wide-skirted dress on the next boardwalk drew her eye. A tight whalebone corset accentuated a generous bosom and impossibly thin waist. *Not impossible.* Annabelle recalled when her figure could be fastened into such proportions before she'd happily shed corsets and petticoats on coming west. Wide skirts were a fire hazard while cooking over an open flame, and corsets always struck her as a cruel torture device. Now when she went out for a day of riding, she wore divided skirts or britches and shirts cut for a young man — a notion that would have scandalized the ladies back home but hardly raised a brow in these more practical parts. Forsaking the trappings of fashion seemed no sacrifice when it had been Annabelle's choice. Confronting an overdressed young woman peacocking before the wide glass windows of the Anaconda Hotel irritated her for reasons she couldn't explain.

The woman's dress was white with accents of crimson roses and a matching silk sash done up in a bow behind her waist. She'd pulled her ruffled sleeves wide to bare her shoulders and plunging neckline. A Wells-Fargo stage headed east on Wallace risked miring in the thick mud so that the driver and shotgun rider could get a better look. Annabelle glared in their direction, but they paid her no heed. She assured herself she could still turn heads if she wished, though a thorn of doubt pricked at her. The woman must be a newcomer, unaware that one of the privileges of living so far from the States was the freedom to ignore the mercurial fashion dictates displayed in *Frank Leslie's Illustrated Newspaper* or *Harper's Bazaar.* Here, women could wear the same dresses year after year, and no one thought less of them for it. Annabelle was debating whether she should introduce herself and enlighten the stranger when the woman turned, and

Annabelle recognized the doll-like porcelain features and golden curls beneath a wide-brimmed straw bonnet.

"Caroline?"

Her young cousin blinked with surprise. Bright eyes nearly disappeared in her squint before recognition took hold and her face split into a hesitant smile. "Annabelle! What are you doing here?"

"I should ask the same of you, Cousin. Is there a cotillion this afternoon I wasn't invited to?"

Caroline responded with a bird-like titter and pirouetted for Annabelle's benefit. "Do you like it? It arrived with the latest stage. Father said it was too pretty for anyone else to wear." Her eyes widened as the effect of her words settled in. "Excepting you, of course, that is. Though I suppose such things seem frivolous now that you're a mother."

Not yet an old woman, though. Annabelle swallowed back her reaction and managed a neutral smile. Caroline had served as Annabelle's living dress-up doll when she wasn't much older than Isabelle, the younger sister Annabelle never had. Though just sixteen, she had blossomed. Annabelle knew she should be pleased, but the sight of a flower in full bloom reminded her that petals are destined to wither and drop.

"Does your father approve of you wearing your new dress about town in the middle of the day?"

The answer came clear enough in Caroline's pursed lips and pinched brow. "You won't tell him, will you? I grew impatient to see how it looked on me."

And to see the reaction you stirred among passing townsfolk. Annabelle had little doubt her uncle Luke would hear of his daughter's display. Recalling how she'd felt at the same age, Annabelle determined to show charity. Her discomfort at the rapid passage of time should do nothing to dull the younger woman's appreciation for it.

"We see too little of each other, dear Caroline. Let's go inside and have a tea." With its white tablecloths and real china settings, the hotel's café was one of the few places in town where a dress like Caroline's wouldn't seem wholly out of place.

Caroline's eyes slid past Annabelle. "You know I would love to —"

"So suddenly concerned with being over-dressed?"

Caroline blinked with incomprehension. "No. I just know how busy you are. I'm sure you need to get home to Isabelle soon, and I wouldn't wish to detain you."

"Nonsense." Annabelle took her cousin's hand in her arm and led her to the door. "I get out too little these days. Tea with my cousin will be a treat."

Midday diners had cleared out of the café, leaving plenty of open settings. Annabelle headed toward a table for two in the back, but Caroline tugged her toward a larger table up front. "Let's sit by the window," she said. "It's such a pretty day."

After a waiter in a crisp white shirt and suit vest took their order, Caroline asked about Isabelle, and Annabelle related the anecdotes mothers are expected to share: doting passages about the wonder of motherhood, spiced with accounts of precocious demonstrations that foretell a child's imminent brilliance. Caroline, no doubt, had heard it all, relayed from Annabelle's mother to Caroline's mother. To her credit, she listened without interruption, and Annabelle forgave her distracted mien as the young woman's eyes flitted among the traffic passing across the window.

The arrival of their tea recaptured Caroline's attention, permitting Annabelle a moment to ponder how she might convince her cousin to return home and change her clothes straightaway without hurting her feelings. Before she addressed the subject, they were interrupted by a new arrival.

"How now. Here's a sight not to be rivaled in Virginia City. Two such pretty belles never made such sweet music."

"Mr. Blake!" Caroline's squeal reverberated across the open room.

Annabelle stood and offered her hand to the gentleman. Henry Nichols Blake had been editor of the *Montana Post* before it relocated and he returned to his previous vocation. He'd studied law at Harvard before the war and had been well positioned as a newspaperman to know all the attorneys and judges who participated in the Supreme Court in Virginia City. Annabelle had been pleased to hear he was building a fair practice for himself. He'd been one of her first friends on arriving in Virginia City, though their relationship had chilled after she'd wed Josey and had the baby.

"I didn't realize you were acquainted with my young cousin," Annabelle said.

"You forget it was my business to know everyone in town." Mr. Blake leaned forward to kiss Annabelle's proffered hand but his eyes never left Caroline. "You can't fault me for paying special attention to the comelier denizens."

Caroline's blush turned her face as crimson as the roses on her dress. The sight of her young cousin playing the coquette so discombobulated Annabelle that she made no objection when Caroline invited the gentleman to join them. Within no time, the waiter arrived at his elbow with a new setting.

Annabelle sat silent while her companions prattled about news of family and acquaintances. Caroline gleamed like fresh snow under a bright sun. Just two years earlier on the journey west, she had been but a wisp of a girl, romping through fields to gather wildflowers by day, leading them in song around the fire at night, and once confessing to Annabelle her fear that she might never have the opportunity to kiss a boy. Well, that no longer appeared to be a concern now that she was a woman nearly full grown. *Too fully grown, in some respects.* Her young cousin's décolletage commanded Annabelle's attention. The corset held her posture painfully erect and squeezed her torso so that with every gasping breath her bosoms threatened to burst free from their confines. Annabelle found it impossible to avert her eyes; no doubt Mr. Blake was even less suited to the challenge. With his thick, dark beard and round, wire-rim spectacles, he had always affected the appearance of an older man. Now past thirty, he was coming into his age — which was far too old to be flirting with a girl of sixteen, no matter how "comely" her appearance.

By the time the couple turned to remarking on the fair weather, the familiarity of their conversation struck Annabelle as not at all like strangers or bare acquaintances come to a chance meeting. Comprehension came slowly, like dawn over the mountains, and when full illumination fired her brain Annabelle nearly choked on her tea.

Mr. Blake hadn't come upon her meeting with Caroline, she realized; Annabelle had preempted *their* assignation.

CHAPTER FIVE

Before accepting the plate of food, Grieve recalled the chain around the woman's neck and said, "Shouldn't we say grace?"

Stoddard frowned as he looked down at a pot of boiled potatoes and beans flavored with the bacon Grieve had brought. "Yes, of course," he said before turning to the woman. "Maria, would you lead us in prayer?"

She bowed her head. Her voice wavered as she spoke, so softly Grieve had to hold his breath to hear. "Bless us, O Lord, and these, thy gifts, which we are about to receive from thy bounty. Through Christ, our Lord."

She paused. Stoddard glanced at the woman, whose head remained bowed. Grieve said, "Amen," and the others echoed him after a beat.

Stoddard crouched and swatted at the green-backed bottle flies that had gathered near the food. "Better get to it before these demons do," he said, heaping potatoes and beans onto a tin plate. "I hope you're hungry, Mr. Grieve. My Maria has outdone herself today." He stood and proffered the plate to Grieve. No one else moved.

"I'm happy to serve myself," Grieve said. "You go ahead."

"I insist." Stoddard thrust the plate toward Grieve. "Guests should come first."

Grieve felt the eyes of the others on him. He reached for the plate with his left hand.

"See that you don't drop it," Stoddard said. His pale eyes sought Grieve's, their color reminding Grieve of a wolf. He took the plate with both hands.

Stoddard's hand slipped to his waist, his right hand crossing his body as if embracing himself, down to where he wore his gun, butt forward on his left side. Grieve flipped the plate of hot food in the man's face and skinned his Colt. The gun's explosion drowned out Stoddard's cry of surprise. A waft of burned powder clouded the air like a perfume as Stoddard fell back. Grieve put a second shot between his eyes to be certain.

Cutting his eyes toward the woman, he gestured to the brothers. Cyrus stood slack-jawed, his mouth beneath the wispy blond mustache open wide enough to catch every fly in Nebraska. Sean's lips were pursed; even his Adam's apple stilled. "Them too?" Grieve asked.

The woman nodded.

The brothers had just enough time to reach for their pistols, but Grieve already had his in hand. He pivoted and fired twice. He'd rushed the shots, so he fired one more time at each once they were down to be certain.

The woman watched him reload without speaking. Grieve holstered the big Colt. He kicked dust over the scattering of beans and potatoes at his feet and looked to her. "I know your name's not Stoddard. What do I call you?"

Their eyes met for the first time. Hers were the color of storm clouds and looked as big as a rising moon in her small face. Finding her voice, she gave her name as Maria Larsson and asked, "How did you know?"

"There were lots of reasons to think something was wrong with this camp," Grieve said, allowing his eyes to trace her slender figure, "for anyone with a mind to look."

Maria rejoined the children in the wagon and sought in vain to soothe their tears. She pulled them close while peering through the opening in the back of the canvas. The man named Grieve sorted through the bodies, taking what he wanted before pulling them off into the brush. He made no effort to bury them. Once done with the task, he filled a new plate, stretching his back with a wince as he stood.

Mr. Grieve was a tall man and well put together, though lean enough to make clear he'd known hunger. His dark hair reached beyond his collar, unruly in a way that suggested he'd once kept it neat. Gray flecked his temples and the thick whiskers that ringed his mouth. She guessed he was older than her Daniel by about a decade. Maria's chest constricted, and she felt woozy to realize she would never see the gray come to her husband's hair. She squeezed the children to her until they protested, then stroked Danny's head while he looked at her. His eyes shone in the dim light of the wagon. So much like his father's. At five years, he might remember his father when he was grown. Astrid, just four, would know him only through the stories they told.

After he was cried out, Danny said, "Mama, I'm hungry."

"I'm hungry too," Astrid said.

Maria shushed them and peered through

the canvas again. She tried to recall what thoughts had woken her that morning. Had she feared for the remaining oxen? Worried over their dwindling supplies? Wondered at the remaining distance to Fort Laramie? Now she longed to open her eyes again, to feel Daniel beside her as he roused himself to see to the animals, blinking in the darkness until she saw him smile at her, the only smile that had ever made her feel loved.

Having lost both her parents at an early age, Maria had grown up in her uncle's household. She was a watchful child who rarely spoke unbidden, as if the sound of her voice might betray her alienation among her three cousins. It wasn't until she was nearly grown and Daniel began to call that she'd even imagined having a family of her own again. His love had enlivened her in a way nothing else ever had, and the children had brought her a joy she had not permitted herself to expect. If only Daniel could have been so content with those blessings, they would still be together in Illinois. She'd agreed to come west, but she'd let him know his decision displeased her. Her fear and resentment had made her shrewish toward him at times. After they'd fallen behind the others and the children were always underfoot with no playmates to entertain them, his eyes followed her, pleading for a moment alone, silently willing her to leave Danny and Astrid after putting them to bed to join him near the fire under the stars, too proud to ask, his need like a fever she stoked to punish him.

Only that morning he'd come to her in the pre-dawn darkness. The children still slept, and she'd risen to fetch water while Daniel gathered the animals. She had found him waiting when she returned from the river. He stooped to take the bucket from her hands and stole a kiss when his head moved past hers. She kissed his cheek in return, the reflexive response of a married woman, but he sought more in the gesture. He set down the bucket and kissed her again, his mouth lingering near hers, waiting for a response.

"The children will be awake soon." She had moved to step past him, but he blocked her path.

"I can be quiet. Do you remember the night before we left Council Bluffs?"

Maria had flushed with the memory of what they'd done, the children asleep beside them, their wagon surrounded by those of strangers. He slipped his arm around her waist and pulled close so that she felt his arousal. He cupped her chin and leaned in to kiss her again. She turned so his lips brushed her cheek.

"With only the two of us, there's too much work to permit time for that," she said.

She'd walked away without seeing his reaction, but she knew how her words had cut him. Now he was gone. There would be no more nights of furtive lovemaking, no chance for Daniel to redeem his decision to bring them west, or for her to forgive him. All that remained to her were these two children, the last traces of Daniel in the world aside from a corpse left to rot in the brush.

Mr. Grieve scraped his plate noisily with a spoon. The rest of the food remained in the pot at his feet. Lucas Stoddard had frightened Maria like no man ever had, yet this man had killed him and his two brothers while showing no more remorse than he would crushing a fly. She had cursed God in the moment before Mr. Grieve's arrival. Now she had to decide: was he an answer to a prayer or a punishment for her loss of faith? Determining that if he meant her harm the canvas cover wouldn't protect her, she loosened the ties and stepped down from the wagon, her back to the man while she helped Danny and Astrid down.

"The children are hungry," she said.

If Mr. Grieve were surprised to see the little ones, he didn't show it. He pointed to the pot. "Plenty here." He stepped back while she filled their plates. Once the children were seated, Maria led them in prayer. She urged them to eat and remain quiet.

"Aren't you going to eat?" he asked.

"I don't think I can."

His eyes flickered to the brush where the brothers had left Daniel. Even knowing where to look, she couldn't see the body.

Crouched beside the fire, Mr. Grieve pointed toward the food. "If you're not going to eat, do you mind . . . ?" She shook her head and watched him fill another plate. He shoveled food into his mouth, opening wide to allow in air to cool the potatoes. He ate as if they'd spent the time before supper playing chuck-a-luck or reading passages from the prayer book. She asked him again how he had anticipated Stoddard's treachery.

"Anyone could see you didn't belong with those men," he said.

If he thought to put her off with such a simple statement, she disappointed him with a look that demanded more. He broke apart the potatoes with his fork to allow them to cool while he elaborated, pointing out how much dirtier the men were than she, how her cross spoke to a faith they seemed wholly unfamiliar with, and other things she wouldn't have expected a man to notice, much less act on in such a violent manner. "You shot three men because one of them had a tear in his shirt that hadn't been patched?"

His mouth half full of potatoes, he said, "Your man ever go more than a day with a tear in his shirt?"

She dropped her eyes to the ground where Daniel had fallen.

Mr. Grieve swallowed. A weariness weighted his words that she understood came from more than weeks of riding. "They weren't the first men who meant to kill me," he said. "I'd seen the look before."

He finished eating without another word while Maria saw to the children.

"I'll sleep by the fire, if you don't mind," he said. "Before first light, I'll be on my way."

"You mean to leave us here alone?" A few minutes earlier, she'd wondered if she could trust this man. Now the thought of his departure terrified her.

His mouth twisted while his tongue worried at some food caught in his teeth. He nodded toward the brush where the Stoddards lay. "Haven't I done enough?"

Maria felt a twisting in her stomach, not hunger but fear fluttering at her insides. She hadn't the strength to yoke the oxen herself. How long would they have to wait before more wagons came along? How could she be sure the next arrivals wouldn't be as bad or worse than Lucas Stoddard? Mr. Grieve's face betrayed no concern for her plight, no kindness for a stranger — but no animosity or avarice, either. He'd displayed a gentleman's manners. He had even suggested they pray before their meal. While she wondered how a God-fearing man could kill as easily as Mr. Grieve did, she had graver concerns at the moment.

Looking to see that the children were preoccupied with their meal, she lowered her voice and said, "If your intent is to leave us here, you may as well shoot us too."

"Is that what you want?" He picked at his teeth with the nail of his little finger, his eyes locked on the horizon.

Maria clenched her jaw, hoping her voice didn't quaver. "Of course not. I don't wish to watch my children starve, either, or fall prey to wild animals — or worse," she said, recalling how Lucas Stoddard had looked at her.

"Look, Mrs. Larsson," he said, his eyes cutting toward her before looking away again, "I didn't come out here to drive a wagon. I mean to move quickly."

"What's the hurry to get to Laramie?" It wasn't like he had to cross mountains before winter set in.

"I'm looking for a man."

After he offered nothing more, she said, "This man must be important."

"He killed my son and father."

Maria blanched. "I'm sorry. I —"

"We've all lost loved ones."

She noticed he didn't mention a wife, and she didn't ask. Growing up in a home that wasn't her own, she'd learned to understand how much people were willing to give, and she was learning that Atticus Grieve didn't have a lot to offer. Yet in her pity, she found hope that her assessment of him had been right. A man who had loved so deeply once couldn't be all bad.

"I was raised to believe God answers prayers that come from the heart," she said. "And he rewards those generous souls who help Him to carry out His works." She turned her head in the direction of the children, hoping to draw his eyes to them.

He cleared his throat and swallowed. "I was raised to believe the same. But I came to learn that a loaded gun in a man's hand can be more effective than any number of prayers from begging mothers and crying children."

Maria swallowed back rising panic before it could dull her wits. If this man would not be moved by pity, she would need to think of something else. She asked, "This man you seek, he's at Laramie?"

"He was. I expect to find news of him there."

Maria spoke carefully, not wishing to stir an anger that might overwhelm Mr. Grieve's better nature. "And you intend to kill this man?"

"I will kill him. Or die trying."

The children had finished eating and were watching them. Maria stepped away from the fire, waiting for Mr. Grieve to follow. "A man so dangerous can't be easy to kill."

"One way or the other, it will be over, and I will find peace."

Still watching the children, she said, "A man traveling with a woman and children could ask questions without raising suspicions. A woman could ask even more." His brows knitted and he looked toward her as if seeing something for the first time. Hoping the warmth she felt in her chest didn't redden her face, she said, "Do you even know his name, this man you're going to kill?"

Grieve looked to the west, toward mountains they couldn't yet see and troubles Maria could only imagine.

"His name is Josey Angel."

Chapter Six

Annabelle's eyes watered from a coughing fit as she tried to swallow back her reaction to her cousin's relationship with Mr. Blake.

"Are you all right?" Concern wrinkled Caroline's face, dimming its glow like a cloud passing before the sun. "You shouldn't drink your tea so quickly."

Struggling to breathe, Annabelle nodded her agreement; she'd nearly drained her cup while the enamored couple had barely taken more than a few sips.

"We've talked so much, we've barely given Mrs. Angliewicz an opportunity to speak," Mr. Blake said. He patted Caroline's hand as if the gesture were an admonishment, his hand lingering long enough for Caroline to brush her thumb against his.

Annabelle swallowed back another cough. "I'm fine."

"Tell us, how is the baby? I was certain motherhood would suit you." Mr. Blake wore his thick beard like a mask, leaving his dark brows as the most expressive part of his face. They arched like a church window. "A rancher woman now. I'm so happy for you."

Forcing a smile, Annabelle replied: "And you, Mr. Blake. I was so pleased to hear you'd returned to your practice of the law. How brave you are to change professions at your age."

Mr. Blake cleared his throat, his eyes sliding toward Caroline. "On the contrary, a friend once told me: 'A lawyer is young until he is thirty.' I feel I've grown into the occupation."

"Mr. Blake's friends in Boston say that in a couple of years he stands an excellent chance for an appointment to U.S. attorney for the territory," Caroline said. "Isn't that exciting?"

"Yes, of course." Annabelle knew more about Mr. Blake than Caroline realized. While he had never been so overt in his flirtations with Annabelle, he'd made his interest clear. Given her well-known attachment to Josey, Mr. Blake contented himself playing the understudy, biding his time in hopes the role might fall to him one day. After Annabelle married Josey, Mr. Blake withdrew any overtures at friendship. She'd forgiven his petulance, but he had to be aware of the inappropriateness of this courtship — how else to explain their covert meeting? And for that she held Mr. Blake more responsible than dewy-eyed Caroline, so flush with pride at meriting the attentions of a gentleman. Annabelle nearly regretted what she must do.

"Tell me, Mr. Blake," she said. "How are your friends in Boston? Do you still correspond so ardently with Miss Clara Clark?"

A silence, heavy like the closing of a church door, fell across the table. Annabelle watched both react: Mr. Blake inhaling sharply; Caroline blinking as if someone had flicked the end of her nose.

"Do I have her name right? I know to you she will always be Kittie." Annabelle offered Mr. Blake her most earnest smile and steeled herself as Caroline rose and departed with an abrupt complaint of dust in her eye.

Even before she'd seen a mountain, Annabelle had understood a man's head could be as thick as one. Whether from ignorance or obdurateness, a man could resist any fact that proved inconvenient to his desires in a given moment. The stronger the desire, the more closed a man's mind became to contradictory truths. *Poor man.* She was tempted to let Mr. Blake carry on with his dalliance, confident that Caroline's attentions — like those of any girl her age — would prove as fickle as a Montana spring and leave him shivering in the cold. Yet it wouldn't do to let things play out. The girl's reputation might not recover if the courtship became public or went too far. Sometimes men needed a clear and forceful demonstration of a woman's will to break through their thick-headedness. They were quick to dismiss such actions as "unladylike," for it threatened their unchallenged dominance of the world.

While her Josey wasn't immune to these intractable bouts, one of the things she loved about him was his reaction on being roused from one. Where other men felt threatened by any show of strength in a woman, Josey valued it, a reaction she deemed sensible. Why should a man speak with pride of a spirited horse but want nothing more than a docile wife? To Annabelle, this proved that most men feared the mare more than the stallion, a weakness she exploited whenever necessary.

Once alone, Annabelle turned in her seat to face Mr. Blake. His brows had fallen flat, his eyes narrowed behind the wire-rim glasses. "I thought better of your discretion," he said, his clenched jaw lending a tightness to his voice. "To think you would succumb to petty jealousy —"

"If you think you can make me jealous by chasing after a girl half your age —"

"It would seem I've succeeded."

His brows peaked. Annabelle wanted to punch his nose. She placed her hands on the table, fingers splayed, and inhaled deeply. As Mr. Blake continued, she held her focus on the unused cutlery at her table setting.

"To suggest anything untoward about my interest in a charming young woman —"

"She's only a girl," Annabelle said, fingers drumming against the knife's silver handle.

"My point is that your vanity won't be fenced in any more than your — what do you call them? *'Dogies'?*" Both eyebrows popped twice to emphasize his clever word play.

Annabelle gritted her teeth and brought her hands to her lap, her fists clenched. "You seem to enjoy thinking me a simple rancher woman."

"It's not that I enjoy it." He took up his cup, swirled the tea around the bowl a moment and made a show of savoring a sip. "We all find our proper station in life, eventually."

Annabelle nearly bit her tongue to arrest the first retort that came to mind. She inhaled and expelled her breath. Leaning forward, her voice dropped to a whisper. "Tell me, Mr. Blake: Do you know the difference between a bull and a steer?"

He waved his hand dismissively. "They're both some sort of bovine —"

She pressed the knife she'd taken from the table against the soft flesh between his thighs. Restaurants in Virginia City served a lot of beef, and the knives at the table settings had to be sharp. "Let me give you a hint."

Blake cleared his throat, squirming beneath her reach until finding it safer to remain still. "I see your point." This time he took no apparent pleasure in word play. He moved his hand toward hers, and she twisted her wrist.

"Keep your hands on the table."

He complied.

"Let me press my point home." She leaned in to him. Mr. Blake no longer breathed. He held his head rigid, his eyes locked on the wall in front of him. His wide forehead gleamed with perspiration in the light from the window.

Compassion fluttered within her breast. Mr. Blake was not a wicked man. He had been kind to her at a time when Annabelle's relationship with Josey was uncertain even in her mind. She doubted that he'd turned his attentions to Caroline only to irritate her — there weren't so many options in Virginia City that a bachelor could afford to be choosy. No matter his intentions, for her cousin's sake Annabelle couldn't sit by idly. Though she'd never bring herself to act on her threat, even if he were a thorough rake, Mr. Blake knew just enough about her past to have his doubts. Certain of his attention, she continued.

"Caroline is an innocent. A sweet and clever girl, but still naïve in the ways of courtship. I won't watch her heart broken because you fancy a 'comely' distraction until Kittie makes up her mind. If any distress befalls my cousin, you will learn more than you care to know about ranch life, especially steers, geldings, and barrows."

She rose on Caroline's return, replacing the knife to the table setting and handing the girl a handkerchief for her red-rimmed eyes. "We must be going, Cousin. I told our fathers we'd visit them at the store." She ignored the look of disappointment on Caroline's face and turned toward the pale gentleman whose eyes remained fixed on the far wall. "Be sure to thank Mr. Blake, who has so graciously offered to pay for our tea."

CHAPTER SEVEN

Josey shivered and pulled the buffalo-skin blanket tight around his shoulders as he gazed out the window. The start of summer turned the days warm enough that he could ride without a coat, yet no matter how hot the sun blazed, night brought a chill, like a bed stripped of a down comforter.

The moon had risen, so bright it nearly hurt his eyes. Its light deepened the shadows among the trees and in the roll of the hills that stretched toward the mountains. During the day, Josey could almost forget that cold and dark filled half the world. Then night came, and he woke to old fears. The happier his days passed, the more intense his nighttime dread became, like the black shadows that hid among the moon's brilliance.

The cabin he'd built when they first settled at Angel Falls had seen them through one winter, but he'd been remiss in maintaining the chinks between the logs, and the house didn't hold the day's warmth the way it should. Annabelle hadn't complained. They'd hired the best masons and carpenters in the territory to construct the permanent home he'd promised her when they wed. The house would be two stories, with a grand staircase and stoves in every room. The workers had made a good start the previous year, and they promised to be done before summer's end. Josey's family wouldn't feel winter's bite in a sturdy house like that. Yet his neglect of the cabin dogged him, a reminder of how ill-suited he felt to the domestic life that seemed to come so easily to most men. The things that came naturally to Josey only brought danger to him and his family.

A week earlier, after hearing Annabelle's story about the lecherous newspaperman, Josey had told her about the confrontation over the sheep with Bouchard's men. He'd tried to pass it off as an amusing yarn, but Annabelle's alarm was immediate. He might have been killed, she'd said. All it would have taken was one lucky shot. Only his understanding of what a fool he'd been shielded him from more of her opprobrium. He'd done well to keep his vow of a more peaceable path until running across

Bouchard's men. In the days that followed, he'd tried to put it behind him, yet he'd awoken tonight believing he'd killed Mc-Cord and the other men at the fence. Lathered in sweat, pulse pounding, he'd been so certain he'd murdered those men that it wasn't until he'd gotten to the window and his breathing steadied that he could sort memory from imagining.

On the day he'd told her about it, Annabelle had asked if he knew why he'd challenged Bouchard's men. He'd shaken his head and tried to pass it off as something noble done in support of a neighbor, but in truth he didn't wish to examine his motives. For now that he'd had time to give rein to his mind, he recalled his thoughts just before he opened fire with the Winchester and the sublime clarity that came from senses so acute he could feel the blood course through his veins. Not even blood. Something richer. *Ambrosia,* he imagined it, like he'd been drunk on the elixir of the gods. In that moment, Josey Angel had felt divine. He'd never considered that those men might best him. Then the moment passed, and his vulnerability settled around him like a mantle of snow. Give a man everything he ever wanted and you hand him something else unwelcomed — the fear that comes from knowing he can lose it all.

No one had ever explained this contradiction to him, had even told him it existed. Before meeting Annabelle, Josey felt his life had been spent learning all a man could know about death, so love was a continuous revelation. It still seemed unreal at times that she could love him. Even after two years, he still had much to learn about even the most natural aspects of relations between a man and woman. His parents had been affectionate but not demonstrative, so the rules of engagement were unfamiliar to him. When was it appropriate to touch or squeeze or any of the other things he longed to do? Alone in the dark it was easy to discern boundaries, but these weren't the only times he desired her. At dinner with her family, for instance, he found pleasure in watching how she moved. He longed to draw her close and feel her body through her thin calico dress. He submersed himself in his desire, like diving into a deep pool, allowing the pressure to build until he felt his lungs would burst from it, anticipating its release like the first sweet draw of breath. At times like these, all she had to do was reach out and touch the bare skin at his wrist and he felt a charge through his body. She knew it, too, and delighted in drawing him on, a brush of fingers against his trousered leg, a musical laugh that led her to lean her head close to his so that he could feel her breath on his neck. His eyes followed wherever she went.

When she was feeling delightfully indecent — or merely sympathetic to his pangs — her eyes would find his in an implicit invitation. She would invent an excuse to slip away from the room where company gathered while he bided his time, pulse racing, breath shallow, before following. He would find her waiting in another room and they would come together in a breathless rush. His hands caressing her face, pushing her hair back, lips sealed so that their breaths became one. Her body pressed to his as if to defy the cloth that separated them. A stolen moment or two. He was never certain if she meant to whet his appetite or if she sensed his need for some release of the building pressure. For when she pulled away, he could not discern whether sweet sympathy or playful wickedness infused her smile. Either way, it left him jelly-legged and drunk with the happiness of a man besotted.

Because any man might admire Annabelle's intelligence, strength, and beauty, Josey recognized that his appreciation for these things gave him no claim on her. No, what made Annabelle his were the things she permitted no one else to see — or hear. He understood this every time he caught her singing. The first time he had come upon her in song she was in her bath in the little cabin he lived in when they first came to Virginia City. Though not yet married, Annabelle often stayed with him while they recuperated from the travails — both physical and emotional — of their journey west. He'd been out hunting one morning and returned sooner than she'd expected. He knew this when he heard her singing *Lorena.* As soon as he entered the cabin she halted, embarrassed, for she knew herself incapable of carrying a tune. It might have been the only thing in the world she wasn't good at despite trying. Because of that, Annabelle never sang *to* Josey, though, in time, with his encouragement, she grew comfortable enough that if she was singing to herself or the baby when Josey came upon her, his presence no longer stopped her. He loved her all the more for that.

This was Josey's greatest revelation: love wasn't a celebration of a person's finest qualities. It wasn't even an acceptance of all the rest. Josey didn't love Annabelle because of her beauty and in spite of her singing.

He loved her equally for all the things that made her Annabelle, that made her *his.*

That conclusion should have been the end of it. How many stories had Josey heard as a child that finished with "they lived long and happily"? People spent their lives trying to achieve such a gauzy denouement, and now that Josey had his he'd learned there wasn't really an ending, other than death. To a thoughtful man, the deepest love is tinged with the deepest sorrow, for no man has loved without losing it in time. Every love story is, ultimately, a tragedy if you play it out to its final scene. The more Josey loved, the more vulnerable he felt to the suffering that stalked him, inevitable as death. Constant vigilance had seen him through the war. Peace and prosperity hadn't changed the need for that. If anything, they had increased the need. At the poker table, a man plays fearlessly with only a couple of bits. Josey felt like a man who played with all he valued at stake, and all the world was arrayed against him to take what he had.

Josey never liked to gamble.

The slightest shift of air in the room signaled Annabelle's approach. She never slept long once he rose, no matter how quietly he stole away. She pressed against him, shielding his back from the chill and filling his head with the scent of lavender and something ineffable he associated only with her. She nestled her head against his neck and followed his gaze.

"It's beautiful," she said, her voice thick with sleep.

His eyes roved from shadow into light. Moonlight reflected off the stream that sliced across the valley, the water's surface shimmering like diamonds where the rush of current over rocks broke its stillness. The light created a halo over far mountain peaks. He said, "I couldn't see its beauty until you were here."

Thinking he was flirting, she rewarded him with a light kiss on his neck. "Are you thinking of John's request?"

They'd had visitors that afternoon. John Hutchins was a mixed-blood guide and trader who had aided Annabelle's escape from the Lakota camp where she'd been held for a month before the Fort Phil Kearny massacre. At that time, Hutchins had moved freely between the two peoples, trading goods with the tribe where his mother lived, while finding occasional employment with the army his father had served before returning to the States and abandoning his Indian child. Hutchins worked only for the government now. He served as a translator for the diplomats sent by Washington to broker a peace with Red Cloud and the Lakota. A diplomat named Grantham had accompanied him on his visit to the ranch. They had spoken of an imminent accord, but Josey doubted the government would accede to all of Red Cloud's demands. The chief insisted the army close the Bozeman Trail and abandon the three forts built along it. The army had never before conceded defeat to Indians.

"What makes Red Cloud think the army will just pick up and leave?" Josey had asked the diplomat.

"The contents of Fort C. F. Smith have already been sold to a Montana freighting company," Grantham said, referring to the northernmost of the trail's outposts. "At Fort Phil Kearny and Reno Station, they're packing up to haul away everything of value."

Josey thought of all the men killed defending the trail and its forts, including his mentor, the Colonel. Red Cloud's warriors had slaughtered eighty-one men in a single day on December 21, 1866, the worst defeat the army had ever suffered to an enemy they'd dismissed as savages. The tides had turned the following summer. That August, another large Lakota army surrounded a small force protecting a caravan of wood wagons. Despite overwhelming numbers, the Indians were repulsed time and again. The difference: the garrison at Fort Phil Kearny carried new breech-loading rifles that could be reloaded and fired at a much faster rate than the old muzzle-loaders left over from the war. After the first round of shots, the Indians had rushed the corral of wagons, believing they had time before the soldiers could reload and fire again. Red Cloud's mistake cost him sixty warriors. The soldiers lost only six.

"Why would the army just leave?" Josey had asked. "They hold the advantage now."

Grantham had sighed, taken off his spectacles, and pinched the bridge of his nose. He was a small-framed, pot-bellied man with a head that appeared three sizes too large for his neck, like a pumpkin impaled on a stick. Josey wondered whether the slump of the man's narrow shoulders came as a result of the burdens of his job — or the weight of his head.

"It's too costly to keep the trail open," Grantham said. "The government has other priorities."

"Would that be the railroad?"

The men turned to look at Annabelle,

who'd been quiet until then. To his credit, Grantham looked more impressed than offended at being questioned by a woman.

"The Pacific Railroad will be completed by this time next year," he said. "Interest in the trails will dwindle. There's no sense guarding roads no one uses."

"And the Indians need peace," Hutchins said. Though dark as any Indian, he wore his black hair too short to braid and dressed in store-bought clothes, like a white man. While barely older than a score of years, he had more experience with the Indians and army than any man in the territory. So long as his mother lived with a tribe of Lakota, no man wanted peace more.

Hutchins continued: "Winning a peace from the soldiers will give Red Cloud the standing among the people that he's always desired. The government's guarantee of land means they can go back to living as they've always lived."

Again, Annabelle gave word to what remained unsaid.

"That sounds promising, but you wouldn't be here if there weren't some kind of trouble." Her eyes passed between her guests as if taking their measure. "I can think of only one man who could cause so much trouble that it would bring you to us."

Josey had flinched even before she'd said the man's name.

CHAPTER EIGHT

Over the first few days Maria and the children traveled with Mr. Grieve, he rarely spoke other than to discuss tasks and their route. At night, after the children were put to bed, he sat and stared into the fire as if its sight transported him to a different time and place. Maria wondered where his mind went, but she learned not to ask him about the war. Even when he didn't speak of battle, his stories of measles, camp diarrhea, and body lice left her either queasy or feeling that she, too, suffered "the itch." One such example came after she pressed him for the reason he refused to eat sausage of any kind.

"While our mess was eating breakfast one day, I discovered a cat's claw in my sausage," he said. "Soon, every man started searching until one found a tooth. Sausage was sold by the weight, you see. Word spread among the camp until reports of similar discoveries were made all over. No matter how hungry we got after that, none of us ate sausage again."

Having heard enough such tales, Maria was happy to do most of the talking. Unbidden, she told him of her life while he sat silently near her. Occasionally, most often after she told a story of the children, he would share something about his son. His eyes shone bright in the firelight when he spoke of Luke, and a smile unfolded across his face, like a flower unclasping its blooms to the morning sun. He appeared as a different man in these moments. He might even be handsome, if he cut his hair and trimmed his beard. While grateful for his help on the trail — she could not handle the wagon and animals without him — his presence at times only reinforced what she had lost.

Daniel was never far from her thoughts. Days spent walking beside an ox-pulled wagon left too much time to ruminate. She mourned quietly for the sake of the children, who didn't seem to grasp yet that their father was never returning. When they buried Daniel, Maria had been too distraught to insist on any kind of ceremony. She'd kept the children away while she wrapped the body in a spare piece of wagon sheet, tying it with heavy cord. Mr. Grieve managed a cross from some spare wood and pounded it into the ground with the hammer Daniel had used for straightening the rims of the wagon wheels. Maria had thought she was protecting the children by shielding them from the burial. Now she wondered if she'd denied them a proper farewell to their father, just as she worried if his soul would find peace without extreme unction.

In those first days after Daniel's death, only the children's needs had constrained her despair. Alone in the pre-dawn darkness when she fetched water for breakfast, she wept for Daniel. Once cried out, for the moment at least, self-pity overtook her. Alone and frightened, she had two children to care for and no prospects for easing her life. This absorption gave way to anger. *Why had Daniel brought us to this awful wilderness?* A stubborn man, unhappy with his lot, he'd placed his pride ahead of the risk to his family. Her rancor left her irritable with the children, with the oxen, with water slow to boil, with sun that shone too brightly, clouds that lingered overly long, rain that soaked her until she cursed the heavens. Finally, her fury spent, she recalled Daniel's fate, and guilt swallowed her anger whole and initiated a new round of grief.

Sensing her mood swings, Mr. Grieve maintained a distance when her temper flared. They worked well together. After breakfast, she prepared a noon meal and stowed it in the grub-box in the wagon while he took the pipe off the little sheet-iron stove, emptied out the fire, and left it to cool. Then he saw to the animals while she readied the children and stowed all their things. Watching him with her children, Maria concluded Mr. Grieve must have been a good father. When Danny and Astrid grew restless from riding in the wagon, he lifted them so they could sit astride the oxen while he walked alongside. At night, he let Danny hold his gun while he showed the boy how he cleaned it. Daniel had never let their son hold a gun, but Mr. Grieve seemed of a mind that the more the boy knew of a weapon, the less threat it posed. After what she'd seen in the territories, Maria agreed. If God would not see to their security in this awful place, they would have to manage for themselves.

One day after a hard rain, the wagon's wheels sank so deep in the mud they had to unload everything and harness the mules ahead of the oxen to pull the wagon loose. Mr. Grieve added his weight to one of the wheels while Maria encouraged the animals. The children stood by the road watching.

Straining against the mired wheel until the veins in his neck distended, Mr. Grieve released a stream of invective that left him more breathless than the effort he'd put to the task. Finally, the wheels began to turn, and the animals pulled the wagon free. Only then did Mr. Grieve become aware of the children's watchfulness. A look of horror darkened his features, and he apologized for his language. Maria struggled to restrain her laughter, for his words had been so exceptional in their vulgarity that they must have struck the children as part of a foreign tongue.

Such mirth proved all too rare. A few days out from Fort Laramie, they came across a way station that Indians had put to the torch. The single log building had a sod roof that had prevented it from burning out. A corral out back with an open-faced shed and wooden trough stood empty. The front door had been wrested from its hinges. A wooden bench sat under the lone window. If there had been glass, it was gone now, permitting a thin haze of smoke to escape.

Mr. Grieve stopped the wagon, though Maria begged him not to, fearing Indians were near or would return.

"It's burned out already," he said, pulling the lever to brake the wagon. "Whoever did this is long gone."

Telling her to wait, he disappeared inside. The children dozed in the back of the wagon, leaving Maria nothing to do but imagine the horrors inside. When Mr. Grieve didn't return immediately, curiosity overcame her fear and she followed.

Inside, her eyes adjusted slowly to the gloom, but the stench hit her straight away. The sickly sweet smell compelled her to pull her bonnet from her head and cover her nose and mouth. A portion of the dirt roof had collapsed, creating a crescent of light across the floor. Particles of dust floated in the sunbeams, swirling up and around with movements that made them seem alive.

They were all that lived in the room.

Mr. Grieve had lined the bodies in a row against a fire-scorched wall. The clothes had been burned away from the corpses, but from their size and shape Maria judged them to be a man, a woman, and two small children. They might have been her family, though the identification was complicated by one ghastly detail: the heads had been removed from each of the bodies. Her throat tightened, and she swallowed back the acidic taste of her breakfast.

"I told you to wait," Mr. Grieve said.

The sharpness of his tone, she understood, came from a desire to shield her from such images, but she'd already seen too much in this savage land to deem herself an innocent. "Let me help you," she said, and they buried the bodies together. They never spoke again of what they'd seen that day, and Maria made sure the children saw none of it.

Without a walled stockade, Fort Laramie appeared less like a fort than a small town, with buildings made of brick and wood frame and the first real houses Maria had seen in five hundred miles.

Yet any illusion of civilization was quickly dispelled. So many wigwams and teepees surrounded the fort that Maria would have thought Indians had the place under siege if she hadn't known better. The soldiers called the Indians who lingered around the fort begging from travelers "Laramie Loafers," and it was difficult to reconcile their slovenly appearance with the horror she had witnessed at the way station.

Delayed at the river crossing to reach the fort, Maria had peeked inside a couple of their homes. The teepees contained no place to sleep, no tables or chairs. Just rolls of blankets, putrid animal skins, camp kettles, and other detritus that looked to have been scavenged from passing wagons. Maria knew she should feel compassion, especially for the women and children, but pity came hard after seeing what had happened to the settlers at the way station.

Once at the fort, Mr. Grieve headed to the stables with the children to trade the Stoddard brothers' lean horses and mules for another yoke of oxen, a transaction Maria deemed a form of divine justice. While they were occupied, she wandered over to the parade grounds to seek out the soldiers idling between duties. Mr. Grieve's discomfort with Union troops was a palpable thing, but they were delighted to indulge her questions about the "cousin" she'd followed from the States.

Nearly every soldier she met had heard of Josey Angel or wanted her to think they knew him. They competed for her attention with increasingly outlandish tales until he sounded like Davy Crockett come to life after the Alamo. One soldier told her Josey Angel single-handedly held off an ambush by more than a hundred Lakota. A clean-shaven private with jug ears told her he had shot more Rebels than any soldier in the Union. A mutton-chopped corporal claimed he had killed a hundred men in a single day at Griswoldville, a place Maria knew from Mr. Grieve's account of where his son and father were killed. The men seemed to need to believe what they told her, the way children drew comfort from tales of angels and Father Christmas.

Yet as much as the soldiers proclaimed to know about Josey Angel, no one could provide practical information about what he looked like or where he lived. Fresh recruits claimed he stood as tall as a grizzly and was not much older than they; a sergeant with a walrus mustache white as cotton said Josey Angel was closer to his age, with thinning hair. The contradictions frustrated her until a young officer broke up the klatch and directed her to the sutler's store, explaining the clerks knew all the news.

Fort Laramie's trading post was a veritable Babel of commerce. Orders were shouted in English, French, and at least two or three Indian languages. She could hardly distinguish the words over the scuffling of so many boots and moccasins on the plank floors. Buffalo, beaver, and wolf pelts were piled on one counter by trappers, their beards as thick as the hides. At another counter, squaws dressed in bright colors hiked up their skirts to create a pouch for carrying cups of rice or sugar measured out by the clerks. Near the back, soldiers argued with a merchant over the price for a case of whiskey while a stern-looking brave stood by the door sucking contentedly on a peppermint stick.

The room was redolent of cheese and herring and a heady mix of delicacies Maria failed to identify after weeks of subsisting on little more than beans, rice, and corn meal. She greedily breathed it all in while her eyes scanned the shelves: clothes, furniture, guns and ammunition, and all types of food. Items that would have seemed commonplace months earlier now struck her as more exotic than spices from China. Cans of tomatoes, lemons, oysters. Jars of peaches and berries. Boxes of nutmeg cream candies. Piles of shirts, trousers, and dress materials that weren't covered in trail dust.

For a moment she wondered how she would manage through the crowd to make a purchase and get the information she sought. Yet of everything on display, the most exotic sight proved that of a white woman who wasn't an officer's wife. Men melted away, nudging those who were slow to notice and forming a path for Maria. Their indiscreet attention was a small price to pay for access to the counter, and within moments two employees jockeyed to assist her. The senior clerk won out. He was an older man with a trim gray beard and Ben Franklin spectacles.

"How may I help you?"

"I don't know where to begin . . ."

Twenty minutes later, Maria had nearly everything she needed. She'd bought fresh provisions for the journey and treats for the children. More importantly, she'd learned what Mr. Grieve needed to know.

While the bespectacled clerk totaled her purchases, Maria slipped in a question about her cousin. At mention of Josey Angel, the man peered over the rims of his glasses, the pupils narrowing. Maria smiled, allowing her dimples to show, and he answered her questions, even if he doubted her account, revealing even more than she could have hoped. After wrapping her parcels, he leaned over the counter, clasping her wrist and drawing her close enough that his breath stirred the loose strands of hair near her ear.

"There are only two kinds of people who go looking for Josey Angel," he said. "Them that need his help are the first."

"And the other?"

"Them that want to die."

Maria pulled back and met the man's

gaze. "I don't want to die."

"Then I hope he can help you."

When she came out from the store, Mr. Grieve waited with the children. "Well?" he asked.

Before responding, she rewarded the children's patience with gingersnaps and pieces of horehound candy. Once they were happily sucking on the hard treats, she said, "Josey Angel settled near Virginia City."

His shoulders sagged. "That's more than six hundred miles."

"There's better news. He may be headed to Fort Phil Kearny for the peace talks."

"How far is that?"

"Less than two hundred and fifty miles."

Maria smiled on seeing Mr. Grieve's face brighten, despite her misgivings. While he'd demonstrated his abilities with a gun against the Stoddard brothers, and she didn't believe half of what the soldiers had told her about Josey Angel, she'd heard enough to be unsettled at the thought of Mr. Grieve trying to kill such a man. Surely, even David faced better odds in challenging Goliath, for he had the Lord to guide his aim, and Maria had concluded that God had no place — nor took any interest — in these lands. If Mr. Grieve's timely arrival in her life had been in answer to a prayer, it was a cruel god who would deliver her salvation in the form of another man to mourn.

They walked together past the front of the store, where men jostled for a turn at going through bushel baskets of mail that had come to the fort. She asked if he'd looked to see if there was anything for him, regretting the question as soon as she saw his face slacken.

"There's nobody who would write to me," he said, appearing even older than his years. "Have you checked?"

"There was nothing."

In truth, she hadn't looked. The only letters she might find would be from Daniel's family, and she couldn't bring herself to read their high hopes and good cheer for a family member no longer living. Inside the store, she had mailed off the letter that would carry the news of Daniel's death to his parents and brothers.

Before their arrival, Mr. Grieve had suggested she remain at the fort to await a wagon train of go-backs who'd given up the dream of riches and an easy life in the west. But without a family to welcome her return, Maria couldn't imagine living in a place where she would feel Daniel's absence even more keenly. It had been her hope to find suitable work at the fort, yet she saw already it was no place for a young widow. Two weeks of traveling with Mr. Grieve had convinced her she was safe with him, at least for a little longer. If only she could persuade him he still had need of her . . .

The children clamored for more candy, and Maria gave them each one piece. To Mr. Grieve, she handed a pouch of tobacco. He'd asked for nothing and seemed embarrassed that she'd bought something for him. Remembering his manners, Mr. Grieve took the parcels from her arms as they continued on.

"You bought a lot of things."

"Food for the road." She eyed him without turning her head.

"Have you found wagons headed back east?"

"We're going with you."

They had turned in the direction of the stables where they'd left the wagon and animals. Mr. Grieve stopped. "It's too dangerous. The Indians won't be like this," he said, a sweep of his arm taking in their surroundings.

"I found a wagon train headed north we can join."

"Soldiers?" He frowned.

"No. It's a medical train of some sort."

"Medical?"

"A doctor is in charge. The wagons have an armed escort, so we will be safe. Once we get to Fort Phil Kearny, if your man's not there, we can join a convoy headed to Fort Ellis. That's near Bozeman, and it's beyond Indian country, at least the dangerous Indians. From there, you can look for Josey Angel in Virginia City."

Mr. Grieve looked off into the distance. The Stars and Stripes flapped in the breeze atop a lofty flagpole in the center of the parade grounds so that he couldn't escape view of it no matter where he went. He asked, "Why do you now want to go to Virginia City?"

"There's nothing here for a respectable woman who's not an officer's wife. I can't settle a farm in Oregon on my own. At least in a city I might find honest work to support myself and the children."

"You can't find work here?"

"Nothing that wouldn't involve lying on my back." She watched him wince at her vulgarity. "You wouldn't want that for me, would you?"

Mr. Grieve fell into a moody silence. His tongue pushed against the inside of his cheek as he considered his options. She'd learned his ways well enough to know he needed time to come to terms with new ideas. He still didn't look at her as he asked, "These men, they will allow us to join them?"

"That's what I've been told. The army restricts travel between the forts, and larger wagon trains are deemed safer."

Mr. Grieve kicked at the dust with his boot. He was almost there but needed another nudge. Whatever value she'd represented to him had been diminished now that he knew where to find Josey Angel, but he could barely look at the blue-clad soldiers, much less speak with them.

"You're not likely to discover much on your own at the next fort," she said. "You still need me."

"I'll go with you," he said, the words clipped by his hard tone. "But I don't need anyone."

He didn't turn from her, not right away, and the softness in his eyes belied his words, reminding Maria of the way Daniel looked at her. Though it comforted her to know he wouldn't leave them, she shuddered on perceiving a tenderness she feared might doom him.

CHAPTER NINE

Crazy Horse.

Josey had first seen the young Lakota warrior two years ago, though he had not yet known his name. Crazy Horse had helped lead an ambush of the army wagons Josey and the Colonel were guiding to Fort Phil Kearny. They'd pulled into a circle and managed to hold off the Indians' assault, but Crazy Horse struck the Colonel in the head with what appeared to be a lethal blow. On witnessing the old man's fall, Josey had been too distraught to even raise a weapon as Crazy Horse rode down on him. The Indian might have killed him, probably should have, but instead of delivering a deathblow, Crazy Horse had merely touched him. Counting coup, the Indians called it.

Their positions were reversed following the massacre at Fort Phil Kearny eighteen months ago. Josey had found the Colonel in the aftermath, soon enough to hear his dying words. Then he'd found Crazy Horse, mourning the death of his friend. The young warrior would have stood out even if he hadn't been alone, with both skin and hair a shade lighter than most Indians. He was a slender man and, like Josey, slight for a warrior. Yet he was no less dangerous for his size. Like Josey.

Seeing Crazy Horse grieve on the same day he'd watched the Colonel die moved Josey to a compassion he had not anticipated. He had every reason to kill him, for it had been Crazy Horse who'd taken Annabelle, plotting to ransom her as a way to gain access to the fort and slaughter everyone inside. Her escape had thwarted those plans, but Crazy Horse still found a way to lure the soldiers into an ambush that shocked the country. Yet those facts had been forgotten in that moment of shared grief, and Josey recalled a different side of Crazy Horse Annabelle had described. How he had never mistreated her and even offered his protection from others who would have harmed her; his gentleness with his elderly grandmother; and his generosity with the old and poor in his tribe. Crazy Horse was known to give away nearly all he took in his raids, a practice that Annabelle compared to a holy man's vow of poverty, despite what it cost the young warrior. The gossip in the village told of how the father of the woman Crazy Horse loved had passed over him in favor of a suitor with greater prospects. Knowing all of that, when Josey had finally come face to face with Crazy Horse on the battlefield, he touched him on the shoulder and walked away. Josey's first coup.

When Annabelle brought up Crazy Horse to the mixed-blood translator Hutchins and the diplomat Grantham, their reaction had made clear she'd intuited the reason for their visit. Hutchins, his gaze fixed on the floor, said, "Crazy Horse's influence could undermine the peace talks."

"It's not like he's a chief," Annabelle said. "Why single him out?"

"His standing has grown among the people since you knew him. There are many warriors who would follow him, if only he would lead."

Annabelle stepped away to the window. Their visitors sought to carry on the conversation with Josey, but he silenced them with a gesture while he watched her. She didn't like to talk about her time with the Lakota. She'd feared for her life nearly every day and had to kill a man who'd attacked her before making her escape, yet she'd come away with greater sympathy for a people whose way of life stood jeopardized by the encroaching settlements of the white men. After a minute of rumination, she broke her silence without turning from the window.

"He doesn't seek to be a leader," she said of her one-time captor.

"Nobody knows what he wants," Hutchins said. "The people don't call him 'Our Strange Man' without reason. He's always gone his own way. His hatred of the *wasicu* runs deep."

"What a who?" Grantham asked, his pumpkin head tilting with curiosity to the point Josey worried he might topple over.

"*Wasicu* — white people," Annabelle said.

Grantham cleared his throat. "Well, his hatred of white men threatens all that the peace commission has accomplished. Isolated settlers and traders have been slaughtered in Kansas and along the trail, some as far south as the road to Fort Laramie. The army believes Crazy Horse is behind these atrocities."

"Atrocities?" Josey asked.

"Unspeakable things," Grantham said.

Hutchins elaborated. "Burned out homesteads and trading posts. The usual raids."

"Not so 'usual,' " Grantham corrected, his emphasis on the last word stoking their curiosity.

Hutchins glanced in the direction of Annabelle, who still had her back to the men. He lowered his voice. "Some of the dead have been found without heads."

Annabelle turned sharply and caught Josey's eye. Mutilations of the dead were common among Indians; they took scalps as trophies and did worse when their hatred burned hot. If real, the beheadings would represent a new level of desecration.

"So far, the incidents have been few, and the army has kept it quiet," Grantham said. "If the newspapers in the States get wind of it, I fear the government will have no choice but to pull out of the peace talks."

"And the Indians would eventually be wiped out," Annabelle said, still looking at Josey.

Wondering if these men had come into his home to request that he commit murder, Josey felt a coldness overtake him. He gritted his teeth to quell his temper as he asked Grantham, "What do you expect me to do?"

The diplomat shifted in his chair, cutting a glance to Hutchins and clearing his throat before speaking. If murder had been one option, he'd read Josey well enough to propose an alternative. "Go with Mr. Hutchins and find Crazy Horse. Convince him to agree to the peace terms, or at least to stop slaughtering white people."

Hutchins placed a hand on Josey's arm. "This is what's best for my mother's people too."

Josey's mind spun like a wagon wheel in loose sand while his thoughts shifted from the prospect of a sinful mission to one that seemed outright impossible. "I never even exchanged two words with the man," he said.

"He didn't kill you when he could have," Grantham said. "That's enough to qualify you as Crazy Horse's favorite white man."

Ignoring the joke, Hutchins said, "What you shared was more meaningful than words. To him, at least."

After their meeting, Hutchins, Grantham, and a troop escort had set up tents near the barn, hoping to get an answer from Josey in the morning before they returned to Fort Ellis. A nightly routine dominated by feeding Isabelle and readying her for sleep had left Josey and Annabelle little opportunity to discuss matters.

Now, as he gazed through the window at the moonlit night with Annabelle, Josey wasn't sure if his interrupted sleep was due to their visitors' request, the incident with

Bouchard's men, or just a general uneasiness. Annabelle wrapped her arms around him from behind, her head close to his so that she could speak in a whisper and not disturb the sleeping child. The clean smell of her comforted him.

"Do you think you can find Crazy Horse?"

"I'm not even sure I want to try."

She pulled away and waited until he faced her.

"Of course, you're going." She clasped his hand and intertwined her fingers with his. Her hands were cold but his were warm, and she drew his hand to her face. "Josey, this is who we are. We're not meant to plant ourselves like acorns."

He studied her, seeking proof that he'd heard her correctly. "Are you saying we should abandon the ranch?"

"No. Angel Falls will always be our home. But your success in building it shouldn't restrict you to a sedentary life that doesn't suit you. It should free you to do what you want."

He considered her words. For a fleeting moment, he wondered if she were testing his commitment to her and Isabelle, but Annabelle had no need to stoop to such chicanery. Josey had reasons to go even if he doubted his influence in swaying Crazy

Horse. Before bidding goodnight, Grantham had sweetened the offer with a promise that Fort Ellis would buy cattle from the ranch. The army paid top dollar for its beef, and Josey had good hands who could run the place in his absence. Plus, he had a personal reason for returning to Fort Phil Kearny.

"I could bring the Colonel back," he said, almost to himself. They had buried the Colonel with the soldiers he'd fallen beside. It had seemed appropriate at the time. Now that Josey and Annabelle were building a permanent home, he believed the Colonel's final resting place belonged with them.

"That's another good reason," Annabelle said. "And once we drive a hundred head to Fort Ellis, we might negotiate an ongoing contract with the quartermaster. If demand dries up in Virginia City, we'll still have a reliable customer."

Josey smiled. He could never match his bride's head for business. He would miss her and Isabelle terribly, but he wouldn't have to be gone long, not nearly as long as he'd been away on the cattle drive from Texas. Grantham said the army hoped to clear out from the fort by mid-August at the latest. Hutchins expected Crazy Horse to be moving north, following the buffalo migrations. If they couldn't find him quickly, it would be too late, and Josey could return home. He kissed Annabelle's forehead and started to thank her for her forbearance when something in her words stayed him.

"We?"

"I'm coming with you."

"But Isabelle . . ."

"She too."

Astonishment at her proposal so befuddled Josey he couldn't articulate an objection before she spoke again.

"We will be safe, Josey. If we travel with John and Mr. Grantham, we'll have an army escort."

Josey's thoughts still trailed behind his wife's. "Bringing Isabelle on the trail . . ."

"You know women who've traveled with newborns much farther than we're going. Besides, Isabelle is no longer a baby, and she's *our* daughter, Josey. If any child was born for the trail, it is she."

Josey smiled at the thought of Isabelle on horseback. Whenever he held her in his lap while he trotted on Gray, she gurgled with glee. Whatever anxiety he might feel at bringing his wife and daughter on the journey would be no greater than what he'd experience leaving them behind. Less, probably.

"We'll tell Grantham we're coming. But when we get to Fort Kearny, you and Isabelle will stay there while Hutchins and I seek Crazy Horse."

"Of course."

She smiled in that way she had that let him believe he made the decisions for them. Josey knew enough to let it pass. He'd been waiting to surprise Annabelle with something, and the moment seemed right. While she stayed at the window, he went to the bedroom and retrieved a parcel he'd hidden on top of the chifforobe.

"What's this?" She loved surprises, though her active mind made it a challenge to catch her unawares.

"You have to open it."

Recognizing the wrapping paper, she said, "This is from Father's store."

He nodded, not biting while she fished for hints. His patience outlasted hers, and she tore into the package. Her brow creased, and her eyes narrowed on recognition of the dress she'd seen her cousin Caroline wearing.

"Your uncle Luke decided it best to sell it," Josey said. "Neither one of us could think of anyone else who could do right by it."

Annabelle held the dress up, admiring the color against her skin even in the pale light. "That's sweet of you, Josey, but it will never fit. I'm no longer sixteen."

"It will fit now. The tailor saw to it."

"How did the tailor know my size?"

Josey waved his hands in matching vertical swipes, pantomiming the curves of a woman. "No one knows your shape better than I."

Annabelle's face flushed as if she were sixteen again. "I suppose you're right."

"Suppose?" He failed to hold a stern expression. "I damn sure better be right."

She laughed with him. "I don't know when I'll have the chance to wear it."

"You could wear it now. If it's all that you said it was, I'll enjoy seeing it on you."

"You want me to go to the trouble of putting on this dress just so you can see it on?"

"If you take the trouble to put it on, I promise I'll spare you the trouble of taking it off." A look from Josey completed her blush. She kissed him and went to change.

Josey returned to the view through the window and cast his gaze east. The logic of Annabelle's arguments for accompanying him to the fort was as clear as the landscape illuminated by the moon. Alone again, though, his eyes returned to the shadows, and he pondered what unseen dangers might lie along their path. Annabelle could placate him by describing the journey in terms of sunshine and summer breezes, but Josey was not a man to enjoy rainbows while storm clouds loomed. No meeting with Crazy Horse would end in a picnic. He forced himself not to dwell on the perils. He would have time to worry tomorrow. He turned away from the window and followed after Annabelle. She might need help with the dress.

CHAPTER TEN

Crazy Horse drew the long knife against the hard stone. He spit. Turned the blade so it caught the light from the fire and brought it toward him across the rough edge in a motion that curved like a half moon. He flipped the blade. Spit again. Repeated the stroke. He continued until the blade felt like an extension of his hand.

His diligence made the white man even more nervous.

"You can keep the knife." The words spilled from the man's blood-rimmed lips. "Keep anything you want."

Crazy Horse ignored him. The binds would hold. He continued working the blade, alternating strokes to sharpen both sides. When finished, he picked up the second stone. He scratched the surface with his thumbnail to test its grit. Satisfied, he repeated the process with the smoother stone, knowing it would bring a keener edge.

The steel blades made by the *wasicu* were stronger and sharper than anything made by the people. That is what they called themselves. While their enemies would label them Sioux or Lakota, they referred to themselves as "the people," for they were all who mattered. Everyone else stood apart. Especially the *wasicu*. Too many of the people had forgotten that.

He continued to work the blade, quickening the pace of his strokes in his agitation. As much as he admired the *wasicu* weapon, a warrior needed to work the blade to hone the steel to its sharpest. Not many young men were so patient. An example of how the white man's things made them lazy. Why would a boy take the time to learn to craft a bow when he could steal a rifle? Why would a girl labor for hours to cure and soften a buffalo skin when she could lay with a white man for a few minutes and get a wool blanket? With each bartered exchange the people risked fading into the *wasicu* world until they were scratching in the dirt for their food, living in houses of wood, praying to the dead god on the cross.

All his life, Crazy Horse had fought to keep the people from becoming like the *wasicu*. Because of his light skin and brown, curly hair, the other children had mocked him as a half-breed, though they knew it to be false. Even before he had seen a white man, he hated the *wasicu*. Yet in the moment of his greatest triumph, the Hundred in the Hands battle when his people killed every soldier who fought against them at Fort Phil Kearny, Crazy Horse found he had never been more like the *wasicu*. The senseless slaughter of an enemy was not the people's way. They fought for honor, for horses, sometimes for slaves. The *wasicu* fought to kill. They had bled themselves white in their war of states, and still they thirsted for more. Blinded by his hatred for the *wasicu,* Crazy Horse now came to see he risked becoming as savage as them.

His day of glory a year and a half earlier had been eclipsed by Lone Bear's death. Arrows shot wildly by overeager warriors had killed his childhood friend. A senseless loss. With his dying breath, Lone Bear shared a vision of more glory for Crazy Horse, an even greater victory over the *wasicu*. But the following summer when Crazy Horse and Red Cloud led warriors in a new attack against the soldiers, they had been turned back. The soldiers had new rifles that they could reload faster. The warriors had tried to overrun the *wasicu* where they hid behind their wagon boxes, but with their new rifles the soldiers killed and wounded too many.

Now the Big Bellies talked of peace. The chiefs said they could make the soldiers leave their forts, but Crazy Horse did not believe them. Not now that the enemy had new rifles. He had given up so much to win a war, yet all he got for his sacrifice was one bittersweet day of glory.

At least Lone Bear died a hero. He had always been unlucky in battle, adorning his headdress with more red feathers for battle wounds than anyone Crazy Horse knew. He died knowing he had played a part in the people's great victory, without tasting the bitter defeat that was to come. *Perhaps you were not so unlucky after all, my brother.*

Crazy Horse had honored his friend by building a high scaffold to encourage his spirit's journey into the sky. He killed Lone Bear's best warhorse and tied its tail to one of the wooden posts so he would be joined by the fleet, barrel-chested mustang in the afterlife. Crazy Horse returned when he could to find solace in Lone Bear's company, but on his last visit he found the scaffold desecrated. Things had been done to Lone Bear's body that Crazy Horse knew only a white man would do.

Lone Bear's corpse was not the only one

121

to be defiled in this way. For months Crazy Horse had collected similar stories. He had traced them to the man bound before him now. Still, he did not have what he sought most. Had it been a fool's errand? Some of the people believed nothing more happened after death than the body rotting, carrion for wolves and buzzards and worms. The *wasicu* believed their worthy dead went to paradise, no matter the state of their bodies in death. That was not the belief most of the people held. Warriors mutilated the corpses of their most hated enemies to deprive them the pleasures of the afterlife. Chop off an enemy's fingers and he cannot pull back a bowstring to kill the ample game to be found in the happy hunting ground. Take his manhood, and he would not enjoy the attentions of the beauties who filled their paradise. Now Crazy Horse had found even worse things that could be taken. Though he could not be certain Lone Bear suffered in death, he could not rest so long as he wondered if it might be true. His friend and mentor High Backbone accused him of using this quest as an excuse to ignore new responsibilities. But Crazy Horse's hatred for the *wasicu* burned too bright to see an uncertain future. The dishonor done to Lone Bear only intensified the hatred.

Once finished, Crazy Horse admired the knife. The blade was as long as his foot, with a sharpened bevel at the tip that would be useful for skinning game. He would keep the white man's knife, the pistol, and the cartridges for the carbine. The rest he would burn — he would not foul himself by wearing white man's clothes.

Knowing his next task would be messy, Crazy Horse peeled off his buckskin shirt and stepped out of the leggings. The man watched; maybe he sensed what was coming, for he bucked like a horse from his prone position, though he failed to move with his hands and legs bound. Crazy Horse knocked him against the head with the solid handle of the knife to still him. He had pissed himself and reeked even worse than usual for a white man. The *wasicu* were such a dirty people. They rarely bathed. Instead of hunting buffalo, they ate the beef of beasts that grazed in pens amid their own shit. The meat had to be foul, and Crazy Horse suspected eating the rotten meat explained why so many white men were as bald as buzzards.

"You don't have to do this. Just tell me what you want."

Crazy Horse had an ear for languages but

preferred to give no indication that he understood the *wasicu* tongue. As a youth, he had learned to speak Cheyenne as well as a native. Through years of fighting the Crow, he had mastered their language as well. He came to know some of the white man's words in the same way, though he did not like to speak them. The sounds felt unnatural in his mouth, as if he were chewing sand when he spoke. He used a few of the words now, telling the man what he sought.

"I have lots of those. Take what you want. Take all of them."

"I want what you stole from Lone Bear."

"I told you I don't have it." The man's voice rose in pitch, and he swallowed. "But I can tell you where you can find it."

Crazy Horse crouched before the man and waited. Though the man's eyes were wide and wild, Crazy Horse saw no dissembling as he told his story, outlandish as it was.

"A medicine man?"

He nodded vigorously, as if he believed his story might spare him.

Hope is the last thing to die in a white man; they are so spoiled in life. Crazy Horse considered this new information. He had thought the men of the *wasicu* god were peaceful, but he knew so little of their

124

beliefs. What he remembered of their god's teachings were the parts he agreed with.

He showed the knife to the man. "Eye for eye, yes?"

The man closed his eyes and shrank away, as far as the binds allowed. He did not breathe until Crazy Horse stood. So much time he had wasted in seeking this man, and for what? Now he would have to seek out another man. He felt like he had been riding in circles for too many moons.

His mind turned to Black Buffalo Woman, as it always did when he thought of lost time. He had loved her since they were children, and it had broken his heart when her father married her off to another man. Even after she wed, Crazy Horse risked shaming his name by being with her. On the night before the Hundred in the Hands, she had offered to run away with him. Alone at night, he wondered what his life would have been like if he had gone with her. Could he forget his hatred for the *wasicu* and permit love to fill his heart? What pleasure did hatred bring? The tribes had scattered after the battle. Black Buffalo Woman and her husband, No Water, had traveled south to live with his father's tribe. Crazy Horse had heard the tribe was returning north for the summer. Perhaps he should seek her out. His body stirred at her memory. He pictured the invitation in her dark eyes, imagined her lithe body pressed to his. Perhaps she would leave with him now. He could not recover the time they had lost, but he could make the most of the days left to them.

It was a pleasing fantasy but too fleeting. An image of Lone Bear replaced the thought. Lone Bear stumbling about the afterlife with no eyes to see, ears to hear, or tongue to taste. A paradise of plenty turned into a hell of deprivation because of what had been stolen from him after death.

Crazy Horse braced his legs as he stood behind the man. He made the first cut at the back of the neck to prolong the suffering. The man screamed like a woman even before the knife hit bone. He thrashed so much Crazy Horse jerked the knife across the man's throat so that he could finish without the man's throes. Only with the body still could he work the blade between the small bones in the neck to sever the spine. He made a mess of it. Blood went everywhere. He had been smart to strip first. When it was done, he cleaned his hands on the man's discarded coat. Then he nibbled on some pemmican while he considered the man's final words and contemplated where he should go next. Before leaving, he wrapped the head in the man's blanket. It was already foul with the stink of *wasicu.*

CHAPTER ELEVEN

Each morning on the trail began with the impatience of a child, the sun rising early where the mountains didn't shield its arrival, and the ground quick to throw off the blanket of chill that descended overnight. The days had been mostly fair since they left Angel Falls, though Annabelle didn't mind inclement weather on the trail. When it was cool or wet, she put on a bright red-patterned Navajo blanket Josey had bought for her in Texas. Josey had cut a slit in the center so she could wear it as a serape. The warm wool proved waterproof against even the fiercest storms, and the colors never ran. She owned nothing else so well made, not even her finery from Charleston.

When she had first come west, Annabelle dismissed Indians as savages. Yet while they might not read or build great cities, she'd learned they were clever in their own ways. Annabelle still feared some Indians — her capture a year and a half earlier haunted her — but now she saw their warriors as soldiers in an enemy army, not unlike the way she'd once regarded Union bluebellies, one of whom now slept beside her each night.

Her views on Indians marked just one way in which Annabelle had changed. Riding out with Josey into open country, she felt the same freedom and contentment she'd discovered on first coming west. Those had been among the happiest days of her life, yet she'd set them aside on having Isabelle to take up the responsibilities of wife and mother. The roles chafed at her like an ill-fitting corset, and she had wondered what was wrong with her because she didn't take to them as naturally as other women she knew.

The invitation to return to Fort Phil Kearny made clear she'd been wrong to try to lead her life as if she still lived in Charleston. There was no going back for Annabelle. While she had loved growing up in such a grand city, her life there now seemed small. Here, possibilities stretched as limitless as the horizons. Was it just her imagination that she could see so far? The air possessed a lightness that beckoned her forth, and she welcomed the invitation.

Returning from the river after washing one morning, she looked over her shoulder to where the sun just crested a ridge that stretched north from the Gallatin range. The air tasted crisp and clean as she stretched. The blanket slipped from her shoulders, and the sun warmed her exposed skin. Even at the first rumbles of hunger in her stomach, she felt a contentment she hadn't known in a long time. This was the life she wanted, not only for herself but for her daughter as well.

The first night on the trail had been fine and clear with a smear of stars stretching like a taut blanket across the sky. After putting Isabelle to bed in their tent, she had brought out a downy comforter and waited for Josey at a discreet remove from the wagon and other tents. He tried to look surprised, but she knew his mind as well as he in these matters.

"What if Isabelle wakes and can't find us?"

"We'll hear her if she cries out. I don't think she'll wake before we've had a chance for some stargazing."

"Is that what we call it now?"

She pulled back the comforter to let him see the thin white chemise she wore. The loose-fitting cotton had ridden up on her legs, exposing a generous view of her bare thighs. "You can gaze at whatever you want."

Afterwards, as they lay watching the night sky, she told him, "This is where I belong." She'd spoken in such a way that it wasn't clear whether she referred to being in his arms or living in the west. When he kissed her, long and deep and with the same hunger she'd sensed the first time they'd made love, she took that as assent.

They'd set out a few days after John Hutchins and Mr. Grantham, who'd ridden ahead to Fort Ellis to give Josey time to organize their party before following. They came with a hundred head and a team of four drovers who'd stayed on as hands after coming with Josey from Texas. They'd left their top hand, Willis Daggett, in charge of the ranch. While not the brightest man, Willis was devoted to Josey and Annabelle after journeying west with them. The remaining hired hands from Texas knew cattle well enough; Willis would see that the men stayed in line.

Being on the trail with Josey, she didn't even mind the daily coating of dust that swirled around the wagons or the nightly attacks of mosquitoes that swarmed any time she strayed from the fire. Josey laughed to hear her declare the fragrant mix of mule sweat and axle grease as sweet as any field of wildflowers.

"You have been too long at home," he said.

After leaving Bozeman, they had passed a well-built farmhouse where an entire family turned out to stare. Riding alongside Josey on an Appaloosa gelding, Annabelle playfully nudged him and nodded in the direction of the settlers. "Don't you think they wish they could come with us?"

Josey tried to look stern when he replied, but the corner of his mouth curled into what she recognized as a smile. "I expect they're glad to have a bed to sleep in and roof over their heads when it rains, like any sensible person would."

"A sensible people would have never left the States to come here in the first place," Annabelle answered. "I'm glad I am not so sensible."

She sat up straight in the saddle and welcomed the settlers' attention. She knew her party was a sight. Strangers considered her a curiosity in her denim pants and a loose cotton shirt that had been cut for a slender man, but she found them more comfortable for travel than a dress or one of the new divided skirts she'd had fashioned in Virginia City. Josey also was something to see with Isabelle perched before him on the saddle and gurgling with pleasure at the bouncy ride.

Lord Byron trailed behind them in a mule-drawn wagon, and if a former slave driving a wagon wasn't uncommon enough, seated beside him was his wife, Red Shawl, a solemn-faced Lakota widow and the mother of four children. While her two young daughters stayed in the wagon, her sons rode along the wagon's flanks on sure-footed Indian ponies. The boys had a tendency to race each other for short bursts, whooping as loudly as a marauding war party.

"Rather than come with us, I think those homesteaders are watching to make sure we don't linger," Josey said.

Isabelle pulled a finger from her mouth and pointed to the boys as they galloped to the front of the line. A circle of drool the size of a ten-dollar gold eagle had pooled on the leg of Josey's trousers, but he was not troubled by a little frowziness.

The sight of them together warmed Annabelle as much as the fire they gathered around at night. Josey had been timid around the baby right after the birth. In his rough hands, he complained that she seemed impossibly delicate. He stood ramrod straight whenever he held her, fearing he might squeeze too tight or stumble while he carried her. Now Isabelle rode in Josey's lap for hours each morning. The exercise left her so exhausted she often napped in the wagon through the afternoon and still slept well at night. On one of the first evenings they took supper around a campfire, Annabelle grew frustrated trying to feed a child whose excitement at living outdoors couldn't be quelled long enough to consume a meal, and Josey took a turn. Annabelle went off to clean dishes, expecting she'd have to resume the task when she returned. Instead, she found Isabelle eagerly eating while Josey delivered spoonfuls of beans, his hand quivering in imitation of a horse's gait, waiting for the child to open the "barn door" and let the horsey in. After that, Annabelle saw to it that the feeding game became a nightly ritual.

Evenings had always been Annabelle's favorite time on the trail. One night after putting Isabelle to bed, she returned to the fire where Byron and his adopted brood lingered, hoping to coax a story from Josey. Though not a natural raconteur the way the Colonel had been, her husband took to the task the way a son might assume a father's duties on his passing. Annabelle assumed her place beside him, feeling his warmth as she rested her head on his chest. The two boys, Chaska and Kicking Bull, sat beside their mother. Byron faced them from the opposite side of the fire with Red Shawl's two daughters, Mina and Dewdrops, pressed against him.

Byron was Josey's closest friend, though they had little in common aside from the years they'd ridden together with the Colonel. Their friendship was built on shared experiences, dangers faced, and troubles overcome. Neither man was voluble by nature. Yet over time they'd developed an ability to leave sentences incomplete, trusting the other understood what remained unspoken. It drove Annabelle mad sometimes to overhear them, and she came to suspect they did it at times just to nettle her nerves. They'd enjoyed the same sport with the Colonel, who, like Annabelle, had left little unsaid.

Annabelle's relationship with Byron had grown closer once she'd overcome an initial awkwardness around him. The slaves who had worked in her family's household never went hungry, received medicine when they were ill, and had a home in their old age. To Annabelle's view, they were better treated than Yankee servants, who earned meager wages and could be dismissed once they became sick or old. Befriending Byron forced her to see that a free man, even one who worked under the meanest conditions, cherished the hope that he could make a better life for his children — a dream denied to even the most tenderly treated slave. The lesson nagged at Annabelle's conscience like an old wound, though Byron's kind nature allowed her to work past her shame and accept his friendship. The two families, who lived on neighboring properties, became natural partners. While Byron wasn't educated, Annabelle respected his insights. In their business dealings, Josey and Annabelle reviewed the contracts and papers. If Byron liked the man they were dealing with, Annabelle knew they could sign without fear of being cheated. When Byron didn't take to someone, Annabelle consulted a lawyer.

Byron's instinct for people probably explained why he'd married so quickly. The winter after the fighting at Fort Phil Kearny had been the worst anyone could remember. As soon as the snows cleared, Josey, Byron, and Annabelle made their way west to Virginia City. Along the way, they came across Red Shawl and her four children. Red Shawl had been wife to a Lakota warrior and bore him two sons. After her husband was killed in a raid against the Crow, she took up with a white trader. She bore him two daughters. During the outbreak of hostilities, Red Shawl's husband had been killed by Indians, who either mistook him for someone else or found he was cheating them. It soon became clear Red Shawl had an instinct for people the same as Byron, and Annabelle credited the Indian woman for sensing the big man's gentleness. She called him *"Matosapa,"* which meant black bear in her native tongue. Before she and Josey even had an inkling of what was happening, their small party had grown into a veritable tribe.

Annabelle came to appreciate the company, even if she rarely succeeded in engaging Red Shawl in more than a sentence or two of conversation. The children more than made up for their mother's reticence. Mina and Dewdrops, who were eight and seven years old, respectively, adored Isabelle and wanted to help with the child as much as they could. The boys maintained their distance from what they deemed women's concerns. Chaska was twelve and Kicking Bull eleven, and they were eager to prove their manhood, at least to each other if no one else paid them heed. While both spoke excellent English, they chittered between themselves in Lakota. Annabelle suspected they enjoyed the idea that no one but their mother could understand what they said. They still identified with their father's culture, though it amused Annabelle how the boys trailed after Josey, watching him with a respect that bordered on adulation.

"Tell us about your first battle," Kicking Bull pleaded once everyone settled around the fire. Though younger, he was the boldest of the brothers. His mother chided his impertinence with a few words in Lakota, but the boy was undaunted. A Lakota boy doesn't feel he's a man until he's earned his first black-tipped eagle feather for slaying a foe, and Chaska and Kicking Bull had an insatiable appetite for stories of battle. Josey preferred to share tales from books or jokes he knew from the Colonel. None of the children had met the old man, so stories of him took the place of memories of a beloved grandfather. Josey rarely spoke of battles in front of the little ones, but the girls were drowsing, nestled against Byron's broad chest, and Josey didn't like to disappoint the boys.

"You've heard that story before," he said. When the boys saw through his protest and pressed him, he said, "Let me think if there's something new I can tell you about that day."

By speaking softly, Josey forced the boys

to remain quiet, and they settled in with the others to listen. "We spent our days marching and drilling, so much marching our boots were broken in and our uniforms dusty and worn. We were young and eager and had won every battle we imagined for ourselves. We were just foolish enough to believe that all the marching and drilling had prepared us for what was coming. The veterans in the other companies knew how green we were just to see our numbers, for it was clear we'd sustained no losses. They called us 'fresh fish.' "

Red Shawl's nose wrinkled. "Why they call you that?"

Josey shook his head. "I suppose it's because they didn't expect us to last long. The older soldiers drew lots to see who would get my Henry rifle after I was killed."

His gaze fell to the fire. The logs had burned out, and the glowing embers that remained pulsated like living things. Annabelle considered asking him to tell a different story.

"I used to dream of that day almost every night. I'd wonder how my life might have been different if the war had ended before I had to fight."

"But then you would not be a great warrior," Chaska said. This was the highest honor the men of his father's tribe could achieve. "Your name would be unknown. Your courage would not be celebrated."

Josey snorted. "I knew little of courage back then." He looked up from the fire and took in the faces around them, as if remembering that he'd set out to entertain them. He cleared his throat, and his lip curled.

"My first time in battle, I was so frightened I forgot to shoot my rifle." Josey spoke the line like the conclusion to a joke, and the mood around the fire lightened as the boys laughed merrily.

"A Lakota would not be afraid," Chaska said. His name meant first-born son, and he yearned to be seen as the man of the family despite his mother's new marriage.

"Even when cannons start to fire?" Josey asked. Artillery terrified Indians, who called them the "guns that shoot twice" for the sound they made both on firing and when the shells exploded.

Chaska fell quiet. Josey leaned forward and placed a hand on the boy's shoulder until he met his gaze. "No man knows how he will respond in battle until he is in one. White man. Red man. Black man. Fear comes to all of us just the same."

"Then how do you know if you have courage?"

"There are ways. They might not always be so obvious as in battle, but you can see bravery every day if you know where to look."

"Do you mean like when we race our ponies?" Kicking Bull asked. "Chaska is more afraid than I of being thrown."

His brother cast a dark glance his way, but Josey spoke before a fight could erupt. "Don't confuse courage with recklessness. Courage could be as simple as speaking the truth to your mother when you have done something that will lead to a disciplining."

Both boys looked down. Their sour expressions suggested they sensed their promised story turning into a lecture. Annabelle interrupted, recalling something Josey had told her of a scouting trip he'd taken in the spring with Byron and the boys.

"Didn't it take courage the time the boys leaped into that mountain lake?"

Kicking Bull laughed, a gleeful, musical sound. "The water was so cold!"

"You made us get in," Chaska said.

"Only because we couldn't stand the stink of you any longer," Josey said.

The boys tried to look insulted, but Josey's laughter proved infectious. Once they quieted, Josey said: "Annabelle is right. There was an example of courage that day, but it wasn't the three of us." He looked to Byron.

"He had fear," Chaska said, pointing an accusatory finger at his stepfather. "He was afraid to jump in like we did."

"You dove in only because I dared you," Josey said.

"You tricked us," Kicking Bull said.

"No, I saved you from fear. I knew the longer you stood looking into a deep, dark, cold lake, the deeper and darker and colder the water would seem. Only by diving right in could you do so without fear."

Everyone now looked to Byron. The girls had stirred, their big, dark eyes blinking in the firelight as they wrapped their arms around his thick neck and waited for Josey to finish.

"*Matosapa* knew how cold the water would be, and he can barely swim. But he jumped into the water after you because he wanted to be certain you were safe. That is why my brother was the bravest among us. We leaped into the water before fear could take us. He jumped in despite his fear. You cannot have courage without fear. Before you can be brave, you must defeat fear, just like any other foe."

Whether out of respect for Josey or drowsiness brought on by the warm fire after a long day, the boys did not object to hearing an allegory in place of the adventure story they'd sought. Snuggled tight to Josey, Annabelle couldn't see her husband's face, but the tension in his body suggested the fears he spoke of were not limited to Byron and a deep pool of water. As she sought sleep that night, her restless mind kept returning to Josey's story and the thought that she was not the only one who had changed.

CHAPTER TWELVE

The wagon train moved at a deliberate pace that Grieve could maintain even walking alongside Maria's oxen. They were two dozen wagons and more than twice as many men, both teamsters who drove the wagons and armed riders who ranged far and wide during the days.

It seemed odd to have so many scouts, but it must have worked; they'd had no trouble with Indians since leaving Fort Laramie. And, on most days, the riders returned with fresh game. They ate as well as Grieve had at any time since before the war. On a couple of occasions, they came back with lantern-sized packages wrapped tight in waterproof canvas that the teamsters described to Grieve as samples for the doctor's work. More than a week out, they camped for an extended rest in a grove of cottonwoods beside a clear-running creek within sight of the Bighorn Mountains while the scouts gathered more samples and the animals rested.

Maria seemed to enjoy traveling as part of a large group. Any concerns she'd had at being the only woman in the party quickly abated. While the men were a rough sort and made Grieve uneasy, having a young mother in their midst inspired their best manners. Someone was always around to fetch water or do other favors for her. The cooks slipped extra treats to Danny and Astrid to win a smile from the children's mother. The armed scouts seemed content just to look at her, as if she were a lone globe mallow blooming bright amid the sagebrush. Grieve often found himself watching, too, though he told himself he should resist the distraction. As much as Maria and the children might relieve the boredom of his travels, it wasn't fair to put them in harm's way after all they had suffered. He told himself that, at least until he found Josey Angel, they were safer with him than on their own, and he disciplined himself against examining any other motives for his actions.

The days had grown hot after they'd moved on from Reno Station, the southernmost of the three forts that guarded the shortcut to Bozeman. Temperatures shot past one hundred degrees each afternoon. Any exposed skin felt like it was being cooked over a skillet after just a few minutes in the sun. Even the children suffered, the sun baking the canvas covering the wagon until they felt like biscuits rising in a Dutch oven. When they could stand it no longer, Grieve hoisted them into Deuce's saddle, charging Danny to be certain his sister didn't slip off the tall palomino stallion. Dust kicked up by the wheels on the dry trail choked the air around them, but at least the air moved atop a horse. By day's end they laughed to see one another looking like chicken parts coated in flour for frying. Even Maria, who never managed to keep their faces as clean as she liked, couldn't hide her amusement.

Water and shade were scarce until they passed beyond the arid sagebrush steppes and the road began to climb into a country creased with deep ridges and coulees. This gave way to a quilt work of rolling, grass-covered hills. The air grew sweeter once the shadow of the Bighorns filled the western horizon. The cloud-shrouded mountains stretched on for some hundred and fifty miles if the caravan's scouts were to be believed.

The new camp lay beside a clear stream

that tripped noisily along a rocky course. It was the prettiest spot they'd seen since leaving Fort Laramie, and the breeze that blew over the water reminded Grieve of standing before the open door to an icehouse. Yet he grew restless at the delay. Thoughts of Josey Angel moving on from the fort before they arrived tested his patience.

A hundred times or more he'd doubted his quest and thought himself a fool. How could he find a single man in all this vastness? How might he best a gunfighter said to have killed hundreds of men? That was before Maria had come back with the news that his quarry might be at Fort Phil Kearny. And it was before he'd shot dead Stoddard and his brothers. He'd never killed men face to face like that. Grieve had served in an artillery unit, attacking an enemy who could be as far as a mile away. He told himself it was the gunner who did the killing, for he aimed and fired the weapon. Grieve's work included carrying the ten-pound balls or the coffee can–sized canisters filled with grapeshot. Ramming the powder and shell to the back of the tube. Sponging the barrel of the twelve-pound Napoleon so it could fire again. No one had ever died from a sponging; believing that had allowed him to sleep and dream of home and the things he would tell Luke about the war.

He'd been no supporter of the War Between the States, but — still deep in mourning for his wife, Chelsea, who had died the winter before — he felt the weight of her absence pressing upon him to the point he awoke breathless in the night. When he told his father of his plans to join the fight, the old man didn't try to stop him, though he was convinced the South would lose.

"There is no earthly show for its success," he had said, predicting what would happen after the North blocked southern ports while it drew on the strength of its factories. "While I have opposed this war, now that it is here you are doing the only honorable thing by taking up arms to defend your home."

Grieve left, calling himself a Georgia patriot, though he knew better in his heart. When he returned and learned both son and father had died fighting Sherman's devils — defending the home he'd fled — Grieve wished he'd been killed. He'd woken the first morning at home with the idea that he would put the pistol to his head and pull the trigger. He might have done it, too, if not for Chelsea. He still felt her everywhere in the clapboard house; he imagined he could still smell her in the walls, though it was probably just the jasmine vines blooming on the veranda. He couldn't kill himself so long as she watched over him, and he couldn't live with himself knowing he'd abandoned their boy to die in his stead.

So he left again. Wandered like a leaf on the wind. Taking work where he could find it. Never staying anywhere long enough that his mind could relax, because then he would start to remember. The idea to kill Josey Angel stole up on him like a summer storm: subtle at first, like a cool turn in the wind and a drop in the air pressure that a man ignores until the roar of thunder and pounding rain push aside every other concern.

He had heard about Josey Angel wherever men gathered to talk about the war. Which was pretty much everywhere. Folks in Macon called him the Angel of Death. Said he'd killed more Southern boys than any other Yankee. Said when he'd run out of Confederates to kill, he'd turned his guns on his own bluebellies. In Atlanta, they didn't use his name, but when they told stories of houses put to the torch while widows and their children slept inside or of old men gunned down where they stood begging for scraps of food from Sherman's passing horde, Grieve knew whom to blame.

At an abandoned train stop somewhere

west of Birmingham, he had picked up a discarded Beadle novel about a western sheriff who hunts down and kills the cattle thieves who murdered his wife and child. He read the book so many times that his eyes glided over words his mind knew from memory. He especially liked the ending, when the sheriff confronts the leader of the gang in the streets of a nameless town, like mounted knights of an earlier era preparing to joust. The murderer draws his weapon, but the sheriff is faster and kills him with a single shot. Grieve had always been good with a pistol, winning plenty of shooting contests during the war when they still had money to gamble. Knowing a good aim wasn't enough, he practiced his draw every day until he could shoot from the hip just as well as taking a careful aim. Then he worked at making himself faster.

He'd surprised himself at how easy it had been to kill Stoddard. He'd felt no remorse at turning the gun on the brothers; they were bad men with evil designs. Afterwards, perhaps for the first time, he felt that his quest to find and kill Josey Angel was more than just some trick he played on his mind to keep himself moving. It was an actual plan. And now that it was real, he wouldn't let an unexplained delay permit the villain to escape. By the wagon train's third day at the campsite, he sought out the doctor to entreat him to get the wagons moving again.

Though seldom seen about camp, Dr. Edward Hamilton was the expedition's nominal leader. He spent his days riding in one of the wagons and his nights cloistered within the cavernous tent the teamsters set up for him. Grieve imagined the doctor's seclusion to be a matter of health, for he did not look well. His yellow hair lay plastered to his head. Skin pulled tight across his face emphasized the plane of his cheekbones and jawline. He wore a blue vest over a crisp white shirt, and, on the occasions when he walked outdoors, his sleeves billowed in the breeze as if there were nothing but sticks within them.

While the doctor commanded the wagon train, supervision for its operations fell to a big Mexican everyone called Mr. Martinez. If he had a first name, Grieve never heard it. The Mexican was as robust as the doctor was frail. He stood six and a half feet tall with broad shoulders and a head roughly the size and shape of a blacksmith's anvil. Mr. Martinez was not a man who invited conversation, so Grieve bided his time, waiting to speak with the doctor when he was alone.

One of the grizzled veterans in the company stood post at the doctor's tent. He was a squinty-eyed man with a wiry red beard that failed to conceal a thin scar stretching from the corner of one eye to his chin. He disappeared inside the tent with Grieve's request for an audience and returned a moment later to lead him in. A whiff of strong chemicals cut through the smell of mildew inside, where the space was dark as dusk despite the sunshine outside. Though they had never spoken, the doctor greeted him as a familiar.

"Mr. Grieve, our southern gentleman. Welcome."

Hamilton had been seated in a camp chair behind a trestle table covered with papers, drawings, and a pair of inkwells. Twin trunks stuffed with books flanked either side of the table. Boxes labeled with writing Grieve guessed to be Latin were stacked like bulwarks along the sides of the tent. They loomed over the doctor so that despite the tent's generous dimensions, his work area felt as tightly enclosed to Grieve as a coffin. Hamilton stood when he addressed Grieve but did not extend a hand before inviting Grieve to take the chair opposite his.

"I am from Texas, you know," he said, as if the geography made them kin.

"Yet you fought with the Union?"

"I am a doctor; I did no fighting." He offered a self-deprecating grunt Grieve interpreted as an effort at laughter. "My father was close with the governor. No one could dispute Sam Houston's loyalty to Texas, but he put country ahead of provincial interests and lost his office for it. We felt the same and left our home until after the war."

The doctor's blue eyes were the palest Grieve had ever seen, bleached like the sky that encircles the sun. Yet there was nothing weak in the man's focus. Under his gaze, Grieve felt like a specimen pinned for dissection to a laboratory table. He swallowed back his discomfort and asked about the delay.

Hamilton apologized and assured Grieve they would depart tomorrow. "We have been remiss in not keeping our guests better informed. The delay was necessary for my work. While I am a doctor, this venture is a scientific expedition."

Grieve had wondered about that. "I thought you were a medical doctor. You're a scientist too?"

"Yes." The doctor's face lit up, adding some color to his clean-shaven cheeks. "I've always considered myself something of a naturalist. Fossils, frogs, birds — I studied whatever was at hand. As a young man, my curiosity knew no bounds."

Grieve guessed the doctor had less than thirty years. "You still seem a young man to me."

"Young in years, perhaps, but short of time, I fear," Hamilton said with a throat-clearing cough. He dabbed at his mouth with a handkerchief, glancing in its folds before returning it to his vest pocket. "I required more samples for my study, and I decided to come west because I thought the dry air would further my recuperation. I am dubious as to its efficacy. Yet the awareness of dwindling time has taught me to discipline my inquiries and focus my work in the area where I can make the greatest contribution."

"What are you studying?"

"Why the Indians, of course."

Grieve tried to hide his surprise. He'd seen no savages around the camp, and he saw none of the animal skins or painted feathers he associated with Indians among the doctor's materials. Besides paper and writing instruments, the table held only a bowl brimming with what looked like buckshot, a tailor's measuring tape, and bottles of foul-smelling liquids.

Hamilton grew animated at his curiosity.

"You are an educated man?"

"I've had some schooling."

"You know how to read and write? You think for yourself?"

Grieve nodded. While the doctor's voice held a pleasant tone, the questions left him bracing for an insult.

"Then my work should interest you."

"I don't even know the nature of your work."

"The nature of my work?" Hamilton rolled the words in his mouth, relishing them like hard candy. "Why it's the very nature of man. Fundamental questions: Who are we? Where do we come from?"

"I'm from Georgia."

The doctor's eyes narrowed with a flash of impatience before his thin lips stretched with the hint of a smile. "You jest because you fear a lecture coming on."

"I wouldn't want you to be disappointed if your work is beyond my appreciation."

He waved a thin-boned hand as if brushing away a fly. "Nonsense. As a southerner, I expect you would have particular interest in the focus of my study. Are you familiar with the theory of polygenesis?"

"Something from the Bible?"

"Not exactly, but you're not far off. *Genesis* tells us that all life originated with Adam and Eve. Do you believe that?"

"I've never given it much thought."

"Think about it now. All the men in the world descended from one man and one woman. The Caucasian and the Malay. The Mongolian, the Ethiopian, and the American, the species we've mislabeled as Indian. Just ponder this for a moment: Queen Victoria on her throne in London sharing the same lineage as the slaves who worked your fields or the savages who ride these plains. Does that strike you as true?"

Grieve shifted in the camp chair, uncertain how he'd been drawn into a Sunday school lesson. As the doctor spoke, his knee quivered with agitated energy. When Grieve did not respond quickly enough, Hamilton slapped an open palm against the table. It was a weak gesture, yet it left him looking spent.

"Dammit, man, you know the answer in your heart, yet you refuse to give voice to it for fear of appearing uncouth. To appreciate science, we must grow beyond the narrow superstitions and childish sentiments that stunt the intellect of lesser men. We must see the world as it *is,* not as we wish it to be."

"It's not that I doubt you. I just can't see how you could prove such a thing."

Hamilton offered a weary smile and lifted an index finger in Grieve's direction, like a salute. "Fortunately, God has given us a way to glean his intent — a trail back in time so that we can confirm the discrete origins of the races and show how each species was intended to serve a unique role in God's kingdom, just as birds were meant to fly and fish were meant to swim and men were meant to walk on two legs."

Sensing a drift in his audience's focus, he paused. "You wonder why this matters? What the application to the world could be?" He did not wait for Grieve's assent. "Recognizing and acknowledging the differences in the races could help us achieve peace in our world, for violence is inevitable when they mix. It is in the nature of our beings, from our very origins, and I intend to prove it."

Certain that expressing any doubt would only agitate the doctor more, Grieve chose to listen without interruption. He was excused from further enlightenment when a coughing and wheezing fit overcame the other man. Grieve started to rise, thinking a good rap to the doctor's back might clear his throat yet fearing the frail body might break at any blow. While Grieve hesitated, crouched half out of his seat, the Mexican rushed in. He threw a black-eyed scowl at Grieve before kneeling beside his charge. The big man brought forth a bottle and spoon from a pocket within his vest and at the moment the doctor's coughing abated helped him to a mouthful of the viscous draught. He whispered something into the doctor's ear while the smaller man held his breath and swallowed with an effort that set his throat and chest to quaking. Older hands in camp said the Mexican had served the doctor's family for decades, and to Grieve the pair looked as close as family. During the long moments until the doctor resumed normal breathing, the Mexican rested his forehead against Hamilton's shoulder. Grieve wished he could be somewhere else but had fallen back in his chair, worried that any movement would break the calm that had descended over the scene.

With a long, trembling breath, the doctor cleared his throat. Without a word of thanks to the man kneeling beside him, he asked, "Do you bring word of Simpson?"

Mr. Martinez shook his head. It seemed to Grieve that the Mexican hadn't breathed the full time he'd waited for the doctor to recover.

"The Indian?"

"No way to know for certain," Martinez said.

"But you fear the worst." Hamilton frowned. His eyes shone brightly in the dim lamplight, but they had lost their sharp focus. "Simpson always brought back the best specimens."

"Maybe too good." The Mexican's voice was hoarse and choked.

"We have our contingency in place?"

"The man from Indian Affairs is seeing to it."

"We may have to see that it gets done."

"Of course."

Hamilton closed his eyes, his face so blank of expression Grieve wondered if he'd fallen asleep. Then his eyes snapped open, and he said, "Help me up."

The Mexican stood, lifting the doctor to a standing position as easily as another man might raise a glass. Martinez towered over his liege, like a nursemaid with a child. With shuffling steps, he guided Hamilton to the rear of the tent, where a tarp provided a screen between the doctor's work area and what Grieve assumed to be his bedroom.

Grieve waited until they disappeared behind the tarp, his mind sorting through all he had seen and heard and failing to discern a coherent picture. He would have thought he'd lingered only a moment, yet in the time he rose and turned to leave, the Mexican called after him with a harsh whisper that stopped him at the tent flap.

Striding forward, Martinez had to stoop his shoulders to prevent his wide-brimmed hat from striking the bracing poles. Grieve had spent little time near Martinez and had only noticed the man's size. Now he took note of his features, realizing he was not only the biggest Mexican Grieve had ever seen but possibly the palest. Besides the hat that left his face in shadow, he wore riding gloves that covered his hands and a kerchief around his neck that left no skin exposed to the sun. He looked down at Grieve. Whatever tenderness had softened the man's manner moments before was gone now.

"Dr. Hamilton pushes himself too hard and does not look to his health."

Grieve shrugged, not feeling he required an explanation. "Perhaps he should be in a hospital."

"No. His work is all that sustains him." He waited until certain he held Grieve's attention. Offset by the paleness of his skin, the Mexican's eyes appeared unnaturally dark. "I will not let anything interfere with it."

On leaving the tent for the fresh air and

sunlight outside, Grieve felt even more anxious to leave the company of their escort. Still baffled by whatever the doctor had been speaking about, he reassured the Mexican before leaving, "Once we reach the fort, I hope to never trouble either of you again."

CHAPTER THIRTEEN

Progress to Fort Ellis was slow, though the work proved easier than any Josey had known on the trail. The hired drovers kept the cattle moving, freeing him to ride with Isabelle in the mornings. While she napped in the afternoon, he loped alongside the herd with Chaska and Kicking Bull, teaching the boys how to round up strays. They made a game of the chore, riding their ponies alongside the steers and notching their arrows as if hunting buffalo. Josey told them to aim just behind the shoulder so that they would strike the animals' lungs and bring down the beasts with a single shot.

Byron wouldn't give the boys rifles of their own yet, telling them that when they could hit grasshoppers in flight with an arrow he would let them hunt with guns. They were too young and resentful to realize his actions arose from respect for their father's culture; Byron wanted them to be as proficient with the bow as any Lakota boy their age. Josey wondered how many years would pass before the boys realized how fortunate they'd been to have Byron in their lives.

Watching Byron, he understood just how hard a road fatherhood would be. Isabelle was still at an age when catching her to steal a kiss was among his biggest challenges. Though still too young to speak in sentences, she stole their hearts every time she let out a "mama" or "dada." Her favorite word, by far, was "no," which she employed anytime anyone asked something of her that wasn't her own idea. It seemed only days ago she still tottered on uncertain legs, fat as sausage casings about to burst, grasping hands outstretched for chair seats or table legs, anything that could still her wobble. Now *she* dizzied *him,* a whirl of motion, like a cattail seed on a restless wind. Keeping up with her made herding a hundred head seem easy.

Their only trouble before reaching Fort Ellis came at a stream Josey had crossed three times over the past two years without aid. This time he found a rough-hewn log hut guarding a ferry crossing. The men who armed it demanded a dollar for each wagon and fifty cents per rider to cross on the simple raft constructed of cottonwood logs lashed together and covered with a pine deck. Ropes were suspended across the stream and harnessed to a team of oxen to tow the craft across the water while the men used long poles to guide it. Josey recalled an excellent ford that had lain just downstream from the ferry, and he rode in its direction. On finding the spot, he saw in the clear water where brush and timber had been thrown in to obstruct the path. He realized the men collecting the toll had dug ditches near the bank to spoil the crossing. He rode his gray Indian pony downstream until he found another safe crossing.

One of the men shouted a warning, "Cross there and you'll mire your horse."

Josey responded with a wordless gesture that made plain what he thought of their extortion. Gray emerged on the other side without so much as a dab of mud on his fetlocks. Chaska and Kicking Bull followed after him on their ponies.

Two of the ferrymen rode over on lathered horses to challenge him, and Josey felt an old, cold fury rise through his chest. He pulled the Winchester from its scabbard and balanced it against the pommel of his saddle as he waited for the men. The riders weren't much older than boys, too young and fit to be making a living by bilking ignorant travelers. Both were heeled with heavy pistols on their belts, and the fingers on Josey's right hand slipped around the Winchester's trigger guard.

The ferrymen arrived full of sand. "Mister, what do you think you're doing?" the first one asked. He reminded Josey of a rabbit, with fidgety hands and a wispy mustache that failed to conceal a pair of oversized front teeth. The second one was jowly with a soft-looking girth and neck so thick he had to tuck the ends of his bandanna into the collar of his shirt instead of tying them off. He added, "You can't cross here."

"I just did," Josey said.

The pair exchanged glances while Josey waited for a response, feeling a calm settle over him like morning dew. A rainbow of wildflowers filled the fields that stretched out over the opposite bank to hills whiskered with evergreens. The air smelled of pine and new grass, and Josey breathed it in. No matter what the young men had to say, he would inform them that if he found they were still bamboozling travelers when he came back this way, he'd tear down their hut and run them off himself. The only question in his mind was whether they'd need a demonstration of the seriousness of his intentions. The breeze off the water felt cool on his neck. A meadowlark warbled unseen from among the flowers. Josey's left hand stroked the rifle's wooden forestock, and his mind emptied of any other thought.

Then, another sound: a horse crashing through the water behind him, followed by a shout. "Josey!"

Shifting his weight so Gray took two steps back, Josey maneuvered to where he could see the newcomer without diverting his attention from the ferrymen. He hadn't recognized Byron's voice, the big man's bass sharpened by an unfamiliar tone that took a moment for Josey to identify.

Anger.

Byron stopped beside him on Annabelle's pony. He'd been driving the supply wagon with Red Shawl and their girls and must have raced the Appaloosa to arrive so quickly. Byron wasn't a natural horseman, and he was out of breath from his haste.

"Just leave it," he told Josey. With a look to the ferrymen, he added, "We'll take the ferry across the stream and pay the fee."

"You saw me cross, Byron. It's not too deep for the wagons here."

Byron faced him, his eyes harder than Josey had ever seen. "It ain't about the water. And it certainly ain't about the money. We don't need no trouble, Josey."

166

"These two? They won't be any trouble."

As if to make his point, the jowly one asked, "Josey Angel?"

"We don't want no trouble either," his rabbit-toothed companion said.

Both men held their arms wide, fingers splayed, to reinforce a preference for peace.

"You see?" Josey said, trying to contain his irritation. "No trouble here."

"Maybe not for you, Josey, but you ain't the only person to consider." Byron's eyes cut to the boys. Josey had forgotten Chaska and Kicking Bull had followed him across the stream. He absorbed Byron's disapproval, cringing at the thought of what might have happened if a stray bullet struck one of the boys.

"I'm sorry, Byron," he said.

Byron wouldn't even look at him. "This is for the wagons and horses," he said, tossing the fat ferryman a gold coin Josey figured was far more than the full cost. "We'll drive the cattle across here. You won't want them making a mess of your ferry."

"That's more than fair," the rabbit boy said.

He looked to Josey for confirmation. Not trusting his voice, Josey nodded. Byron had already ridden off, gathering the boys and leading them back to the ferry, leaving Josey to reflect on what had happened over the days that followed.

They reached Fort Ellis without further incident. The meeting with Captain La-Motte, the fort's commanding officer, went as well as the diplomat Grantham had promised, and Josey soon had an ongoing contract to provide cattle to the fort. Annabelle had been the one to set the terms, though Josey closed the deal, knowing no officer would deign to negotiate with a woman.

With that task completed, the drovers turned back to the ranch while Annabelle, Josey, and Lord Byron's brood continued on for Fort Phil Kearny, now accompanied by a patrol of soldiers, the diplomat Grantham, and the Indian translator John Hutchins.

Following the Yellowstone River east, they basked in the warmth of the season. The leaves on the cottonwoods shimmered in the breeze off the river, and Josey didn't think he could be happier, except for the coolness he felt from Byron after the incident at the ferry. Having apologized, Josey didn't know what else to say to make it better between them. Friendships didn't come easily to him. After losing his closest comrades to battle or illness during the war, he'd held himself back from most people. A friendship with Byron probably wouldn't have been possible if not for the Colonel, who held both men in his orbit with his easy manner and gregariousness. After the war, the three men headed west on an odyssey with the unspoken goal of helping Josey leave behind his memories of the war and what he had done to survive it.

With a smile, Josey recalled the night the slave, who'd been called "Ol' Hoss" because of his size and stolid manner, settled on what he called his "free man's name." With the Colonel, they were gathered around a fire, the horses grazing nearby on long pickets, the warmth of the flames and full bellies engendering a level of camaraderie Josey had not found matched anyplace else. On nights like these when the Colonel wasn't philosophizing or sharing a story they'd already heard, it was Josey's habit to recite poetry. On that night, he had shared a short poem he'd memorized that had always pleased the men in his company.

When a man hath no freedom to fight for
   at home,
Let him combat for that of his neighbors;

169

Let him think of the glories of Greece and
of Rome,
And get knocked on the head for his
labors.
To do good to mankind is the chivalrous
plan,
And is always as nobly requited;
Then battle for freedom wherever you
can,
And if not shot or hanged you'll get
knighted.

The Colonel, who'd heard it before, chuckled, as much at Josey's performance in emphasizing the rhymes as the word play. It was Byron's first time hearing it, and the big man's face widened into his gap-toothed smile before erupting into a deep rumbling laughter that shook his whole body. Byron generally lacked the vocabulary to appreciate the work of the British Romantics; about the highest praise he offered was to call the words "pretty." On that occasion, his laughter proved so infectious Josey and the Colonel joined in.

"I'm so pleased you enjoyed that," the Colonel had said once he'd regained his breath. "Tell us what you liked about it."

Byron had needed a moment to catch his breath before he could speak. The Colonel and Josey grinned at each other at the anticipation their friend built without being aware of it. Still grinning, he had said, "It's just funny to me to imagine a man sitting around with the time to think up such things. That man must have a good life."

From that night, his fascination with the poet Lord Byron was secured, and the new name followed. Josey's Lord Byron may never have appreciated his namesake's word play as much as his pen name, which he once described as "the freest name" he'd ever heard, but the Colonel had delighted in the choice. He'd never needed much prompting to repeat the story to new acquaintances whose curiosity was piqued at hearing the black man's name. As for Byron, Josey doubted he appreciated the irony in his choice so much as the joy it gave the Colonel. His friend was generous that way.

Josey had come to depend on Byron more than he realized until the big man was gone. Not gone. Just not there all the time, as he had been. Something had been lost, though Josey wasn't sure he could explain exactly what. Long before the ferry crossing, the friendship had changed in the Colonel's absence. Josey brooded on the matter off and on for the rest of their journey, and it occupied his mind again as they drew near

Fort Phil Kearny.

Josey had wished for another way to approach the fort. But after turning south into Wyoming east of the Bighorn Mountains, the Bozeman Trail passed through the valley where the Indians had set their ambush just north of the fort. On a small rise, Josey saw the rocks where the Colonel had concealed himself long enough that he still drew breath when Josey found him. He put his heels to Gray, and the pony kicked up loose stones as it ascended the hill. From the crest he saw Byron following him on an Indian pony that looked too small for such a big man. It was the first time since the incident at the ferry Byron had left the wagon to ride. He fell in beside Josey at the spot where the Colonel had died. No words were needed.

They continued on once the wagons caught up, Josey still pondering what the Colonel might have said to set things right between his surrogate sons. Failing that, he said, "Do you miss our talks much?"

Byron's heavy features knotted with thought. "Neither one of us is much for talking, Josey."

"I suppose the Colonel did most of the talking for both of us. I think he preferred it that way."

"I miss him too," Byron said, inferring Josey's meaning without being told. "Now that we have wives and children, we can't just pick up and ride somewheres like we used to."

"Those girls adore you," Josey said.

"The boys prefer you."

"That's because I don't sleep with their mother."

Both men laughed. Red Shawl was an energetic and enthusiastic lover — at least to hear her. For all her stoic ways during the day, she held nothing back when alone with her man, no matter who was within earshot. Byron quickly changed the subject, his focus on what lay before them. "I don't like this place," he said.

Fort Phil Kearny stood a little east of the midway point along the spine of the Bighorns on a slightly elevated plateau between Big Piney and Little Piney creeks. The creeks meandered through a valley with high rolling buttes that buckled and folded into the horizon. From this distance, the fort appeared impossibly small for the hundreds of soldiers and workers who'd sheltered there during the worst of the Indian raids. Today, an encampment of a couple of dozen wagons and even more tents lay beyond the fort's eight-foot-high wooden stockade. More than once, Josey had given thanks for the engineering skills of the commander who oversaw Phil Kearny's construction, with firing platforms and loopholes for rifles built into that stockade, and a pair of blockhouses where mountain howitzers covered the approaches. The Indians had never dared a direct assault on Fort Phil Kearny. In the end, they hadn't needed to.

A pang of guilt thrummed through Josey's chest, and he recognized there'd been more on Byron's mind the past few days than what happened at the crossing. It had never occurred to him Byron didn't want to accompany him on the errand to retrieve the Colonel's body, though he saw now he'd left Byron no choice. "I had to come back, don't you understand? He was like a father to me."

"He was as much a father to me as to you," Byron said. "But dead is dead. The dead ask nothing of the living but what we choose to give them."

"Won't it be good to have the Colonel with us, to remember him by?"

"What I remember of the Colonel don't have nothing to do with a box of dried up bones. I'll remember him just as well whether he's buried here or in our valley."

174

"I'm sorry I made you come." Josey heard the bitterness in his voice but could do nothing to sand its rough edges. "I wouldn't have asked if I'd known you felt this way."

"You never have to ask. I'd have come anyway. It's just that every time we come to this place, we find trouble."

Josey tried to lighten his friend's mood. "That's when we were younger and eager for trouble."

"Trouble don't care if you go looking for it. Trouble has a way of finding you."

Josey recalled that Stephen Chestnut had told him the same thing not long ago, and he sulked at recalling the ferry crossing again. He held too many responsibilities now to be inviting trouble, and he let down Byron and Annabelle anytime he forgot that.

They took in the scene, speaking while waiting for the wagons and soldiers to draw up. The prairie below was as silent as a church. Though Josey couldn't hear it, he could see a wind blowing across the level ground from the way the long grass folded and unfolded before it, the green deepening and lightening as the blades swayed in the breeze. The journey had been pleasant and easy, yet as Josey descended the hill to the fort his mood altered, the way a fast-moving storm cloud can blot a sunny day and bring on a sudden chill.

CHAPTER FOURTEEN

On arriving at Fort Phil Kearny, Maria and Mr. Grieve camped with the rest of Dr. Hamilton's party outside the fort's walled stockade in a grassy field speckled with wild pea. A creek of cold-running, clear water wound around the backside of the fort, and along its banks grew thickets of chokecherry, bullberry, and willow. It was a welcome respite from the trail, though she understood their stay would be brief, and she already worried about their next move.

The soldiers were preparing to abandon the fort for the long march back to Fort Laramie — the wrong direction to suit her needs. But their preoccupation with packing and tallying inventory meant almost any other need could be had for the price of a smile and a kind word. From the cooks seeking to lighten the load of their wagons, she accepted sacks of flour, rice, and beans. From the soldiers who maintained a lackluster vigil at the gates, she gleaned news of Josey Angel.

What she learned only agitated Mr. Grieve more; Josey Angel hadn't been at the fort for more than a year. With the fort nearly ready to be vacated, it appeared the rumors she'd heard at Laramie of his coming here were as fanciful as some of the stories of his deeds. At least she confirmed that Josey Angel had settled near Virginia City. She learned something else about the gunman that she held back, unsure of how Mr. Grieve would react and figuring it better to wait to deliver that news after they found safe passage west. Even with the peace talks all but concluded, the soldiers advised against a lone wagon traveling through Indian country.

While they rested from the journey, the days passed pleasantly enough. Maria took long walks with the children and partook in the riding lessons Mr. Grieve gave Danny. The wind blew so hard and steady Maria gave up any attempt to keep a hat or bonnet in place, and all their faces turned brown as acorns in the summer sun.

One day they rode with some of the doctor's men south to a large lake where their approach stirred flocks of ducks and geese to take flight, thousands of birds wheeling and turning like a feathered cloud. With peace nearly secured, a small band of Indians had camped along the lake's banks, closer to the fort than they ever would have come before the treaty. Their little village consisted of dozens of tepees that reminded Maria of a small military encampment she'd seen in Nebraska. The notion of familiarity was soon dispelled when the entire village turned out to greet them. Squaws with papooses loaded on their backs and older children at their heels came pouring out, waving written papers from the fort that attested to their status as "good" Indians. The young boys were naked but for a small piece of buckskin around their waist. The women wore skirts of buckskin with trimming of every imaginable ornament. They were desperate to "swap," as they called it, and proffered leather moccasins adorned with beads, holding up a pair of fingers to indicate they wanted two dollars. Maria bartered instead, securing moccasins for herself and the children in exchange for some of Daniel's clothes and an old wool blanket. She held out for an extra pair for Mr. Grieve, whose boots were wearing out from walking so much.

Aside from the young boys and old grandfathers, Maria didn't see any men in the camp, and their absence alarmed her. When they'd set out from the fort, she'd noticed flashes of brilliant light from among the surrounding hills. One of the doctor's scouts explained that Indians used hand mirrors they'd gotten in trades with white men to reflect the sunlight and signal one another. While the women's presence near the fort could be explained by their hope to secure handouts of food and other goods, the thought of the warriors skulking about the surrounding hills left Maria even more anxious about finding companions for the journey to Virginia City.

With that in mind, she set out alone one morning while Mr. Grieve saw to a wagon wheel that had been making a steady clicking sound on the trail. Leaving the children in his care, she told him she needed to go to the sutler's store at the fort for supplies. She planned to make her way there eventually, but first she hoped to cross paths with Dr. Hamilton, who she knew took a constitutional every morning after breakfast. Word had spread among his men that he planned to remain at the fort briefly to continue his work before returning to Laramie. As accommodating as all the other men had been, she hoped convincing him to continue on to Virginia City would prove as simple as asking.

She recognized the doctor's slight form as he walked the path that extended from their encampment toward the fort, his head down as if counting his strides. Mr. Grieve had told her of the doctor's strange behavior and tried to explain his work, though his account struck her as so odd she doubted he'd related it correctly. A man so young who presumed a premature death might be excused some eccentricities. Setting aside her trepidations, she approached him directly and greeted him.

Hamilton looked up, his eyes blinking with surprise. His gaunt features made him appear older than his years, but his face brightened on seeing her. "You must be Mrs. Grieve. I've heard so much about you."

Maria permitted a blush in response. She'd asked Mr. Grieve to pass her and the children off as his family to shield her from unwanted attentions, but she was still unaccustomed to the name.

"Won't you join me?" Hamilton asked. "I find the air here to be quite fine, particularly in the morning before the heat of the day settles in."

Falling in beside him, they spoke of the weather, the landscape, and how both differed from lands they'd known as children. Seeing an opportunity, she asked, "Have you considered continuing farther west? I understand you study Indians. Wouldn't your work benefit by venturing into the lands of the Crow and other tribes?"

Hamilton's pale eyes studied her with an intensity Maria found unsettling, as if she were a patient to be examined. The moment passed, and his lips pulled back to expose a row of even teeth not much larger than a child's.

"You are correct about my fascination with Indians, but I have found little variation among them. No matter the tribe, their appearance is striking and similar. Broad face. High cheekbones. Tumid lips."

Recalling all the different faces she'd seen in the Indian village, Maria hesitated before deciding she hadn't considered the matter enough to contradict the doctor. Before she could construct another argument for his heading to Virginia City, Hamilton continued. She sensed he was unaccustomed to having someone — particularly a woman — take an active interest in his work. The words gushed from him like a mountain stream after the spring thaw.

"My work builds on the groundbreaking study of Dr. Samuel Morton of Philadelphia. I can see by your expression you're not familiar with him. It would surprise me if you were. His is a specialized field. You should visit my tent sometime, and I will show you his *Crania Americana.* It's a sumptuously illustrated volume and his most important publication. I first read it as a boy, and it changed the way I viewed the world."

Awaiting an opportunity to turn the conversation to a journey west, Maria determined to keep him talking. She asked, "How so?"

"Dr. Morton taught me to seek out the small differences that lurk beneath the skin of things. Whether it be fossils, frogs, birds, or even rats. You must get beneath the surface to truly understand their nature."

The doctor's enthusiasm reminded Maria of the way Danny basked in her attention while she pretended to be fascinated by an arrowhead or some disgusting bug he'd discovered. No matter the passage of years, men were not so much different from the little boys they had been.

"If this doctor is in Philadelphia, why come here?"

"Sadly, Dr. Morton died before I could meet him. All I can do is carry on his work, which was limited by incomplete data. For all his brilliance as a writer, Dr. Morton was not a field man. He relied on others to send samples to him. By coming west, I have been able to achieve a significant sample size of indigenous peoples to ensure the accuracy of my measurements."

He had lost her, but Maria didn't worry. Rather than be offended, men expected women to be ignorant of their interests and were flattered by any level of curiosity. Before she could ask his meaning, they were interrupted.

Mr. Grieve called out and loped alongside them on his tall palomino, dismounting in a graceful arc that left him breathless after greeting the doctor and Maria.

"Why aren't you with the children?"

Mr. Grieve's eyes went to his boots. "I told them to stay with the wagon while I went to see the wainwright about that wheel. I found a break in the iron, and I'm not sure it will make it to Virginia City."

"That couldn't have waited until I got back?" Even to her own ears, Maria sounded like a harridan. She granted the men a smile so that the doctor wouldn't think this her usual mien.

Hamilton cleared his throat. "I see that I am intruding on a private conversation. Please excuse me." He doffed his hat toward

Maria. "It was a pleasure meeting you, Mrs. Grieve." He showed his child's teeth again and turned back toward the encampment.

Maria replied, "May the Lord hold you in the palm of his hand."

Mr. Grieve watched him go. He spoke without looking at her. "I thought you were going to the sutler's."

"I was on my way when I came across the doctor."

"I don't think it's a good idea for you to be alone with him."

Maria might have been flattered by his pique of jealousy if she hadn't been so irritated with the interruption. With a deep breath, she set aside her disappointment and laid a hand on his arm. He tensed for a second before his entire body relaxed like after a deep sigh. She softened her voice. "I only meant to see if he might be persuaded to continue on to Virginia City. It would be safer if we moved on as part of a large group. You were right; he is an odd man."

"I fear he's more than odd. I'd rather be rid of him and his men."

Maria offered Mr. Grieve a placating smile. His agitation seemed rooted in more than jealousy, and it wouldn't serve to argue now. "That's fine, Atticus." He liked when she used his given name. "Something will turn up. 'All things work together for good, to those who love the Lord.' "

"You're right. We'll find a way," he said, brightening like a man hearing his reprieve. "I'll go back to see to the children if you'll visit the wainwright. He might come out to look at that wheel himself if you were to ask."

"I'll see him on my way to the sutler's."

Mr. Grieve nodded and remounted the palomino. In his haste to please her, he put Deuce to the gallop in the direction of the wagons. Maria quickened her own pace as she continued on to the fort. The morning was getting away from her.

The Bighorn Mountains filled the horizon beyond the fort. When the rising sun shone on the snow-peaked mountains, they gleamed like golden altars. Now they looked almost blue in the shadow of a passing cloud and close enough to touch. She knew better. On the day when she first saw mountains on the road to Laramie, she'd celebrated with the children until Mr. Grieve told them the peaks were still some hundred miles away. It seemed impossible that they could be so far when they were plainly visible as the sun sank behind them, yet he would be proved right when days passed before the mountains seemed to

186

draw any closer.

Appearances could deceive. Mr. Grieve had looked jealous to her, but perhaps his distrust of the doctor sprang from something more than she perceived in the wan-looking man. She'd thought Mr. Grieve dangerous even after he'd saved her from Stoddard and his brothers. Now she counted on him nearly as much as she had Daniel.

She might count on him entirely if it weren't for an affliction that might yet prove as deleterious as whatever affected the doctor. Mr. Grieve would swim across the Pacific Ocean if he believed he'd find Josey Angel on the opposite shore. She wished the soldiers had told her Josey Angel had died. Such a violent man must put his life at risk all the time, and that news might be the only thing that could cure Mr. Grieve, for she viewed his murderous quest as an illness, like a man who's been bitten by a snake. The venom gets in them. Some it kills. Others just need time for it to run its course.

She believed she could help draw the venom from him. She noticed him watching her after supper as she cleaned up before bed. In time, Mr. Grieve might find he wanted to live with her and the children more than he wanted to risk his life to avenge deaths he could not be certain were Josey Angel's responsibility. She didn't know how long that might take. In their time together, she had learned much about him. He had been a farmer before the war. He worked a small plot of land — no great plantation for him — but she warmed to the pride in his voice when he declared that it had been his. And she heard his heartache when he spoke of his wife, Chelsea, who had died in childbirth along with their stillborn daughter. After supper, he enjoyed sitting by the fire, listening while Maria read to the children from the Gospels. Sometimes she led them in a hymn. Mr. Grieve never joined in, but one night she had seen his lips moving as they sang a Fanny Crosby hymn.

"Had earth no thorns among its flowers,
"And life no fount of tears,
"We might forget our better home
"Beyond this vale of tears."

Once they had finished, she asked him, "Does that song appeal to you, Mr. Grieve?"

"*Our Better Home Beyond* was a favorite of our minister. He often spoke of heaven."

"Tell us what he said," Danny had urged.

"I can't recall all he said." Seeing the disappointment in the boy's face, Mr. Grieve had added, "I do recall one story, I suppose."

Danny's face had brightened, and Astrid moved closer. Warming to their attention, Mr. Grieve began.

"The reverend dreamed that he had died and gone to heaven. He was led into a large house. It was empty of furniture, but there were paintings on all the walls like in a palace. He realized the drawings displayed moments from his life. Some of the events he recalled had been hard to understand while he lived. But they were made clear to him in this house, where he could see the hand of God had been guiding him all along. When he woke, he was comforted to know God had a reason for all that happened, even if he wouldn't understand it until he found his place in paradise."

Maria had thanked him for the story, believing at the time it had been for the benefit of Danny and Astrid. Yet later, as she lay awake listening to the children's steady breaths, she understood the story had been an offering to her as well, a chance to believe Daniel's death might not be senseless. Mr. Grieve's gesture meant even more because she understood he no longer shared her faith, a loss she rued on his behalf as she mourned for her husband. She recognized now that for all the violence he'd demonstrated in their fortuitous meeting, Mr. Grieve had a good heart. He was gentle with the children and treated her with kindness. In time, she might even grow to love him. Once the venom of Josey Angel was out of him, they might build a life together. She hoped the journey to Virginia City would be long enough to cure him.

Maria passed through the fort's main gates with a dimpled smile for the sentries, who'd recognized her and stood ramrod straight long before she reached the high wooden walls. Once inside, the fort resembled a small rural village more than a military outpost, with clapboard houses for officers' quarters, pine log warehouses, and quarters for the enlisted men and a military band. Blue-clad soldiers moved about in every direction while dusty teamsters loafed in what shade could be found while waiting for their wagons to be loaded. The stables were on her left. Beyond those was a gate to the quartermaster yard where she would find the wainwright's shop. If he'd completed his work in preparing the army wagons, he might be enticed by an offer of supper to come visit their camp and assess their rig.

Just ahead and obscuring her view stood a well-equipped train of wagons in the company of soldiers on horseback. She'd spotted them earlier as they approached the fort on the north road. She'd thought nothing of them at the time, but now hope bloomed within her. The newcomers might be from Fort Smith, the northernmost fort along the Bozeman Trail, or the other fort she'd heard of to the west in Montana. If they intended to return that way, she and Mr. Grieve might accompany them.

On drawing closer, she saw something that startled her: not all the newcomers were soldiers and teamsters. Among their ranks Maria saw two women, one an Indian, surrounded by a cluster of children; the other a white woman, close to Maria's age to look at her. She held a squirming child eager to be set down to explore her new environment. Maria smiled at the sight, remembering when Danny and Astrid were so young. While eager for women's talk, Maria restrained herself. The new arrivals would be too preoccupied now for conversation, and she'd lost too much time already in her visit with the doctor. If she wished for an audience with the newcomers, better that she should return once they were settled from their journey. Better still that she should come calling with her children and "husband" so that they might make friends with this soldier's family. Perhaps they might find traveling companions more to Mr. Grieve's liking than the doctor and his men.

CHAPTER FIFTEEN

The diplomat Grantham had arranged for Josey's group to billet in a vacated company barracks near the fort's bakery. At first Josey considered it a magnanimous gesture — such a large building, still equipped with cots and coal-burning stoves, meant plenty of room, and a party that included a black man, a squaw, and practically a tribe of Indian children didn't normally warrant such hospitality from the army.

On arriving at the building so far removed from ongoing activity at the fort, Josey sensed an unspoken agenda of minimizing contact between the remaining soldiers and their "guests." Grantham, he realized, would always have more than one reason for doing a thing. Sometimes that would be best for everyone, but Josey wondered how often that wasn't the case.

Leaving Annabelle to see that everyone settled in to their temporary quarters, Josey headed off to check in with the fort's commanding officer. He was accompanied only by Grantham because two days earlier John Hutchins had veered off the trail to visit his mother's village in hopes of learning Crazy Horse's whereabouts.

Josey measured his steps to match the heavier man's pace across the grassy parade grounds. After so many days in the saddle, it felt good to stretch his legs. The long ride seemed harder than he recalled from the last time he'd come to the fort, and he walked with one hand pressed to his lower back, as if he could squeeze out the lingering ache.

The fort had known better days as well. Fort Phil Kearny was roughly rectangular and divided into two parts. The fort proper, where they were, stretched about four hundred feet square, its high walls enclosing barracks for the company, quarters for officers, stables for the cavalry, and all the warehouses and administrative buildings necessary to support them. On the eastern half of the grounds, separated by an inner wall, were the quartermaster's yard and quarters for the civilian teamsters, their stables, the hay and wood yards, blacksmith, wainwright, cooper, and others.

At the center of the fort, a sun-bleached

Stars and Stripes, big enough to cover the roof of one of the buildings, hung limply in the midday heat from a hundred-foot flagpole. Abandoned equipment lay scattered about it. Broken wagon wheels. Extra neck yokes for oxen. Empty barrels with busted staves. Rusted log chains from the pinery. A mowing machine that had been used to gather hay. They all spoke of a place that had served its purpose and had no more to give.

The fort's first commander, Colonel Henry Carrington, had felt invulnerable behind his high stockade until Captain Fetterman and his eighty men were massacred four days before Christmas two years earlier. After that, many in the fort believed the Indians would come for the rest of them. Josey had tried in vain to assure them the Indians would go off and celebrate their victory, but the shock of that day's defeat drew out the commander's worst instincts. While Carrington managed to swallow back his fear and venture out the following day to oversee the recovery of the bodies, he left orders that, if the Indians attacked, the women and children were to be gathered in the powder magazine, a storage room buried beneath a corner of the parade ground where all the fort's spare munitions were stored. If a final stand failed, the soldiers had orders to blow the place, providing the women and children with the quick death Carrington believed preferable to capture and whatever came afterwards. Josey and Byron had been so alarmed at hearing of the plan that they had stood sentry over the powder magazine that day to ensure no one got panicky enough to follow Carrington's orders prematurely.

Recalling those dark days reinforced Josey's bitterness at seeing the fort's deteriorated state. All the trouble that went into building the fort. All the lives that had been lost protecting it. What had been the point?

Grantham must have sensed Josey's reservations. The diplomat was the sort of man for whom silence is a foreign land wherein one shouldn't stray for long. "Abandoning the forts is a necessary step," he said. "Red Cloud won't sign the treaty until it happens."

Travel responsibilities and family matters had prevented Josey from spending much time with Grantham on the trail outside of one exchange. It had come one evening after they'd made camp near the Bighorn River, when Josey returned on horseback from scouting the surroundings to find Grantham walking with a small trout on a string.

Though hardly worth keeping — cleaning the fish would strip most of its flesh — he had displayed it as proudly as if he'd brought back Melville's whale.

"I haven't fished since I was a boy," Grantham had said.

"I wouldn't have guessed."

Along the walk to the commander's office, Josey reminded Grantham of the conversation. "There's good fishing nearby. You might improve on your catch here."

Grantham's breathing had grown ragged from the effort to maintain his footing on the uneven surface, and he waved off the suggestion with his free hand. "I won't have time for that. I'm to return straightaway to Fort Laramie once the soldiers are packed and ready to leave."

The news stopped Josey. John Hutchins had reassured him they would know soon enough if their mission had any hope for success, but if Grantham and the soldiers were leaving so soon . . . Josey said, "I hope you don't expect me to bring Crazy Horse all the way to Fort Laramie."

"There's no need for that."

Josey began to understand. "You don't expect me to succeed in bringing Crazy Horse here."

Grantham's eyes widened, whether with

surprise at Josey's acuity or apprehension over how he'd react, Josey couldn't tell. He spoke quickly. "It's not for any lack of confidence in your diplomatic skills. I'm quite impressed. You surround yourself with such a" — he paused as he considered his words — "diverse assortment of companions."

Josey let the comment go.

"It's just that it's difficult for me to project success when I can't fathom the nature of your relationship with Crazy Horse."

"We don't have a relationship," Josey said. "At best, you might call it a mutual respect."

Still fixated on the account of Crazy Horse touching Josey when he might have struck him down, Grantham asked about it. "If he considered you a threat, why not rid himself of that concern?"

"Some warriors believe they can capture the 'magic' of a foe by counting coup. To them, killing is easy. It's a greater test of courage to get close enough to their enemy to feel power over him."

"Does Crazy Horse still hold power over you?"

Recalling the last time he saw Crazy Horse, Josey said, "I believe we are even now."

Grantham shook his oversized head, leaving Josey to wonder how he maintained his balance. "I've met many times with the Indians, and I'm no closer to understanding all their ways. These 'visions' that inspire their actions. The mythologies that form their religion. It's all a bunch of hocus-pocus to me."

"We worship a god who died and rose from the dead. The Indians have nothing on us when it comes to imagination."

Grantham chuckled. "I suppose it's that attitude that gives young Mr. Hutchins so much faith in your ability to sway Crazy Horse."

"I'm not sure I share his confidence. Now that we're even, Crazy Horse is just as likely to kill me the next time he sees me as listen to what I have to say — especially if you expect him to put his mark to a treaty."

"Don't be discouraged. Terms have already been settled. Some of the more peaceable tribes have already signed on. What's most important is convincing Crazy Horse to stop his raids."

"So he doesn't need to sign — only agree not to do anything that would jeopardize the peace?"

"A holdout as charismatic as Crazy Horse could be a dangerous thing. The disaffected warriors might rally around a man like that, and the terms of the peace deal wouldn't be worth" — Grantham paused again — "well, the paper they're written on. I won't have this peace spoiled by one rogue Indian."

"I suppose it would be good for a diplomat's career to broker a lasting peace with the Indians."

"Lasting peace?" Grantham chuckled. "Until you came along, I feared it might unravel in the time it took me to return to Washington by train. But, yes, a peace that sees us through the completion of the transcontinental railroad would be a credit to my career. There's nothing wrong with wedding self-interest to the greater good. You strike me as a practical man who understands that."

Josey wanted to debate the point, but the quickness with which he'd negotiated a contract to provide beef at Fort Ellis stopped him. He had become more practical with age and the advent of new responsibilities. Peace would be good for the territory, and he had no great affection for the Indians. And yet he felt troubled at Grantham's description of terms. Maybe Annabelle's safe return from her time in captivity had softened his views.

"So your treaty," he had said, "it's meant to stand only a few years?"

"It will stand as long as it's in the best interests of both peoples."

Josey paused. The headquarters lay just ahead along the path that bisected the parade ground. "The Indians will want it to stand in perpetuity."

"Perpetuity is a long time."

Grasping how little his mission mattered, Josey said, "Maybe Crazy Horse is right to carry on the fight."

Grantham fell uncharacteristically quiet. His expansive brow furrowed while his mind went to work. He cleared his throat as they resumed their walk. "The news of my imminent departure may have given you the incorrect impression that your mission holds no value or that the treaty is not an earnest compromise."

Josey's bitterness over Grantham's gamesmanship overshadowed any amusement he drew at the diplomat's verbal contortions.

"I can assure you that the treaty provides genuine benefits to both peoples," Grantham continued. "Besides closing the forts, the government will establish an agency to look to the care and education of the Indians. Each family will be given a cow and tools for farming."

Nothing the Indians seek, Josey thought.

"And, of course, the Indians would retain

hunting privileges in the Powder River country, and, and" — Grantham was speaking so fast Josey feared he might choke on his words — "the Black Hills, sacred to their people, the Black Hills would remain theirs forever."

"In perpetuity?" Josey asked.

"Why, yes. Of course." Grantham's face had turned an unflattering crimson that left him looking like an overripe tomato.

They reached the headquarters, a long, narrow structure built of one-inch plank board. Josey gestured for Grantham to lead the way, but the diplomat first grabbed his sleeve with surprising force. He spoke in a throaty whisper.

"I admire your capacity to sympathize with a people you've warred against, but you need to know this: If Crazy Horse continues murdering every white man he can find and these negotiations fail, the army will return. In greater numbers. And those who favor more extreme measures than this treaty will have their day."

"More extreme measures?"

Grantham cleared his throat again, the sound nearly choking off his response.

"Extermination."

CHAPTER SIXTEEN

Josey and Grantham were greeted at the post commander's office by a young private not much thicker than a flagpole. The pants he'd drawn from the quartermaster were so large he'd hiked them around his waist and bunched the excess fabric so it stuck out like a cartridge box. Holding his drawers in place was a three-quarter-inch peg carved from hard wood, what some soldiers called a "Kentucky button." From the worn appearance of his square-toed brogans Josey figured the soles were so thin he'd wince at every nail in the floorboards. His face lit up at seeing them, and he extended a bony hand.

"You're Josey Angel! The sergeant told me you was expected, but I didn't think to meet you myself." The young soldier flashed a grin pocked with missing teeth, telltale signs of scurvy along with his fetid breath.

Josey shook the hand and replied, "The

pleasure's mine, private."

"The pleasure's *his*," the soldier said, turning his grin onto Grantham. "They still talk at the sutler's about what he did at Crazy Woman Creek. How he held off more'n a hundred bloody Sioux single-handed with his rifle."

Pulse quickened by the memory, Josey sought to maneuver through the open door, but the private blocked their way. "People do like to stretch the blanket when they tell a story," Josey said. "Especially soldiers."

"But I heard from them that was there. They say you work that rifle almost like 'twas one of them Gatling guns. How many did you kill that day?"

Josey took a deep breath, the air escaping through his mouth in a long, low whistle. "I don't know."

"Too many to count, I expect."

Grantham warded off another question with a gentle reminder. "Soldier, I believe the colonel is expecting us."

The grin fell away. "Yes, of course, sir. The colonel's just finishing another meeting." He stepped back so that they might pass. "Maybe I'll see you around, Mr. Angel, and you can finish telling that story."

Josey nodded without responding, his mind far removed from the fort's stockade walls and wood-frame barracks. As they stepped into the room, he was relieved to find the colonel occupied, affording him time to settle his thoughts. He felt Grantham's eyes on him as he took in their surroundings.

The room was largely as he remembered it: a smell of coffee and cut pine; the space dominated by a large table covered with stacks of papers and an inkwell; plank floors off of which every boot scuff reverberated like a rifle report. One new addition: a finely wrought, upholstered chair, the sort Josey associated with the sitting room of a well-furnished house. It sat alone in a corner, leaving Josey to conclude the commander's quarters weren't large enough to accommodate all the furniture his wife had brought with them from their last posting. Pondering its incongruity helped refocus his mind on their meeting.

Colonel John Eugene Smith was a trim, fit-looking man with a bristly beard and mustache that masked the lower half of his face. He stood on the opposite side of the long table, flanked by a major and a lieutenant, who shuffled through papers while briefing him. He acknowledged the newcomers with a flick of his dark eyes before returning his attention to the men beside him.

The major, a portly quartermaster with a thick beard and a hairline in full retreat, had been speaking when Josey and Grantham came in. His voice carried across the spartan room so that even at a discreet distance they heard every word.

"With companies B and F already departed, we have more than enough provisions for the remaining three companies of infantry and the cavalry company," he said. "Especially if it's still your intention to depart so soon."

"It is," Smith said with a firmness that brooked no dissent. "We have already exceeded our original orders to vacate by the end of July."

The major straightened his back and cleared his throat at the implied censure. "The general's expectation that anyone would bring a train of wagons to such a remote outpost and purchase our excess supplies and hardware was, shall we say, optimistic at best."

"It is a general's prerogative to be an optimist." Smith cut a glance at his guests, a hint of amusement in his eyes as if he meant to include them in his jest. "It is his officers' duty to see that he isn't disappointed."

The lieutenant, a small-boned man with a pallid complexion that indicated his duty lay more with pencils than rifles, interjected with suggestions of how both of his superiors might be appeased. The major parried each proffered solution with a curt shake of the head and dismissive grunt.

While they dithered about numbers of pack mules and sacks of flour and sugar, Josey recalled the private with the scurvy-riddled teeth and shook his head at the pointlessness of the discussion. The army had brought these men to a land that, while sacred to the Indians, held worth to the white man measured only by the miles saved on the route to Montana's gold fields. The whole endeavor of building forts to protect a dusty trail had been a waste of time, money, and lives.

Most of all lives.

Now they spoke of excess sacks of rice and beans and outdated armaments as if their loss would be the ruin of the United States. That all countries and all armies behaved the same provided cold comfort to Josey.

An outburst from the major drew Josey's mind back to the moment. "We simply don't have enough wagons for everything," he told the lieutenant, the palm of his hand going to his bare forehead to wipe away a sheen of perspiration.

All eyes turned to Smith to serve as arbiter, but Grantham stepped forward and spoke first. "If I may, Colonel: Have you considered giving away some of the excess supplies to the Indians? Instead of being faulted for waste, you'd be credited for a grand gesture that puts the stamp on a final peace."

Smith rubbed his whiskered chin, a gesture that failed to fully mask a smile at Grantham's wiles. He said, "Make an accounting of what we can spare and see that it's done, Major Grimes. Foodstuffs only — we will leave behind no arms for the Indians." He straightened and pulled on the end of his tunic, smoothing out the fabric and looking pleased with himself.

Stepping away from the table so that his officers could see to the remaining paperwork, Smith led Josey and Grantham to his private office. The door to the smaller room scraped against the pine-plank floor as he pushed it open.

Grantham made formal introductions. Smith had taken over command of the fort a year earlier, a few months after Josey had left. He said, "I've heard so much about you, Mr. Angliewicz, I feel that we are acquainted. Your reputation precedes you."

Josey offered a tight smile. "A reputation can be a heavy burden, Colonel, especially when it's exaggerated by soldiers' gossip. From what I've heard, the accounts of how your men turned back Red Cloud last summer outstrip any tall tales you may have heard of me."

Smith waved away the compliment, though his eyes were alight with pride. "All credit goes to the men who kept their heads under fire, and the new breech-loading Springfields that arrived with me."

Josey thought again about how different things might have been a year and a half earlier if the soldiers at the fort had been equipped with modern rifles. Grantham seemed to sense his melancholy and interjected: "I expect you'll be glad to leave this place behind, Colonel."

Smith responded with a *tsk*. "No one will miss this posting. The men went nearly six months without pay because of snows that prevented the paymaster from getting through until the end of March. Then they got the news that everything we've been fighting for here was for naught. We're to pack up and leave with our tails between our legs."

"There is no dishonor in peace," Grantham said.

"Yet there's no honor in retreat," Smith parried.

"It's not a retreat, Colonel, it's a —"

Smith cut him off. "You haven't heard the latest report from the mail courier team."

Josey looked at Grantham, who appeared braced for a blow.

"Seeing smoke from the trail, they went to investigate a site a few days north of Fort Reno. Wagons had been set ablaze. Eight men slaughtered."

"*Eight* men?" Grantham's eyes closed, as if he could will away the news if he couldn't see it.

Smith's voice betrayed his frustration. "Does that sound like the work of a single malcontent Indian?"

"You suspect Indians?" Josey asked.

"The site was littered with arrows," Smith replied. "The riders said the bodies looked like pincushions."

"Who were the victims?" Grantham asked.

"They appear to have been miners, too impatient to get to the gold fields to abide by the orders at Laramie to wait for a larger wagon train. They were panning in one of the streams when they were attacked."

Josey shook his head. "Fools. If there had

210

been gold in Wyoming, it would have been found long before now."

Grantham's mind had turned to darker portents. "The bodies," he said, "they were found in the same condition as . . . before?"

Smith spoke through a jaw clenched so tight his response was inaudible.

Grantham took this as an affirmative. "Could your men tell when it happened?"

"They didn't linger at the site." The tightness in Smith's voice was a warning against Grantham pushing too far. "It doesn't take long to confirm that a man's head is missing. And there's not much sense in waiting around to lose yours next."

He pulled again on the end of his tunic, smoothing the fabric as if to restore order where he could. He took a deep breath before concluding, "This is why our orders feel like a retreat. Rather than punishing the perpetrators of such heinous acts, I fear we are conveying weakness to an enemy who will find that irresistible. How long, after we are gone, before these savages prey on unprotected homesteads or begin to harass the new rail lines? I can't say I hold out much hope for the durability of your treaty, Mr. Grantham."

Before Josey could ask what the news meant for his mission to seek out Crazy

Horse, a ruckus of shouts and cries erupted from outside. Josey and Grantham followed Smith from the building, where they found a scene even wilder than the noise had indicated.

Josey didn't know where to look first. Five men moved before him in an elaborate dance of violence that confused him as much for its chaos as for the disparate identities of its participants. To his left, two enlisted men fought a losing battle to restrain a civilian built roughly on the proportions of an upright grizzly bear. To his right, a sergeant in a dusty McClellan cap shielded a bedraggled old Indian, who at turns cowered behind the soldier, then popped out to shout what Josey interpreted as profanities at the bear-sized man, his intervals of courage and cowardice dictated by how determined the other man appeared to get at his quarry. For his part, the civilian seemed less inconvenienced by the straining soldiers than by indecision, as if torn between choosing whether to rip the old Indian apart by the limbs or crush him life-less with hands big as hams.

Colonel Smith's bellowed orders brought a moment's détente to the spectacle, at least long enough for the combatants to catch their breath. "What's the commotion, Sergeant?"

The dusty sergeant placed a restraining hand on the Indian's frail shoulder. With a nod in the direction of the big man he said, "We found that one beating the savage outside the main gate." He paused to draw another breath. "He looked like he would have killed him if we hadn't broken it up."

"He is a spy," the civilian said with a trace of accent Josey couldn't immediately place.

The Indian responded with more shouted gibberish. *"Natá. Natá. Wanági."* He had a half-starved look and appeared too old to fight, but now that the clash had been confined to a verbal contest he exhibited no fear toward the man who towered over everyone.

The tall civilian dressed too well to be a teamster or drover, with clean dark pants and a matching vest over a bright red shirt of the sort Josey had seen frequently in Texas. His heeled boots were high and black and adorned with a silver buckle and rowels the size of a silver dollar. He must have weighed at least three hundred pounds, so maybe he needed the oversized spurs, though Josey pitied any horse he rode. Before Smith could address the combatants, Grantham was in his ear, speaking so softly

Josey doubted anyone but he overheard.

"That is Mr. Martinez, the doctor's man."

Smith nodded before addressing the newcomer. "He doesn't look much like a spy."

"I've seen him around the teamsters' camp," the sergeant said. "He's a bad egg, Colonel, always loafing around, looking for handouts."

"Who better to spy on the fort than an Indian beggar?" Martinez said with a snort. An extra-wide brim on his hat left his clean-shaven face in full shadow, but hearing him speak a few more words confirmed the man's origins from south of the border. Josey doubted he'd ever seen such a big Mexican.

The old Indian had calmed enough that the sergeant unhanded him. He apparently spoke no English and kept pointing to his forehead and repeating a word Josey took to be his name. Moving down the stairs to get a closer look at the old man, Josey detected a musky, wild animal scent. He approached and asked, *"Natá?"*

The Indian's leathery face wrinkled with confusion. He shook his head and pointed to Martinez, repeating the word or something close to it.

"Natá. Natá. Wanági."

The man's agitation made Josey wish John

214

Hutchins were there to translate. "He acts like he knows you," Josey said to Martinez.

The Mexican stood more than a head taller than Josey — and loomed even larger with broad shoulders nearly as thick as a horse's haunches. Martinez had made his own assessment of Josey and seemed to find him wanting, ignoring him to address the Colonel: "That is because he is always skulking around our camp when he isn't spying on the fort."

"What would be the point of a spy?" Josey asked. "The army is abandoning the fort. The Indians can see all they need to know from the surrounding hills. Surely, you've seen the flash of their hand mirror signals."

Martinez stared him down without responding.

"Perhaps he's aligned with Crazy Horse," Grantham suggested.

The Indian's agitation increased, his voice rising with what Josey interpreted as a mixture of anger and indignation. The words still made no sense to the English speakers, though Josey picked out the same word or a variation of it again and again.

"Natá. Natá. Wanági."

"I'd sure like to know what's got this old man so worked up," Josey said. "John Hutchins should be here tonight. He'll be

215

able to tell us."

Smith appeared relieved to postpone a decision on the old Indian's fate. With a perfunctory nod, he ordered the enlisted men to escort the captive to a holding cell.

Only Martinez seemed displeased with the verdict. "A dirty Indian like this is no more than a thief — or a murderer, if you gave him the chance," he said. "You should let me finish him and be done with it."

"There will be no summary executions under my watch," Smith said.

After the soldiers left with the Indian, Josey and Grantham returned inside with the colonel. The interruption had left Smith irritable, and he concluded their business quickly, giving Josey no chance to satisfy his curiosity about Martinez or his employer. He waited until he and Grantham were alone and making their way back to ask about the man.

Grantham replied: "The family that employs Mr. Martinez has personal ties to President Johnson. I have specific instructions from Washington to afford his employer every courtesy, and I conveyed those to the colonel."

"You said he worked for a doctor."

Grantham nodded his oversized head. "The father's heir and only child. He served the Union as a surgeon. Now he's conducting some kind of scientific inquiry. I hear it's garnered interest from the Army Medical Museum. Mr. Martinez has worked for his family for many years. He's said to be fiercely loyal."

After turning off the path that stretched before the headquarters, they walked along a narrow alley formed by the high stockade walls and the wide, two-story buildings that housed the fort's remaining infantry companies. The sound of voices raised in anger echoed between the buildings. Josey rushed ahead.

He found Martinez standing over the old Indian, a boot on his back to hold him in place while the smaller man's spindly limbs flailed like an upside-down tortoise. Beside Martinez stood a new man, a red-bearded fellow with what looked like a saber scar stretching the length of his face. The two privates charged with the Indian's care were sprawled on the ground, looking none too eager to continue whatever confrontation had preceded Josey's arrival.

"You see?" Martinez told them. "I told you he could not be trusted."

"He would have been fine if you weren't so rough with him," a pock-scarred private said.

Martinez drew his gun.

"Wait," Josey ordered. His hand slipped to the revolver on his belt to reinforce his command, but he stayed the impulse to draw. Escalating tensions with a heedless challenge had gotten him in trouble with Lord Byron at the ferry crossing. He swallowed back his instincts, held his voice calm, and said, "There's no need for guns."

Martinez studied him a moment. The lowering sun gave Josey a better look at his face. His eyes were dark, but his skin pale, more like a European than a Mexican. His wide nose flared, and he smiled, his misshapen teeth yellow against the whiteness of his skin. He tilted his head in Josey's direction and lifted his boot off the Indian.

Then he shot the old man in the back.

Before Josey could react, the pistol was pointed at him. The red-bearded man drew his pistol too. Still smiling, Martinez paused a moment, as if inviting Josey to reach for his gun. He said, "You would shoot a white man over an Indian? I do not think so."

The shot must have passed through the Indian's heart, killing him instantly. Not even a drop of blood could be seen. Martinez holstered his gun, but the bearded fellow kept his aimed at Josey. Uncertainty stayed Josey's hand. The big man no longer threatened him, and nothing he could do would help the dead Indian. "You had no cause to do that," he said.

Martinez snorted. "You think yourself a good man, do you?" His tone made clear his words conveyed no praise. "A man of honor and courage. Is that what you tell yourself?"

He showed his teeth again in what Josey understood was supposed to be a smile before turning his attention to the soldiers, both of them still so stunned by what had happened neither had spoken nor moved. "He was trying to escape. Be glad I was here to take care of things." Hearing no challenge to his words, Martinez turned away. He told the man with the scar, "Send a couple of men over to retrieve the body. Dr. Hamilton will wish to study the remains."

Before leaving he looked to Josey, his eyes black as the hole at the end of a gun barrel. "Do not make me draw on you again," he said. "I will not hesitate a second time."

CHAPTER SEVENTEEN

When Maria paid a call to the woman she'd seen arrive at the fort, she found her at work removing her wagon's contents and wiping them clean of the dust and grime that had accumulated over the course of her travels.

Maria called out with a shy wave, "Now there is a task I find even more onerous knowing it will need repeating an hour after returning to the road."

The woman looked up, her surprise at the interruption giving way to a smile that invited an approach. Maria had assumed the woman to be an officer's wife of some status from her manner and means. Wanting to make a good impression, she spoke with the crisp articulation of a schoolmistress. "Excuse my boldness, but the sight of another woman at a chore with which I'm too well acquainted stirred a sympathy within my breast that overcame my manners."

The woman responded with equal formality. "Your boldness is well received," she said, setting aside her dust rags and wiping her hands on an apron. Coming forward with a proffered hand, she introduced herself as Annabelle Angliewicz.

Maria sighed with relief when Annabelle insisted she call her by her Christian name. She reciprocated after giving her name as Grieve and mentioning a husband and children to reinforce their bond. She dismissed a twinge of guilt over the deception, telling herself God would forgive a fib motivated by concern for her children's well-being and the need for safe passage to Virginia City. Until she knew Annabelle better, she dared not share too much of her situation.

She said, "I apologize for calling unannounced, but I saw your arrival, and, having been deprived for so long of proper female companionship, I could not resist."

"Do not apologize. Any excuse for a reprieve from this tedious exercise is to be welcomed." Annabelle exhaled with an exaggerated sigh, blowing a loose strand of dark hair from her fair face.

Maria guessed Annabelle to be no more than a few years older than herself. She was an attractive woman, tall with a lean build accentuated by the divided skirt she wore beneath her apron. Maria had at first thought it a dress with an unflattering cut until she saw the other woman move in it. Clearly designed for riders, it also emphasized Annabelle's long legs and the rangy strength demonstrated in her success at removing the contents of the wagon by herself. Her clothes and appearance conveyed a hardiness that, while not exactly fashionable, suited the woman and place perfectly. *A couple of years living out here, and I may look the same.* Recalling the black man and Indian woman she'd seen with Annabelle earlier, Maria said, "I'm surprised you don't leave such a job to your servants."

Annabelle's brow knitted with a moment's confusion before her face relaxed. "I believe you speak of Lord Byron and his wife, Red Shawl. They are not servants but our friends." Seeing Maria's reaction she added, "Do not be embarrassed at the error. It is a long story."

"A fascinating one, I'm sure."

"No one arrives in the territories without a tale to tell."

You've no idea. Maria forced a smile and tried to keep her face blank. "May I inquire more regarding yours? Is your husband an officer?"

"Not anymore. We have a ranch just west of Bozeman. My husband has some business with the army, part of his negotiations in securing a contract to provide beef to Fort Ellis."

The casual familiarity with which Annabelle spoke about business matters increased Maria's admiration. Here was a woman who exuded strength and competence without apology — the way a man might.

A child's fussing drew their attention to a bed Annabelle had fashioned from blankets in the shade beneath the wagon. "Isabelle is finished with her nap," Annabelle said with a weariness Maria recognized.

Maria spoke of her children while Annabelle saw to her daughter, who looked as precious as Astrid had been at that age. With a wistful stirring, Maria wondered if Daniel would have been content to remain in the States if they'd had another baby's needs to consider. She was glad when Annabelle accepted her offer to feed Isabelle once she had finished swaddling the child. Isabelle smelled of powder and milk, and Maria pulled her tight and breathed deeply to recapture the sense of completeness her life held when Astrid had been barely more than a year old. *Not so long ago, and yet so far away.*

Annabelle seemed more than content to return to her cleaning while Maria fed the child a porridge with stewed apples and gave her water flavored with lemon juice to mask a slight mineral taste. Between bites, she tickled the soft rolls of skin beneath Isabelle's chin, winning a wet smile she wiped with a handkerchief from her pocket.

"She takes to you like blood," Annabelle said. "She's fascinated with your yellow hair. It's beautiful."

Maria deflected the compliment. "She is such a pretty child. I can tell she favors her mother — oh, and I see she has new teeth coming in."

"Really?" Annabelle dropped her dust rag and wiped her hands.

Bouncing the child in her arms to elicit a smile, Maria ran her index finger along Isabelle's lower gums. "Right here, on either side of the lower middle teeth."

"Oh, yes. We've been expecting those to come in," Annabelle said, though she sounded uncertain and made no move to reclaim her daughter.

Fearing she'd embarrassed the other woman, Maria changed the subject. "They grow up so fast." She resumed feeding Isabelle, and they lost themselves in conversation. Maria steered its course with frequent, impersonal comments and questions that avoided any queries about her own life. Even within those limits, Annabelle proved a fascinating source for news about the fort and the army's imminent departure, relations between the Indians and settlers in the area, and the weather and conditions Maria could expect in Montana, including women's fashions.

"I've been admiring your skirt. It's so cleverly constructed," Maria said.

Annabelle accepted the compliment at face value and told of how she'd instructed a tailor in Virginia City in its specifics after seeing an advertisement in *Frank Leslie's Weekly.* "I still prefer to wear boy's pants while riding, but this is more versatile — and I don't think it would cause my old friends in Charleston to collapse from vapors to see me in it," she added with a knowing wink.

"I think it's wonderful," Maria said, careful not to sound too effusive. Being generous with praise was usually the surest way into a woman's good graces, but Annabelle struck her as someone with a limited appetite for high approbation. "You will have to introduce me to your tailor in Virginia City."

"Is that where you plan to settle?"

"We are considering it."

Maria told a strategically abridged version of the aborted journey to Oregon. Shared intimacies were even better than praise at securing a woman's friendship, and she hoped someday she might confide all with her new friend. The journey to Virginia City would be so much more pleasant with another woman. Maria already imagined Astrid and maybe even Danny amusing themselves by helping to attend to Isabelle. She sensed in Annabelle's confident nature a kindness that would make her not only a valued friend, but a potential lifeline if Maria could not dissuade Mr. Grieve from his deadly quest. Surely, it would be no imposition for a woman of such obvious means to help a new friend establish herself in some honorable occupation. First Maria would have to figure out how to tell her about Mr. Grieve. Annabelle must know of Josey Angel, at least by reputation, and might provide the intelligence Mr. Grieve required; better yet, if Annabelle's husband proved a persuasive man, he might dissuade Mr. Grieve from his deadly quest — though Maria held little hope for that. Women as strong-willed as Annabelle typically found themselves matched with men who were easily cowed, and such a man would never

226

move Mr. Grieve from his intentions.

She'd been thinking of ways to broach the subject and finally saw an opportunity. She asked, "Is Virginia City safe? One hears such horrifying stories in the States of outlaws and gunmen in the west."

"It's as safe as any town. You will hear of how vigilantes took things too far in their pursuit of justice, but that was a few years ago, before we arrived. The town has quieted since then and is more focused on commerce and the governing of the territory. Virginia City is the capital of Montana now and about as civilized a town as you'll find in the west."

Annabelle regaled Maria with tales of Virginia's City's theater, literary society, and new schoolhouse. Maria listened patiently, understanding a person's inclination to praise to a stranger the home they carp about among neighbors. With murmured gasps of wonder and delight, Maria encouraged her to continue. When Isabelle finished eating, Maria moved the child to her shoulder while she continued listening and took in the sights around the fort. In the distance, soldiers shoveled lime into the pits beneath the latrines behind the barracks. Across the parade grounds, others hauled boxes out from an underground storage area. Through

227

the crowd milling about the main gate, she recognized the form of a man accompanied by two young children.

"I think I see my husband and children back from the sutler's store," she told Annabelle. Balancing Isabelle with one arm, Maria waved, calling out, "Atticus!" He returned the gesture.

Annabelle came and relieved her of the child, smiling at the sight of the children breaking into a run to reach their mother. "Oh, that is excellent news," she said. "My husband should be returning soon from his errand. I'm sure Josey will be delighted to meet you."

Maria had taken a step in the direction of the children when her knee caught and nearly buckled. She turned sharply and looked at her new friend as if seeing her for the first time.

"Did you say Josey?"

CHAPTER EIGHTEEN

She came to him in a secret place within a copse of mulberry, far enough upstream from where the women gathered water that they would not be seen or heard. While Crazy Horse had waited, he twined blades of sweet-smelling grass into his hair, yet even their scent failed to dull his impatience. He knew from the position of the sun through the thick leaves when to expect her, yet it seemed the sun was tethered in place and would not move for him. He had been waiting so long. A lifetime.

On finally seeing her Crazy Horse said, "I feared you would not come."

"You would only seek me out again if I did not come." Black Buffalo Woman wore a finely beaded buckskin dress, her dark hair in two long braids that hung down over her breasts. Her eyes looked hard as acorns. "I cannot have you mooning over me in the village like a mare in heat."

He winced but could not deny her words. Seeing her, even among all the other women and the children in the village, had taken him back to when they had no more than fifteen winter counts and he had first loved her. Black Buffalo Woman was no longer a maiden. She had birthed three children. Lines fine as spider's silk stretched out from the corner of her eyes, and the creases around her mouth were deeper. Years of stretching hides, stripping bark from willow, and other women's chores left her hands as rough as whetstones, yet he longed to feel them on his body again.

"You should be with the rest of the men on the buffalo hunt."

"I have been away."

"Lone Bear is dead," she said. "Nothing you do will bring him back."

He was not surprised that she knew of his quest. He could only imagine how her husband, No Water, ridiculed him. Worse, he had little to show for his efforts, for he had failed to find the medicine man he had sought after taking the white man's head. His voice sounded meek even to his own ears when he said, "I sought to spare Lone Bear an afterlife of deprivation."

"You should know better. If our gods are

so strong, why do they allow us to suffer so?"

He felt the sting of her words but could not rebut her. The roots of Crazy Horse's faith reached deep. His father had been a medicine man and had helped him interpret the visions he had on becoming a man after thirteen winters. Crazy Horse had seen a man on horseback ride out of a lake. The man had instructed him to be modest about his accomplishments, to keep no more from his raids than he needed. This, he and his father had agreed, would be the price of Crazy Horse's greatness in battle. While most men adorned themselves in eagle feather war bonnets and sang of their victories, Crazy Horse wore no more than a single feather and left it to others to speak of his valor. While successful warriors enriched themselves with horses stolen in raids, Crazy Horse would grow wealthy in the gratitude of those in need to whom he gifted his spoils.

The magical man on horseback had told him other things, too, even how he would die, and those words had guided his behavior ever since. Yet now when he recalled the vision, he wondered if the man from the lake had been no more than a hallucination brought on by hunger or the urge to see something — anything — that would mark him as a man. He had been so eager to prove himself, so determined to outshine the boys who had taunted him because of his light skin and hair. The vision had reinforced his belief in his own importance, even as it prevented him from speaking of it. Black Buffalo Woman, perhaps alone among the people, saw through his modesty and generosity. She knew he had always been greedy above all things for the acclaim that came to a brave warrior.

"You have a proud name, everything you ever sought," she said. "All of the people speak of your greatness."

"They see now what you always saw."

"Every girl wants to see greatness in her first love."

He winced again. She had not meant to wound him, and for that her words relegating him to her past cut even deeper. He said, "You are my first and only love."

Her chin quivered as the hard set of her jaw relaxed. She called him by the boyhood name she had used the first time they made love. Hearing her speak it still held a power over him. "Oh, Jiji, any woman who seeks to claim you can only be a mistress to the ambitions of your visions."

"That is no longer true. I have done all I

can do for Lone Bear. There is no more to be gained from fighting the *wasicu*. I am no longer bound by my visions."

"So many times I longed to hear you say that." Her dark eyes glinted with moisture that had not been there before. "It is too late for us, Jiji. I have my children to think of, and I am no longer a young woman. Find yourself a pretty maiden and make her happy."

"I do not want anyone else. I have never wanted anyone else."

He thought back to when she had come to him on the eve of the Hundred in the Hands, the battle named for the vision of a seer who had predicted they would kill that many soldiers. Crazy Horse had anticipated his destiny in that triumph, while Black Buffalo Woman had feared for his life. A Lakota woman could divorce her husband by simply turning out his possessions from the tepee they shared, and that night she had offered to come away with him. In his vanity, Crazy Horse had spurned her. He had been raised by the people to the status of a *wica,* a man who demonstrates the virtues of generosity, courage, fortitude, and wisdom. Another man might steal a woman with no more sanction than the loss of a horse or two if the Big Bellies who judged such things ordered it to keep the peace. More was expected of a *wica;* he had felt the shame of betraying the honor bestowed upon him every time they had been together, yet he could not give her up. He had turned from her on the eve of battle, convinced in the heat of his hatred for the *wasicu* that she diminished him and threatened the greatness his vision had promised.

"It was not so long ago you offered to come away with me —"

"And you refused me."

"I was wrong."

His admission unsteadied her. She turned from him, as if she did not trust herself to meet his gaze, and placed a hand against a mulberry's deeply furrowed bark. "We could not stay. Where would we go?"

"Wherever you wish. North, perhaps, away from the wars that are coming. The *wasicu* settlers make for easy raids, but more will come when their iron horse is built. Their army will protect it in numbers not even Red Cloud can match, and they will drive away the remaining buffalo. Living among one of the northern tribes would be best."

Her fingers traced the bark's deep grooves with a light touch he envied. She sounded amused. "You have given much thought to this."

He moved closer, less than an arm's length away, though he did not reach for her. Not yet. "I have thought of little else."

"That is not true. You have demonstrated more loyalty to a dead friend than to the people who look to you as a leader."

"I have come to realize my place is with the living." His hands went to her shoulders.

"You abandon a purpose that kept you from the people only to take up with a woman who will force you to flee. Is it me you desire or merely an escape from your duty?"

He tightened his grip and pulled her close. Dropping his voice to a harsh whisper, he spoke into her ear, "Let me show you."

Her body tensed, then relaxed, molding against him. He kissed her neck, and his hands traced her contours until they found the familiar holds at her hips. His desire pulsed like war drums, and he pressed against her. She turned her head enough so that his mouth found hers. The kiss left them breathless. He loosened the drawstring to his leggings and tugged up on her dress before her hand found his in a firm grip.

"No."

He kissed her again, pulled her even

tighter. In all the years they had been lovers she had never denied him. She had refused to see him at times. He had avoided her for long periods. But they had never resisted one another when alone. He held the skirt of her dress in place with one hand, while the other caressed her bare thighs. The heat between her legs nearly scalded him.

"No, Jiji. Stop." She pushed his hand away and tried to back away from him.

He held her fast. "Do not ask me to stop."

"I must."

His grip relaxed and she slipped away, far enough for her skirts to slip down and cover her legs. His eyes searched hers for answers veiled behind the hardness she had shown when she first came to him. Bitterness got the better of him.

"Is this because I refused to go with you before?"

"No, Jiji. But as you had then, I have duties I must attend. I cannot leave my children now. If this winter is as hard as the last, they will need me. I know you will not like to hear this, but the soldiers have offered food from their winter stores before they abandon the fort. I must go with the women to receive this gift so that the children will not go hungry."

His anger flared. "The buffalo hunt will —"

She stayed him with a finger to his lips. "Do not be angry. And do not speak of the buffalo. You know as well as I that since the *wasicu* came, the hunt provides less meat for the people each year. Our men are too proud to take handouts from the fort, and so the task is left to the women. Do not permit your pride to expose the children to hunger."

He knew she was right, though it chafed him to think the *wasicu* believed themselves so strong — or thought the people so weak — that they could sustain an enemy they might later seek to kill on the whims of the Great White Father.

"I will go with you. I will stay with you this winter."

"You know that cannot be."

She watched him fill in the reasons: How No Water could not abide such a loss of dignity and had a large family to support his feud; how the elders would object to open hostilities within the tribe; how his love would always be tainted by the shame it would cost him to have her.

Without a word, she turned from him and walked away. He watched her, shifting a step left, then a step right to keep her in view through the trees while her image receded. Watching. Waiting. Knowing she would not change her mind but hoping. Hoping she might look back.

"You are all I have left," he said, so softly not even he heard the words.

She never looked back.

Chapter Nineteen

Josey saw Annabelle by the wagon from across the parade ground.

She wasn't alone.

He didn't know the newcomers. A pretty woman, hair shining like gold in the sunlight, who looked anxious to leave; a pair of towheaded children, a boy and girl, a little younger than Mina and Dewdrops and perhaps just as shy as Byron's girls; and a man, tall and lean, if a bit haggard, wearing a big Colt '60 on his belt that looked better cared for than its owner. The man stared off into the distance, then his head snapped in Josey's direction as if called by a whistle. His gaze brought to mind a hawk, perched atop a lodgepole pine, just before taking wing.

"There's trouble," he said, barely loud enough to be heard.

"What's that, Josey?" Lord Byron, walking

beside him, saw the strangers and stopped too.

"Remember that discussion we had about whether I go looking for trouble or it finds me? If I don't win that argument after today, I never will."

He was later than he'd told Annabelle he'd be. A pang of guilt for leaving her alone to the chores of cleaning the wagon pricked his conscience, but it couldn't be helped after all that had happened.

Grantham had been in a hurry to avoid any more trouble with Martinez, urging Josey to leave the dead Indian to the soldiers. Josey had gone along. He had a strong sense Martinez would face no consequences for his murder of the old man given his employer's high ties with the government, and Josey couldn't stomach watching that play out.

Grantham had told Josey, "You did the proper thing. Martinez is a dangerous man. You shouldn't chide yourself for backing down. He wasn't even pointing the gun at me, and I was afraid."

"That wasn't fear," Josey replied. "It happened too fast for me to be afraid."

"Yes, of course." Grantham's arched eyebrows belied his quick agreement. Josey couldn't expect a paper-collar man to understand how it was worse for Josey to confess being ill-prepared than afraid. Josey had survived the war in part because he'd been alert to things other men didn't see. His failure to anticipate Martinez's intentions had cost that Indian his life. And while he had no love for Indians, the episode discomfited him for what it might portend.

"All I'm saying is that a sensible man allows his fears to guide his actions," Grantham continued. "Live to fight another day, that's what I say."

"You know nothing of it."

"I beg to differ. Fear is a subject I dare say I know better than you."

Josey had spun on the diplomat in a way that cowed him into silence. "In that you are wrong. Now keep quiet or leave before I lose my temper and further your education on the subject."

Grantham had chosen the second option, his big head bobbing like a scarecrow come to life as he scurried off. Josey had headed to the barracks in hopes of finding Annabelle. He took the long way along the stockade wall, needing time to sort through his thoughts. Even without understanding why, Grantham had struck a nerve with his talk of fear. The problem with diplomats and the politicians back East is they viewed

241

fear as something to be avoided or denied. Josey knew better. Fear had dominated his life for years, though it had taken different forms. As a "fresh fish" in an unblooded regiment, he'd feared turning coward and embarrassing himself before his brothers-in-arms. Later, his fear became failing the Colonel. He'd have rather died than live with the thought he'd let down the old man. That kind of fear made him a better soldier. The sort who is always ready. Never taken by surprise. Ever vigilant.

The kind of soldier who might have saved that Indian from Martinez.

His failure to do so exposed just how much he had changed now that his responsibilities were to Annabelle and Isabelle. They didn't ask him to charge an enemy line or keep his head when canister shot exploded all around. The opposite, in fact. They required a gentle man who provided them with a safe home that stayed warm through winter. A father who could comfort a crying baby and feed an obstinate child. A husband who was both loving and could be counted on to return home every night.

These roles did not come naturally to Josey. When he had first met Annabelle and her family while scouting for their wagon train, he had seen his place in their world as a dog in the yard, a necessary safeguard against foxes or wolves but too dangerous to be allowed in the house. Annabelle had taken it upon herself to tame him. *Or at least housebreak me,* he thought wryly. She wasn't suited to be a soldier's wife. Her father was a merchant, and, while a merchant's wife could find herself a widow before her time, it wasn't a fate she had to contemplate every time her husband left the house.

As much as Josey wanted to be that man for Annabelle, he couldn't escape his old fears of failing those he loved most. Had blunting the sharp edge of his vigilance dulled him to life's dangers? An Indian had died because he'd been slow to recognize a threat. That created a whole new set of fears for Josey.

By the time he had reached the barracks, Annabelle was gone. He had found Red Shawl with the girls, setting up house in the empty soldiers' quarters while the boys, as usual, had gone missing when there were chores to do.

Lord Byron had offered to come with Josey. "Maybe Chaska and Kicking Bull have gone to help Miss Annabelle with the wagon," he said.

That hadn't sounded like the boys, who

243

were more likely to be up to some mischief than volunteering to clean a wagon. Josey didn't say anything. He didn't have to.

"I know," Byron had said. "But I'm just as likely to find them walking over to the wagons as anywhere else I might look."

Josey had increased his stride to fall into step alongside the big man, relieved to have someone else's problems to focus on. Byron knew him too well not to pick up on his mood.

"Something go wrong in your meeting with the commander?"

Josey had hesitated, but the need to talk through what had happened proved stronger than his taciturn nature. He told Byron about the encounter with Martinez, ending with the Indian's death.

"What's done is done. No sense letting this eat away at you," Byron said. "We won't be here long. Keep clear of this Mexican, and there won't be no trouble."

"I wish it were that simple. We have good lives, Byron, and I know the Colonel would be proud of what we've built for ourselves. Martinez reminded me how quickly that can be taken away if a man isn't careful. I hope all this easy living hasn't dulled my senses, so that if the time comes that Annabelle needs me the way I used to be, I won't fail her the way I failed the Colonel."

"You didn't fail the Colonel, and you ain't going to fail Miss Annabelle," Byron said, his deep bass giving his words the solemnity of Gospel. He started to shake with a hearty laugh. "Don't you see, Josey? So long as you all knotted up about it, you haven't really changed. When those you love have need, you'll do what you must. You always do."

Josey had felt better for the talk — at least until he spotted the watchful man at the wagon with Annabelle.

Josey moved forward alone, his eyes never leaving the tall man. Gray streaked an unruly beard, and he had a faraway look in his eye anytime his gaze wasn't directed toward the blond woman at his side. Josey recognized that look, and his hand dropped to his gun belt. The revolver was so heavy, he'd worn only the one for walking about the fort and hadn't even brought his rifle. He chided himself for growing so complacent. God seemed determined today to remind him of his place in the world.

Josey came directly to Annabelle, slipping his left arm around her waist and planting a light kiss against her cheek. His eyes remained fixed on the tall man. His right hand hung free at his waist, just above his gun belt.

Pretending to be embarrassed by the public display, Annabelle leaned away from him.

"Josey. Finally. I was afraid you'd lost your way."

Her dark brow arched to signal a jest, but her eyes narrowed when she saw his attention diverted. Josey took this in as well as everything else around him. The rich scent of horses carried on a slight breeze from the stables. A strip of cloud that passed over the sun, leaving the children in shadow where they played near the wagon bed. The way the blond woman watched him, her eyes big as pools, as if he were Hugo's hunchback come to life. And how a man he'd never seen before gazed at him with the certainty of recognition. Such a look, Josey knew from weary experience, usually augured trouble.

Annabelle cleared her throat and began making introductions. She knew his moods like a favorite poem, and the way she sensed his alarm yet continued the conversation without stumbling over a syllable would have caused no one to think anything was amiss. Except they already knew. Unfamiliar with the arena of violence the way he was, Annabelle was last to discern the undercurrent of charged atmosphere, yet Josey never doubted her fierce intelligence would rally. His heart swelled and ached for her in the same instant, his adoration prompting seemingly discordant thoughts of love and death to twine like ivy between the rails of a garden fence. Love: his for her knew no bounds, moral or otherwise. Death: he had killed for this woman and would kill again without remorse if even the shadow of a threat darkened her path.

He'd managed to set aside many of these concerns during days made largely carefree by the absence of war and the comforts that came with a degree of wealth. Yet at times, especially at night when nothing distracted him from the fear of losing what he had or the remorse for the things he'd done, he felt something coming for him. Like watching a gust of wind trace a path through the tall prairie grass that bent before it, he knew he couldn't run from what pursued him. All he could do was turn his face to it and hold his hat close to his head and hope he was strong enough to weather it.

After Annabelle concluded her introductions, a silence fell over them, heavy as the moment between the priming of a cannon and its firing. She had called the man Grieve. The name suited him.

Josey had let down his guard with Martinez because the imminent threat had not been directed at him, and he'd underestimated the man's taste for violence. Now he saw that it had been a useful reminder; he wouldn't make the same mistake again. As his hand hovered over his gun, he looked on Grieve not as a stranger but as an anticipated messenger whose delivery had been too long delayed. He nodded toward him and took a step forward, shielding Annabelle as he spoke.

"You come to kill me?"

CHAPTER TWENTY

Josey Angel looked nothing like Maria had imagined. She'd expected an older man. A larger man. She'd built him up in her mind to be the embodiment of death itself, yet what stood before her was just a man, not so many years removed from youth. He was clean-shaven and handsome in a boyish way, with a slender frame and middling height, no taller than his wife. He looked hardly old enough to have fought in the war, though she had no doubt he had for he wore the same sadness that Atticus did. It wasn't anything she could point out, just an impression of a man weighed down as if made heavier by life. His hat shielded his eyes so she could not discern their color. They never alighted on any one spot for more than a moment and kept returning to Atticus at her side.

"You come to kill me?" he said, as casual as he might ask about a Wells-Fargo post.

Josey Angel acted like he'd been waiting all spring for death, while Atticus stood stupefied. His jaw practically came unhinged. Seeming to find an answer in silence, Josey Angel said, "You're not the first." He sounded more weary than afraid.

Atticus found his voice. "I'll be the last," he said, sounding more like an actor on a stage than the man she'd seen shoot down the Stoddard brothers.

The corner of Josey Angel's mouth twitched in imitation of a smile. "You believe that? Or is that just what you say so you can sleep."

"I don't see why it should matter to you." The set of his jaw gave Atticus the appearance of a hard man, but Maria could tell from the way his tongue pressed at the inside of his lip that something troubled him.

"Killing me won't heal whatever's hurting you," Josey Angel said. "It won't help you sleep, either."

"That will be my problem."

Josey Angel's eyes flicked in Maria's direction. He said, "You sure of that?"

Maria shuddered. Josey Angel didn't seem to notice, but Atticus did. He looked to her, only for a moment, but it was time enough for her to see an ocean of pain welled in his eyes, stirred up in a frothy maelstrom of confusion, regret, and something else she wouldn't name lest she break down in front of them all. Her breath caught with a twinge of pity, for she realized how his words rang with the brand of courage men draw on to save face in a crowd. The soldiers had told her Josey Angel had married and settled down, but, uncertain of how Atticus would respond to the news, she had not shared this with him. She had counted on there being time once they set out for Virginia City to draw out the venom of his vendetta before he threw his life away or committed a murder he'd regret for the rest of his days. Though confident neither man would draw with women and children around, she realized Atticus, who'd thought of little else but finding this man when she'd met him, hadn't conceived how the denouement would play out.

He was trapped.

This should not have surprised her. A dog might chase its tail with single-minded determination without knowing what to do should it succeed. In truth, Maria hadn't given the moment much thought, either. Josey Angel had been little more than a myth in her mind, a useful motive for binding Atticus to her as travel partner and protector.

So long as Josey Angel had remained an abstraction, she'd consigned her curiosity to the back of her mind. She never asked Atticus how he knew Josey Angel was responsible for the deaths of his son and father. He was as sensitive as a new wound on the topic and flinched at any questions about it. The how of the matter had seemed unimportant until now. That Josey Angel had killed Atticus's loved ones was simply a fact of the man, no different than his age or origins. Yet now that they stood face to face with a flesh-and-blood man, his friendly wife, and adorable child, she began to challenge the premise. How would Atticus know Josey Angel had killed his son and father? He hadn't been there. Who had told him? How could anyone be certain? And what did it matter now? There had been a war. Men on both sides had killed. Was either side more in the right in the eyes of God when it came to murder?

Beneath the sharp light of interrogation, all sense of a godly pursuit of justice fell away like leaves in autumn to expose the ugly bare branches of vengeance. At best, Atticus would make a widow of a young mother. At worst, he would deprive Maria of any hope she harbored that he might stand as a father to Danny and Astrid. Had he spared a thought for how his senseless death would affect her and the children? Of course not. A man's selfishness recognized no boundaries. This confrontation, she realized, was as pointless as two cocks in the yard pecking and kicking each other bloody.

Atticus seemed to recognize it too. He'd never been a bad man, just a father, a son, and at one time a husband, drowning in sorrows no one could tread. He'd grabbed hold of the idea of killing Josey Angel as some flotsam to keep from going under. Now that the moment had come, instead of confronting evil like that wolf Stoddard and his brothers, he faced just another man as full of pain and regret as he.

All of these thoughts flashed through Maria's mind in the time it took to blink back the hot tears that obscured her sight and left her incapable of conjuring a way to stop events from unfolding.

"You'll find no solace in vengeance," Josey Angel said.

Atticus looked away from Maria and coughed. "You know where I can find solace," he said, "I hope you'll tell me before you die."

Josey looked past him, and Maria felt his eyes on her again. He looked as if he knew her, and she squirmed beneath his gaze.

Too late, she realized he wasn't looking at her. She sensed the other man's presence before he brushed past her from behind. Atticus must not have heard the heavy footfalls, for he made no move before the plywood board struck him in the back of head, dropping him like a scarecrow off its perch.

The big black man she'd seen walking with Josey Angel at a distance crouched over Atticus, close enough to see he still drew breath. She'd forgotten all about him as she'd watched Josey Angel's approach. The man looked up at her with a wide face made friendlier by a prominent gap between his front teeth. "He's going to wake with a hateful headache, but he be good enough after a spell," he pronounced.

Josey Angel came to her. "When he wakes, take him away. If I see him again, I won't take the time to talk."

"You're not going to kill him?"

Josey Angel shook his head. "I promised my wife I wouldn't kill another man, not unless he's got it coming." Something in her reaction prompted him to add, "You'd be surprised how many have it coming."

"No, I wouldn't."

He studied her a moment, long enough that she felt her face redden. "I suppose not," he said, his voice softening. "Convince him we fight to protect the living, not to avenge the dead."

"I don't know that I can do that." Her glance sought out Annabelle. She had gone to see to the children, who seemed blissfully unaware of the drama that had unfolded. Recalling the pain of watching Daniel gunned down, she tasted bile in her throat, and her face grew hot with shame to consider how she would feel if the same fate befell Annabelle.

"How do you know he won't come after you again?" she asked.

"Killing's a lot easier when you've got nothing to live for."

"Killing you is all he lived for. He told me that the day we met."

Again, she saw that twist at the corner of his mouth that she took for the start of a smile. "Maybe it was true then. I don't think so now."

CHAPTER TWENTY-ONE

The rain, thick as cheesecloth, started before dawn. By the time Josey made his way to the stables and saddled his horse, pools of water deep as Gray's fetlocks mired the road that led out the gate at Fort Phil Kearny. John Hutchins waited for him there. He wore a waxed canvas slicker, his shoulders hunched against the chill. The half-blood translator wished him a good morning. Josey barely made out the words over the percussion of raindrops, big as nickels, beating against his hat. The water pooled on the brim, and when he nodded in reply rivulets poured down in a sheet before his face.

Hutchins's mouth twisted in a wry grin. "Guess we picked a fine day to set out." He felt in the breast pocket of his duck coat for tobacco and bent at the waist to create a cover so that he could roll a cigarette. He offered it to Josey, who refused. "I hope this rain is not a sign."

"I don't put much stock in signs," Josey said. He clicked his tongue, and Gray set off, leaving Hutchins to match his pace. "I'm sure I've set off on distasteful tasks on sunny days too."

"Tell me about one of them."

"I can't recall any at the moment."

They rode in silence after that.

In truth, the weather matched Josey's mood and outlook for their mission. Even if Hutchins managed to find Crazy Horse, Josey doubted he'd be able to convince the warrior to preserve the peace, especially when his instincts told him the treaty was doomed before it was even signed. He rode out on such a miserable day anyway for two reasons. First, he'd told Grantham he would try his best, and the diplomat had delivered on his promise to help Josey secure the beef contract with the army. Once Josey gave his word on a matter, it was settled in his mind.

His other reason was the tall southerner who wanted to kill him. Before they'd parted yesterday, the pretty blond woman had told him about the man's father and son. Josey couldn't say if he'd killed them, but, even if he weren't responsible for their deaths, plenty of others weighed on his conscience. He figured their paths would cross again if he lingered at the fort, and he saw no advantage in having to kill Grieve. Better that he leave and give time for the woman to show her companion life held better options than a deadly vendetta. Taking his own advice on the matter, he'd decided it was just as well if his path didn't cross with the big Mexican, Martinez, either. A little rain was a small price to keep the peace. At least it kept the mosquitoes away.

They followed the Bozeman Trail north toward Montana. They rode through fields of prairie bunch grass and wild rose and sage, the sodden trail stretching before them like a dark river beneath a bruised and swollen sky. The rain let up by midmorning, and the day lightened, though the sun never broke through. The parched earth sucked down what moisture the skies had offered, and they moved at a fair pace, loping through brush along open prairie and climbing wooded hills. Hutchins said he hoped they would find Crazy Horse at a village encampment near the Tongue River, a distance of two days' ride.

They stopped near midday to water the horses at a stream swollen from the morning's rains. Josey left Gray's saddle on but loosened the girth. He'd kept his pistols in a tar sack in his saddlebag and checked them to make sure the powder had remained dry. He sat on a wide rock beside the stream and chewed on some dried meat and drank from his canteen. Hutchins joined him. He took off his hat and shook it, sending beads of water flying out. His dark hair lay plastered to his head in thick, wet strings.

"How far we going today?" Josey asked.

"We will stop before nightfall. I know a place. A half-day ride tomorrow will bring us close enough. I will ride on alone to seek word on where Crazy Horse might be. He has family in the camp. If I can find him, I will bring him to you. It will be safer that way."

While they rested, the sky darkened again. Great ragged masses of clouds gathered like penned cattle over the Bighorns to the west. The approaching rain smelled like clean laundry. Wind began to whip along the path cut by the stream, and Josey pressed his hat more snugly on his head. Thinking Hutchins might have been right about what the weather foretold of their chances he said, "If you can't find Crazy Horse, we'll call that proof this wasn't meant to work out and head back to the fort."

Hutchins followed his gaze across the

mountains. The coming storm looked even worse than the one they'd ridden through. "I thought you did not believe in signs." He watched for Josey's reaction and was rewarded with a roll of the eyes.

"Even a stubborn man has to listen when all the world seems intent on telling him something. Besides, I don't want you getting your hopes up that we'll convince Crazy Horse to agree to this treaty."

Hutchins laughed. It was a small sound, almost apologetic, a man accustomed to speaking for others and not drawing attention to himself. He said, "Crazy Horse will never put his mark to paper."

"But you at least think he'll agree to stop the raids?"

The laughter stopped. Hutchins's eyes narrowed as he appraised Josey, as if weighing the sincerity of his curiosity. "I cannot say. No one hates the *wasicu* more. He has seen too much to ever forgive."

"Tell me."

Hutchins did.

Josey recognized the story. Every soldier posted to the territories knew it. A cautionary tale veterans told the fresh fish in their regiment to rouse them from a complacency that could prove fatal when fighting an enemy armed largely with stones and sticks.

In the version Josey knew, about thirty soldiers from Fort Laramie were dispatched to a nearby Indian camp after a cow had been stolen from a wagon train of Mormons. The soldiers tried to arrest the thief, but hundreds of Indians stood in their way. In the standoff that followed, someone fired a weapon. Then everybody started shooting. The Indians killed every member of the detachment.

In Hutchins's telling, the cow had wandered into the Indian encampment, running amid the tepees and knocking over meat racks until a young warrior killed and butchered it, sharing the meat among those who were hungry. Knowing there would be trouble, an old chief named Conquering Bear went to the fort and offered one of his own horses as compensation for the lost cow. Despite the generosity of the offer, the fort commander demanded that the Indian responsible for killing the cow be turned over for punishment. Because the young warrior was from a different tribe, Conquering Bear could not fulfill the demand even if he'd wished.

The next day the soldiers came, toting a pair of cannons. Conquering Bear went to the soldiers, again seeking to broker a peace. He offered two horses in payment for the cow, but the translator the soldiers had brought with them was drunk and failed to share the offer with the officer, a lieutenant named Grattan. The officer ordered the soldiers to aim the cannons at the camp. The first great gun blasted, shattering the tops of the lodge poles on Conquering Bear's tepee. Warriors who had gathered in anticipation of trouble loaded their rifles and brought out their bows. Conquering Bear tried to forestall a fight, but he was struck down when the second cannon roared. He would later die of his wounds. The angry warriors fell upon the soldiers, killing them all.

Josey took in the story without interruption. He understood how accounts of battle varied depending on who did the telling. He'd never thought much about what had become known as the "Grattan massacre." The version he'd known made sense, he realized now, only if the audience shared an assumption that the Indians were eager to slaughter white men without provocation. In Hutchins's telling, Josey recognized points of the story he'd known that didn't hold up to critical review. Hell, Indians didn't even care for the taste of cow. If they were going to steal from a wagon train, they would have gone after horses or mules. He tried to recall when the slaughter had occurred. It must have been more than a dozen years earlier.

"Crazy Horse was there?" he asked.

"He was still a boy then. Too young to go out on raids. His friend Lone Bear used to tell of how they watched the attack that day. He said they never forgot their anger at the injustice. Their thrill of the triumph."

"And their fear," Josey added.

"Yes, fear of consequences. They knew the soldiers would return in greater numbers."

Josey knew that part of the story too. As he recalled, the army tracked down the tribe responsible for the massacre more than a year later in Nebraska. "Was Crazy Horse also at Ash Hollow?"

"The people call it Blue Water Creek. You know what happened?"

Josey nodded and listened as Hutchins told the story anyway. How the army, determined to avenge itself, sent General William Harney and six hundred soldiers against an encampment of half as many Lakota, many of them women and children.

"Many of the warriors were away for the buffalo hunt when the soldiers attacked," Hutchins said.

The men who remained attempted to hold off the soldiers while the women and children sought to escape, but Harney had sent a regiment on a flanking maneuver so they could sweep down on the fleeing Lakota. Josey winced while Hutchins described the mutilation of women and children. Even newspapers in New York labeled it a massacre.

"Did Crazy Horse fight that day?"

"If he had fought that day, he would have died that day," Hutchins said, his tone displaying the reverence with which the Lakota held the young warrior. "He had gone off alone to hunt and returned to find the camp destroyed."

Josey imagined how he would have reacted if he'd experienced something similar. He had seen terrible things during the war. Men mad with fear and battle lust acted savagely. He had lost his own head at times. But it was nothing compared with the inhuman torture he'd witnessed and heard described in the Indian wars. The differences between the peoples stirred a loathing that drew out the worst in men. Behavior that would have been criminal at Bull Run or Gettysburg was practically encouraged at Ash Hollow and Sand Creek. Josey had questioned his mission's chances for success because he believed Crazy Horse too clever to be duped into a bad treaty, but he saw no harm in trying. Now that he knew how deep the roots of Crazy Horse's hatred for whites reached, he wondered if he'd been a fool.

"You're telling me Crazy Horse has more reason to want to kill me than speak with me," Josey said. "So why are we here?"

"I am not here for Crazy Horse," Hutchins said. "I am here for my mother."

Josey looked at him, a little slow to make the connection.

"I do not want some ambitious general seeking to make his reputation riding through my mother's village, killing women and children. We might win single battles, but we cannot win a war. There are too many of you. We have no match for your weapons. And if we do not die by the sword or rifle, we die from the pox or cholera."

"Do you think Crazy Horse understands that?"

"Warriors like Crazy Horse know only one way to be a man: by fighting. If I have learned anything from the *wasicu* it is that a man can be defined by more than just battle. It is too late for Crazy Horse. He should hope to die fighting, a single, glorious death. For if he lives to be an old man, he will taste death every day he has to live on a reservation."

"You had better let me do the talking when we find Crazy Horse," Josey said, forcing a tight smile to leaven the young man's mood. The seed of humor fell on infertile ground. "You foresee a bleak picture for your people."

"And yet that is better than the alternative for the women and children. The treaty will give us a home. The Black Hills, while worthless to the white man, are sacred to the people. We will live in peace, and the women will not have to watch their children starve. Their children will learn about letters and numbers and your god on the cross. The boys may discover another path to manhood other than through a fight they cannot win."

Hutchins described a world for his mother's people where he might finally belong, where his command of English and white man's ways could make him a leader. Josey wondered if this was Hutchins's way to restore himself to the good graces of his mother's people. Josey couldn't fault him for it, since coming to Annabelle's aid had been the reason the Indians looked askance on Hutchins now. But was it unrealistic to imagine Crazy Horse and men like him making a home in the white man's world? After the Great Rebellion, Josey had doubted that a world at peace held a place for him. Then he had met Annabelle and slowly, with help from her and friends like Byron, he felt he was finding where he belonged. Could Crazy Horse, who had no wife or children, be made to see that continuing to attack the whites would only put more Indian lives at risk? There was a time, not so long ago, Josey thought he should have died in the war. Maybe Hutchins had a point about Crazy Horse seeking a glorious death.

"Did you tell the army Crazy Horse was leading these raids because he hoped to die in battle?"

"I did not tell the army anything. They already knew. Grantham was the one who told me about Crazy Horse's raids."

"How would he know?"

Hutchins's shoulders raised and dropped. "It must have been in a report from a patrol. I never saw it."

Josey turned over this new information, beginning to see the outline of something not yet clear in his mind, like a shadow on the ground cast by a cloud on a bright day.

The first drops from the clouds he'd seen approaching began to plunk against his hat. The rain pricked like ice where it struck his exposed skin. He stood. No sense contemplating questions he didn't have enough information to answer. The man who could tell him what he wanted to know was out there somewhere.

CHAPTER TWENTY-TWO

From under the wagon, Grieve heard the nickering of a horse and the soft clomp of hoof falls before he saw the rider. He expected it might be one of Dr. Hamilton's men, come to share some news about when the camp would be moving on. He'd just finished setting up the wagon jack beneath the rear axle. The wainwright from the fort had repaired the wheel — free of charge, after Maria asked about his home in Vermont and stayed with him while he fixed the break in the iron. Grieve didn't think he could walk another mile hearing the click-click-click the break in the tire iron made, like a drip of water in a darkened house. While reinstalling it, he planned to remove and grease the other wheels with the mixture of pine resin and lard stored in a covered wooden bucket they hung from the rear axle. Anything to stay busy.

The horse halted beside the wagon. All

four legs were marked with white socks, with fetlocks too narrow to be one of the big eastern-bred horses Hamilton's men rode. Craning his neck for a better view, he saw the belly was also white and covered with black spots, like splotches of paint. An Appaloosa. He didn't see many of those and associated them with Indians. He crawled out from under the wagon.

And stared up into a rifle pointed at his chest.

"Good afternoon, Mr. Grieve. I apologize for calling unannounced."

Annabelle Angel, as he thought of her, offered no apology for the rifle. It was one of those repeaters the Yankees loved so much. The Rebels had had nothing like them, so he hadn't seen many during the war, and he'd never seen one from this angle.

"Nice rifle," he said, trying to focus on anything but the black hole at the end of the muzzle. "I didn't think Josey went anywhere without it."

"Oh, this one is mine. An engagement gift of sorts."

Grieve nodded as if this were a typical exchange of betrothal presents. He decided he'd never met anyone quite like this woman or her husband. As if to reinforce the point, she was wearing trousers and a denim work shirt with her hair tied up beneath a wide-brimmed hat. From a distance, he would have taken her for a young man.

Unfazed by his attention, she continued: "I prefer the rifle to a revolver. I find my aim is better."

He made to stand but stopped when she leveled the gun at a point he judged to be between his eyes.

"Don't move. I can fire off four shots in the time you can stand." Her eyes snapped off him for a moment before returning to him, pinning him in place. "Well, Josey could lever off four in that time. I can probably shoot twice. I expect that would be enough."

He found her candid assessment more convincing than any amount of boasting. Her words snuffed out his thoughts of spooking the horse and trying to disarm her. Instead, he rested his back against the spokes of the wheel. "You would kill a man?"

"Only when I feel I must."

"And you feel you must now?"

"I won't spend my life, or even the next few months of it, looking over my shoulder for you."

"I would never harm you. Or your child."

"Josey is my husband. You come after him,

you come after me."

He had no response to that. She'd spoken with no more emotion than he'd expect from a clerk tallying purchases at a dry goods store. As with her assessment of her shooting skills, he found himself more convinced by her measured tone than any screamed threat or ultimatum. She sat astride the Appaloosa watching him, making no motion to lower the gun.

"So what happens now?" He repositioned himself against the rim of the wheel. "Are you just going to shoot me?"

"That depends."

He felt like a mouse under the gaze of an owl perched on the widow's peak of a barn. Unsure what she wanted, he decided talking was his best option. The rifle must be getting heavy. "Depends on what?"

"It depends on you." She adjusted her grip. "Are you still determined to kill my husband?"

The only question that mattered. And he didn't have an answer. Two days earlier when Maria roused him from the blow to his head, he'd been angry and ashamed. Angry at himself, mostly, for not acting on the promise he'd made to the memory of Luke and his father. When he'd first heard of Sherman's march, he'd wanted to come home, but they said he'd be a deserter if he left, that he'd be arrested and shot. So he stayed, figuring the war had to be over soon and trusting to God he'd return to his son when it was done. Except his boy was already gone. His father too. Having failed to protect them, he vowed to avenge them.

Now he had failed in that as well.

Shaming himself in front of Maria made it worse. He wondered what she must think of him, but, dreading to see the disappointment in her eyes, he wanted to be gone from her even more than he wanted to ask. He would have left that day if he hadn't been so unsteady on his feet. His head had throbbed like a train rattled through it. Maria had waited with him until he could stand. Then she and the children had walked him back to their camp. No one spoke about what had happened. No questions about what would come next. The walk must have taken a long time, but he recalled hardly any of it. She had made a place for the children under the wagon so that she might lay him in the bed. He was too muddle-headed to object to kindnesses he didn't deserve. She stayed with him, holding him until he fell asleep.

He had slept until almost noon the next day. His head ached, but he managed to get down some food. It rained all day, yet Maria had left while he slept, bringing back news that Josey Angel had departed on some business for the army. He braced for some ruse, almost welcoming the possibility of Josey Angel doubling back and putting an end to him. Yet nothing had happened until this morning, when Maria received a hand-written invitation to tea with Annabelle. He'd not wanted her to go, but he wanted her to stay with him even less. As soon as he could stand, he'd started busying himself with chores. While the effort to keep his mind off Josey Angel had met with limited success, at least his activity prevented Maria from trying to talk with him about what had happened. His shame was too great to entertain the subject before he even knew his own mind on the matter. Maria saw the visit among the women and children as an opportunity to broker a peace among them all. He had felt too indebted to her to object.

Now he wondered what Maria must be thinking to find Annabelle gone. Did she assume some misunderstanding or error in the time or place in the invitation? Could she even conceive of such a deception? Perhaps a woman could.

Annabelle looked down on him, awaiting an answer to a question that hurt his head to contemplate. Would she have the sand to do what he had blanched from? Her manner suggested yes. Practically screamed it. He had thought her pretty when he first saw her smiling at Maria. Now he saw a sternness to her features that reminded him of his wife. Chelsea had given that look to Mr. Bowers at the general store any time he cited a price for goods that was higher than what he'd quoted when she'd placed the order. The gimlet-eyed coot was notorious for chiseling customers, but he never got so much as two bits more from his Chelsea. Grieve envied Josey Angel; life was a lot easier for a man with a good horse and a strong woman.

He refocused on the gun, almost willing Annabelle to shoot so that he might be reunited with Chelsea and their children, or at least be removed from the world where their memory could so easily steal upon him. His hands dropped to his sides, palms flat against the dirt that might soon cover him. Would Chelsea even recognize the man he had become?

The rifle held steady while Annabelle waited for an answer.

"I wish I could tell you no," he said. "I wish I could tell you I've found forgiveness and some kind of comfort. For him. For

275

me. For all of us who fought in that damn war. The truth is it still hurts. I don't know how I'll feel if I see your husband again. Maybe I hope to be dead before that happens."

His hand went to his face. His thumb and middle finger pinched at the outside of his eyes to stay the tears he felt welling. When he looked up, she had lowered the gun.

"I thank you for your honesty." With a nudge of her knee, the Appaloosa pivoted away.

He stared at her back a moment before calling. "You heard me clear? I said I don't know what I would do."

She halted and looked at him over her shoulder. "I heard all I need to know."

With a click of her tongue, the Appaloosa broke into a canter. Grieve watched her ride away through a smear of tears he no longer tried to stop.

CHAPTER TWENTY-THREE

Crazy Horse raced the sorrel gelding to the top of the mesa, leaving the half-blood translator behind. He paused at the crest, turning his horse to face the wind, where it would be refreshed more quickly in the moving air. He preferred geldings because they had more endurance than mares and stallions. The horse's flanks soon steadied, and he moved east to watch the clouds carry away the last of the rains. If he held his breath and turned his ear from the wind, he could hear the thunder, like the hoof falls of an enemy in retreat. He sensed the younger man's arrival from behind, but John Hutchins did not approach. He still waited for an answer. Crazy Horse had agreed to ride with him to the camp he shared with the white man, but he had not yet decided if he would speak with him.

He dismounted and left his horse with Hutchins. The white man called Angel was nearby. Crazy Horse saw his horse grazing in the shade of a copse of aspen. He admired the animal, a gray mustang gelding. Angel was not a fool; the Indian pony was more sure-footed in the hills than the big American horses, and it could travel farther and lighter, for it did not have to be fed the oats or corn that the long knives fed their mounts. He amused himself with the thought that instead of speaking with this man, he should steal his horse.

He had been angry that Hutchins had sought him out for such a foolish reason. Yet he felt a strange kinship with the young man whose father had been a soldier who abandoned his Lakota wife and son. While Hutchins had the hair and skin coloring of his mother, children had taunted him because of his father, just as they had teased Crazy Horse, whose lighter skin and hair drew whispers about his parentage. Children could be cruel to anyone who brought to mind the fear they'd been taught by old grandmothers, who admonished the disobedient with the warning, "If you do not behave, I will allow the white man to come and take you."

His sympathy for the translator had been the reason Crazy Horse set aside his suspicions that Hutchins had aided in the escape of the white woman he had taken captive two winters earlier. He had intended to use the ransoming of the woman in a ploy to destroy the fort. Whatever anger he had felt toward Hutchins at the time was lessened by the triumph at Hundred in the Hands. Now Hutchins wished for him to meet with a white warrior, the husband of the woman he had captured. Their paths had crossed before. Crazy Horse had never seen a man fire a rifle so fast and with such accuracy. Wishing for some of that magic for himself, he had counted coup on the man when he might have more easily killed him. Later, after Hundred in the Hands, when Crazy Horse found Lone Bear's body and mourned for his friend, a soldier who had survived the massacre by feigning death tried to kill him before Angel and his black-white-man brother intervened.

Crazy Horse walked in the opposite direction of the camp so that he could be alone with his thoughts before meeting Angel. He recalled playing among the meat-drying racks with Lone Bear as a boy, sneaking up on the women while they scraped hides stretched out on the ground. He had envied his friend's dark skin and glistening black hair and was grateful that Lone Bear had never teased him about his appearance. His friend understood that Crazy Horse had hated white men before he had even seen one, though they held a fascination for both boys, like wanting a closer look at a rattlesnake in spite — or, perhaps, *because* — of the danger it posed.

He and Lone Bear would crawl up to the edge of the tepees when the Big Bellies gathered to tell stories of the white men. Even more terrifying than tales of battles and the white man's big guns were those about their diseases. Hearing how the Kiowas lost half their tribe in a single summer. Or the Lakota who lived along the Great Muddy who lost a thousand people in a single winter around the time the boys were born. The old chiefs bickered over how close a raiding party could draw to the white man's wagons without catching a sickness that could kill even the strongest among them in only a matter of days.

The summer the people camped near Fort Laramie the boys watched the soldiers from a distance, mocking their habit of marching together like birds in flight. "They are so foolish," Lone Bear had said. "You could fire one arrow among them and cannot miss." The boys did not laugh the day they saw the great guns fire and Conquering Bear go down.

280

As he walked toward the stony ledge of the flat-topped hill, a fallen tree blocked the path. Lone Bear's spirit must have been watching over him, guiding him to step onto the log rather than stepping over it. On the opposite side, stretched out in the late afternoon sun, was a rattlesnake, about the length of his arm from fingertip to shoulder and about as thick as his wrist. The snake was pale brown with darker patches that formed rings near the tail. On becoming aware of his presence, the snake coiled and raised its wide, triangular head in warning. Crazy Horse froze, waiting until the snake showed no interest in a challenge, uncoiling and slithering toward the rocks where it probably had a den. Crazy Horse pulled out his bow and killed it with a single shot through the head. He used the end of the bow to pin the head in place while retrieving the arrow and decapitating the snake with a chop from his knife. He kicked aside the head with the toe of his moccasin and hefted the thick body. Using the sharpened white man's knife, he cut a slit along the length of the snake's pale belly. Once he peeled away the skin from a section of the body about as long as half a handspan, he was able to grab the exposed meat with one hand and the peeled skin in the other and pull the two apart until he reached the tail. He tossed the skin aside. A pink strip ran the length of the snake's body along the middle of the underside. He used his fingers to dig it out, pulling down its guts and leaving only meat and bones. He left this intact, deciding to roast the meat over a fire on a skewer.

Now he felt ready to meet the white man.

Crazy Horse recognized Angel more from his manner and bearing than his face, which he had never taken the time to study. He was not a good judge of white men's ages; their hairy faces made even the dark-haired ones look old to him. While this man was smooth faced like an Indian, he was still nearly as ugly as most of the white men Crazy Horse had seen up close.

He stood when he saw Crazy Horse approach, raising his right palm in an awkward greeting. Crazy Horse noted that he was not wearing his gun belts, nor did he carry the rifle that he used to such great effect. Hutchins said his name was Josey. Crazy Horse had never heard of another man with the name.

"Tell him we come in peace," Angel told Hutchins.

"He knows that already. He would not

have come if he did not believe that."

Crazy Horse gave no indication that he understood. It was not easy as they continued to bicker.

"Well, I don't know what else to tell him."

"What were you thinking of all that time we were riding?"

"Nothing that I thought would make a difference."

Crazy Horse let out a long sigh until he had Angel's attention. His eyes were the color of a bay pony, and Crazy Horse saw no signs of the dissembling he associated with most white men. He determined Angel did not know what to say because he did not intend to lie.

Aware that he was being studied, Angel said to Hutchins, "Tell him what you told me. About the women and children."

Before he spoke, Hutchins invited them to sit. Crazy Horse found a white-barked limb from an aspen that he carved into a spit to roast the snake. Only once they were settled did Hutchins begin, expressing his concern that if the war with the white men continued, the women and children would suffer most. The treaty would guarantee that the women could live in peace and their children would not starve.

"I will not put my mark to the paper, but

if the white man leaves the people in peace, I will no longer make war on them," he told Hutchins, who translated for Angel.

He meant his words. When he was young, all he thought about was going to war. Like everything else, the white men had stolen that from him too. His idea of war was not the same as the white man's. To him, war could be as simple as a raid to steal a few horses from another tribe. To charge headlong into danger so that the men who rode behind him would tell the people about his daring. War was how a man made his name. The *wasicu* had changed everything. They were too strong to be confronted head-on. He had learned that after Hundred in the Hands. While the people had won the day, the whites came back even stronger, in greater numbers and with better rifles. The people could not win. They could take no satisfaction in raiding other tribes, either, for war between the tribes only left both weaker for the day they must face the *wasicu*. Without a war to fight, Crazy Horse did not know what to do. He did not know where to go. Lone Bear was dead. Black Buffalo Woman had rejected him. Though still a young man, he felt weary of life.

"The people are melting like snow on the hillside, while the white men are growing like spring grass," he told Hutchins.

Angel took in the translated words, nodding as if he believed them. "Tell him the raids must stop to protect the peace."

Crazy Horse listened to the translation, as confused by the words in Lakota as he had been in English. Other than some stolen horses and mules, the only raids he knew of were taking place far to the south, in the lands the whites called Nebraska and Kansas. It was only after Hutchins mentioned heads cut off bodies of the dead that Crazy Horse understood.

"I have killed one white man, and, yes, I cut off his head. I did this because he stole the head of my friend Lone Bear, which I hoped to retrieve so that he might lie in peace."

Hutchins began to translate, but Angel interrupted him. "What was that he said? *Natá?*"

"Yes. It means head."

"There was an old Indian at the fort who kept repeating that. *Natá. Natá.* I thought it was someone's name or a curse. Martinez killed him for it."

"Who is Martinez?"

"The big Mexican who works for the doctor camped outside the fort. They've been —"

"Pejuta wacasa?"

Startled by his outburst, both men turned to look at Crazy Horse, who asked Hutchins to repeat what the Indian at the fort said about the doctor. Hutchins translated.

"The Indian wasn't speaking about the doctor," Angel said. "He kept repeating himself to Martinez. *Natá, natá* and then another word."

"What was the other word?" Hutchins asked.

Angel closed his eyes and covered them with his hands. "Let me think."

Crazy Horse watched him carefully. The white man he had killed had told him he had given Lone Bear's skull to a doctor. White men often spoke of an Indian medicine man not when they meant a healer but when they meant a holy man. Crazy Horse now saw he had made the same mistake, believing the white man spoke of a holy man when he meant a healer.

"*Natá. Natá. Wanági.* I think that's the word. *Wanági.*"

"You must be mistaken," Hutchins told Angel. "*Wanági* means ghost. 'Head, head, ghost'? That makes no sense."

While they debated alternate words, Crazy Horse considered what Angel had said. Maybe in speaking the word for ghost, the

286

old man had meant the head of a dead man. *Ghost heads.* A doctor with the heads of dead men.

Crazy Horse interrupted to say he would accompany them to the fort. They took this to mean he had changed his mind about putting his name to the paper, and he did not correct their mistake. They made plans to set out at first light.

Exhausted by the white man's talk, Crazy Horse set out alone with his bow. He had not eaten since before dawn. Now that evening approached, the meat from the snake would not be enough for them. He had seen a stream from the mesa's perch, and he suspected it might be a good spot to wait for game. He could build a driftwood blind along the water's edge and wait for a whitetail deer or maybe an elk to come. As he began to descend from the rise, he saw between the leaves of the cottonwood trees an antelope standing motionless along the water's banks, its ears erect and alert. He had thought his movements had been silent but clearly not. He crouched to wait. He could sit for hours without moving while hunting. Then, without warning, the thin-legged animal burst from its cover, and three more antelope followed in the wake it stirred among the tall grass beyond the trees, scampering in every direction across the field.

Crazy Horse began to make his way back up the rise, not as quietly as before, for he suspected haste was now more important than stealth. At the top he saw Hutchins and Angel approaching. He motioned for them to take a prone position from where they could look down from the rise. He drew from his belt a far-seeing glass he had taken long ago from a dead soldier. He trained it on the area near the trees where he had first seen the antelope. The others moved beside him. He told Hutchins what he had seen and listened while he translated.

"He saw antelope. The way the game moved, it was as if they had been disturbed."

"Indians? Perhaps there is a hunting party."

"The antelope would not have heard Indians."

Crazy Horse looked over his shoulder, and the others followed his gaze. Some of the wood they had used to build a fire was still wet from the recent rains, and it threw off a visible smoke. Crazy Horse looked again to the trees below. He spoke, as much to himself as the others.

"What did he say?" Angel asked John

Hutchins.

"He said he believes we are being hunted."

CHAPTER TWENTY-FOUR

Making amends with Maria cost Annabelle. She blamed her upbringing.

She didn't regret confronting Mr. Grieve about Josey. It had to be done. Either Maria would recognize that and forgive her, or she would hold a grudge and prove herself an unfit friend. That's what Annabelle told herself. Then, in the next moment, she heard her mother's voice in her head, admonishing her about even well-meaning deceptions. Back and forth the arguments played in her head until Annabelle felt like the pendulum within the grandfather clock in her family's home in Charleston.

She made her peace with Maria during a walk with the children along Little Piney Creek, just outside of the fort. A frost coated the exchange as Annabelle apologized, and Maria said she understood her protectiveness. The silence between them deepened until the gurgling stream sounded as loud as a cascade. If Maria hadn't been so desperate to travel with companions to Virginia City, Annabelle expected they might have parted and never spoken again. The children might have relieved the silence, but they had drifted off after Danny found some rocks at the creek's edge and attempted skipping the stones across the water. Astrid led Isabelle to his side to watch. Her mother's voice still echoing in her head, Annabelle apologized again and asked about something that had been troubling her since the encounter: "How does Mr. Grieve know Josey killed his father and son?"

The question must have plucked a chord, for Maria's response spilled out in a rush. "I confess I do not know. He won't talk about it. Grief does strange things to a man. A woman might blame God but knows she's helpless to do anything but carry on. Men take it on themselves, and the feeling of helplessness twists them up inside. Some it destroys."

"Do you believe it's destroyed Mr. Grieve?"

With a candor that reminded Annabelle of Mr. Grieve, Maria said, "I wish I could answer you. I hope not."

They watched the children play. The way

the water tripped across the larger rocks in the fast-moving creek denied Danny any success in skipping his stones, but Annabelle gave thanks the children had a distraction.

"I know Josey better than anyone else, and yet at times I don't understand him at all." She told Maria about the nightmares that kept Josey awake so often. "He takes nothing for granted, and I usually take comfort in that because most men aren't careful enough. They always overestimate themselves, even as they're constantly underestimating women. But Josey is too hard on himself. He imagines he can see all the men he's killed, even those whose faces he never saw in real life."

"Should it surprise you that it weighs on his soul? Killing a man must be a heavy burden."

"I've killed men." Annabelle counted them in her mind. One had been an act of mercy, a dying man whose misery she ended. Killing her first husband had been an act of justice after he'd threatened to kill her. She'd shot and killed one of the Indians who tried to capture her and another who tried to rape her. Those were acts of self-defense. "I still have nightmares about them, but their deaths don't trouble my conscience the way they do Josey. I don't know why."

Danny had run out of stones, and the girls returned to their mothers. Annabelle stooped to lift Isabelle, who would soon need a nap.

Maria reached out and tickled Isabelle's chin, winning herself a smile. "Maybe your answer is here," she said. "You brought this life into the world. A man can't make life. He can only take it. Maybe that's why it weighs on them so, the good ones, at least."

Afterwards, they led the children back to the barracks for lunch. While Isabelle went down for a nap, Astrid stayed with Red Shawl to play with Mina and Dewdrops. Maria went to check on Mr. Grieve, leaving Annabelle — her conscience still getting the better of her — to volunteer for the task of minding the boys and seeing they didn't get into any mischief. Inspired by the walk to the creek, she led them on an expedition to search for arrowheads and other objects of interest by the water's edge. The outing started well enough; Chaska and Kicking Bull didn't mind having a tagalong, though they delighted a little too much in torturing the smaller boy with their rough games. Danny appreciated any attention from the older boys and didn't seem to mind the bruises their "play" left on him. All Anna-belle had to do was ensure they didn't hurt themselves too badly and stayed out of the way of the soldiers, who were making final arrangements to depart the fort. What could be simpler?

The soldiers had cut down most of the trees along the banks of Little Piney so that the Indians could not steal upon them under cover. As she walked the treeless path, she felt the heat of the sun on her neck beneath her bonnet. The breeze that blew steadily down from the mountains carried a whiff of pine that she breathed in greedily. She wished she were on horseback and could ride as far as the pinery. Away from the fort, she would have discarded her bon-net and dress in favor of her riding hat and trousers. She loved summers in this country. The sky across the valley beckoned her and seemed to stretch forever. The air had a lightness to it she didn't recall in South Carolina. Here, the sun could feel hot as a branding iron, but it wasn't the moist heat of the South that left her drenched after any exertion.

Recalling her home and how confined she'd felt as a young woman, it pleased her to know Isabelle would know no such boundaries. Isabelle could choose to marry, raise children, and run a household — or she could learn to ride, chase cattle, and run a business. She would wear a corset and bustle only if she desired — not because her mother and the fashion of proper society dictated it. She smiled to think how blessed they were. Maria had spoken of blaming God in her grief, and Annabelle had felt the same after her brothers were killed during the war. She had cursed God for the war and all it had done to her home. Yet now she heard the echoes of old sermons about God's mysterious ways, and guilt twinged her conscience over her ingratitude for all her blessings. After a miscarriage years earlier, she'd thought herself incapable of bearing children. Isabelle had seemed a miracle. Now, seeing Maria with her children, Annabelle's thoughts turned to what it would be like to give Josey a son. As much as she enjoyed watching him with Isabelle, Annabelle imagined he would be delighted with a boy. He was so good with Chaska and Kicking Bull . . .

The thought stopped Annabelle. Her breath quickened, and her heart raced. *Where were the boys?* She whirled around, taking in the fort's tall stockade, the meandering stream, the open fields of waving grasses, the tents and wagons that marked the boundaries of the doctor's camp, the dusty road that led into the hills.

The boys weren't anywhere to be seen.

She'd had just one task, a chore so simple she had thought she'd gotten the best end of the afternoon's distribution of labor. How had she allowed this to happen? The boys had wandered off, of course, just as she had allowed her mind to wander, and her attention with it. But where had they gone? Surely, not back to the fort. They had been eager to escape its confines. She walked in the direction of the doctor's camp. Its tents and wagons provided the only screen that might hide the boys from her view. She increased the pace of her stride as much as her dress permitted, knowing the camp also offered the greatest opportunity for mischief.

She saw surprisingly few men moving about the camp given its size and usual level of activity. The wagons sat idle on the borders created by the rows of tents erected in the square pattern favored by military outposts. Dogs lay in the shade beneath the wagons, watching her. Their open mouths panted a steady beat in time with thumping tails. It was too hot for them to come out and satisfy their curiosity. She strode on. Her destination was a makeshift corral where the wagon train's horses were kept. She thought that might attract the boys' attention, but already she could see that there were few horses in the pen. Most of the doctor's men must be out somewhere.

Just as she began to wonder if her instincts had been wrong, she spied Chaska and Kicking Bull running among the tents, playing some game in which they pretended to be frightened and running from the *wasicu.* Relief mixed with anger at the fright the boys had given her, and she decided it would be good for them to know a little fear once she got hold of them and learned where they had left Danny.

Noting their direction and pace, she calculated how to cut them off as they emerged between two of the tents nearest the fort. Chaska eluded her, but she managed to grab hold of his younger brother, who seemed surprised by her agility.

Surprised and frightened. Genuinely frightened. His eyes were wide with terror, and his face twisted in agony when he believed himself caught by the collar by whatever he was fleeing. Hot tears streaked his cheeks, and she thought he might cry out until he recognized her. It crossed Annabelle's mind to wonder if the boys had taken something from one of the tents, but she immediately regretted the notion. As full of mischief as the boys were, they were more honest than her brothers had been at their age. She masked her guilt while asking Kicking Bull what was wrong. The boy was so disconcerted he answered her in his mother's tongue. Annabelle knew enough Lakota to recognize one of the words: *wanági.*

Ghost.

He pulled against her, eager to be away from the place.

"Where's Danny?" Kicking Bull pointed to a tent in the middle of the encampment. Before releasing him she said, "Go find your brother and wait for me by the wagons."

She headed toward the tent he had pointed out, the largest in the camp, which she assumed belonged to the doctor. She had seen a guard posted outside it previously, but there was no one today. Stopping outside, she called softly, "Danny?"

No answer.

She called again, a little louder. "Danny? Hello?" She entered with soft foot falls as she might an empty church.

Beneath the heavy canvas, it was dark and at least ten degrees cooler than in the sunshine. The place had an earthy smell, like a fresh tilled garden, cut with something sharper that reminded her of a hospital.

Hearing a man's soft, patient voice, she stepped into the gloom.

A large wooden table filled the space before her. It served as a desk with a lamp burning brightly despite the daylight hour. Books and papers were scattered across its surface. Dr. Hamilton and Danny were behind the desk near a shelf filled with boxes. The doctor had taken a knee so that he was at eye level with the boy. Even in the glow of the lamp, the doctor's face looked so pallid Annabelle wasn't sure if the ghost Kicking Bull mentioned had been a reference to the doctor or the human skull he held in his thin-boned hand for the boy's inspection. Danny reached out tentatively with his index finger to touch the hollow-eyed, grinning visage, as if it might respond to any pressure.

"It's all right," the doctor reassured him. "The bones have been thoroughly cleaned." He explained to the boy how the task had been completed, speaking so softly Annabelle couldn't hear all of the words. Something about using soda or caustic potash after boiling the flesh off. "Another method I've discovered is to put the skull in a box near an ants' nest and wait for them to eat the flesh from the bones."

Annabelle shivered; Danny seemed enthralled.

"Romantics talk of the heart, but scientists understand that it's the brain that gives man — and woman" — he added with a nod toward Annabelle, who until that moment hadn't been sure he was aware of her presence — "the capacity to love and the consciousness to dominate the world as God intended."

Almost afraid to hear the answer, Annabelle asked, "Where do you find these . . . ?"

"My specimens? My scouts find them. Most come from old battlefields or abandoned gravesites." He returned the skull to its place on the shelf and withdrew another from a box beside it. "No two are the same."

"They look the same," Danny said.

"They share similarities, for certain. To look at these bleached bones, I would wager you couldn't tell me which one came from an Indian and which one came from a white man like you and me."

Danny shook his head.

"Does it matter?" Annabelle asked.

The doctor turned to look at her, his face so gaunt it seemed an effort for him to swallow. Or perhaps he was just annoyed at the interruption. "It matters to a scientist," he said, "because we study the differences."

"Why?" Danny said.

The doctor ruffled the boy's hair, a gesture that might have passed as playful, even paternal, yet something in the doctor's manner made Annabelle shudder. "Why?" he repeated with a laugh. "I never considered that question. I suppose the answer is to learn all we can. Let me show you."

He opened a few more of the boxes. Each contained a bleached skull. A cord was wrapped around them to hold the jawbone in place. Notes were scrawled across the forehead that marked the gender, age, race, and location of discovery. "Among the differences I study is size. While similar in form and structure, each is unique in that way, though the irregular shape makes it difficult to discern an accurate measurement."

"Couldn't you wrap a cloth tape measure around it?" Annabelle asked.

The doctor's smile revealed a row of small, yellowed teeth but couldn't conceal his patronizing tone. "These bones are but the shell for what is truly important. I seek to study what is no longer present — the brain — by measuring the cranial cavity." He turned over the skull in his hand to display the bowl-like opening underneath. "Some of my colleagues use water, but I've found that it can soak into the porous bone or settle into the squamous sutures and leak out the sinuses. Of course, you can try to solve for that with a rubber coating, but stuffing too much putty into the eye sockets will distort one's measurements. That's why I prefer buckshot. So long as you're consistent with your methodology, you will achieve a fair comparable."

Annabelle moved to stand behind Danny. She was certain the boy didn't understand much of what the doctor said — she knew she didn't — but he was held rapt.

"Why does the size of the brain matter?" Annabelle asked.

Hamilton's enthusiasm for the subject brought color to his cheeks. "By determining which species has the largest brains, we will demonstrate which is the most intelligent and the most well adapted to thrive in the modern world."

"How can you be certain that's true?"

"I should think that would be self-evident," he said, no longer attempting to disguise a patronizing tone.

Annabelle's irritation got the best of her. "Then how do you explain that most women's heads are smaller than men's heads, with presumably smaller spaces for brains, and yet I've known many men who couldn't tell their head from their backside without wearing a hat — a big hat, generally."

The doctor stared at her a moment, the line of his jaw so tight his next words escaped through compressed lips. "How charming."

"You'll have to forgive me, Doctor; I forget my manners sometimes," she said, placing her hands on Danny's shoulder and pulling him against her. "I assure you I find the topic fascinating."

His face relaxed, and he displayed his childlike smile again. "Do you really think so?" He stood. "It is my manners that call for forgiveness. I don't often have the opportunity to play teacher, and I was so caught up with this young man that I have forgotten myself. I am Dr. Hamilton." He offered his hand, which Annabelle took lightly in her own. His fingers were softer than hers, the fine bones reminding her of a wounded bird she had held once. "Of course, you knew that already. Just as I already know you to be Mrs. Angliewicz."

She nodded an assent.

"Reputation of your beauty precedes you," he explained. His head turned back to the shelves of samples. "I realize as a woman you didn't have the benefit of a formal education, Mrs. Angliewicz, but your insights suggest an aptitude for science."

Years of dealing with powerful men had taught her to overlook the qualifier that circumscribed any compliment directed toward a woman's intelligence, and she bowed her head. "Thank you, Doctor."

He stepped closer, studying her features with an intensity that most men would attempt to obscure. "You have the most striking face," he told her. Men never needed to wrap praise of a woman's beauty in a caveat. He reached out and nearly cupped her face in his palm before catching himself when she began to lean away. She had the sense the doctor was more comfortable with his "specimens" than a warm, breathing woman.

He returned his attention to Danny, touching the boy's head as if petting a favorite hound. "You are a fine specimen too," he told the boy. "I can tell just by looking. I wonder how much larger your brain would measure than those of the Indian boys you were racing around with."

Though he smiled as he spoke, Annabelle shuddered again. She began to guide Danny away from the doctor. "I'm sure you wouldn't know about children. You probably don't have any samples."

"Oh, I do have some." He cocked his head as if offering an apology. "Just not enough."

Annabelle made her excuses and left quickly with Danny.

CHAPTER TWENTY-FIVE

Lying prone on the edge of the mesa, Josey used binoculars to scope out the spot where Crazy Horse had seen movement. Frothy masses of low-lying clouds swept overhead in waves, casting bands of shadow and light on the land below. The cottonwoods growing along the river shivered in the breeze, their leaves, bright green on one side, a paler shade beneath, flickered like candlelight. The foliage obscured any movement, so he watched for color.

He expected to see Indians, perhaps angered at the encroachment into their lands and unaware that Crazy Horse traveled with them. The army no longer sent patrols to this region, and they were too far from the trail for random travelers. About the time he began to doubt Crazy Horse's suspicions, a flash of color drew his eye: a navy blue he knew all too well. *Soldiers?* He couldn't be certain. Plenty of Indians took to wearing the Union blues they stole from corpses.

While he sought a break among the trees where he might see more, Crazy Horse spoke and Hutchins translated. "Do not stare at the enemy's eyes too long," he said. "He will feel your stare. He will know you are looking. No matter how far, eyes have the power to draw other eyes."

Josey looked over to where the men lay beside him, more annoyed with his inability to see than with any Indian proverb. "What does it matter? Whoever they are, they already know we are here."

"But they do not know that we know," Hutchins said after a quick exchange in Lakota. "He says we should kill as many as we can before they know."

"We don't even know who they are."

"He says they mean to kill us."

With a shake of his head, Josey wondered again how well Crazy Horse understood him. "What if they're Indians?" He peered again.

"He says they are not Indians."

Before he could ask how Crazy Horse knew that, Josey found a thin spot among the trees where he saw horses and men, maybe as many as a dozen. They were white men, but not soldiers. "They're not Indians," he said, telling himself he only imagined the smug look on Crazy Horse's face.

"He says we should wait here and kill them when they make their ascent."

"What if they were sent from the fort with a message?" Josey asked.

John Hutchins sucked in his cheeks in deep thought. It was a moment before he translated the question. Crazy Horse's response was immediate.

"He says they were sent to kill us."

Josey envied Crazy Horse's certainty, and if he'd shared it, he would have agreed with his tactics as well. Certainty was a soldier's armor against doubts that could prove fatal, and it had come easily to Josey, too, when he'd been at war. Shoot first. Think of the ramifications later. That's what he had done at Griswoldville. That battle had been on his mind since meeting Grieve. He'd been marching with Sherman through a South bereft of Rebel armies, and the panicked townspeople sent a militia of old men and boys against the Union lines with no better odds than wheat before scythes. He'd fired his rifle so many times that day in Georgia the barrel burned his hand. Black powder smoke had obscured the sun.

The battle haunted him more than any other, even though he knew he had done nothing wrong. They were at war, and anyone who marched against them did so with murderous intent. Kill or be killed. That's what they had told themselves, he and everyone else who stood beside him that day. And he knew, riding alongside Lord Byron or watching his friend take joy in life with his new wife and adopted children, that the war had not been in vain. Violence could be justified sometimes. He had felt no sin after fighting to protect the wagon train from road agents on their journey from Omaha or fending off the ambush at Crazy Woman Creek. So why should the appearance of a stranger, come to accuse him of murder on a day of battle, seem like a form of divine judgment? Why didn't he feel absolved for what he had done?

The problem, as he saw it now, was that a man couldn't always know when a fight was justified until it was over. And once a man inured himself to serving as a sword of justice, that reasoning couldn't so easily be sheathed. Now, every instinct screamed in agreement with his unlikely ally — these men were here to kill them, or at least Crazy Horse — yet his conscience held him back. He was not at war today. If he killed any of these men and they turned out to be messengers from the fort, how would he live with that?

Josey shouted down the slope. "We know you are there. State your intentions if you value your lives." He ignored the stares he felt from his companions, while a rustle of movement from among the trees confirmed that he'd been heard.

A man stepped out. He wore a blue Union coat, but its tattered condition marked it as a vestige of service completed. A thick head of red hair with an unruly beard of matching color created a distinctive appearance. Taking a closer look with his binoculars, Josey was certain he recognized the man from the fort. An angry pink scar stretched from above one eye past the side of his mouth. He called out, his words thick with the brogue of a distant homeland. "Gies th' Indian 'n' ye kin go."

While John Hutchins translated the demand to Crazy Horse, Josey replied, "He is under our protection. We're on official army business."

"Nae anymair."

Not anymore? What did he mean by that? Josey looked to Hutchins, who shrugged.

"You can't have him," Josey called down. "Now leave this place. We don't want a fight."

"If ye dinnae gie him up, a rammy is whit ye'll git."

The skin across Hutchins's forehead crinkled with confusion that mirrored Josey's own. He wanted to believe this was a misunderstanding, but a darker possibility settled in his mind. The redheaded Scot had been with Martinez when he killed the Indian at the fort, a connection that stirred more worries than for just Crazy Horse's safety.

With a nod toward the Indian he told John Hutchins, "Tell him to go. We can hold them off while he escapes off the backside of the mesa. He can be gone before they have time to encircle us."

Josey reached for his rifle while the other men spoke and checked the supply of cartridges. He had more in his saddlebag at the camp, and he had a feeling he would need them. After the chittering in Lakota ended, Hutchins said, "He will not go."

"It sounded like he said a lot more than that."

Hutchins looked away from him. "It does not matter."

"Tell me."

When Hutchins looked back, his eyes pleaded for understanding, a translator who did not wish to be held responsible for the

311

words he spoke. "He said he wishes the white men would grow their hair longer so that there might be more honor in taking their scalps."

CHAPTER TWENTY-SIX

Dr. Hamilton set a generous table from his well-stocked provisions. Grantham delighted in a variety made downright exotic by so much time away from Washington's diplomatic circles. His fingers beat a drumbeat across his ample belly while he took in the sight. Atop a trestle table adorned with white linen were dishes of fresh bread with preserves, pickles, and dried fruit. A first course of oyster soup was followed by roasted antelope with oyster dressing, then custard for dessert. The rich aromas masked the earthy smell that usually permeated the doctor's quarters, a scent that reminded Grantham of plucking weeds from his mother's rose garden as a child when he wished to earn her favor.

The doctor ate as if impatient to return to his studies, in contrast with Grantham, who was accustomed to conversation at a meal. Decorum dictated that his purpose for seeking an audience with the doctor wait until after the meal, and he preferred to work up to his request the way a man eases into a hot bath. Failing to moderate his host's pace over soup, he resorted to a winding interlocution that invited the doctor to lecture on topics as varied as the local climate and national politics. In this way, at least, he could savor the fresh antelope — and chew his food before swallowing.

Grantham found an unwitting ally in the person of the young man who had been assigned the task of serving. The swarthy youth may have been Mexican — he never spoke to betray an accent, if he had one — with eyes that were nearly black; long, sleek hair; and a wide mouth with a full upper lip that imparted a feminine quality to his features. He made a game effort of delivering courses without fumbling the cutlery or spilling the dishes. Yet each of his intermittent appearances halted all dialogue while both diners cringed in anticipation of a soup dousing or dish-smashing pratfall. It felt like watching a performance of "the daring young man" from the song about the flying trapeze. Grantham's nerves were frayed by the time the dishes had been cleared and they could relax with brandy snifters. He breathed deeply to help settle his food, praised the quality of the meal, and thanked his host again. Finally, the time had come for business. He opened the negotiation as if setting the pieces on a chessboard.

"The soldiers are leaving tomorrow," he said. "I will be departing with them."

Hamilton watched him, unblinking. "Yes, I am aware."

"Don't you intend to accompany us?" Grantham had seen no sign of the doctor's men making the necessary preparations.

"I still have work to do here."

Better acquainted with the doctor's work than he wished, Grantham asked, "Don't you think you've done enough?"

"Not until I've finished."

"Good God, man. You can't have too much time left." Grantham took in his host. Hamilton had never been a robust man. He'd been ill as long as Grantham had known him. Now, emaciated and wan, he looked barely a step or two removed from his collection of specimens. Only his pale eyes displayed signs of vigor, maintaining the intensity that Grantham had always found a touch unsettling. They suggested something within Hamilton burning so hotly that it threatened to consume him. "Wouldn't you rather spend your final days surrounded by your family in comfort rather

315

than" — he paused to take in the stacked boxes filled with dusty bones, the mildewed contours of the tent's darkened corners — "than in a place like this?"

Hamilton's thin lips stretched by the smallest of measures. "You make my point for me, Mr. Grantham. My work is all that matters now. It represents my hope for immortality, for it will outlive me if I can complete it. You must understand that."

Grantham arched his eyebrows, an expression he'd adopted long ago in place of a nod so as not to draw attention to his head. The boys at school had mocked him ceaselessly about its size. As if that weren't enough to place a target on him, his fair complexion left him susceptible to a bright blush. The boys learned that by redoubling their taunts, they might incite a florid reaction they labeled his "tomato head." The teasing had served a purpose, though, motivating him to work harder at his studies than any of his peers. He was not a natural intellect, but his work ethic helped him surpass others with greater natural gifts. It also meant he understood better than most a man driven by ambition.

"If I can't appeal to your health, let me try to appeal to your reputation. Out of an obligation to your father, I have looked the other way, even as your expedition has grown increasingly brazen. It was one thing when your men were merely robbing graves. But the slaughtered family at the Laramie trading depot, the miners on the trail — your methods risk exposure that will forever overshadow your work."

Hamilton leaned back in his chair, his eyes momentarily losing their focus. "I will concede my scouts have been overeager at times to earn the bounty I offered, but I needed additional specimens of all races, genders, and ages." He pivoted in his chair, looking to where Grantham knew the boxes of skulls were stacked on their shelves. His eyes had regained their focus. "For such a comprehensive study, I can't have too many samples. You were under orders to help ensure the success of my expedition."

"And I have forestalled or misdirected official inquiries."

"Aid that came at the direction of the president."

"Johnson is a lame duck. General Grant won't be so indulgent of anything that threatens the peace." Grantham inhaled slowly, hoping his pique wouldn't bring on a flush. "If you feel your work must continue, so be it. All I ask is that you relocate

317

your operations so as not to jeopardize *my* work."

"Are you forgetting what I have done for you?" Hamilton demanded. The set of his jaw accentuated the tightness of the skin across his face. "You said Crazy Horse threatened the peace, and I have taken action to solve your dilemma."

"The Indian posed an even more direct threat to you after one of your 'overeager scouts' stole the head of his friend. He would have found his way to your camp one day if I hadn't arranged to lure him out."

Hamilton looked away. "Yes, and shortly my men will return with news that our mutual concerns have been remedied. Surely, *that* warrants some consideration if I wish to tarry a bit."

Grantham pulled at his paper collar and shifted in his chair, for he understood what motivated Hamilton's desire to linger near the fort. Even with no one to overhear, his face warmed to speak aloud of their understanding. "Of course, I am grateful for your efforts. But the deaths of women and children will not go unnoticed."

"The range of my samples will be incomplete without them. Besides, people die every day, Mr. Grantham. In these forsaken lands, life is particularly cheap."

"Then don't be greedy with it. Too much work has gone into forging this peace. You speak of immortality; the treaty is my legacy, Dr. Hamilton."

"It is a paltry legacy then."

Grantham swallowed and cleared his throat. "Men can't always choose their path through history. A great man makes the most of the path he finds himself on."

Hamilton tilted his head and turned his pale eyes up, a supplicating gesture that Grantham figured was as close to an apology as he could expect. The doctor's voice softened. "Don't mistake me, Mr. Grantham. I see for you a legacy that will outlive that of most men."

Blinking rapidly at the flattery, Grantham replied, "While I appreciate your confidence, my work here is not secure."

The tight skin across Hamilton's forehead crinkled above the bridge of his nose. "I do not speak of the treaty. Once the railroad is completed next year, your treaty will have served its purpose and hold no more worth than yesterday's newspapers."

The insult, following so soon after praise, overturned Grantham's normal restraint. "Your arrogance is exceeded only by the blindness of your single-mindedness. My treaty will prove of greater value to the

American government than your scientific dalliances." The shouted words had winded him, and he needed a breath before continuing. "I only wish you could live long enough to recognize the futility of your life's work."

He sat back, exhilarated at the rare opportunity to speak his mind without reservation. His attack had set off a coughing fit in the doctor, whose breath came in great wheezes until he hawked up a bloody dollop of phlegm.

Once recovered, Hamilton said, "I see you fail to grasp the meaning of my work."

Grantham always did his homework, and before meeting the doctor he'd read the appropriate volumes to better understand the man. "By failing to concede any evidence that contradicts your prejudices, you are the one who has failed," he said, enjoying the opportunity to peacock the depth of his research. "You propose to prove that human races represent different species. Yet if that were true, how do you account for the mating of a trapper and a squaw or a slave owner and his chattel? Science instructs us that, if different species, their offspring would be as sterile as a mule."

Grantham leaned back in his chair, so pleased with himself he forgot his prohibition against holding his head high. The doctor sat immobile, his shoulders slumped. Grantham felt a twinge of pity for taking from a dying man what meaning he found in his last days. Diplomatic principle dictated leaving a recalcitrant party some semblance of accomplishment, and Grantham had forgotten that. Now, rather than concede defeat, Hamilton would dig in his heels.

"It has not been proven," he said, his voice almost inaudible, "that the offspring between races are not less fertile. More study will be required."

In deference to his host, Grantham stifled a chuckle.

"Besides which," Hamilton continued, "it is no certain thing that interfertility should be a criterion for the establishment of distinct species."

"Now who's rejecting the science?" Grantham replied, permitting himself a guffaw. "I suppose you believe if you collect enough samples, you will establish your racial order's logic to your fellow craniologists."

A dark look passed over Hamilton's wan face. "It is not only a matter of the number of samples," he said. "It is their quality."

"A skull is a skull, no?"

"You of all people should know better."

Grantham shuddered as a droplet of

perspiration trickled from his armpit, cool against his side.

The doctor continued. "Your condition — I suppose you are aware that it's called macrocephaly: a head circumference two standard deviations larger than the average. It's rarely fatal in cases like yours."

Grantham withdrew a handkerchief from his pocket and dabbed at his forehead. "I am aware."

"I've theorized," the doctor said, "whether expanded cranial capacity could indicate enhanced intelligence. I must say, however, that in the time I've known you, I've seen no confirmation of that."

Grantham returned his handkerchief and began to object. Hamilton cut him off.

"Please, don't take offense. I spoke earlier of your legacy, and you misunderstood me. I did not speak of the treaty or your skills, such as they are, as a diplomat, but of your value to your species in demonstrating the superiority of the white race."

The doctor reached into the pocket of his coat. Earlier, he had withdrawn a handkerchief; this time his hand emerged with a pistol. It looked unnaturally large with his bony fingers wrapped around its grip. The intensity of his gaze softened into something benign, affectionate even.

"You will find your immortality as part of my collection."

The sound of a gunshot startled Grantham. He flinched, expecting to catch a bullet between the eyes. But no, of course, the shot had not been directed to his head. The impact knocked him back in his chair, followed by a burning, as if he'd been impaled through the chest by a red-hot poker. Time slowed. He wanted to reach to the source of his pain, but he couldn't command his arm to move. Hamilton placed the handgun on the white linen beside his cutlery. His hands reached up to straighten his necktie. He gazed upon Grantham, his lips pursed in a way that conveyed impatience. Mr. Martinez appeared at his side. The pair spoke, but the words were lost to Grantham. The Mexican drew near, his movements languid, as if he were passing through water, until he hovered overhead, looking down from a great height that seemed to stretch to infinity as the scope of Grantham's vision narrowed, like looking through the wrong end of a spyglass, until only a pinprick of light remained.

Then all was gone.

CHAPTER TWENTY-SEVEN

Everywhere Annabelle looked she saw soldiers and wagons, horses and mules. The din of shouted commands and responses over the whinnying horses and mules added to the confusion. The garrison and civilian workers would be setting out soon for Fort Laramie, if the level of activity within the fort was any indication.

On a clear, cloudless day when even the winds that usually blew across the valley seemed to have abandoned the fort, Annabelle choked on the miasma from so many animals and the dust they kicked up. She drew a handkerchief from a pocket in her dress to cover her mouth. Making her way across the parade grounds, she passed pairs of men straining with crates of weapons and ammunition. Others toted sacks of feed for the horses. More led mules from the stables, harnessing them into their collars. They filled the wagons with all of these things, plus household goods and personal effects. Furniture, bedding, valises stuffed with clothes. Shovels, saws, hammers, and other tools. Churns, wash buckets, straw brooms. The big wagons were so weighted by their loads, their wheels left indentations marking their passage in the hard dirt.

Annabelle weaved her way among the masses to the commander's headquarters. Josey and John Hutchins were a day late in returning. She hadn't wanted to believe the soldiers would leave before they returned, but contrary evidence surrounded her. What was the point of seeking out Crazy Horse if the soldiers weren't going to wait to learn whether the effort had been successful?

A barrel-chested sergeant with a bulbous nose greeted her in the outer room of the headquarters. Informing her that Colonel Smith was occupied and would be with her presently, he ushered her to a chair in the corner. Its elaborately carved wooden legs and embroidered upholstery identified it as a Louis XVI replica. She sat gingerly, as if she suspected the ornamental piece would not bear the weight of her concerns.

She'd had two such chairs at her home in Charleston, authentic items, nearly a century old, imported from France by her first husband's grandmother. Their golden-hued wooden arms and legs were carved like Greek columns, and the seats and backs were a bird's egg-blue upholstery embroidered with elaborate floral patterns. The pair had cost an obscene fortune, yet no one could sit in them due to an accident during shipping that snapped one of the legs. Attempts to replace the leg with an exact replica failed to meet the matriarch's exacting standards, and the carpenter resorted to gluing the pieces together so that the chair at least *looked* none the worse. Richard's grandmother relegated the restored chair and its mate to opposing corners of her parlor like rooks on a chessboard, where their beauty could be admired but no guest would be tempted to sit upon one. By the time Annabelle took possession of them as lady of the house, no one recalled which chair was the broken one, and so no one sat in either.

The chairs were an afterthought until after the stillborn birth of her baby. Having been raised to believe a woman's duty was to birth children — sons, in particular — the news that she could no longer bear children devastated her. Afterwards, she hated the chairs, seeing in them a reminder that her damaged state left her no more than an adornment to be admired for its fragile beauty. While raising funds for her family's journey west, she finally found a purpose for the chairs, selling them to a Yankee carpetbagger with more ill-gotten funds than good sense.

She stood abruptly, smoothing the fabric of her dress and abandoning the chair for a window that looked out over the grounds. Her unfocused eyes took in nothing of the scene while her mind plied over memories normally locked away. In truth, it wasn't the chair or the thought of her lost baby that troubled her. Josey's absence forced her to confront how she'd never felt loved for who she was before he came into her life. Though she'd never doubted her parents' love as a child, she'd felt she owed them something, an expectation that was hers to realize. In contrast to her brothers, who it seemed could do no wrong in their doting mother's eyes, Annabelle had felt a drive to be perfect in every task she undertook. After meeting Josey, she'd avoided telling him she believed herself barren, fearing that he would reject her. When instead he'd responded by saying he would love her even if they never had children, she'd felt a worth in their shared life she'd never known, even before Isabelle came along.

Yet the sharpness of that joy cut two ways.

For the love that strengthened her also exposed her to a weakness that might shatter her if it were lost. She wanted to view herself as a woman capable of making her way in the world if she must. It was her choice to love Josey and be loved by him. But that choice forced her to acknowledge that she was her best self for having his love. The two were indelibly linked. No matter how strong she stood on her own, she was stronger with him.

The only thing that made this bearable was the knowledge that he felt the same. Josey was not a demonstrative husband. Long ago she'd realized he possessed a poet's heart, but whatever inclination he might have had to freely express his feelings had been stunted by the war, which left wounds that still hadn't healed. Yet even if she didn't always hear the words, Josey said "I love you" every day. He said it when he vowed to build an icehouse for her, then set about the task each morning until completed. He said it as he drove her to town to look at baby clothes when she knew he would have preferred seeing to chores at the ranch. This and a hundred other examples spoke of his love as prettily as any words composed by a poet.

She had relied on that reassurance at

times: when her body expanded to the point she thought she might explode; when the baby came and she always felt tired. Now that Isabelle was grown a bit and Annabelle felt herself again, she wondered if she hadn't asked too much of Josey. Through her time of insecurity, even as she grew into what she believed was her true nature, she'd asked him to deny a part of his, and he'd acquiesced by way of saying "I love you."

Now he was gone, possibly in danger. The rational part of her brain offered a hundred different harmless reasons why he might be delayed, but she found no reassurance in them once her imagination — saturated with the juices of her fear and dependence — conjured any number of threatening scenarios. She allowed these irrational thoughts to preoccupy her because they were preferable to what dwelled within the darkest part of her mind: that Josey one day would ride off and choose to never return. She'd never given voice to the fear. She'd told herself it was a silly thought all women — and maybe even some men — harbored in their weakest moments. Yet the idea stalked her like a wolf in the woods, waiting for the moments when her exhausted mind grew still and careless and the wolf could pounce.

Without thinking, she'd left the window and begun pacing, her steps across the pine wood floors pounding a beat that nearly matched her racing heart. She'd drawn the attention of the poor sergeant, who sat at a table covered with papers he'd been trying to organize, now watching her as he scratched his swollen nose, one brow arched in an unspoken plea for quiet. Casting her eyes to the ground, she returned to the chair and disciplined herself to remain in the seat. She retrieved her handkerchief, twisting it in her hands in a vain attempt to steady them.

She had no cause to question Josey's devotion; she knew that. Josey wasn't like men who sought their entertainment in town, where they could put from their minds thoughts of wives and children. In the rare moments when he could relax, he preferred to be at home. She recalled evenings when they sat together in the growing dusk. The house faced east, but the day's last light cast a glow on the horizon before them, as if the river and the clouds suspended over the Madison peaks were afire. She didn't always know what Josey thought in these quiet moments, and she'd learned not to ask, content with the knowledge that he was where he wanted to be.

With her.

With that understanding came the realization that her fears of losing him were merely a projection of the constraints she'd placed on her own life after becoming a mother, like a corset worn too tight. Some day she would tell her daughter the story of what her parents did this summer, and it would be a better story than if she'd spent the time confined to a routine where the day's most exciting events were meals and changes of soiled underclothes. Through her example, Isabelle would never see herself as a useless adornment, no matter what troubles life sent her way.

The sound of groaning hinges broke her reverie, and she looked up to see Colonel Smith emerge from his office. If he was happy to see her, his thick beard and mustache masked his pleasure. She rose to greet him, slipping the twisted handkerchief back in her pocket, and gracefully accepted his apologies for her wait. He invited her into his private office, though his haste and abrupt manner made clear he believed he had more pressing matters than placating a hysterical woman.

Before following her, he turned on the sergeant. "Egad, Northrup. I thought you said you had seen to my personal belongings." He pointed to the chair. "My mother-in-law would have my scalp if I abandoned that to the Indians."

The sergeant's nose turned florid at the upbraiding in front of Annabelle, whose amusement he no doubt misconstrued as being at his expense rather than the rococo chair. "I'll see to it at once, sir," he said.

After niceties were exchanged, Colonel Smith made clear his haste. "What is it that I can do for you, Mrs. Angliewicz?"

"I realize you have much to attend to before you depart today, but Josey and John Hutchins have not yet returned."

"I fear that cannot be my concern."

She blinked rapidly at his curtness. "It was the army that sent him on this mission."

The gold-trimmed epaulets on the colonel's shoulders rose and fell in a display of apathy. "Not the army. The Office of Indian Affairs," he corrected. "It was Mr. Grantham who asked your husband to seek out Crazy Horse. I was never consulted. You might think a fort commander would merit being included in such decisions, but apparently all Washington believes a soldier is good for is following orders."

"We are splitting hairs, sir," she said, her chin thrust out to prevent a tremble in her voice. "Josey is a full day overdue. Fearing something must be wrong, I sought out Mr. Grantham before coming to you. If you could direct me —"

He interrupted. "I have no idea where Mr. Grantham has gone off to." Irritation clipped the enunciation of his words like pruning shears. "I sent a messenger round to his rooms to alert him to our departure, but he was not there. I can only deduce that he's accompanied the doctor's men to the Indian village to discuss the distribution of our leftover provisions."

"You've left that task to the doctor?"

"He will be perfectly safe," Colonel Smith said, misinterpreting her concern. "Mr. Grantham believed the transaction would go more smoothly if handled by civilians, rather than soldiers. No doubt the doctor's men are capable of dealing with a horde of women and children."

"Women and children?"

"The warriors won't deign to accept handouts at the fort," he said, guiding her from the room and closing the door behind them. "The doctor has more than enough men in his camp to see the task done, and you will be safe until your husband's return."

"It is not my safety that concerns me, Colonel."

Smith's beard parted, and his dark eyes lit with amusement. His body, which he'd held rigid while prepared to deflect her entreaties, visibly relaxed. "I forget whom I address," he said with a bow of his head. "I imagine your husband's safety is not a concern, either, for I can think of no man more capable of protecting himself."

"Could you not at least send a scouting party to ascertain that no trouble has occurred?"

He raised a hand as if to cup her shoulder with a gesture of comfort but held himself back. "My lady, I wish I could do more for you, but I have my orders, and I intend to fulfill them. The army is through with this place, and I must make all haste to Fort Laramie. I am confident your husband will return shortly, and then I trust you will quit this place too. It has brought to us all nothing but grief."

Colonel Smith saw her out, offering the parting advice that she check with Dr. Hamilton to learn if his scouting parties or envoys to the Indian village had produced any information about Josey and John Hutchins. After her last visit to the doctor's tent, Annabelle had no desire to return, but circumstances left her no choice. She went to the campsite outside the fort but was turned away by Hamilton's hulking Mexican foreman, who said his liege was preoccupied with his work and would send word when he could meet with her.

Thoroughly frustrated, Annabelle returned to the barracks to check on Isabelle and confer with Lord Byron. In Josey's absence, he had undertaken the responsibility of exhuming Colonel Long's body so that it could be brought back to Angel Falls. It was a distasteful task, and Annabelle knew Josey had not intended to leave it to Byron alone.

When she found him, he had already loaded the pine case into their wagon and was setting about plans to pack for their departure, confident Josey would return at any moment. After she informed him of her lack of progress, a messenger arrived from the doctor's camp. The young man, his upper lip covered with a downy fuzz that reminded her of a caterpillar, carried a handwritten note from the doctor. She bid he wait while she composed a response. Only after he'd left did she share the contents of the note with Byron.

"It seems I've been invited to dine tonight with Dr. Hamilton."

Knowing of her last visit to the doctor's tent, Byron frowned. "I'd feel mighty better if you told me you've refused," he said, the resignation in his voice implying he knew better. "First Josey running off to Indian country, now you running off to that spooky doctor. He tryin' to tell me this family don't go looking for trouble."

Annabelle smiled at the affection revealed in his consternation. "I don't see that I have a choice if I wish to glean any information about what's happening."

"Josey will be back tonight, by noon tomorrow at the latest — you'll see."

"You can't know that for certain."

"If he's not back, I'll go find him myself."

She went to Byron, laying a hand on his arm. "You sweet man. I couldn't ask you to leave your family to —"

"Josey is my brother. If he's not back by noon tomorrow, I'll go after him."

"We will seek him out together then," she said, her tone making clear she'd brook no objection.

"Then you'll stay away from that doctor?"

His words, more request than directive, drew another smile. "You know me too well to imagine I can sit still until tomorrow while Josey is unaccounted for. Perhaps the doctor knows something that will aid in our search, should it come to that." She squeezed his arm before turning away.

"Besides, it's only a dinner invitation. What could go wrong?"

CHAPTER TWENTY-EIGHT

As Josey looked down on an uncertain number of enemies hidden among the cottonwoods, John Hutchins made the case for staying and fighting from the top of the mesa. "We have the high ground," he said.

"They won't attack from here," Josey said. "A few of them might try to hold our attention while the rest flank us and come from behind. We'd be surrounded and exposed on this ridge."

The half-blood translator's mouth twisted as he contemplated this. "Then we should run. Get our horses and flee down the other side before they can get behind us. By the time they know we are gone, we will be too far ahead for them to catch us."

"Ask what he thinks of that." Josey nodded toward Crazy Horse, who lay prone beside them seeking the white men through a spyglass.

While they talked in Lakota, Josey played

out the scenario in his head. The hour already was too late to make it far before full darkness. After that, they would have to move slowly to protect the horses from unseen dangers like stepping into a prairie dog hole. One felled horse would be a disaster for them, but not for their pursuers, who had enough numbers that they could continue the chase even if they lost a horse or two. The pursuers also had the advantage of knowing their quarries' destination; they could race ahead in the dark and lie in ambush on the road to the fort. Josey waited while Crazy Horse explained the situation to Hutchins.

"So what do we do?"

Josey stood and took a step in the direction of the camp. It lay far enough from the ridge to provide open sightlines on the flat-topped hill no matter where their enemies ascended. They could dig rifle pits to create a defensive position where they could fend off their attackers, he told the others. Crazy Horse rose, bow in one hand, two arrows held in the palm of the other while he clenched a third in his teeth. A quiver bristling with more arrows hung from his waist beside a stone-headed tomahawk. With a nod of his head toward the enemy below, he made clear what he thought of burrowing into holes.

Josey felt his face redden. He'd always preferred charging at an enemy, too, trusting that his aim under fire would be better than his foe's. That was when he had little concern for whether he lived or died. Now that he had Annabelle and Isabelle to think of, the rifle pits seemed a more sensible option, particularly without knowing how many men were aligned against them. An organized defense might be enough to drive away their attackers with little risk to themselves.

He appealed to Hutchins. "Tell him there are too many. If we don't fight together, they will kill us all."

While they spoke, Josey moved off, trusting the others would follow. Whether convinced by the argument or merely curious about Josey's plan, Crazy Horse came. They checked that their canteens were full and moved the horses to provide them with what cover they could among some brush and boulders within their campsite. While they worked, Josey kept time in his head, imagining how long it would take their enemies to encircle them and begin their ascent up the ridge. They would be slow about it, careful to maneuver under cover in case Josey had taken a sniper's position from above, an idea he'd rejected so that he would have more time to fortify their position. They used knives to loosen the dirt and dug trenches that encircled the camp. Josey showed them how to throw the dirt into a mound on the outside of the ring. On top of the loose dirt, they placed what logs or loose branches they could find, leaving small gaps so that they could shoot from a protected position.

When they paused to rest, Josey wiped his face on his sleeve, took off his hat, and slipped his fingers into the crown to straighten the crease. He nudged John Hutchins and pointed toward Crazy Horse. "Tell him it was rifle pits like these that allowed us to hold off his raiders at Crazy Woman Creek."

"I am not telling him that. He might leave just to make a point."

The sun hung low over the horizon when Crazy Horse called and pointed. He'd seen movement on their left. Behind their makeshift bulwarks, Josey took inventory. He had his Winchester and four Colts, all fully loaded. Crazy Horse had a bow, a pistol, and an old Sharps. The single-shot rifle wouldn't be much good in a siege, but Josey trusted that the Indian's aim was true. Hutchins carried a new Colt revolver that hung heavy on his belt and a seven-shot

Spencer carbine.

"How many spare cartridges?" Josey asked, pointing to the short-barreled rifle favored by cavalry.

Smiling with pride, Hutchins held out a box of twenty-five .56-56 cartridges.

Josey unslung the saddlebag he'd retrieved from Gray and emptied the contents from one of the pockets. A pile of .44 Henry cartridge boxes spilled out.

Hutchins whistled. "Anyone who figures they can outlast us until we run out of ammunition has not fought against Josey Angel."

Josey tossed a box of cartridges to Crazy Horse. "Tell him these will fit in his rifle too." He looked at Hutchins's single box. "You'll have to ration your shots."

Dusk slipped upon them, long shadows reaching out to overtake the fading light that cast the western mountains in a purple glow. After all their digging and building, they welcomed evening's chill at first. Then the cool air dried the sweat beneath their clothes, and the cold burrowed into their bones. From the protection of their rifle pits, they took turns watching for movement among their would-be killers.

Before settling in, Josey saw to his horse, watering it from the spare canteen he'd filled before they ascended the mesa. Then he raked up a thick pile of pine needles to spread across his spot. The needles were dirty and a little damp from the previous day's rain, but they made a softer mattress than the rocks and fresh dirt from where they'd been digging. He spread out his bedroll, laying down the gum blanket first to protect against the cool dampness.

Hutchins fidgeted. He shifted his guns between hands and holsters, checking and rechecking them, though he'd already cleaned and loaded them. When done with that, he peered overtop of their screen in case anyone tried to steal upon them. Before he could repeat his gun check again, Josey said, "My guess is they won't come until dawn. They have the numbers. No sense attacking in the dark when they might shoot one of their own in the crossfire. They will wait for light."

Nodding as if he knew this already, Hutchins pulled his tobacco pouch from his coat before abruptly changing his mind. "I'm going to check the other side of the camp," he said, moving off in the crouching run of a man whose bowels are loosening on him.

Crazy Horse watched all of this with no change of expression.

"I suppose neither one of us expected to end up like this," Josey said, before rummaging through his saddlebag and pulling out a cold supper of dried meat and cheese.

Crazy Horse spoke a few words that were gibberish to Josey's ears.

"If you're telling me I'm crazy for talking to an Indian who doesn't speak English, I will concede the point." Josey took another bite of dried meat and offered what was left to Crazy Horse. The Indian stared a moment before leaning forward and taking the food. He sniffed it before taking a bite.

While both men chewed the dried meat, Josey's thoughts turned to the mystery of their predicament. The redhead in the old Union blues had been with Martinez at the fort. Josey couldn't imagine that his grievance with the big Mexican inspired this ambush, so he assumed the man spoke the truth in saying they'd come for Crazy Horse. What he couldn't understand was the why of the matter. Had they been so certain Crazy Horse would reject Josey's entreaties to remove himself from the fight? They had been wrong, if that had been the case. Crazy Horse had agreed not to undermine the peace treaty more easily than Josey had expected. No matter which way Josey turned the puzzle in his head, he could not determine what the picture was supposed to be. He concluded there was more at work than he could see — and he worried that whatever he was missing might mean danger for Annabelle and the others at the fort.

Lord Byron had been right; Josey never should have brought them to this place. Byron held a stubbornly practical view of the world that provided a healthy dose of perspective at times. The idea of bringing the Colonel's remains back to Angel Falls held a chivalric appeal to a boy raised on stories of Lancelot and Hector, but Byron had seen through that, identifying the vainglory behind Josey's motivation for returning to Fort Phil Kearny. Josey had wanted to believe the army needed him to secure a peace. He'd wanted to believe he was the only white man who could win Crazy Horse's respect. Yet Lord Byron never challenged him on it, supporting Josey's decision and watching over his family in Josey's absence.

On looking up from his reflections, Josey realized Crazy Horse had been watching him. He had finished the dried meat Josey had given him and sat motionless, his face impassive, looking as patient as the Bighorns. From the other side of the camp,

Josey caught a whiff of one of John Hutchins's cigarettes. The smell could carry for miles, though there was no point in concealing themselves now. They could even light a fire if they'd wanted, though Josey preferred to keep his eyes adjusted to the dark, just in case one of the men surrounding them got it into his head to sneak upon them.

"Why don't you try to get some sleep? I'll take the first watch," Josey said to Crazy Horse, placing his palms together and laying his head against them in a gesture he could only hope would signal sleep in the Indian sign language.

The Indian warrior's expression did not change, and he made no move to go off with his bedroll. Josey settled in and tried to relax, but his limbs felt heavy from the riding and digging, and his mind remained too active to sleep. Night sounds his ears normally ignored clamored as distinctly as hearing his name called. The remnants of yesterday's rainwater dripped from the thick tree canopy where it had pooled. A coyote yipped from the next hill. A squirrel rustled among dried pine needles. Its movement flushed a bird, its wings beating against the air in rapid thumps. The breeze whispered through the tree branches, and where the trees grew close branches rubbed together like the groaning of a wounded man. Eventually, he slipped into the half-waking state of a sentry, a mind at rest yet alert to any discordant sound. They sat like that for what must have been hours. Every so often one of them would rise and make a circle within the camp, watching and listening for any strange movement in the dark. Without a word spoken, they fell into taking turns. That was how Josey learned that John Hutchins had found escape in sleep on the far side of the camp.

After Crazy Horse returned from one of his rounds, they sat facing each other. The moon had risen over the horizon, and its glow plus that of the stars was enough for them to watch each other. In the near-dark, Josey could see nothing in Crazy Horse's profile — the slope of his nose, the curve of his ear, the shape of his eyes — that distinguished him from any other man Josey had known. He might have been a Frenchman or Italian, with language and diet separating them more than anything physical. Annabelle had lived among the Indians for nearly three months, sharing the same tepee with Crazy Horse for most of that time. If Josey thought of it that way, he had more in common with this man than any other, saving Byron.

"Do you understand me? Annabelle said you understand more English than you let on."

Crazy Horse watched him but did not react.

"Indians fight for honor. That's what I've always heard. You fight so that you will be esteemed by your people. And you fight to survive. If you don't fight to protect the best hunting grounds, your people will go hungry. There is honor in that."

He paused, waiting for something, though he wasn't sure what. He felt no more ridiculous speaking his mind to a man who probably didn't understand a word than he did speaking aloud to his horse, with no greater expectation of being understood or eliciting a response, just trusting that the sound of his voice might impart some sense of his meaning.

"I don't know what white men fight for anymore. We also speak of honor. We speak of faith. We speak of patriotism, but I'm not sure I believe it. Where is the honor in taking this land from your people? What patriotic purpose is served? Some men will be made wealthy, but that shouldn't justify the loss of so many lives. No one wants to admit that, so we talk of honor, faith, and patriotism. We imbue these words with such meaning that they can justify anything. But what if they are intended merely to rationalize actions that are done for greed?"

He'd been turning these thoughts over in his mind for days. The army had come to this place to protect emigrants who demanded a quicker route to Montana's gold fields. Now the army wanted a peace treaty that would safeguard the railroad the country wanted so it could move people even faster. If honor, patriotism, and faith were merely the inventions of men who used them to serve their ambitions, what about other abstractions he took for granted? What about love? Is it real — or merely a concept invented to reinforce belief in things like honor, faith, and patriotism? He couldn't speak this aloud even to a man who didn't understand him. Giving voice to such a doubt felt like a betrayal of Annabelle and Isabelle.

Crazy Horse's face offered no hint of reaction. Josey had noticed before that Indians seemed less expressive than white people. He wondered if that was always the case or true only when they confronted white people. He would have asked Crazy Horse if he'd expected an honest answer.

"Do Indians believe in love? Do you love your children, love your women, the way we do? If you do, what kind of villains does that make us? Annabelle told me you loved a woman. Maybe she just wanted to believe that. A woman needs to believe in love even more than a man. Without the hope of love, their lot in life is a hard one. It makes me wonder if it's not an invention intended to control their behavior the way talk of honor, faith, and patriotism directs a man's."

These were dark thoughts, and, even as they nagged at Josey, he wondered if they were a product of weariness and his fear of failing Annabelle, Isabelle, and everyone else who counted on him. For questioning the reality of love did not mean that he loved them any less, just as some people found comfort in prayer even as they questioned the existence of God. These were matters to be pondered by men of greater wisdom than Josey possessed. At least these questions had helped him put from his mind for a little while thoughts of what the morning would bring.

"If you understand me, you must think I am crazy. They call you Crazy Horse, yet clearly I am the one who is going mad." His lip curled, and he was struck by the thought that, normally, he was the one accused of not speaking his mind. No wonder Annabelle had come to feel comfortable with Crazy Horse. "I have told you things I have never said to another. Probably because I'm not certain you understand a word."

The sky began to lighten. A whip-poor-will called from the trees, its first note followed by a staccato string like echoes through a canyon. The Indian still watched him. A flick of his dark eyes in the direction of where the sun would soon rise spoke his thoughts more effectively than any words.

"Yes," Josey said, gathering himself to stand. "They will be coming for us soon."

CHAPTER TWENTY-NINE

With the children asleep, Maria returned to the fire, a wool blanket wrapped around her thin shoulders. Atticus didn't appear to have moved since she left, his eyes transfixed by the dying light. He'd been quiet all evening, speaking only in response to a question from Danny or Astrid, saying only enough to satisfy them before losing himself again in his thoughts. Maria moved to his side of the fire, upwind from the slight breeze that pushed the wood smoke. She sat far enough away so as not to disturb him, yet near enough to hear a whispered word. She would not press him; a man would speak his mind only when he believed it was his idea. A sprinkling of feeble stars low on the horizon winked beyond the glow of their fire. As she waited for more to appear in the darkening sky, she imagined them to be distant campfires lit by other lonely travelers, seeking warmth, yes, but also sending out a light into the universe so that they would not feel alone.

"The soldiers are gone now," Atticus said.

"Yes. I hadn't realized Josey Angel had returned." Taken aback by his words, she'd spoken without thinking. She'd known he'd been preoccupied with something but had imagined — *perhaps hoped?* — it pertained to her. She attempted to cover for her poor choice of subject. "I wonder if he found the Indian chief he was seeking."

"They ain't back."

"I thought the soldiers would wait for his return before leaving."

"So did I."

Atticus had found a twig that had fallen loose from the kindling he and Danny had gathered to start the fire. He turned his attention to snapping it into increasingly smaller pieces, as if he had no more use for their conversation than the stick he held in his hands. Maria didn't know what to make of the army's absence and Josey Angel's failure to return; only one question mattered to her. "What do you propose we do?" she asked, holding her breath while waiting to see if he challenged her use of pronoun.

"I don't know, Maria." He rarely used her given name, and it startled her. "If we leave in the morning, we could catch up to the soldiers. At Fort Laramie we could find a wagon train east." Having broken his stick into as many pieces as he could, he began casting the pieces, one by one, into the center of the fire. Their addition had no evident effect on the dying flames. She felt his gaze on her but didn't dare meet it. He said, "Would you return to your people?"

"I have no one." Daniel's family would welcome the children, but she had always felt like an outsider among them, just as she had growing up in her cousins' home after the death of her parents. She might endure that for the children's sake, if that were her only option, but she knew Atticus also had no one back in the States. Needing to hear him say it, she asked: "Would you return to Georgia?"

He stared into the fire as if watching the scenes of his life play out in the ember glow of the charcoal. Within his closed mouth, his tongue passed over the front of his teeth, like the sweeping of an arm. "There is nothing there for me."

They sat in silence for a spell. With the fire fading and the night growing darker, more stars blinked on. Maria drew courage from their light, feeling less alone. She asked, "Do you think we should continue on with the doctor's wagons?"

"I'm not sure I trust them any more than the Indians," he said. "Maybe less."

"They can't be worse than Indians."

The strange doctor and his brooding Mexican foreman unsettled her. She recalled the dispassion with which the doctor discussed his work, as if he studied butterflies pinned to the pages of a book rather than humans. For all his talk of the study of mankind, the doctor displayed little affection for people. He sought only their admiration and respect. Still, the company of the doctor and his men had to be preferable to traveling alone through roads infested by both Indians and road agents. So many dangers filled Maria's world, she didn't want to conjure another, and after what happened to Daniel she wouldn't know a moment's peace traveling alone again. Only one alternative remained. Could this man set aside his need for vengeance and find forgiveness in his heart?

She said, "You know I won't travel alone, Atticus."

His eyes cut to her before returning to the fire. "Annabelle will let you accompany them." He wouldn't even speak Josey's name.

"I said I will not travel alone."

He heard her, she knew, for his eyes closed

355

as if wincing from a slap. During his conva-
lescence, he had permitted her to cut his
hair and trim his beard. She had been right;
he was still a handsome man once he looked
kempt. Her mind sought the words of Luke.
She needed to speak them aloud to be
certain she had them right.

"Judge not, and you will not be judged.
Condemn not, and you will not be con-
demned. Forgive, and you will be forgiven."

His eyes remained closed, as if to shut out
the light before him. When that wasn't
enough, he covered them with his hands.
His body shook, and his breath came in
great heaving gulps. She went to him.
Kneeling beside him, she placed her hand
on his arm.

"I promised I would avenge them," he
said.

The anguish in his words cut her. "That is
not a promise to God," she said. "That is a
promise to the devil, who prowls around,
seeking some soul to devour."

She wrapped her arms around him, and
whatever still held him firm dissolved between them. His body trembled with sobs
he failed to restrain. He gripped her tightly,
like a drowning man grasping a piece of
driftwood, so tight the breath was forced
out of her, and she had to wait for his body

to relax between sobs before she could draw air. She held him so long her knees grew sore against the hard ground, but she did not mind. She rocked him as she'd done when she cradled Danny and Astrid to her breast. The motion, as gentle as reclining in a rowboat on a lake, soothed him.

When he finally leaned back from her, he looked away, ashamed, wiping at his eyes with his palms, where his hands were cleanest. "Don't turn away from me," she said.

In the faint light, his eyes looked dark, and they widened with understanding as her words sunk in. She thought he might protest, that he might react with anger for exposing weakness to her, but instead he pulled her to him. It was the first time she'd been held by a man since Daniel's death. The warmth of his body both filled and covered her, the way caulking between boards keeps the cold out of a home. She gave herself over to the heat and did not protest when he laid her back, making a comfortable place for her and resting his head on her shoulder. She couldn't recall Daniel ever lying with her like that. He'd always positioned her head against him. She waited, knowing she must not pry if she wished to hear his thoughts. When he finally spoke, his voice was thick with phlegm. He coughed to clear it.

"I proved a better soldier than I was a farmer, but I was content then."

She had wondered where his mind would go and was surprised at the answer. "You liked working the land?"

"I hated it." He coughed on what might have been a laugh. "If I wasn't worried about floods, I worried about drought. And when nothing went wrong, the county had a surplus and the price at the market dropped."

Knowing he wasn't done, she waited, her fingers twining the gray hairs at his temple that shone in the firelight.

"None of it mattered because at the end of the day I had Chelsea. She didn't have to say anything. She could just look at me, her blue eyes holding me as close as any embrace. On nights she knew I was troubled, she pulled me close and traced the worry lines on my brow until she had rubbed away the bad thoughts and I could sleep."

His hair was too short now to wrap around a finger, so she drew circles on his temple with her finger, applying pressure as he spoke until the lines that stretched out from the corner of his eyes faded and his face relaxed. With his eyes closed, she wondered if he imagined the fingers that played in his hair belonged to his dead wife. She decided that it would be all right if he did.

"I was not a good farmer, and I knew I would never be a wealthy man. For whatever reason, God had chosen to give me Chelsea, and that was enough. In love, I was as wealthy as Prince Albert, probably even richer, for I doubt Queen Victoria could be as kind and loving as my Chelsea."

His breathing had evened. With his body nestled against hers, she could feel his heartbeat, so slow she wondered if it might stop.

"I needed her more than a man will admit aloud, and I thought she would be with me forever. It hurt so bad when I lost her, my only consolation was to think I would never have to mourn like that again. I still had our boy, and he would outlive me."

He fell silent. She knew he feared his voice would betray him if he tried to speak more. After Daniel's murder, she had wished for death, if only to spare her from the pain of his loss. Only in the thought of her children did she find the strength to live. His grief must have been all-consuming.

When he continued, he did not speak of his boy's death or his father's, could not even bring himself to name them. "I had nothing left. I didn't care if I died. I didn't know what to do or where to go. I couldn't stay. Not where their memories were rooted to the very ground, like seeds that could sprout with each new season. The only reason I had to rise each morning was the hope of avenging their deaths."

In the silence, she listened for his heart. Slower than seconds, she wondered if it was strong enough to love again. She waited until she heard the steady thump before she asked, "Do you still have a reason to rise each morning?"

He opened his eyes and faced her. "You know I do."

His eyes found and held hers, a question asked yet not spoken. In response, she pulled away the blanket that shrouded her. She wore only a light cotton shift dress, and the night air gripped her as if she wore nothing. Her skin puckered against its chill until his hands covered her, everywhere at once it seemed in their greedy need, then his body tight against her until her hands claimed him too. He might have imagined the memory of a dead woman soothed his troubled mind, but it was a living woman he sought now. Once she acceded to his desire, she was surprised at how much her need matched his. They made love, at first with a breathless hunger of an appetite long denied, then with movements of a sweet accord, like music softly played lest they wake the children.

As they lay together afterwards, his words echoed in her mind, a question answered indirectly, allowing her to infer its meaning. She had wanted to believe the venom had been drawn from him, that this was a man who no longer had only revenge in his heart. Yet she feared what the light would bring, when time had dulled his passion, and the memory of his losses hollowed him out like a man so starved that a full meal would make him ill. At last, she slept, soothing her restless mind with the hope that soon he would need her more than he needed to kill Josey Angel.

CHAPTER THIRTY

Annabelle sat at a table set with wine glasses and china plates. A young man with a pretty mouth poured a blood-red wine. Hands and face still pale from the washing that removed the layer of dirt that still creased his wrists and ruddied his neck, he managed to snatch the bottle away before leaving a trail of spots across the white linen tablecloth. Seated across from her, Dr. Hamilton drew in a whistle between gritted teeth.

"He means well," he said once the young man retreated. "I assure you the cook is more skilled than the server." His thin lips spread to reveal a row of child-like teeth.

Annabelle endeavored to return the expression. The reception had exceeded her expectations. She felt underdressed in a simple calico dress given the formal setting and Hamilton's appearance in a long frock coat with matching vest and a silk puff tie. He sipped from his wine and set the glass beside the table lamp, its flickering light passing through the liquid so that shadows of garnet floated across the linen. None of the niceties assuaged her discomfort at being with the man, who'd evaded her questions about Mr. Grantham, explaining that the diplomat had accompanied some of his men to the Indian village to arrange for distribution of the fort's supplies.

"Mr. Grantham doesn't speak Lakota. Wouldn't it have been better to wait for John Hutchins to return and translate?"

"We have others who can speak enough Indian to be understood," the doctor said without naming anyone. "In fact, the Indians are already here. They made camp in the quartermaster's yard after the soldiers left. In the morning my men will hand out the food, and they will be on their way."

Annabelle had not seen the Indians, who must have entered through the eastern gate, behind the wall that divided the civilian work buildings from the military compound. She had been watching the soldiers leave, vainly hoping the sight of her forlorn figure might convince Colonel Smith to send out a scouting party. The commander had evaded her stare, leaning forward in his saddle as he passed to run a gloved hand over his horse's shoulder as if something were amiss with the animal's gait. The line of blue-clad soldiers and wagons seemed to stretch as long as the Yellowstone River. She had watched until they disappeared into the hazy brown cloud their passage kicked up over the valley. Now Hamilton used the Indians to justify his rejection of her request that he send a scouting party to look for Josey and John Hutchins.

"I'm sure they will return of their own accord before I have an opportunity to arrange anything," he said, appearing relieved to be cut short by the delivery of an oyster stew.

Over the stew, he regaled her with stories intended to demonstrate the precocious curiosity of his youth. He told her of the frogs he caught at a river by his home and "studied" in his bedroom until his mother, drawn by the odor, discovered their bloody remains.

"After that, Mr. Martinez was ordered to build a workshop for me beside the stables. Mother made a point never to visit." He chuckled at his anecdote, forestalling any interruption by speaking of "experiments" conducted on rats and even a cat that his sister had taken in. Annabelle resisted pressing him on the nature of his studies. She enjoyed a good oyster stew and anticipated his response would ruin her appetite. Besides, if she held out any hope that he would send scouts tomorrow, she figured it best to indulge him now.

By the time a main course of roasted duck had been served, she'd begun reevaluating his motives. All she'd sought were answers to questions, yet like a frustrated teacher he clearly enjoyed an audience for his lectures, deeming her attention the price of his hospitality. As he maneuvered the conversation to the subject of his work, his apparent need to impress her left her wondering if his invitation had been a prelude to a seduction. He wanted something from her; she recognized that. The idea that it could be a dalliance seemed absurd. His manner reminded her of a boy, just old enough to recognize the differences between men and women but too indifferent to find any appeal in them. The type of boy who, once grown into manhood, lost himself in books and study so that he could retreat from conversation whenever it suited him.

Yet such men often married and fathered children, and she'd yet to meet a man who, under the right circumstances, didn't enjoy preening before a woman. Just as the cardinal bares his crimson chest while airing his song, men sought a way to draw women's attention to themselves. A show of strength or valor suited a strong man's vanity. Men with nimble minds wooed with poetry and decorous manners. Men of faith employed Scripture to demonstrate a public virtue that made any fall to temptation when alone with a woman all the more irresistible. A man like the doctor would wield his intellect, trusting that the less a woman understood, the more enthralled she would become.

If the doctor had any such designs on her, he concealed them well. She could usually read a man's thoughts by tracking his eyes as they roamed her body, yet the doctor's pale eyes never left her face, hovering over the point of her chin, the slope of her forehead, the plane of her cheeks — but never meeting her own in the fashion she'd expect of a man entertaining carnal interests. She might have dismissed his timidity as a failure of confidence but for the discomfiting intensity of his gaze, a reminder of the boy whose insatiable curiosity drove him to play with his specimens before cutting them apart.

Suddenly feeling flushed, she found her patience for indulging the doctor's idiosyncrasies running out. Glancing past him to the shelves of boxes that extended into the dark corners of the tent, she said, "Tell me, Dr. Hamilton, how do you come by so many specimens?"

He cleared his throat and looked down, pushing slices of duck around on his plate with his fork. "Many of our samples come from scouring the sites of old Indian battles. While the victors tend to remove their fallen from the field, the vanquished are often abandoned."

"Doesn't that skew the results of your study, if all of your samples are presumably young men fallen in battle?"

Hamilton coughed politely into a handkerchief and offered a small-toothed smile. "I fear by speaking of my work, we might hinder our digestion."

Using her knife to pick away at the bones, Annabelle found she had little appetite. Her thoughts turned to Colonel Long's remains, just exhumed by Lord Byron, and how devastated he and Josey would have been if they'd discovered his pine box empty or missing . . . parts. She rested her hands in her lap, so that Hamilton wouldn't see her clenched fists. "Is that why you've come west? Because people's frequent movements mean there is less attention paid to cemeteries or burial sites."

He set down his fork. For the first time,

his pale eyes sought out hers and held them. "It's nothing personal."

"It's personal to the family and friends of the deceased."

The doctor's gaze returned to his plate. "I'm disappointed, Mrs. Angliewicz. I thought, as an educated woman, you would appreciate the need to further the boundaries of science. As a woman of the Confederacy, I thought you would endorse my theories."

"I don't see how your work can do anything more than promote some ghastly freak show display."

"A woman like you so hewed by convention?" His body shook with anger as he stood. For a moment, Annabelle thought she had secured a quick dismissal and escape from any more tedious lectures. Instead, Hamilton went to his shelves and retrieved a large wooden box he set on the table before her. He lifted the lid to reveal a set of skulls and withdrew the largest, its skinless visage set in a harrowing grin.

"This is one of the prizes of my collection. It belonged to an honored Indian warrior, one of the few to die at the massacre here. You see how well-formed the skull is. Note the facial angle here and the larger-than-usual zygomatic arch," he said, running a finger across the thin bone that extended across a concave gap where the jaw hinged. "I defy you to find a difference between it and the skull of any of the white men."

"If there's no difference, then —"

"Ah, but that's what distinguishes a scientist from a layperson. We must test our observations. Through careful measurement I've determined that, despite the apparent size of the skull, the cranial cavity of the red man, on average, has a smaller capacity than the white man. It is the same for Negroes and, I suspect, Chinamen."

"Why should that matter?"

"The cranial cavity is where the brain is encased. By measuring the average capacity for each race of men, I will be able to demonstrate which possesses the greatest innate intelligence. An obvious conclusion, I admit," he added, with a modesty that rang false, "but I will be providing the scientific basis to prove it."

She waited for him to continue, assuming there must be more, for she had known many large men with proportionately sized heads who displayed all the brain power of a milk cow chewing cud. And she had lived among Indians long enough to see intelligence and stupidity among her captors in equal measures to what she'd experienced any other place. When it became clear the doctor had concluded his case she said, "If you spent more time with the people you purport to study than with just their bones, you would understand that Indians, while not formally educated, are no less intelligent than you or I."

Ignoring the comment, the doctor stood and moved behind her. She thought he meant to gather other specimens for her inspection until she felt his hands brush away loose strands of hair at her neck. Annabelle froze with a sharp intake of breath.

"You see the world as a woman's kind heart wishes it to be," he said, in a tone he might employ to lecture a slow child. "By studying the theories of Dr. Samuel Morton, I learned to see the world as it is. His efforts were limited by a scarcity of specimens. Once I can collect an adequate supply with suitable variety, I expect to glean God's logic in establishing a racial order. Then you will understand that I am right."

She tensed at feeling his fingers tug at the pins that held her hair. Shock at his audacity held her in place, giving time for her racing thoughts to settle into coherence. If she could keep him talking, she might learn something — for she now sensed the doctor knew more about Josey's activities than he let on. She kept her hands clenched beneath the table, enduring the touch of his bony fingers while he removed each pin with a delicate motion.

"I am disappointed you fail to recognize the value in my work, but I am not surprised. The cranial capacity of a woman is even smaller than that of the average male Negro or Indian." He raked his splayed fingers through her hair so that the strands fell about her shoulders. "That's better."

She braced for what came next, her dread compounded by her confusion. Where another man might be emboldened to reach for her breast or lean in for a kiss, the doctor's desires were unfathomable. She shivered at his cool touch against her scalp, the hairs on her head feeling electrified by some mélange of fear and anger.

"Your skull's dimensions are ideal, slightly larger than the average woman, I would say. Of course, I can't conclude anything until I take thorough measurements."

Annabelle rose to flee but felt the full weight of the man leaning down on her, surprising strength holding her to her seat. A coughing fit overcame him, and she twisted in her chair to get out from under him. Just as she thought to break free, she halted at the click of a revolver hammer being drawn back. The doctor moved before her, one hand with a handkerchief to his mouth, the other holding a gun pointed at her breast.

"I'm afraid I must insist that you stay, Mrs. Angliewicz," he said, his voice hoarse from the cough. He sank into his chair, keeping the gun leveled at her chest. He took a sip of wine to clear his throat. The glass shook as he returned it.

"You see now why I am so anxious to brook no delay." He nodded toward the blood-speckled handkerchief and steadied his hand by laying it flat against the table. "My time is limited, and the scope of my work is too important. Shortcuts are necessary if I am to accumulate a sufficient sampling of skulls, particularly among native women and children. By this time tomorrow I will have them."

The horror behind his meaning eclipsed even Annabelle's fear of staring into the barrel of a gun. "You have no intention of distributing food to the Indians," she said, the words spoken deliberately as she absorbed a truth that nearly defied belief. "How can you speak of God while you plot murder on such a scale?"

He cocked his head to the side, as if

pondering an equation. "There might have been a time when that would have troubled me. I believed God found such value in my work that He would see I had sufficient time to complete it. Mr. Martinez helped me realize that God had enforced a deadline that compelled me to disregard normal scientific methodology."

While it was clear now Hamilton held no compunctions about murder, the revolver frightened her less than the man's cold-blooded nature. The world was a laboratory to Hamilton, and all its living things nothing more than specimens for his study. She needed to get away and warn others.

"If you harm me, Josey will come for you. You fear not having sufficient time to complete your work. He will see to that."

His frown was meant to evince pity, though Annabelle now understood Hamilton was incapable of emotions; he merely mimicked what he deemed appropriate for the circumstances.

"Your husband is most certainly dead, a victim of what the diplomats call 'collateral damage.' You see, they needed Crazy Horse dead to preserve any hope that the treaty would last until the railroad was completed. And he was drawing uncomfortably close to realizing we had taken his late friend's head." He nodded toward the Indian skull on the table before Annabelle. "We used your husband to lure him out. While I held nothing against him, I couldn't afford any delays caused by Crazy Horse or an Indian office investigation into reports about my collection methods. It was nothing personal."

The news, delivered in such a matter-of-fact manner, hit Annabelle harder than the bullet could have. *It can't be.* She would know if Josey were dead. The premonition she felt in his tardiness convinced her something was wrong. But not dead. *No.* Hamilton's words echoed in her head, and she parsed them like a lawyer seeking a loophole. *"Most certainly dead."* That's what he'd said. That means he doesn't know for sure. He would need a whole army to kill Josey, especially if Crazy Horse were with him.

Still frowning, the doctor watched her. The crease between his eyes relaxed with what she might have identified as empathy in a man capable of it. "If it's any consolation, I expect your sample will be the primary display model for your gender and species at the Army Medical Museum. You will, in a sense, live forever."

The last word was nearly choked off as he

cleared his throat to suppress another cough. In that moment, Annabelle struck. Withdrawing her hands from her lap, her right arm pivoted like a windmill in a blur of motion. Powered by an anger that burned white hot, she plunged the knife she had secreted from the table into the doctor's left hand with all the force she could muster. The blade impaled the back of his flattened hand, embedding itself deep into the wooden table with a satisfying thud.

All that followed occurred so quickly Annabelle had to reconstruct it later in her mind. Still recovering from the cough, the doctor's mouth opened in a silent scream, his pale face burning sanguine from a lack of air. He dropped the gun so that he might pull the knife from his other hand, but from a sitting position he lacked the strength to withdraw the blade. Annabelle pounced. By the time he stood, she faced him, revolver now trained on a point between his eyes, her legs braced to absorb the recoil.

He froze at the sight. His open jaw came nearly unhinged in his desperation to suck in air, stretching the gaunt skin across his face and accentuating his resemblance to one of his samples. His pale eyes widened with a need to communicate thoughts he could not give breath to.

"You don't live with a gunman without learning some things." She lowered the gun so that the sight lined up with his heart, rather than his head. "Maybe someone will find value in your specimen. It's nothing personal."

She pulled the trigger.

Chapter Thirty-One

Josey figured their attackers were smart enough to encircle them before advancing. They seemed to know they faced only three men, who would be unable to protect all sides at once. They started firing on the camp from more than two hundred yards out. The rifles were good from that range, but they were shooting up a slight incline, which made for a difficult shot. Secure in his rifle pit, Josey held his fire. The rimfire .44 cartridge loaded in his Winchester was a large, slow bullet with a fast-dropping trajectory. Its effective range was no more than two hundred yards, though with time for a careful aim Josey had learned to compensate for that.

A steady spray of bullets kicked up the dirt in front of his position, but he sensed the men were doing little more than throwing lead in his direction, hoping to keep him from drawing a bead on any of them.

Another shot thwanged off a limestone boulder to his left. He didn't bother to duck, just kept watching for the smoke so he could discern the pattern to the men's advance.

They were smart about that, too, moving forward in turns. While two men shot, another raced to whatever cover he could find. Josey continued to bide his time. Patience was his ally. In his fortified position, the men advancing on him couldn't be sure where he was until he shot and the smoke from the exploding powder gave him away. For now, they may even wonder if they were advancing on an unprotected front. He hoped so. That would make them careless as they drew closer.

The cover on top of the mesa was limited. Boulders were scattered here and there, along with some scrub and spindly trees whose trunks were too thin to hide a man's girth. Recognizing this, his attackers kept moving, quickly cutting the distance to the camp in half. Fixing his aim on a boulder, big enough to shield a man's head, but only that, Josey waited. He didn't have to wait long.

The man who came was a slender, nervous-looking fellow who ran forward in a zigzag pattern. He threw himself into the dirt behind the rock, exposing only his shoulders and legs while he caught his breath. Josey waited. Soon enough it was the man's turn to take aim and provide the cover for another to advance. He shifted around the rock, using it to steady his rifle as his head and face peeked overtop. Too far away to see the muzzle of Josey's rifle barely extending beyond the pile of dirt and logs at the edge of the camp, the man couldn't be sure where exactly to aim. Josey already had his shot lined up. He pulled the trigger.

One down.

His shot drew fire from the other two men advancing toward him, but Josey's single shot wasn't enough to give them a good gauge on where to aim. Armed with repeating rifles, they maintained a steady rate of fire, but they were shooting blindly while Josey sought a new target.

A heavyset man in a black derby hat with a brightly colored feather in the band took shelter behind a thick growth of mountain mahogany. Other than the top of his hat, he was nearly invisible behind its wild, silvery plumes, but Josey doubted the thin branches offered much protection against a bullet. He watched for the smoke from the man's rifle to judge his position. Waited. Waited. Saw it.

Josey fired twice.

The derby hat disappeared, and he heard the man's yell from across the distance. No more smoke came from behind the mountain mahogany. By the time Josey looked for the third man, he saw only his back as he raced away, already beyond Josey's effective range.

Backing out of his rifle pit, Josey slithered over to the unprotected side of the camp, trying to keep lower than a snake. The cover for the attackers was better here, but a few well-placed shots proved enough to deter the two men who were approaching from this side.

Josey rolled onto his back and stared into the sky. The sun still hung low over the horizon, yet with few clouds he had to squint against the brightness. A trio of buzzards already smelling death circled in a tight spiral. He wondered if Crazy Horse or John Hutchins had added to their bounty. He wiped his face with his kerchief, knowing it would be smeared from a mixture of sweat and black powder. Feeling as tight as a telegraph wire, he closed his eyes and breathed. The sound of steady gunfire from the back of the campsite prevented any respite and drew him on.

He crawled in that direction, seeing John Hutchins popping up like a prairie dog to fire his carbine from two spots along their makeshift wall. With all that movement, he was drawing heavy return fire.

"Hutchins, stay down!" Even shouting, Josey wasn't sure he'd been heard over the sound of the rifle shots. He scooted forward as fast as he could on his belly, careful not to lose his hat — or his head — to the flying bullets.

The translator sensed his approach and looked back. "I got one!" A look of triumph brightened his powder-stained face.

"Get down!" Josey waved his hand in a sharp downward swipe to illustrate his warning over the noise.

He was too late.

The bullet must have caught Hutchins in the neck. He dropped his rifle. A hand went to the wound like smacking at a mosquito. He slumped to his knees and then fell to his back. Josey rushed toward him, firing his rifle as fast as he could to suppress the attack, and fell in beside Hutchins. His side was covered with blood, bright red and frothy. His face looked as pale as a full-blooded white man.

"I got one," he said again, his voice a

hoarse whisper. "Did you see?"

"Stop talking." Josey pressed the other man's hand flat against the pulsing wound. He tugged free his neckerchief and applied it to the source of the bleeding, feeling for the bullet hole so that he might stuff the fabric into it. He risked a glance up; a blue-coated gunman had stepped out from the cover of a boulder twenty yards away to advance on them. Josey drew his pistol and fired twice, intent more on driving the man back than hitting anything.

Crazy Horse appeared on the other side of Hutchins. On seeing the wound, his grimace slipped into a blankness that Josey interpreted as sorrow. He realized as much as Josey that they could provide little more than small comfort to Hutchins, and that they'd all be dead if they allowed their attention to be diverted for long from their attackers. Crazy Horse looked away and fired his rifle in the direction of the man behind the boulder. Before he could reload, Josey tossed him a fully loaded revolver. "Hold them back while I reload," he said, trusting the Indian would know what to do even if he didn't comprehend the words.

A handgun at that range wasn't much of a threat, and the man saw an opportunity to break for cover closer to the campsite. Josey was ready by then. His first shot caught the man in the thigh. He went down in an awkward tumble, landing on his shoulder and lying immobile a moment, enough time for Josey to lock in his aim.

The man looked up. A full head of red hair revealed the Scotsman's identity even before Josey recognized the scar that puckered the length of his face. He felt he could read the man's mind in the moment: *move forward or go back?* Or maybe he just wanted to face the death he knew was coming. When they believe it is inevitable, some men welcome death, like an escape from a lifetime of weariness and suffering.

Josey released him.

He knew without seeing what a rimfire .44 cartridge could do, for his Winchester had been chambered to fire the same ammunition as his old Henry. The conical-shaped bullet was more accurate than the old balls fired from smoothbore muskets, and this one entered at a spot just above the bridge of the Scot's nose. But that was not its most devastating effect. While the solid balls fired from rifles a generation earlier could pass through a body almost intact, the newer, tapered bullets flattened on impact, shattering bones and shredding tissue. The star-shaped, almost delicate-looking wound that punctured the man's forehead would be matched with a vicious tearing at the back of the head, spraying blood and brain matter onto the ground behind him.

The sight of it was enough to convince the rest of the Scot's comrades to withdraw.

Josey lay watching, waiting to be certain the men weren't rallying for another charge. His limbs felt leaden, and it took great effort to move even once his breathing evened. By the time he returned to John Hutchins, the translator was dead. His sightless eyes stared up as if watching for the buzzards' approach. A cloud of black flies had gathered where the sticky blood stained the side of his shirt. Josey closed the man's eyes. He retrieved a blanket from the nearest rifle pit and used it to wave away the flies before covering him. They'd killed at least four of the mercenaries who attacked them, but it felt a poor exchange for the life of one good man.

The rest of the morning passed more slowly than any Josey could recall. From the camp, there was no way to tell if their attackers had abandoned their mission or were simply waiting them out, and Josey didn't relish the idea of riding across open land to find out. The smart move would be to wait them out, allow the intervening hours to wear down the defenders, hope they might do something stupid. Josey fixed a blanket over one of the rifle pits to create shade and lay down. He noticed Crazy Horse watching him, impassive as ever. He said, "Wake me if anything interesting happens."

The Indian offered no response before going off to position himself on the opposite side of the camp. Despite his grief and weariness, Josey recognized the irony: He had come here, half expecting to be murdered by this Indian, who now represented his best hope of surviving until the next day. He almost missed the Indian's company as the hours dragged on.

Josey tried to doze, but worries preyed on his idle mind. If their attackers returned, he doubted two men would be enough to stop them — but they'd cut down a few first, and Josey had already killed the man who'd spoken for them. These were hired guns. Eliminating their leader and so many of their comrades might have convinced those who remained to cut their losses and flee. Nothing a man could get paid would be worth losing his life over. The more time that passed, and the more Josey thought about it, the more convinced he became that they were gone. If he waited until dusk, he might sneak to the tree line without being seen to figure out if he was right.

In the meantime, he had other things to occupy his mind. On recognizing the betrayal, his first thought had been that powerful interests wanted to eliminate any threat from Crazy Horse, and he had been duped into aiding their cause. Grantham was an obvious suspect. He had the most to gain from the treaty's success, and John Hutchins said it was he who had provided the intelligence that Crazy Horse was leading the raids — an accusation that Crazy Horse denied. Yet the threat of Crazy Horse's raids seemed an inadequate motivation for all this trouble, and it didn't explain why Martinez's henchman would lead the ambush. Grantham had seemed to know a lot about Martinez and the doctor he worked for, but Josey didn't understand the connection. All he knew was that there had to be one — the dead Scotsman was proof of that. And if Grantham and Martinez were somehow allied, and neither one was here, that meant they were still at the fort . . . doing what, exactly?

Josey jolted up, too uneasy at the new thought to wait out his attackers. He looked back toward the tree line — still no activity

— then hurried off to the cover where they'd picketed the horses. He was saddling Gray when Crazy Horse approached. Josey slipped the bridle over Gray's head. "I'm going to ride hard to the north. If anyone shoots at me, we'll know they're still there. If not, I'll circle back into the trees and make certain they're gone."

He nudged the bit into Gray's mouth and looked to see if Crazy Horse understood. The Indian had already slipped a thick blanket onto his pony's back. He stopped when he felt Josey's eyes on him. "I will ride south," he said.

Josey's mouth dropped open. He'd heard the words without seeing the Indian's lips move and wondered for a moment if he'd imagined the response. Crazy Horse's face was set as stone. Recalling how the Indian had understood the word for doctor yesterday, Josey smiled. At the time he'd thought it might have been an exception, the way he had recognized the Indian words for head and ghost without understanding their meaning. "You've been having fun, but your game is up now that I know you understand me."

He swung up on Gray and waited for Crazy Horse to mount his ride. "If they're gone, we'll meet back here. We'll bury John

Hutchins together."

"I will take him to the village. To his mother. The people will build a scaffold to make it easier for his spirit to reach the sky."

Josey nodded, liking the idea of Hutchins being reunited with his people, even if it was in death.

Crazy Horse continued: "Then I will follow you to the fort."

"You don't have to do that. These men were here to kill you. You will be safer at the village."

"I will seek this doctor you speak of," Crazy Horse said. "And there is a small tribe staying near the fort. I fear for their safety."

Josey looked back to the tree line, trying to gauge where the men might be and lessen the risk of their getting a clean shot at him. "What do you want to do if they're still out there?"

Crazy Horse stooped to pick up his war club and with his free hand drew out the long Bowie knife that had been tucked in his belt. "I will kill any I find," he said. "Those who are in our way will die."

Crazy Horse leaped onto the back of his gelding. The pony pranced sideways but under control, its nostrils flared, as eager for the fight as his master.

CHAPTER THIRTY-TWO

Martinez heard the gunshot sooner than he'd expected. *Dinner over already?* Edward usually took his time. The boy had a need to explain his intentions to his victims, as if he expected them to embrace their fate once they comprehended the importance of their role. That he was always disappointed didn't stop him from seeking a kindred spirit in the world. Martinez attributed their failure to understand to a lack of intellect; that he didn't understand it any better did not matter.

He hurried to finish tying off the spare canvas sheet he'd been preparing. He would wrap the woman's body in the canvas in case there was much blood. Her dark-haired beauty reminded him of Clara when she'd been that age, so he preferred not to make a mess of things. She was lighter than the fat diplomat, so it would be a simple matter to carry her body to the spot by Little Piney

Creek he'd picked out. It was far enough from both the camp and the fort that he would not be seen. His saw would make quick work of her delicate neck. He had an old blanket for the head. Edward would decide the best method for cleaning the flesh from it. After rewrapping the body in the canvas, Martinez would bury her in the hole he'd dug earlier. He'd have to do the work himself because McDougal and the rest of the men he'd sent after the Indian weren't back yet. He had a bad feeling about that, but he tried not to dwell on it. He still had enough men to finish the job tomorrow, and he had a long night ahead of him.

Tucking the wrapped sheet under an arm, he paused at the edge of his cot and withdrew from beneath the threadbare pillow a silk scarf of the sort gentlemen wore to dinner on a cool night. Unwinding the scarf revealed a palm-sized frame. It was round with a carved bow on the top in matching gilt brass. The image was a dark-haired woman who stared unsmiling at the camera, her fair skin almost ghost-like in the daguerreotype. His breath quickened, and his chest constricted with an old sorrow even as the image recalled the happiest days he'd known. He rewrapped this most precious possession in the scarf and returned it to its place beneath the pillow.

His tent faced the rear flap of Edward's so that no one else could go in that way without his knowing it. He had to duck his head to enter, being quiet about it in case the shot he'd heard was just a warning and Edward was still at his game. In the darkness at the rear of the tent, his nose wrinkled at the smell of moldy canvas and Edward's chemicals. He didn't trust the noxious liquids. Edward's hero Morton had used mercury to calculate the volume of his skulls, and it had nearly driven him mad. In a concession to Martinez's warnings, Edward used buckshot for his measurements. Yet whenever Martinez pressed him on his use of chemicals, Edward laughed him off like an old grandmother. "I'll be dead before I go mad," he said with a fatalism that always cut through Martinez. He blamed himself for the boy's illness; God's punishment for his sins.

The tent was still. Too still. A canvas curtain divided the large space into a bedroom and a workplace that Edward converted to a dining area when he wished to entertain. Dingley, the boy who served Edward's meals, knew from experience to return to the kitchen tent as soon as dinner was over and keep his distance until Martinez called on him to clean up. The gunshot meant the woman was dead, or dying. Why could he not hear Edward? Driven by the strange silence, Martinez advanced toward the curtain with quiet footfalls. He peeled back the canvas with a premonition of dread he could not explain.

After the darkness of the back room, he squinted against the warm lamplight. Edward liked the room bright even when he wasn't reading. The table was still set: plates of unfinished duck, wine still in the glasses, and Edward, seated alone at the table, slumped in his chair, his head drooped painfully to his left, as if he had fallen asleep and would wake with a crick. No sign of the woman. Martinez took a silent step forward, reaching out to gently rouse Edward, the movement giving him a clearer view of the table and the doctor's extended left arm, the arm held in place by his hand, the hand held in place by —

"Edward!"

Martinez rushed to his side, prying loose the knife from Edward's hand with a powerful jerk, freeing the boy to slump against his chest in a cold embrace.

"Edward!"

He leaned Edward back in his chair, taking his delicate face, so much like his mother's, into his large hands, frantically searching the doctor's pale eyes for some sign of recognition but finding nothing. He shook him by the shoulders, understanding coming slow against a parapet of disbelief until the boy's head lolled to the side.

"My boy, my boy," he managed through streaming tears. He could not remember when, if ever, he had cried. Not even when Clara sent him away did he cry. At least then he still had the boy. Their boy. He still had his son, even if Edward would never know. He clutched the frail form tighter to his chest, finding outsized hope in the shallow breaths the boy still drew, taking refuge a little longer in disbelief, unprepared to contemplate what he would tell Clara.

"I promised your mother I would never tell you, that I would protect you with my life. Now you must know. I am your father. I loved your mother. She was the only woman I ever loved. And I loved you. Hamilton employed me, and he gave you his name, but it was always you I served, my son, my brilliant, beautiful boy."

He pulled Edward to his chest, wrapping him in his thick arms. "You will be fine now. I will get you help, and we'll make you strong again, my son."

He swept him into his arms and stood, the weight nothing to arms and shoulders strengthened by fear.

"Eduardo?" T'was barely a whisper.

"Yes, that's right. You were named for me. Your mother couldn't let me hold you, but she honored me in her choice of a Christian name."

"No . . ." The word escaped the boy's colorless lips like a gasp.

"I am sorry. I have hurt you. I will be more careful." His mind whirled through options. Edward, of course, was the man who saw to any serious injuries in the camp. "I will take you to Silva. He helped treat wounds in the war."

He strode past the table to the tent flap and stopped. He would need Edward's medical bag. He pivoted, Edward's legs swinging out in a circle, seeming weightless in his panic. Maybe it would be best to bring Silva here. Treat Edward in the well-lit room with his medicines and instruments nearby. But he found now that he held his boy, he couldn't let him go. He cursed his indecisiveness. Time was running out.

"No . . ." Another gasp of pain.

"You will be all right. You will see." His eyes rummaged through the corners and across the surfaces of every shelf and table seeking the medical bag. He kept talking, hoping the sound of his voice might serve like a rope cast to his drowning son. "Hold on, my sweet boy. Hold on."

In his fantasies about telling Edward the truth, Martinez had been on his own death-bed, Clara had spoken the words, and the news had been a revelation to Edward, who finally understood that it was he, Eduardo Martinez, who had always loved him, who had protected him, who had endeavored to see his dreams realized. In these imagin-ings, Edward cried tears of gratitude and cursed the heavens that he would not have more time with his father now that he knew the truth, and Martinez died happy for knowing that, in the end, his love had been returned.

With Edward cradled like the baby he'd never been permitted to hold, Martinez kicked his way through the canvas that divided the rooms, stomping on the fabric where it gathered loose near the ground until his weight tore it free and allowed the lamp to light his way.

"Your mother and I . . . we loved each other, but we could not be together. She swore me never to tell anyone, not even you. I would have gone to my grave without tell-ing you, hoping that perhaps she might tell you after I was gone. But now I must tell you how proud I am. My son, a doctor. A man of science. I never understood all that moved you, but I made certain you had whatever you needed. The man who called you his son gave you money, but I gave you love."

"No . . ." The next breath came with a rattle Martinez recognized.

For months now, he'd understood he would never realize his dream of a deathbed reconciliation, that Edward would go first. He had consoled himself with new fantasies. That on helping Edward complete his work, he would take him home to his mother. The deathbed scene played out the same, only with the roles reversed. Edward, grateful to see his life's work completed, would understand all that his true father had sacrificed to see it done. In Martinez's vision, he heard his son's final words: "I always wished that you had been my father."

Finding the medical bag beside Edward's cot, Martinez balanced Edward against his shoulder and stooped to retrieve it. It was a leather valise with handles stitched into the sides. He looped them over his wrist and turned to the exit. He had to find Silva quickly.

With another gasp, the loudest yet, Edward spoke again. "You . . . are not my father."

"It is true. You are small, like your mother, and you have her color, thank God. But you are my son, and I have loved you."

"No . . ."

"Hold on, my child. I will find Silva. He will help you get strong."

Martinez hurried past the table, cursing the woman for spoiling everything. She would suffer for this. She and all her people would pay for what she had done. He pulled Edward against him to free a hand so he could open the tent flap, and his son thrashed against him.

"No . . ."

"Be still, my son."

It was no use. With surprising strength, Edward shook and kicked so that Martinez had to go to the ground to better secure him. "You must be still, Edward. I have to get you to Silva, who can save you."

"You not . . . my father."

Shutting his eyes as if to close his ears to his son's words, Martinez said, "You do not understand, my sweet child. We have the same blood. We —"

"I . . . not . . ." The last word escaped his lips in a final release of breath. ". . . inferior."

Martinez pulled his son to his breast to

still Edward's thrashing and silence him. He shushed him with a breathless whisper, like calming a baby. Tightening his grip, he rocked on his haunches to soothe the boy. "You don't understand, my son. Once you are well, I will take you to your mother. She will explain things. We will live like a family, and, once you are strong, we will go to Washington, where you can present your work. You will see. We will be happy, and you will love me as your father."

All movement by the boy had stopped, and Martinez released his breath in a long, deflating sigh. His arms were sore from having held Edward so tightly. He relaxed his grip and gazed into his son's face. His pale eyes, so much like Clara's, stared back at him, yet he saw no love there, no hatred, either. He saw nothing.

"Edward?" He shook the weight in his arms, gently at first, his spasms intensifying with his frustration until the head snapped forward and back with such violence the bones of the neck crunched.

Martinez screamed, an inhuman howl that would soon draw to him the bravest of his men, who feared a wolf had made its way into camp. By the time they arrived, armed and ready to kill, Martinez knew what must be done. He would gather the rest of Edward's samples. He would take them to Washington himself. And he would avenge his son's death on the woman who had robbed him of his dream.

CHAPTER THIRTY-THREE

"I killed the doctor."

Annabelle's confession made no sense to Grieve as he attempted to put his clothes on while Maria comforted the woman. How could she have killed Dr. Hamilton? Granted, he was a weak man, near death, perhaps, and not too long ago she had pointed a rifle at Grieve. But that had been different. He had threatened her husband, and he still wasn't certain she would have followed through with her threat.

"He meant to kill me. I didn't have a choice."

Recalling the cold gaze of the doctor's pale eyes, Grieve's shock abated, though he still wondered how she'd managed it without dying at Martinez's hands. Thoughts of the big Mexican prompted Grieve to hurry. Annabelle had said nothing about killing Martinez, and that meant he would be coming for her — and no one around her would be safe from that monster's fury.

He had no idea of the time, though he guessed the hour wasn't as late as it felt. His lovemaking with Maria probably hadn't lasted as long as he imagined; as he recalled, it never did. As he lay with her afterwards, he pretended to sleep so that she wouldn't ask him questions he couldn't answer.

He hadn't intended to seduce Maria. He'd been speaking of Chelsea just before, yet she'd listened so intently, that heart-shaped face turned up to his with as much interest as if he spoke of her. Then she'd lifted the blanket, offering her slender body to him, and in that moment he wanted her more than anything. In the madness of his lust, he would have sworn off his need for vengeance against Josey Angel if she'd demanded it; he would have denied his love for Chelsea if she'd challenged him; he'd have made any vow she required so that he could have her. And it would have been worth it in those minutes that followed.

Then it ended, and that single-minded focus had splintered into a thousand conflicting thoughts. He held great affection for Maria; he would wish to lie with her again, if she would have him. Yet he also felt the heavy weight of guilt, like an ox collar around his neck. Chelsea was dead; lying with Maria represented no betrayal of her. And yet he felt it in his heart, among so many other things. He had spoken no words of love to Maria, nor she to him, but did his assent imply a promise of something more? Would she expect now that they would be wed? The idea was by no means distasteful to him. She was a beautiful woman, and he found comfort in her companionship. He adored her children. Good marriages had been built on less. He simply hadn't given the matter much thought while he had been seeking out Josey Angel.

That name raised another question he couldn't answer. Maria wanted him to set aside his quest for vengeance. He couldn't even be certain the man had killed his son and father, and meeting his family had shown Grieve the evil in his pursuit. Killing Josey Angel would be nothing short of murder. Yet he could not imagine himself settling in as neighbors, like Maria wanted, waving howdy-do with the man who may have killed his boy should they pass on the streets of Virginia City. Every sight of Josey Angel would only remind him of Luke's absence. Killing Josey Angel might be murder, but living near him was an invitation to madness.

Given his dread of being asked to discuss

a future so tangled in his mind, Annabelle's interruption had been almost welcome. The moment of her arrival at their campsite had played out like a stage farce. Grieve had left the blanket to Maria while he retreated, still unclothed, from the faint light cast by the dying fire. Maria had somehow managed to dress herself beneath the cover, all the while assuring Annabelle that her arrival had not disturbed them. The obviousness of the lie had been alleviated only by Annabelle's preoccupied mien. If she had noticed anything awry, her manners and breeding prevented her from commenting on it.

Her story had soon enough doused any comedy from the scene. When she reached the point that the doctor revealed his intentions to slaughter the Indian women and children camping in the wood yards, Maria objected.

"You must have misunderstood him. It doesn't make any sense that the doctor would be killing people."

Grieve, fully dressed now, returned to the fire ring, adding a log and a few broken sticks to revive the flames. "The doctor's men are killers, Maria. I'm almost certain of it," he said. "Those settlers we found murdered by Fort Laramie — the Indians didn't do that. I think it was the Mexican."

"Why would you think that?"

"His men talk — they feel like I'm one of them by now — and I hear things, especially after they've been drinking."

"What did they say?"

"Enough for me to suspect what was happening. I didn't want to believe it." He nodded toward Annabelle, for it felt awkward speaking her name so soon after she'd held a gun on him. "What she's said confirms my fears. I don't know what hold the doctor has over the Mexican, but the man will do anything for him."

"But he's a man of medicine. He values life."

"He's a dying man. Life holds no value to him beyond his work, and he's losing patience. He'll do anything to complete it."

Maria absorbed this. Her delicate features, scrunched with doubt only moments before, relaxed into acceptance as his words took root in some conclusion she'd already reached about the man's character. She went to Annabelle. "I didn't mean to doubt you, it's just —"

"I know," Annabelle said. "I was slow to see the evil in him as well. It nearly cost me my life."

The women embraced.

"Are you certain he's dead?" Grieve asked.

Annabelle tilted her head to one side as if seeking to retrieve a memory from the same angle she'd perceived it in life. "I didn't linger to check. I feared Mr. Martinez might arrive before I could escape. But if he wasn't already dead, he won't survive his wound." The certainty of her tone reminded Grieve that this was a woman with firsthand experience.

"That is good," Maria said with a curt nod. "With the doctor's death, his men will have no reason to carry out the murder of the Indians, and you have nothing to fear."

"No. Mr. Martinez will come for me. He may come for all of us. That is why I am here: to warn you. I do not trust how he will react."

Grieve agreed. "You are not safe, and I have no intention of waiting around to see who else he decides to kill." His mind turned to logistics, and he thought of the black man and Indian woman. "Have you warned your companions?"

"Not yet. I came here first."

"Go to them now." Grieve found he could almost set aside thoughts of Josey Angel by thinking of him only as the husband of the woman before him who needed his aid. "We will pack our wagon and meet you at the fort. If you can be ready, we'll set out before morning. With luck, we will come across your husband on the way."

After loading the wagon and yoking the oxen, Grieve led them in a wide circle outside the entrance to the fort so that the wagon pointed north, toward Montana. A three-quarters moon hung like a lamplight behind him, throwing long shadows from the fort's stockade like outstretched arms also seeking escape from this place. The hour was nearing midnight, and the day's heat had been stripped from the valley like a quilt from a bed. He didn't notice the chill so long as he kept moving, but he was glad Maria had taken the time to dress the children in their coats. He helped them down from the wagon, and it crossed his mind that there was a better way — at least for him, Maria, and the children. They could never hope to outrun Martinez and his killers in wagons. Their best chance was if the big Mexican never thought to come after them. And the only way that would happen was if Martinez found what he sought here at the fort.

Grieve dared not speak the thought to Maria, convinced it would diminish him in her eyes. With Astrid in her arms and Danny trailing behind, she had already set off to find Annabelle and the others. Maria would never agree to abandon them unless she believed it was the only way to save her children. After setting the wagon's brake beam and blocks, Grieve followed, wondering if it might yet come to that. Before he walked through the fort's gates, he stole a glance back in the direction of the doctor's camp, dreading what he might see before turning away to help Maria.

They found Annabelle with her wagon outside the cavalry stables a short walk from the main gate. The wagon sat heavy in the dusty cart path that led from the stables to the gate. The mules were already hitched. Annabelle stood beside them. Dressed in trousers, a loose-fitting shirt with vest, and a wide-brimmed man's hat, he wouldn't have recognized her if he hadn't expected to find her. She held her sleeping child to her shoulder like a sack of flour, rocking side to side in a motion that looked unconscious. The big-eyed Indian girls stood by her like hand maidens while the boys hung back.

"Where's your Negro?" Grieve would feel better having another man around, even though the big black had struck him when he faced Josey Angel.

"Lord Byron and Red Shawl went to warn

the Indians in case the doctor's men still come for them."

Grieve's head swiveled in a vain search for the pair. "I'm not sure we have time for that."

"We must make time for saving lives," Annabelle said.

"Martinez won't need much time for taking them." He felt the passing time like dirt piling upon his grave, each second adding the weight of another shovelful.

The set of Annabelle's jaw reminded him of Chelsea in the moments he knew he had lost an argument. She said, "Then we will find another way."

He considered arguing the point, but Annabelle was ahead of him. After a brief discussion between the women, she urged them to go on ahead, making the same arguments Grieve had entertained. Maria objected until Annabelle reassured her that, given the slower pace of the oxen, her mule-drawn wagon would catch up with them on the road after Lord Byron and his squaw returned. Eager to be gone, Grieve added his assent. His breath had turned shallow at the press of passing time. He picked up Astrid so that they might return to the wagon faster. Danny trotted beside him while Maria quick-stepped to keep up.

On reaching the gates, he saw the wagon just as he'd left it. Even though he'd set the brake beam, until he actually saw the wagon he'd dreaded that somehow the beam had slipped from place and the oxen had wandered off. He drew a deep, shuddering breath, the cold air sharp against his throat.

Then he stopped.

To his right, just emerging from the shadow and gloom, he saw riders. Four, six, at least eight. The horses advanced at an unhurried pace, their shape indistinct yet unmistakable. The rider at the center of their midst loomed a full head taller than the rest, leaving no doubt about their identity. Maria had seen them too. She stopped and looked at Grieve, eyes wide and mouth open as if to speak, though no words emerged.

Grieve turned back to the fort. "I sure hope your friend has found that other way."

CHAPTER THIRTY-FOUR

Josey rode as hard as he dared, desperate to reach the fort as soon as possible. Along with Crazy Horse, he had charged out from the camp that afternoon, flinching with every stride in anticipation of gunfire that never came. By the time he veered off into the cover of the trees and circled back, it was obvious the attackers had abandoned their mission. Josey had cursed himself for not riding out earlier, his imagination running wild with thoughts of what disaster might await him.

Once they had cleared out the camp and descended from the mesa, Crazy Horse had set off to the Indian village with John Hutchins's body, vowing to meet Josey at the fort. "I will not come alone," he had said.

Josey stopped only once while he still had light, at a stream crossing where the cold, clear water snaked between high, curving bluffs striped with layers of different rocks. Trees grew from the edge of the ridge and out from the side of the bluff to cast shadows along the water's edge. While Gray drank, he filled his canteens and thought about what he might find at the fort.

It could be that nothing was amiss, though every instinct warned him something had to be behind the attack beyond a desire to kill Crazy Horse. Grieve might bear some responsibility; he had wanted Josey dead and had been traveling with the doctor and his men. Yet a face-to-face confrontation seemed more the gunman's style. Grantham and Martinez were more likely suspects; the diplomat had played him from the start, and one of Martinez's men had led the attack at the mesa. Something connected these men, but Josey struggled to identify a motive that explained Grantham's role, and, if Martinez wanted him dead, he would have seen to the task himself. The uncertainty roused Josey from his rest.

Riding up from the stream, he crested the ridge. The hills that stretched out ahead were a blurred blue line on the horizon that mocked him for every moment he'd tarried at the mesa. He pushed on the rest of the day and into the night, testing Gray's limits. It was past midnight by the time he reached

Lodge Trail Ridge. In the dim light of the gibbous moon, the fort appeared below him in the Piney Creek valley like a child's toy, and just as lifeless. The soldiers must have left, he realized. Would he still find Annabelle and the others there?

As he studied the tableau, bright orange flames shot into the night sky from the northwest corner of the fort. The fire flashed in a lively dance that originated near the bakery, not far from the barracks where his family and friends were ensconced. His alarm increased with the fire's spread, but it also heightened his sense of caution. Even as he hurried down the ridge, he decided against riding directly through the main gates. He tied Gray to an ox-drawn wagon he found on the road leading to the fort, another mystery to add to his growing list of questions.

After ensuring no one stood sentry at the gates, he stole into the fort on foot, carrying his rifle in a scabbard over his shoulder. He figured by now anyone inside would have been drawn to the flames, which soared into the dark sky. Distant shouts from men seeking to contain the fire proved the fort wasn't deserted. The smell of wood smoke enveloped him, and he struggled to suppress a cough that might alert others to his presence as he made his way in that direction in case Annabelle was still there. He slipped between the guardhouse and the high stockade and paused. A man skulked among the shadows cast by the cavalry stables and laundry building to his left. From the man's awkward gait, Josey guessed his hands were full. Drawing one of his revolvers, Josey followed.

He moved as quickly as he could manage across the open ground between buildings. The weight of guns and his need to stay quiet made for an awkward gait. He paused on recognizing the wagon and mules they'd brought from Angel Falls. Annabelle had been clever in leaving them out of view from the front gates, but Josey still had no answer to where she had gone. He continued to follow the furtive figure, who moved south along cover provided by the empty cavalry stables. The man appeared so preoccupied that Josey hardly worried that he'd be spotted as he pursued him to the southern side of the fort where the non-commissioned staff had been quartered.

The tall silhouette stopped outside a barracks building. Moonlight reflecting off glass globes and fonts revealed he'd been carrying oil lamps. He set them on the ground and removed the globe from one so he could light it with a match. Once he'd coaxed a flame, he covered the wick with the glass chimney and stood. He swung the lamp in a wide arc, releasing it high overhead so that it flew up and disappeared overtop of the barracks. Josey flinched at the crash of shattering glass, and the man stepped back to observe his handiwork. Josey smelled the kerosene before he saw the flames, but soon enough the roof began to glow.

Josey recognized Grieve's lean features in the light. He stepped forward, his gun still drawn. "I suppose you have a reason for what you're doing. What I want to know is are we allies or foes?"

Grieve whirled at the sound, his hand reflexively reaching toward the heavy Colt '60 at his waist but stopping once he recognized Josey. He said, "I'm not sure."

"At least you're honest." Josey closed the distance between them. In the fire's glow, Josey saw sagging features and slumped shoulders that spoke of a man overtaken more by fatigue and sorrow than anger.

"My boy and pa are dead. Someone should pay for that."

"You don't know I killed them. I don't even know." Recalling how many times he'd fired his rifle that day in Georgia, Josey added, "I suppose it doesn't matter."

How many deaths could one man carry on his conscience before the weight of them dragged him down? Annabelle had sought to distance him from his murderous past, and he'd told her that's what he wanted, even as a secret part of him resisted. During the fight on the mesa, he'd recognized again how he never felt more alive than when death hovered over him like a circle of buzzards. In war, he'd told himself the invigoration of these moments helped keep him alive. Yet, even in times of peace, he felt their pull the way some men feel the need for tobacco or coffee. He didn't know how to quit their thrill any more than the army knew how to put an end to pointless wars. He'd never told Annabelle this, fearing she would see him as monstrous. She and Byron had tried to tell him it was his choice whether to live as a man of peace or a man of war, but the world wasn't as simple as that.

Sometimes the war came to him — and sometimes he *wanted* to answer its call.

His hands would never grip a lariat as naturally as a repeating rifle, but Josey told himself he could learn to use the weapon only when it was justified. If he could resist the allure of an unprovoked fight, he might even find forgiveness for the times he'd failed to live by that principle. Preachers said God forgives all sins. Could Josey forgive himself?

Josey holstered his gun.

"You shouldn't do that." Grieve's right hand hovered at his waist, and his eyes locked onto Josey. "You might be a better aim, but I expect I'm faster on the draw." From the way his fingers twitched, he looked eager to discover if he was right.

"You're not going to shoot me." Josey had felt certain of it when he'd holstered his gun; now he wasn't so sure. "You'll kill to protect those you love, but that doesn't make you a murderer."

"I don't know that." Grieve squeezed his eyes closed a moment, maybe hoping to change what he saw — or alter his thoughts. "He was just a boy. He'd never even killed a rabbit."

"I shot them that shot at me. That's how it was. You know that."

"I never shot a boy."

"Then no boy ever shot at you." Josey's voice rose, and he clenched his fists to prevent himself from reaching for his pistols.

The black powder smoke had been so thick that day at Griswoldville, Josey never saw the faces of the soldiers he shot at. It wasn't until the next morning, after the Confederates had withdrawn in the night, that he walked across the open field to the ravine where the militia had taken cover from the canister shelling, and he saw how many of the dead were too young even to grow a fuzz of whiskers on their lips. The sight might have made him ill earlier in the war, but by then nothing touched him. At least he thought so at the time. Only later did he begin seeing the boys' faces in his sleep.

Josey felt the anger leach from his body. Now he was the one who stood slumped by sorrow. "I never expected to outlive the war," he said. "I thought God had a role for me, and, when it was done, He would take me. After the war, there were times I wanted to die."

"You don't feel that way anymore?"

Something in Grieve's voice made clear Josey didn't have to explain wanting to die. "I found a reason to live." He pictured Annabelle holding Isabelle. "Then I found another." He raised his arms wide, exposing himself to the armed man before him. "Now I'm surrounded by them."

Though his hand still hovered by his waist, Grieve made no move to his gun.

"My only reason to live has been to kill you."

"I know," Josey said. "But I told Maria I don't think that's true any longer."

Shoulders sagging, Grieve looked diminished somehow. Josey thought of logs in a fire, how the heat hollows them out before they collapse onto themselves. He asked, "Where's Maria?"

Eyes that had been staring at Josey with the intensity of a raptor now couldn't meet his. "She's with Annabelle and the children. Your black friend and his woman went to warn the Indians. Annabelle killed the doctor. Now the Mexican means to kill her and anyone else he can find."

Killed the doctor? "He must have had it coming."

"He did. After, she took the children to hide in the powder magazine."

"Good place for it," Josey said, though he winced at a memory. Women and children had been sent there once before with thoughts they might die. "Come with me. Let's get them away from here."

"You go," Grieve said, his boot drawing Josey's attention to the remaining oil lamp. "I'll finish stirring up some more trouble and meet you."

They stood a moment looking at each

other. The growing fire had cast a warm glow over their half of the cavalry yard. Someone would be coming soon. Josey turned to leave, confident enough the man didn't mean to shoot him in the back, though he still couldn't say how their next meeting might end. As big as the world is, he wasn't certain it was big enough for them both.

CHAPTER THIRTY-FIVE

After parting ways with Josey Angel, Grieve took his remaining oil lamp and crossed to the far side of the fort.

Twice now he'd faced the man, and both times he'd felt unprepared to take the action that had been his focus for months. Did that make him a coward? Or was it like Josey Angel had said — he wasn't cut out to be a murderer? He had no time to think of that now. Seeing Martinez and his men approaching the fort had spurred Grieve into action. He'd hatched a plan with Annabelle: while she led the others to a hiding spot in the powder magazine, he would create a distraction. He'd taken the oil lamps from the packed gear in the back of the wagon, figuring he could use them to set fires that would draw away Martinez's men long enough for him to retrieve the women and children and slip out of the fort unnoticed.

He had lit the first of Maria's three lamps and tossed it onto the bakery's roof, where the glass font had shattered and spread burning oil across the surface. The wood-frame building, dried out from summer heat and wind, had been engulfed within minutes. A breeze out of the west had carried burning embers onto the roof of the company band's headquarters. He'd known it wouldn't be long before that building went up in flames that might then spread to the sutler's store and guardhouse. He'd torn himself away and disappeared into the darkness before the first of the doctor's hired men arrived to check on the commotion.

That had been in the northwest quadrant of the fort. Next had come the barracks building in the southeast where Josey had found him. Now, moving in the shadow of the stockade wall, he stopped at the south-western corner of the fort before the chapel. He had told himself setting his third fire here, as far as possible from the gate, would spread confusion among Martinez's men and draw them away from his intended escape route. But it was also true that for a long time he'd had no use for God. Putting His building to the flame provided a special satisfaction.

Yet something stayed his hand now.

The last thing Maria had said before they'd parted was that she would pray for him. The words might have been reflexive, like wishing someone a good night on parting, but Grieve had not taken them that way. He stepped back from the chapel, curious how her faith had survived the death of her husband. He knew she had struggled in the days following Daniel's murder. She had questioned aloud if by going West they had exceeded the range of His vision and come to a godless place. He had assured her that God had abandoned him long before he'd come West. Yet she had said she would pray for him, and he was moved by more than her words. It was the way she'd looked at him in that moment, her eyes meeting and holding his. Earlier, he had wondered if their lovemaking would bind him in a commitment he didn't feel prepared for. Yet there had been nothing constraining about the love he saw in her eyes. Instead, he saw a meaning to which he felt wholly unworthy: in her eyes, God had allowed Daniel to be taken from her, and He had delivered Grieve in his place.

Grieve stood before the chapel, the lamp set at his feet, the match quivering in his hand. Abandoned and emptied of anything of value, was the chapel even a place of God any longer? Just an empty building, it was no different than the company quarters or bakery he had incinerated. Yet he knew better. He had thought himself hollowed of his faith, no longer one of God's creatures, yet his inability to murder Josey Angel and the love he felt for Maria and her children had proved that wrong.

He turned around. He lit the last lamp and threw it onto the adjacent barracks roof. A fire here would be just as effective at diverting Martinez's men as burning the chapel.

The dried-out wood went up as quickly as the other buildings had. He stood transfixed by the flames' frenetic dance. The crackling of the wood gave way to a whoosh, like a giant expelled breath, and the roof collapsed in a shuddering of sparks that flew high, tumbling on the air, orange and red mixed with black ash. It felt like staring at some vision of hell. The walls cratered, collapsing on themselves and almost smothering the fire under their weight until, moments later, new flames, even brighter than before, leaped into the night with renewed hunger.

As his face flushed from the heat, he recalled cold mornings when he'd lingered in the kitchen near the stove on Chelsea's baking days. The wistful sorrow of the memory gave way to something else, and he pondered whether Maria possessed any baking skills. There was still so much he didn't know about her, things he'd never bothered to ask but now found himself curious about.

The wind shifted, and the smoke from the burning building swallowed him. He coughed and turned away — and stopped. A figure loomed ahead, just beyond the fire's glow. He couldn't see the man's features, but there was no mistaking the hulking silhouette with the extra-wide brimmed hat.

Oversized spurs jangled when Martinez stepped into the light holding a heavy revolver that glinted gold in the reflected flames. He was dressed as ever, with his formal dark pants and vest over a crisp shirt. In the dim light, the skin he so carefully shielded from the sun appeared darker, and he more resembled a Mexican.

"When I realized what was happening, I figured you must be Josey Angel. I never expected to find you doing his bidding. Now I suppose I will have to settle for killing you."

Grieve drew and fired, the motion as fluid and natural as slipping an arm into his sleeve. All those months repeating the same movement until he could pull a pistol and shoot as quick as a blink had found their purpose in this moment. He had shot without thinking, just as he had the day he killed Stoddard. The explosion of the Colt sent a tremor through his arm to his shoulder, waking him to what he'd done. The Mexican doubled over, his face hidden beneath the brim of his hat. The big man slumped to his knees, a wet stain across his waist glistening in the light.

Grieve had imagined himself in this moment standing before Josey Angel, even before he knew what the man looked like, before he even knew if the man were real and not just some frontier myth. After shooting down the Stoddard brothers, he had felt certain pulling a gun on Josey Angel would be just as easy, for he'd felt no regret at killing the Stoddards, Lucas in particular. He'd sensed evil in the man's wolfish grin. Smelled it on him, too, if evil held a stink. He'd smelled the same evil on the Mexican, and he'd reacted as much to preserve his own life as to dispense this wickedness from the world. Maybe the reason he hadn't drawn on Josey Angel was that he hadn't sensed the same in him, only a coldness beyond anything he'd felt from another living thing.

Martinez's head hung down, chin almost

to his broad chest. He emitted a low, guttural sound that Grieve took for spasms of agony. Pity stirred in him, and he lowered his gun as he advanced toward the dying man. His chest swelled on his next breath. He would have been fast enough to gun down Josey Angel after all. No man could have bested him. Maybe knowing that was enough.

Standing over Martinez, he reflected on whether it would be more merciful to finish him quickly with a shot to the head. The gut shot would kill him, but the death would be slow and painful. Even a man who stank of evil deserved the mercy of a quick death, didn't he? Grieve had made up his mind when a subtle change in the rhythm of Martinez's breathing alerted him to his mistake. The Mexican wasn't moaning in pain; he was — *laughing*?

Martinez's head snapped up at the same moment he raised his gun and fired. The bullet struck Grieve like a hammer blow to the chest. The next moment he was on the ground, blinking as if roused from sleep, not recalling how he'd wound up on his back. His gun was still in his hand somehow; he holstered it without thinking. His chest felt afire, and he reached for the flames but felt a warm moistness instead. He closed his eyes, hoping that when he opened them he would be someplace else, but the Mexican's voice intruded on his dream.

"You were fast. Maybe the fastest I've ever seen."

Grieve tried to stand but found that he had no use of his left arm. He managed to roll over, bracing himself with his right hand so that he could get to his knees, crawling with his one good arm away from the voice that stalked him.

"You were fast, but you were stupid. Good men always are. You should have finished me when you had the chance."

The words echoed in Grieve's mind. He kept crawling, until his momentum allowed him to push off and regain his feet. He stumbled, nearly went down, fearing that if he lost his footing again he might never rise. He had to get to Maria. He pictured her heart-shaped face, the pert nose, cheeks that dimpled when she smiled, eyes that were too big for the rest of her features. He had tried to deny her beauty so that he might not covet what he could not have. The memory of her in his arms drove him forward, into the grassy field of the empty parade grounds. The flagpole loomed to his left. The powder magazine should lie just ahead. Is that where he would find her? He steadied himself against a busted caisson, confused by the unfamiliar surroundings. Had they reached Virginia City already? His memory failed him until the smell of smoke brought him back. *We are still at the fort. She is near!* He pushed off from the broken wooden chest, stumbling forward until he recognized the gentle rise of grass that covered the powder magazine. *Yes.* That is where she waited for him. If he could see her again, everything would be all right.

CHAPTER THIRTY-SIX

Annabelle knew of the powder magazine only because of a story Josey had told her about Colonel Henry Carrington, the commander who oversaw construction of Fort Phil Kearny. Carrington was a better administrator and engineer than a soldier. Though almost always short of ammunition, he buried the fort's magazine for storing munitions eight feet beneath the parade grounds to protect against an accidental discharge. A dirt ceiling covered the square storage room, leaving only a sloping grassy rise to mark its location.

On the day after Indians ambushed the eighty-one men he'd sent out to relieve a party of woodcutters under attack, Carrington conceived of a darker use for the magazine. While she and Maria led the children to the grassy square in the middle of the fort's grounds, Annabelle decided it best not to share the part of the story about the colonel's orders to blow up the place with women and children inside if Indians had overrun the fort. All that mattered now was her belief that Mr. Martinez and his men would be unlikely to look for them in the magazine — if they even knew of its existence. She could think of no safer place to hide while Byron and Red Shawl warned the Indians and Mr. Grieve distracted their enemies.

The magazine had been cleared out before the soldiers abandoned the fort. A bull's-eye lantern in hand, Annabelle led the way down a few bowed wooden stairs to the cellar-like door set beneath the slope. The door was unlocked but thick and heavy. She put her shoulder to it to force it open, the hinges creaking as they gave way. She had to crouch to pass through into a space that looked to have been built for dwarves. Dust glittered like a golden fog in the light of the lantern. She coughed as she reached into her pocket for a handkerchief and called back to the others, "Watch your heads."

Behind her came Maria, holding Isabelle tight to her breast. Danny helped Astrid negotiate the stairs. Chaska and Kicking Bull led Mina and Dewdrops. Only the younger children could stand upright in the space. Annabelle estimated the width of each wall at three times her height. The room was empty but for the ruins of a few wooden crates and some tools used to open them.

"Once we close the door, I hope the dust will settle," she said after the others joined her. Among them they had two lanterns and enough bedding materials, food, and water to make themselves comfortable while they waited. Annabelle brought her rifle, just in case.

"Once it's safe, we will find your father," she told the boys, who, for once, did not object to hearing Lord Byron referred to in that manner. Maria caught her eye, the unspoken question suspended between them with the dust motes, for neither knew when that might be. If Mr. Grieve's plan didn't work, Annabelle could only guess at how long it would take before they felt safe enough to flee.

Settling in among their blankets, they encouraged the children to sleep. In time each of them nodded off, no doubt worn out by the excitement of the night and the tension they sensed among the adults. Annabelle knew she would not be so fortunate. She laid her head beside Isabelle, listening to the child's little breaths, regular as the hoof falls of a trotting horse. Annabelle's mind moved even faster, alighting on new worries with each passing second until she'd exhausted the list and began anew. She'd had no time to plan their flight, and she was certain she'd forgotten something. More than just one thing, most likely. She questioned her decisions as well. Given a choice between secrecy and security, she'd picked the former; now she realized that, if she were wrong, no escape would be possible should anyone find them here.

She also worried about things she couldn't control. Would Byron and Red Shawl warn off the Indians before any harm came to them? If something happened to their wagons, would they have to take to the woods and hide? And what about Josey? Where was he?

She tried to quiet her mind by staring at the lamp in the farthest corner. It held the least amount of oil, and as she watched the lamp slowly burn itself out, the wick became a red glow, and the glass chimney filled with curls of black smoke until that corner of the room snuffed into darkness.

By the time Josey reached the powder magazine, his body shook with yearning to know his loved ones were safe. He crouched down and pushed through the solid wood door and stepped into the dank room. The groaning hinges had silenced everyone, and his eyes needed time to adjust to the gloom. He first saw Annabelle, who glowed in the dim lamplight like an angel in a church painting. An angel with a rifle at the ready. He went to her, pulling her into a rough embrace, allowing its warmth to permeate his body and still his quaking knees.

"I knew you'd come back," she said before startling him with a kiss in front of the others.

"It wasn't always a certain thing," he said, his eyes drinking her in. Even surrounded by unseen dangers, he felt whole in a way he never did anywhere else.

He relinquished his hold on her to greet the children and check on Isabelle, who slept through the ruckus in a swaddle of blankets on the dirt floor. He told Maria of seeing Grieve and reassured her that he would join them soon. He assigned Chaska and Kicking Bull the duty of serving as sentries on the steps that led to the underground magazine, the boys eager to be charged with something they deemed a man's responsibilities. Mina and Dewdrops, awakened by the activity, snuggled against him as he sat on the floor beside Annabelle. She wanted to know where he'd been; he wouldn't talk until he knew what happened between her and the doctor. He had to control his anger in hearing the story. They were interrupted by Chaska before he could finish his.

"Someone is coming," the boy said, urgency lending a breathless quality to his voice. Even Kicking Bull seemed shaken by what he'd seen. "He moves as if wounded."

"Is it your father?" Josey would never forgive himself if any harm befell Byron during his absence.

Chaska shook his head. "This man is not so big as *Matosapa.*"

That news delivered only short-lived relief. On reaching the top of the stairs with the boys, he recognized Grieve. He looked bad. Josey tried to hold him as he stumbled down the stairs and through the door, but his dead weight was too much, and they collapsed together onto the ground. Grieve looked up, his eyes glazed until recognition provided a focus.

"I shot the Mexican," he said, a raspy rattle in his voice. "I was so fast. I would have been faster than you."

"Shush," Josey said. "Save your breath."

Grieve cut loose with a string of profanities that, even as a fellow soldier, Josey found remarkable. Maria fell to his side, taking Grieve's head in her lap, her hands caressing a face so wan and drawn Josey wondered how he'd managed to make his way to them. Looking to the wooden stairs, Josey saw something that almost made him wish Grieve hadn't.

"I'm sorry, Maria. I shouldn't use such language in front of the children. It don't hurt so bad when I am cursing."

"Hush," she said. "I'm going to take care of you now."

"Too late for that."

"No. You will be fine, Atticus. I prayed for you."

Hovering over him, her tears fell onto his face like the first drops of a cleansing rain. Blinking with the effort to see her clearly, he said, "Your prayers have been answered. Don't you see?"

Josey tried to look away, not wishing to eavesdrop on such personal matters. Only a couple of days ago, Grieve's death might have fostered a sense of relief, one less threat in a world that reeked of them. Yet now he felt only pathos at watching the couple. The way Maria's thin shoulders shook while she tried to control her breathing brought to mind imaginings of Annabelle tending to his own death, and he couldn't wrest away his attention.

"The story I told you and the children," Grieve said, his throat constricted with spasms as he fought for breath amid the words.

Maria's hands moved over his face, a caress less gentle than desperate. "Don't speak, dear. Save your breath."

The slightest movement conveyed the shake of his head. "I see God's meaning now." He swallowed, his Adam's apple stretching the length of his throat at the pace of a caterpillar on a tree branch. "He did not send me out to murder a man. He brought me here so that I might save you and the children. You have given me my place in paradise. You saved my soul."

Maria kissed him with a fervor that imparted a life's worth of love in the moments left to them. As she pulled away, Grieve's face fell slack, and a final breath escaped his lips. Maria fell atop her man as if to shield him from the call of death's messengers, her weeping now unrestrained.

Josey turned away. Annabelle had been watching him, Isabelle held tight to her shoulder. Her free arm reached to him, and he moved into her embrace, breathing in the comforts of her.

Watching Grieve's death brought into focus his own thoughts from the past couple of days. He recognized now that he had not feared death during the war because his life had held no meaning. Rather than courage, his lack of fear at that time had signaled apathy. Grieve had been treading the same path until love imbued his life with the strength to face down a killer like Martinez, the compassion to forgive Josey, and the hope for a new life with Maria. Recalling the words he had spoken to Crazy Horse on the mesa, Josey now realized that love and hope and all the other abstractions that might move a man to risk his life had not made Grieve a weaker man. Even though his hope had been snuffed out before he could realize it, his love had provided him the only comfort that can bring solace at a man's end: the understanding that life had been worth living.

Holding Annabelle, he closed his eyes and breathed in lavender. The scent of her woke him to responsibilities not yet met. He pulled himself out of her embrace and said, "We should be going."

Annabelle's eyes narrowed with confusion. "We can't ask Maria to leave him so soon, and we can't take him with us."

"We can't afford to linger any longer."

"But Josey —"

He moved away from her, cutting off her

437

objections, and stepped to the door. Crouching before the bottom-most step, he pointed to a dark stain against the dried wood.

"Josey, what are you doing?"

He pointed to another stain on the dirt floor, his finger gliding along a path that led from the door to where Grieve had fallen. Annabelle lifted the bull's-eye lantern and directed its light to where he'd pointed.

"It's blood," he said. "His blood. Maybe no one knew we were hiding here before, but they will figure it out soon enough."

Chapter Thirty-Seven

"We're too late."

Annabelle watched Josey close the powder magazine door behind him. After seeing the path of Grieve's blood, he'd ascended the stairs to peer out the opening across the parade yard to check if the dying man had been followed.

"What did you see?" Annabelle asked.

"Some of the doctor's men are out there. Five, maybe six. We'd be gunned down before we could take two paces."

"Did they see you?"

He nodded. "They were waiting."

"Was Martinez with them?"

He shook his head, his expression distant as he thought through the problem.

"Maybe Mr. Grieve killed him."

"Then why are his men still fighting?"

"It doesn't matter. They can't get in." Annabelle's voice sounded more hopeful than certain even to her own ears. "We can

439

hold them off with the rifles."

"They can set fire to that door and burn us out anytime they want."

Annabelle glanced back at the children to be certain they didn't overhear this. They had gathered around Maria, the girls to comfort her, Chaska and Kicking Bull because they couldn't resist the opportunity to glimpse a dead body up close.

Josey stalked about the room like a caged predator. Hunching beneath the low ceiling, eyes pointed to the ground, he stopped when his boot kicked one of the metal bars that had been used to open crates of ammunition. He picked it up and went to the door.

"Chaska, Kicking Bull — come help me." The boys leaped up, pleased to be taken into his confidence no matter what he had in mind. "Help me remove these hinges."

With a nod to the black metal that connected the door to a wooden frame, he positioned the bar's claw end beneath the hinge and left it to the boys to put their weight behind the lever and pop off the first one. They adjusted the bar to take on the second hinge.

The door was all that protected them from whoever was outside, but Annabelle trusted Josey enough not to question him. A look was all it took to elicit an explanation. "Once they fire that door and try to smoke us out, it will be too late," he said.

As he spoke, he was methodically checking the safety peg between the cylinder chambers of his revolvers, though Annabelle had never known him to carry a gun that wasn't fully loaded and ready to be used. When he anticipated a fight, Josey wore two gun belts fitted with two holsters apiece. He slung his rifle in its scabbard over one shoulder, an ammunition belt over the other. The first time Annabelle had seen him outfitted this way, ambling like an ox weighted down by a wagon collar, she'd thought of a boy playing at bandit. Only after she'd seen him fight did she understand what little time he had for reloading pistols with powder flask and cartridge box, and how many times he might shoot when outnumbered. The Colonel had once told her Josey was the equal of a score of men in a firefight, and Annabelle hadn't doubted him, even as she prayed the claim would never be tested.

His task completed, he looked up and flashed a crooked grin that looked forced to her. "Don't worry; I have a plan."

"So long as it doesn't mean you going out there alone."

He holstered the last of his revolvers. "I must."

"I will go with you." She thrust her chin forward to prevent it from quivering. "I have my rifle." Reading the refusal in his eyes, she added, "I go where you go."

His hands caught her arms at the elbow. "I want that, too, once this is done. But this is something I can do only if I know you, Isabelle, and everyone else I love is safe. Can you keep them safe for me?"

She nodded, not trusting her voice as her vision smeared with tears. *Damnable dust.*

He went next to Isabelle, dropping to his knees to where she sat with Mina and Dewdrops beside Maria. Placing a hand on her head, he brushed a stray curl from her eyes. From his knees, he hoisted her high above his head, a position that never failed to elicit giggles. But on this occasion, with her father's rifle protruding over his shoulder and directly before her, she burst into tears. Josey removed the rifle scabbard and pulled her to his chest, but the intensity of his embrace made her wail even louder. Annabelle took the child from her father, who stood stoop-shouldered beneath the low ceiling with a sheepish look.

"I don't even wear a plumed helmet," he said.

Annabelle blinked before she recalled the day on their journey west when Josey took her riding to see Scotts Bluff, a wall of sand and rock rising eight hundred feet above the North Platte River. At a distance, it resembled the high walls and battlements of a fortress city and reminded them both of Homer's Troy. Annabelle compared him to Hector, defending his home and family at the city gates. But Josey had insisted he was more like Achilles, a man born to war, who did not fear death so much as failure. Hector, he told her that day, never stood a chance against Achilles, the son of immortal Thetis. Now, perhaps without meaning to, he had compared himself to Hector, whose horsehair helmet frightened his child when he embraced his family a final time before fulfilling his fate. Annabelle pulled her husband near, her voice a fierce whisper.

"I need you to come home to us." She grabbed him by his shirt collar and pulled his mouth to hers. The kiss was quick, but she tasted love in their mingled breath. "I need you to be Achilles today."

A loud thunk echoed through the enclosed room after the boys succeeded in prying the final hinge from the door. Josey went to them and praised their work before bidding them to stand back with the others. The door was barely more than half the size of an entryway to a house. He tested its heft, lifting it by its iron handle and balancing the weight against his shoulder. He had to turn it on its side to maneuver it through the open doorway.

He left it there and returned to her. "Wait for me," he said.

"What do you plan to do?"

The corner of his mouth curled into the smile she recalled from that day at Scotts Bluff. "I thought once that Hector's love made him weak by putting fear in his heart. I see now that love gave him the courage to face a god." He kissed her again, then picked up his rifle, slipping its scabbard and sling over his shoulder. "No gods stand against me today."

CHAPTER THIRTY-EIGHT

Crazy Horse and his companions rode hard all afternoon and into the night only to arrive at the fort to find it burning. He frowned; whenever he had imagined this sight, he had been the one to put the torch to the place.

He had taken the body of John Hutchins to the translator's mother, who wailed and cut her arms in her grief. Though moved by her sorrow, he didn't linger, leaving her in the care of the other women in the village so that he could seek out his brother Little Hawk and friend High Backbone. They joined him without question, along with six young warriors eager to distinguish themselves in whatever raid rallied such renowned warriors to action. Each man rode his best traveling horse and led a second so that he could change mounts whenever one tired. In this way, Crazy Horse had expected they might overtake Angel on the road to the fort. The raging fire suggested he had underestimated the white man again.

The warriors found the women leading their children and packhorses away from the fort, their possessions stacked atop travois built with lodge poles. Even the tribe's larger dogs moved with poles attached at the shoulder, dragging smaller loads behind them. Crazy Horse stopped a young mother walking with her baby strapped to her back. She held the bridle of a heavily loaded horse in one hand and a thick roll of animal skins and clothes in the other.

"Tell me mother, what has happened here?" he asked.

Without speaking, she half turned and nodded to a woman he did not know in the company of a black-white man he recognized as Angel's brother. The man sensed Crazy Horse's eyes on him and approached. He spoke a little of the people's tongue, yet even with the help of his woman the story he told did not make sense. A doctor who would kill women and children to steal their bones? Crazy Horse had him repeat it until he realized the parts of the story he assumed were misspoken were true. Little Hawk, whose blood always ran hot, asked only where he could find the white men to kill. High Backbone remained skeptical until

Crazy Horse reminded him of what had happened to Lone Bear's body. No matter how much he despised the white men, they still had the capacity to surprise him with how terrible they could be.

"Where is this doctor?" he asked, but the black-white man did not know.

He had a question of his own. "My brother look for you. Where is he?"

Responding in the white man's tongue, Crazy Horse told him Angel had gone ahead. With a nod toward the burning fort he said, "I believe we will find him there."

The black-faced man's mouth split, his teeth shining in the light of the moon. "I should have known. Josey has a way of finding trouble."

"Let us seek it with him."

While the black-white man spoke with his woman, Crazy Horse went to gather the young warriors who had come with him. He stopped at the sight of a woman with three children. The oldest child, a boy, stood beside a packhorse he led by a rope. The younger children sat on the ground, waiting on their mother, who stared at Crazy Horse.

"You came for me," Black Buffalo Woman said.

Meaning to sweep her into his arms, he took two steps toward Black Buffalo Woman

447

and stopped. He had never been with her in front of her children, and uncertainty held him back. Yet their watchful eyes had no restraining effect on her; she closed the distance between them, throwing her arms around his neck and folding herself into him.

"You came for me," she repeated.

"You are my woman, even if you are another man's wife."

She leaned back, and he recognized in her eyes the look that never failed to beckon him. He imagined himself alone with her again. It had been so long his body ached for her. Aware of the attention they drew, he freed himself from her embrace.

"I am pleased you are safe, but you must see to your children."

She misunderstood his coolness. "I am sorry I did not heed your warning. We should not have come here."

He did not blame her for seeking the white man's handouts. While he could never trust the *wasicu,* he did not bear responsibility for hungry children the way she did. She had believed the white man's words of peace because she needed to believe them, but needing to believe something does not make it so.

His expression must have softened, for she

448

pressed herself to him again. "Come with me, Jiji," she said. "The people are safe now; let us leave this terrible place together."

He cupped her cheek in his hand, stroking its softness with his thumb. He had never loved another woman. The Big Bellies of the tribe would have him take a wife, but he knew none could claim his heart when it already belonged to her.

"I cannot leave yet. I have a debt to repay. You go. See to your children's well-being, and, if you still wish it, I will come for you."

She kissed him, pulling him to her again so that he felt the full length of her body against his. Before letting him go she said, "I will wish it."

CHAPTER THIRTY-NINE

Josey lifted the wooden door and made his way up the stairs with the awkward weight. After the stale confines of the powder magazine, the brisk night air puckered his skin. He crouched at the top and waited for his eyes to adjust to the darkness. Not a total blackout. The clear sky revealed a forest of winking stars, and the three-quarters moon at his back cast a thin shadow in the shape of the door before him.

As he caught his breath, he smelled smoke; the orange glow of Grieve's fires lit up the sky over his left shoulder and to his right in the direction of the cavalry yard. Voices, indistinct at a comforting distance, carried across the emptiness of the parade grounds before him. The men he had seen earlier must have taken cover between the barracks buildings some forty yards away, waiting with their rifles for targets to emerge from their hiding place. They wouldn't wait for

450

long; if Josey and the others cowered too long in the powder magazine, it would become their tomb. The thought pushed him forward, into the open. Gripping the iron handle, the weight of the wood solid against his shoulder, he ran forward a half-dozen steps before the cumbersome mass forced him to stop.

More voices, this time raised in shouts. He tried to make himself small behind his shield. A rolling thunder of black powder explosions produced a thunk of bullets striking the thick door, like heavy rain on a roof. He steadied himself against the impact. Wished he could be even smaller.

The temptation to remain in this spot weighed down his limbs and lulled his mind. Here he was safe. The moment he moved, his legs and maybe the crown of his head would be exposed to the sharpshooters. He recalled lying in a trench once before a charge, praying that he could close his eyes and awake somewhere else, anywhere else, considering for the moment what would happen if he burrowed into the dirt while those around him rose and raced into the face of death. But when the order came, all of them moved as one, the pull of their numbers as inexorable as a turning tide. Here, he stood alone. No one ordered him forward. No one shared the burden of fear that outweighed even the door he held tight. He'd rested long enough but still heaved for breath. His knees quaked where he crouched, and he settled into the ground to steady them. His right arm shook from the strain of holding the door. It was too heavy. Maybe if he waited, the men shooting at him would go away. Maybe someone would come to his aid. Byron might return from warning the Indians. Crazy Horse might arrive with his warriors.

Another round of bullets knocked splinters from his shield, and Josey remembered he wasn't alone. Annabelle waited for him, their child held tight in her arms. Byron's children — Josey's nephews and nieces — waited with her. And another woman, a widow twice over now, looked to him to keep her children safe. If he lingered much longer, his attackers would destroy his shield or flank him in the darkness. They'd probably begun to move already, and once even one of them got behind him, he was done, along with those he held dearest.

At the next pause in the rain of bullets, he ran forward again, purposely advancing in an uneven line to confuse the aim of his predators, biding his time until he could turn them into prey. He stopped, straining to listen for the source and number of thunder strikes. Someone hunted him with a buffalo rifle. Its single shot roared like a cannon and nearly wrenched the door from his grip with each impact. Only the wood's thickness prevented the heavy cartridge from piercing through. By contrast, the blast of a repeating rifle — no, two repeating rifles — struck with an almost percussive beat. No sense trying to count bullets to anticipate when the shooter had to reload with two of them out there. Josey had been holding the door with his stronger right hand. Now he took it in his left and drew his first pistol. He flexed his fingers around the grip and rebalanced the weight of the door and waited until he could gauge the source of one of the rifles.

He risked a quick look, drawing fire so quickly splinters from the top of the door landed on the brim of his hat. Three buildings were aligned before him, a cavalry barracks in the center with infantry barracks to either side. Gaps between the buildings created natural cover for two of the shooters. The third, the buffalo rifle, he judged, had taken position on the far edge of the northernmost infantry barracks. He had the worst angle, and Josey calculated a course toward the nearest building that would best take advantage of that. He launched himself forward, firing blindly from behind the door, more in hopes of silencing the repeating rifle in front of him than of hitting anything. A heady whiff of burned powder invigorated him like breathing the aroma of a favorite meal. After he'd emptied the first six-shooter, he dropped it and drew another, maintaining a steady fire in the direction of the gap between the nearest buildings. He flinched at the cannon's roar from the buffalo rifle, but his quick movements had thrown off the rifleman's aim. He stumbled beneath the steady blows from the second repeater but used his momentum to carry him forward.

He risked another glimpse ahead. He was nearing the gap between the cavalry barracks and southernmost infantry barracks. An abandoned caisson, one busted wheel leaning against it, formed an ideal cover. In the half-second peek he'd allowed himself, he'd seen the silhouette of a rifle protruding behind it and imagined the man who waited there counting pistol shots until he believed it safe to pop out and kill Josey while he reloaded.

Josey was counting his shots as well.

Ten . . . eleven . . . twelve . . .

Dropping both the door and the second

six-shooter, Josey rushed for the cover of the barracks just as the man behind the cart stood and trained his rifle in Josey's direction. Josey read the man's shock at seeing a third pistol already pointed at his face — *Who carries more than two pistols?* — and his shock created a lethal delay as Josey fired twice at such close range the man's head burst like a crushed melon.

Chest heaving as much from bloodlust as exertion, Josey scrambled to recover the second pistol he'd dropped and collapsed against the wood-planked cavalry barracks, safe and out of the line of fire for the moment. His hands shook as he drew his powder flask from his belt and opened his cartridge box. The practiced routine of reloading his guns always steadied his nerves, and his breathing evened while he weighed his options. Would his adversaries come for him or wait? He holstered his weapons, his senses strained for any hint of a man's approach, and decided he couldn't wait. He retrieved the door and carried his shield to the rear of the building, hoping the shooters were still focused on the front. Flames from Grieve's firing of the non-commissioned staff's quarters leaped toward the heavens behind him, but the darkness was nearly complete in the shadow of the cavalry barracks. He drew his pistol and inhaled deeply before setting out, moving as quickly as he could without making a racket. He stopped at the edge of the building and peered around the corner.

Nothing.

The man with the second repeating rifle must have joined the one with the buffalo rifle. *Smart.* Together they could watch each other's back. Josey hoisted the door again and moved to the rear of the infantry barracks, the last of the three buildings. He advanced along its length, stopping only when he reached the corner. He dropped the door and fell to his belly, not wanting to present an easy target in case they were watching for him to step out. He crawled forward and looked.

From the barracks it was a straight shot of about a hundred feet to the fort's main gate. That's where he saw two men, running without looking back, their rifles still in hand. With the doctor dead and Martinez shot and maybe dying, they must have decided facing him down wasn't worth the risk. Josey rolled over and closed his eyes, his exhaustion pinning him to the ground. He glimpsed in that moment what it would feel like to be an old man. The fire from the barracks crackled in the distance, the intermittent pops of splitting boards creating a feeble imitation of gunfire after the fusillade he'd just survived.

Then he heard another pop, sharper and deeper than the sounds of the fire. This was no imitation of a gunshot. It was a large pistol. With a sharp twisting in his gut, Josey realized he'd heard that pistol fired before.

CHAPTER FORTY

Inside the powder magazine, Annabelle sat at the base of the stairs and stared through the opening where the door had been. A field of stars filled the sky, and the night had turned as quiet as the stars. After Josey had left, Annabelle flinched with every rifle shot, especially the big gun that sounded as loud as the artillery she remembered at Charleston's battery. The gunfire had lasted so long, she feared the door Josey carried would be blasted into kindling. The flatter report of the pistols had comforted her. Their rapid fire had to have come from Josey. Then the gunfire had ceased, and she didn't know what to think. She had her rifle and Mr. Grieve's heavy pistol, and she kept them close, prepared in case any of the gunmen got past Josey.

She tried not to think about what that would mean.

At the back of the room, Maria cried

quietly over Mr. Grieve's body, while her children lay against her. Isabelle slept, along with Mina and Dewdrops. Their brothers, alert to the tension the adults had shielded from the younger children, sat with their backs against the wall, their dark eyes big as dollars while they watched Annabelle. They looked both eager to be called upon to do something and apprehensive about whether they could carry out what was needed.

Minutes passed like hours. *God, I hate the waiting.* It preyed on her, a wolf gnawing on the bones of her sanity. The sky darkened, and she wondered for a fretful moment if something was going wrong with her eyes before she concluded that a cloud had passed over the moon. She wanted to envy Josey, for in taking action at least he didn't have to suffer the torture of waiting. But she knew the dangers he faced, and she knew he was safer for not having to fret over her and the children. So she bided her time.

The blinking stars brought to mind the night they'd stargazed on the journey to the fort. Even though she tried to steel her mind against pessimism, she wondered if she would lie with him again. She squeezed her eyes tight against the thought, hoping she might hear the sharp crack of Josey's rifle or his voice calling out that all was well if she shut down every other sense. Instead, she heard only Isabelle's steady breaths. They whistled between parted lips when she slept on her back. Annabelle counted. On the two hundredth breath, she rose, driven as much by a fear of madness as the conviction that Josey must have taken the fight beyond the range of her hearing.

The boys' eyes tracked her movement.

"Stay here and watch over the others," she said. "I'm going to check if it's clear."

She tucked the pistol into her belt beneath the Navajo blanket she wore as a serape against the chill of the cellar-like room. The pistol's length and heft pinched against her as she crawled up the stairs one handed, her rifle gripped in the other. She stopped before reaching the top, peering out over the edge across the grassy parade ground. The view had brightened, with breaks in the thin clouds permitting a ghostly moon to peek down on them. Nothing obscured her line of sight for nearly a hundred yards to the guardhouse that stood near the main gate. The fires before her — one to her left near the barracks where they had stayed, the other to her right, south of the cavalry stables — lit up the sky with an orange glow. She saw no one but waited for her eyes to adjust to the night to be certain. She

460

climbed to the next step to enhance her view. The ground sloped up behind her over the roof of the magazine, and she climbed to the top step so that she might see over it to the south where the officers' quarters were lined before the stockade. She scanned the horizon in every direction but saw no movement. Either the fort had been abandoned, or the doctor's men had been diverted by the fires as Mr. Grieve had intended. Either way, it meant she could lead the others back to the wagon and out the gate. With luck, they might even find Josey, Byron, and Red Shawl there.

She descended the stairs and roused the others. Maria objected.

"I can't leave him," she said. Mr. Grieve's head still lay on her lap while she stroked his hair and caressed his face.

"He gave his life for ours in drawing away our enemies. Do not allow his sacrifice to be wasted. We will return for him when we know it is safe."

To demonstrate she would brook no debate on the matter, Annabelle helped up Daniel and Astrid from where they lay beside their mother. She brushed the dirt off them and handed to them the small packs they'd carried into the magazine. Next, she roused Isabelle, stooping with her

461

pressed to her shoulder so that she might keep sleeping. When Maria reluctantly rose, Annabelle handed her child to the other woman.

"I'll need my hands free for the rifle," she said. "Just in case."

Annabelle led them out. Chaska and Kicking Bull helped the little ones negotiate the steps, while Maria carried Isabelle. They stared to the northwest, where the fires raged out of control. The smell of smoke was stronger now that she stood on the parade grounds. "That's another reason we should leave while we can," she told Maria. "Between the breeze and these dried-out buildings, those fires are only going to get bigger."

She herded the children north toward the gate and the cavalry stables where they'd left the wagon and mules. She stopped at the pull of Chaska tugging on her blanket.

"A man is coming," he said.

She whirled back in the direction from which they'd come. A long silhouette moved against the glare of the barracks fire. At first, it seemed too large to be a man. She swallowed back the taste of panic that rose in her throat like bile. The shadow grew even bigger as it drew nearer, its shambling movement confirming the dread that tightened her chest so that she could barely draw a breath.

Wishing Martinez dead had not made it so.

"I knew you would come out if I could be patient," he said.

Though his face remained in shadow, there was no mistaking his voice, nor the revolver he held in his right hand, its blued steel gleaming in the firelight. From the angle he stood and the wet bloodstains reflecting light at his waist, she could tell he'd been gut shot. Mr. Grieve had killed him after all, just not fast enough.

Without taking her eyes off the man, Annabelle said to Maria, "Continue with the children to the gate while I speak with Mr. Martinez." Maria began to protest, but Annabelle cut her off. "Don't argue with me."

Martinez interrupted with a gunshot into the air. He pointed the weapon at Maria but spoke to Annabelle. "Drop the rifle first."

Annabelle let her rifle fall to the ground. "Get the children away, Maria," she repeated.

"Which one is your child?" Martinez demanded.

Hoping he wouldn't recognize the child in

463

Maria's arms as hers, Annabelle answered, "I had Red Shawl, our Indian woman, take her to safety while the rest of us hid here. We were afraid the baby's cries would give us away."

The silence that followed as Martinez allowed this new information to filter through his brain seemed to last forever. Without realizing it, Annabelle had been holding her breath until she saw him nod.

"Go!" she told Maria in a harsh whisper that commanded immediate obedience. She hurried off, but Chaska and Kicking Bull lingered beside her. She looked at them. "This man needs medical treatment. I'm going to see to that, and then I will join you."

The boys appeared torn between their disbelief of her words and the understanding that they could do nothing to help her. To encourage their departure, she raised the side of her Navajo blanket just enough for them to see the pistol tucked in her belt. She'd yet to form a plan, but if she could distract Martinez and get him to lower his pistol, she might finish with the same gun the task Mr. Grieve had started.

"You know the way," she told the boys. "Please see that everyone gets to the wagon safely."

The boys nodded, though it took some effort for them to pull their eyes away from Martinez and the gun pointed at Annabelle. She waited until they disappeared into the gloom with Maria and the other children before turning back to Martinez.

"You're going to die if you don't see to that wound."

He pulled his left hand away from his waist to look at the blood that covered his fingers. "I'm going to die anyway. You killed the only doctor." He tried to laugh, a wet, phlegmy sound.

"Dr. Hamilton was insane."

"He was my son."

Annabelle blinked with surprise, though the news explained much.

"I loved his mother, but I could never tell him. I could never give him the life he had with her husband's name. At least his work will outlive him."

Hoping Martinez might grow careless if roused to anger, Annabelle said, "He was a failure. He allowed his science to be clouded by his prejudice."

Martinez raised the gun, redirecting it from her heart to her face. "You should cherish what time remains to you."

"You should go now, while you can. Josey will be back soon."

"I'm counting on that," he said. "I only hope my men have not been too eager in their efforts to draw him out."

He stole a glance beyond her, as if mention of Josey's name might conjure him from the darkness. Annabelle held the pistol tightly beneath the folds of the Navajo blanket, but he didn't give her time to pull it out and take aim.

"You have taken from me my son, and now I will take the man you love — but only after I expose him as a coward."

The intensity with which he stared at her reminded Annabelle of a hungry dog watching people eat. He couldn't have signaled his appetite for her fear any more than if he had licked his lips. The image hardened her against his threats. She would not gratify him by giving in to a panic that would only cloud her mind from what needed to be done.

Let him keep talking. He will let his guard down.

"You think I am wrong," he continued. In his pain, his breaths came steady and shallow. "You think, 'My husband is no coward.' And that is why I will savor killing him. For a good man will believe himself brave — right up until the end. That is the best part. That is when he comes to see his courage

466

has been nothing more than a mask he wore, like a player on a stage. In the end, all good men are cowards, and, when you show that to them, they are broken. They are almost grateful for death. No meal is so delicious, no woman so satisfying as that moment when you have broken a good man."

Shifting her balance from one foot to the other to ease the weight of the hidden gun, Annabelle bided her time. So long as Martinez believed he was torturing her with his words, he might keep talking until he bled out. Or until his attention wavered just long enough for her to get off a good shot. Or until Josey returned. *Keep talking, you evil bastard.*

"It is always the same, the death of a good man. First, he will seek to appeal to my better nature. Tell me no good will come from our fighting."

Martinez barked a bitter laugh. "No good for him, it is true," he continued. "In failing with his appeal, he will try to strike a bargain. He will offer me something. What does your husband have to offer?"

She resisted looking at him, leaving him to answer his own question.

"Money, I think. He will offer me money. But, of course, I have no more need for money now." He looked again at the blood on his hand and spit into the dirt, rubbing out the moist spot with the toe of his boot. "Finally, he will offer his life in return for yours. Not every man does, but I think yours will, especially because you are watching.

"After all else has failed, he will threaten me, and that is when I know he is ready to die." He barked another laugh that left him more stooped, his free hand pressed tight against his wound. "Do you see how funny that is? A man shows his cowardice to the world — then he seeks to reclaim his courage. By then it is too late. And when he sees that, he will beg. They pretend they are begging on behalf of the woman or the child, but it is for themselves that they beg. Because they are afraid to be exposed as cowards. Fear enfeebles all men, especially those who believe they have something to live for."

In the distance, a shadow emerged from beyond the far barracks a good two hundred feet away. It was just a silhouette against the bright orange flames of the fire beyond, but Annabelle could not mistake the shape. She tried not to look, but something in her manner must have given her away. Martinez pivoted so that he might take in the image while still watching her. He stood taller at the sight of the other man and lifted the bloody hand he had pressed to his gut. He kept the gun trained on Annabelle.

"Josey Angel," he called. "I have been waiting for you. Your woman has been waiting for you. Come and let us finish this."

Josey stopped on hearing Martinez's voice, but only for a moment. Without responding, he resumed walking toward them, his stride even and steady. He carried his rifle loosely before him with both hands. He closed to about a hundred feet, approaching the larger man at an angle that left Annabelle out of his firing line. If Martinez noticed, he ignored it as he sidled over to her, his gun still pointed at her chest from two arm's lengths away.

"Look at how bravely your man comes." Martinez's wide face split into a grin, his thick mustache flattening over his open mouth. "Watch him try to bargain with me, then watch me take him from you."

He looked toward Josey, who had closed to fifty feet and gave no indication of stopping. Martinez no longer had to call to be heard.

"Josey Angel. At last. I thought you might run away from me again. I am glad to see you have the courage —"

Josey pointed the rifle and fired from the

waist so quickly Martinez failed to get out another word. The bullet knocked the big man back two steps. The arm directing the pistol at Annabelle fell to his side. At the same time, Annabelle pulled free Grieve's pistol and fired from beneath the Navajo blanket, striking Martinez through the back. He started to fall forward, but Josey had already shot a second time. Martinez sunk to his knees, then toppled over onto his side. Without breaking stride, Josey cocked his rifle once again, waiting until he hovered over the prone body. He relaxed his grip so that the rifle hung at his side in one hand. The bright brass receiver glowed with the reflected light of the flames, and he pulled the trigger a third time. Then he tucked the rifle beneath his armpit and slipped new cartridges into the loading gate.

Annabelle waited for his mind to return from the place it went when he had to forget everything that made him human. It was only long enough for him to finish reloading and draw a breath or two. Then he turned to her, his face hidden in the shadow of the flames behind him. His shoulders sagged, and he lowered his head before raising an arm. She went to him, folding herself into the circle of his embrace, closing her eyes as if to shut out the memories of this night and breathe in the scent of smoke, sweat, and something more that was only Josey. She lost track of how long they remained like that. He leaned away from her, kissing her lightly before stepping back to look at her. He fingered the bullet hole in her serape.

"I knew when I couldn't see your hands that you had a surprise. But you ruined your blanket."

She shook her head. "It's more precious to me now than ever."

CHAPTER FORTY-ONE

Josey and Annabelle caught up with Maria and the children on their way to the wagon. Together, they found Lord Byron and Red Shawl. The arrival of Crazy Horse and his warriors had driven off any of the doctor's surviving men. The reunion was heartfelt but brief. Josey wanted to be clear of the place as soon as possible before the winds that came with the approaching dawn could spread the fires any farther. He had cut short the exchange of stories so that the men could retrieve Grieve's body.

Only once they led their wagon through the fort's gates could Josey share with Annabelle the news of John Hutchins's death.

"I judged him too harshly," he told her, recalling how he had seen opportunism in the translator's efforts to live in two worlds, moving among the Indians as a trader when it suited him and working for the army when he found advantage in it. He became something of an outcast among his mother's people after aiding Annabelle in her escape from captivity, yet he had given his life to foster a peace that he believed would save them.

"I saw his desire for peace as a selfish thing, a way to become a leader among his people if they took up the white man's ways. But I was wrong to see him as changing sides, for he never saw a divided world as a natural or lasting thing. Instead of doing what he thought was best for one side or the other, he did what he thought was right."

"Maybe he saw the world the way it should be," Annabelle said. "The way it will be one day."

"I hope you're right, but I fear that day will be a long time coming."

They halted alongside Maria's ox-pulled wagon that Grieve had left pointed toward the Montana road. The sight brought new tears to Maria's eyes. She said, "I don't have anywhere to go."

Annabelle took the other woman in her arms. "Yes, you do."

The eastern sky had begun to lighten, casting a gray light over the horizon that caused the stars to fade. A few Indians on horseback had gathered to watch the fort burn. Josey and Annabelle found Crazy

Horse among them, giving instructions to a pair of younger men to torch the remaining buildings within the fort. A couple of the buildings had burned out. To the Indians' frustration, the stockade wouldn't hold the fire, so a couple of other warriors had starting pulling down the pine-log walls and piling them like a bonfire. Chaska and Kicking Bull — fascinated by the young warriors from their native tribe — had wanted to help, so Lord Byron accompanied his sons. Crazy Horse looked contented as he dismounted to speak with them.

"If you leave the fort standing, your enemies will never be able to defeat you here," Josey told him.

Crazy Horse's mouth twisted as if he'd just eaten a bad egg. "I promised my people we would burn this place to the ground and spread the ashes until nothing remains but the memory of it. And that will fade with time."

Josey had no reason to cherish memories of Fort Phil Kearny either, but a place where so many had died was not easily forgotten. Annabelle withdrew a small bundle wrapped in white linen that she'd retrieved from the wagon and handed it to Crazy Horse.

"I took this from Dr. Hamilton's tent

after . . ." She didn't finish the sentence.

"Pejuta wacasa?" he asked, rubbing his hands together. Josey recognized it as an Indian sign for wiping out a foe.

"Yes," Annabelle said. "The doctor is dead."

Crazy Horse unwrapped the folds of linen, which had disguised the shape of the object within. Josey understood the significance of the gift only after Crazy Horse uncovered the skull. He held it aloft, turning it in his hand as if he recognized the man who once was.

Speaking in English for their benefit, he said, "Lone Bear, you will be at peace now."

"What about you?" Annabelle asked. "Will you agree to the peace treaty?"

It might have been a trick of the light, but his hard eyes seemed to soften for a moment. "I will honor the peace, so long as the white man does."

He is right to add that caveat. Josey kept his thoughts to himself.

Crazy Horse looked at Josey, who held Isabelle, asleep against his shoulder. Annabelle seemed to know his mind. She said, "A woman's love can bloom fully only in a time of peace. If you go to Black Buffalo Woman now, I don't think she can refuse you."

Crazy Horse gave no indication that he heard. They stood together in silence, watching the fort burn. One of the Indians had put the torch to the blockhouse that overlooked the main gate. The soldiers had kept a mountain howitzer there that could spray canister shot across the approaches to the northeast side of the fort. While they watched, the beams that held it upright gave way, and the flooring and roof collapsed under their weight. The sight of the toppled structure brought a chorus of triumphant war cries from the Indians. Josey stole a glance at the man beside him, figuring the look of grim satisfaction was as close to a smile as he'd ever see on the young leader's face.

Feeling his eyes, Crazy Horse turned to them. "Farewell," he said. "No one will trouble you on your journey."

Josey extended his hand, but the Indian brushed by him without a word. Annabelle cocked her head with a question unasked. Josey shrugged. "I wouldn't blame him if he never shook the hand of a white man."

Annabelle twined her fingers around his free hand, and they turned back to the wagons. The glow of dawn in the east nearly matched the shade of fire behind them. The dirt road before them, lighter than the scrub and grass it bisected, emerged from the darkness to mark the way.

"What are we going to do now?" he asked.

"Go home, of course. Home to Angel Falls."

He squeezed her hand. "To plant ourselves like acorns?"

Her eyebrow arched as she replied, "Only until the next adventure calls."

ACKNOWLEDGEMENTS

Writing is a lonely pursuit, but publishing a book is a team effort. I'm grateful to count so many talented and patient friends as teammates. My gifted circle of fellow writers who indulge me with extra turns when I'm on a roll: Jeff Boyle, Sandy Smith Hutchins, Ginger Pinholster, and Jennie Erin Smith. The beta readers who act like it's Christmas when I deliver, unannounced, a three-hundred-page manuscript and ask for their feedback yesterday: Sheri Catron, Heather Doughton, and Renée Lyons. My editors at Five Star: Gordon Aalborg and Tiffany Schofield. And my first, last, and most enthusiastic reader, my love, Lori Catron. You keep me going.

ABOUT THE AUTHOR

Derek Catron, author of the critically acclaimed *Trail Angel* and *Angel Falls,* has hiked and camped throughout the West to research his novels. A career journalist who's won numerous awards for reporting and feature writing, Catron is an editor on the *USA TODAY*'s investigative team. He lives in Florida with his wife and daughter. Read more about the author and *Avenging Angel* at derekcatron.com or on Facebook at Derek.Catron.Author.

CPSIA information can be obtained
at www.ICGtesting.com
Printed in the USA
BVHW050001171122
652169BV00003B/5